RUBÁIYÁT
OF
OMAR KHAYYÁM,
THE
ASTRONOMER-POET OF
PERSIA.

鲁 拜 集 之 美

［波斯］欧玛尔·海亚姆
原著

［英］爱德华·菲茨杰拉德
英译

钟锦
译解

R U B Á I Y Á T

北京时代华文书局

RUBÁIYÁT
OF
OMAR KHAYYÁM,
THE
ASTRONOMER-POET OF PERSIA.

Rendered into English Verse.

【校勘版本】

用第五版为底本，汇校各版异文，兹列各版版本信息于后

FIRST EDITION.

RUBÁIYÁT
OF
OMAR KHAYYÁM,
THE ASTRONOMER-POET OF PERSIA.
Translated into English Verse.

LONDON:
BERNARD QUARITCH,
CASTLE STREET, LEICESTER SQUARE.
1859.

On the verso:

G. NORMAN, PRINTER, MAIDEN LANE,
COVENT GARDEN, LONDON.

SECOND EDITION.

RUBÁIYÁT
OF
OMAR KHAYYÁM,
THE ASTRONOMER-POET OF PERSIA.
Rendered into English Verse.

Second Edition.

LONDON:
BERNARD QUARITCH,
PICCADILLY.
1868.

On the verso:

JOHN CHILDS AND SON, PRINTERS.

THIRD EDITION.

RUBÁIYÁT
OF
OMAR KHAYYÁM,
THE ASTRONOMER-POET OF PERSIA.
Rendered into English Verse.

THIRD EDITION.

LONDON:
BERNARD QUARITCH,
PICCADILLY.
1872.

On the verso:

LONDON:
G. NORMAN AND SON, PRINTERS, MAIDEN
LANE,
COVENT GARDEN.

FOURTH EDITION.

RUBÁIYÁT
OF
OMAR KHAYYÁM;
AND THE
SALÁMÁN AND ÁBSÁL
OF
JÁMÍ;
RENDERED INTO ENGLISH VERSE.

BERNARD QUARITCH; 15 PICCADILLY, LONDON.
1879.

On the verso:

LONDON:
G. NORMAN AND SON, PRINTERS, MAIDEN LANE,
COVENT GARDEN.

On the title page:

RUBÁIYÁT
OF
OMAR KHAYYÁM,
THE ASTRONOMER-POET OF PERSIA.
Rendered into English Verse.

FOURTH EDITION.

FIFTH EDITION.

LETTERS
AND
LITERARY REMAINS
OF
EDWARD FITZGERALD
EDITED BY
WILLIAM ALDIS WRIGHT
IN THREE VOLUMES.
VOL. III.

LONDON:
MACMILLAN AND CO.
AND NEW YORK.
1889

[All Rights reserved.]

目　　录

前言

- 同一充满着思索了世界人生后的幻灭，沉浸于醇酒妇人后的伤感，而出以乐观的态度，健康的情调…… 6

序言

- OMAR KHAYYÁM, THE ASTRONOMER-POET OF PERSIA. 14
- 欧玛尔·海亚姆：波斯的天文学家诗人 22
- 奥玛珈音：波斯之天学诗客 28

正集

- 插图
- 菲茨杰拉德英译文诗歌
- 文言译文诗歌
- 白话译文诗歌

33–358

删稿

- 插图
- 菲茨杰拉德英译文诗歌
- 文言译文诗歌
- 白话译文诗歌

359–379

前言

同一充满着思索了世界人生后的幻灭，沉浸于醇酒妇人后的伤感，而出以乐观的态度，健康的情调，不过，海亚姆的《鲁拜集》是质朴之美，菲茨杰拉德的《鲁拜集》是爽若哀梨、快如并剪之美。两者相辅相成，成就了一段文学史上的奇缘，翻译史上的奇迹。

波斯原本是诗的国度。不仅诗人众多，似乎个个还才思泉涌，下笔动辄上万行。菲茨杰拉德就把波斯诗人和希腊诗人相比拟，说他们像饶舌的孩子，奇情异彩散发起来仿佛有无限精力。海亚姆又质朴又短小的四行诗，势必淹没其中，我们也就无须惊讶他的诗名一直隐而不彰。波斯文学史旧有“诗坛四柱石”之说，指的是：菲尔多西、鲁米、萨迪、哈菲兹。爱默生讲过“波斯七大诗人”，还要再加上安瓦里、内扎米、贾米。无疑，这些才是波斯的一流诗人。如果有人想把海亚姆加进去，那真是一件不可思议的事情。

虽然海亚姆生前不以诗名，直到死后 50 多年才有人提及他的四行诗，但这件不可思议的事情居然成了真。随着《鲁拜集》的风靡，海亚姆变成了一个响亮的名字。他不仅跻身一流诗人之列，甚至成为波斯诗人的代表。这个转变发生在 1859 年，英国诗人爱德华·菲茨杰拉德翻译出版了《欧玛尔·海亚姆的鲁拜集》。在此之前海亚姆的诗名，在此之后菲茨杰拉德自己的诗作，都少有人知，而菲茨杰拉德的《鲁拜集》译本却越来越辉煌，成为诗坛和翻译界独一无二的事件。160 多年后，仍然留给我们无尽的反思。

一

欧玛尔·海亚姆全名阿甫尔法塔赫·欧玛尔·本·易卜拉欣·海亚姆·内沙浦里，十一世纪后期生于呼罗珊的内沙普尔，塞尔柱王朝最著名的天文学家、数学家、医学家、哲学家，自然，后来也是最著名的诗人。他一生事迹不多，大概著述就是他的生平。现存著作，《鲁拜集》之外，还有命名为“马立克·沙希星算表”的天文图表，以及一些论文，其中《代数论》比较知名。

所谓“鲁拜”，波斯文的意思就是“四行诗”，是波斯的一种诗体，每首四行，每行十一音节，多为一、二、四句押韵，也有四句全押的，形式上很像我们的绝句。由于唐帝国和西域的密切关系，杨宪益等很多学者认为鲁拜和绝句有着共同的渊源，不过这很难得到确切的证明，所以更多的人还是持怀疑态度。也有学者如王蒙认为，我国新疆，乃至塔吉克斯坦、乌兹别克斯坦、哈萨克斯坦等国家流行的“柔巴依”（波斯文“Roba'i”，英文“Ruba'i”），和鲁拜更为接近。黄杲炘先生认为它们其实就是一回事，而且柔巴依的译音更准，他的译本坚持叫《柔巴依集》。张晖从波斯文直接翻译的译本，也叫《柔巴依诗集》。不过，郭沫若的《鲁拜集》译名已经约定俗成，不论事实真相如何，大家广泛采用的还是“鲁拜”。

菲茨杰拉德译本的序文《欧玛尔·海亚姆：波斯的天文学家诗人》，对海亚姆的介绍足够满足我们知人论世的要求，对《鲁拜集》的介绍也极有见地。让人疑惑不解的是，虽然《鲁拜集》中译本众多，这篇序文却很少译出，他的介绍并未得到应有的重视。这里，除了提醒我国读者稍加注意外，还要补充两点。第一，序文中最动人的尼查木和哈桑的故事，其实并不可靠。伊朗学者们考证，即使欧玛尔和哈桑可能同学，那时尼查木已经四十开外，早已做了首相。但是，由于菲茨杰拉德的讲述，这个故事已经广为流传，似乎只要提到海亚姆，就一定会提到它。第二，菲茨杰拉德对《鲁拜集》的看法，和一些学者，比如著名的法文本译者尼古拉斯等，还是有较大差异的。他更倾向于认为海亚姆是无神论者，另外的学者则认为是神秘主义者，是个苏菲派诗人。双方各执一辞，各有道理。其实这跟如何认定海亚姆的作品有很大的关系。归于海亚姆名下的鲁拜多达上千首，但可以确认出自海亚姆之手的不会超过 150 首，伊朗文学家伏鲁基进行了严格的考订，认为只有 66 首。多达上千首的鲁拜既然思想各异，如何认定又颇具争议，必然导致学者们对海亚姆的不同认识。不过，一致的观点是，海亚姆语言质朴、理趣浓厚，在波斯诗人里独树一帜。

现存《鲁拜集》最早的写本曾经认为是收藏在剑桥大学图书馆的公元 1207 年抄本，共收录鲁拜 252 首。自从 1957 年苏联科学院根据这个抄本出版波斯语俄语对照本后，1207 年抄本引起学者们的广泛研究，最终被认定只是一个早期古写本，不过抄写年代肯定比 1207 年晚很多。尽管如此，这个版本还是在我国产生了很大的影响。著名波斯语学者张鸿年根据这个版本翻译的《鲁拜集》，在 1991 年（文津出版社）、2001 年（湖南文艺出版社）、2017 年（商务印书馆）三次出版。另外一个重要的早期写本就是“乐园”本。按照波斯人根据阿拉伯字母计数的方法，“乐园”一词的七个波斯字母所代表的数字之和是 867，正好是写本抄成的希吉来历 867 年，即公元 1462 年。抄写者的名字也留了下来，叫亚尔·阿合玛德·本·胡赛因·拉希迪·大不里士。这个抄本年代可靠，数量又多，共 554 首，影响也很大。四川人民出版社 2017 年出版了张鸿年、宋丕方的中译本。菲茨杰拉德没有提过这两个抄本，根据他的序文，他翻译依据的主要是另外两个抄本。“我们知道只有一本在英国，就是牛津包德勒图书馆编号乌斯利第 140 号的写本，公元 1460 年写于设拉子。这里包括 158 首鲁拜。有一本在加尔各答亚洲协会图书馆，我们得到一个副本，包括仍不完备的 516 首，还被各样的重出和劣制品种充斥。”他的译本自第二版起，还参考了法国学者尼古拉斯 1867 年出版的法译本，那里收了 464 首。根据爱德华·赫荣－艾伦的考订，菲茨杰拉德译本中的 49 首能够合于或基本合于原文，44 首经过了加工、组合，另外还混入阿塔等人以及菲茨杰拉德自己的所作。

二

菲茨杰拉德在他译本的第一版序文里，谈到了海亚姆的诗歌在波斯乃至东方并不流行的原因，不知道为什么，从第二版开始，这段文字被删除了。无论如何，菲茨杰拉德在写这段文字时，或许根本想不到，正是他自己的译文让海亚姆风行世界。

爱德华·菲茨杰拉德，英国萨福克郡布莱德菲尔德镇人，生于 1809 年 3 月 31 日。1826 年就读于剑桥大学三一学院，同学中后来的名流甚多，比如著名桂冠诗人丁尼生和小说家萨克雷。1851 年他出版《幼发拉诺尔》，写的正是这段生活，只是假托了古人而已。连续印过三次，也都是匿名的。大概剑桥生涯对他后来最大的影响就是结识了爱德华·B. 考威尔。考威尔的东方学造诣甚深，他敏锐地发现了海亚姆和他的诗，菲茨杰拉德的翻译正是受他引导。

菲茨杰拉德家境优裕，但为人温良，生活简淡，在伍德布里奇附近过着隐居式的生活。他的友人伯纳德·巴顿，是位贵格会教徒诗人，菲茨杰拉德因为答应巴顿照顾他的女儿，没有慎重考虑就和她结了婚。不久，因为菲茨杰拉德孤僻不偶的性格不适合婚姻生活，与女方的性情也不合，双方友好地离了婚，他以后也没有再娶。巴顿身后，菲茨杰拉德帮助印行了其诗集，附有他所写的巴顿传略。他独居的生活不过是读书写作，偶尔和两个水手放舟海上，一去一两天，有时也会跟考威尔一起，所带不过一块大饼，几瓶红酒，当然也少不了书。

1852 年他出版《珀洛尼厄斯》，近于书话，从中可窥见其读书之一斑。1853 年出版翻译的《卡尔德隆戏剧六种》，大概在友人的勉强下，这是他唯一的署名作品。1856 年出版翻译贾米的《萨拉曼和阿布萨尔》。1859 年出版《鲁拜集》，后来，这本一再重版的小册子为他带来了全部声誉。1876 年出版修订译本《阿伽门农王》（初版为自印，时间不详）。他还翻译过《俄狄浦斯王》和另外两种卡尔德隆戏剧，生前并未定稿。

菲茨杰拉德和诗人乔治 · 克雷布的孙子克雷布教士是朋友，他去莫顿教区看望克雷布时，想着手写一本《克雷布读本》。未能完成，就于 1883 年 6 月 14 日在克雷布家中辞世。1889 年，友人威廉 · 奥迪斯 · 赖特编辑出版了他的三卷本文集，1903 年又出了七卷本的文集和书信集。

1858 年，菲茨杰拉德把 35 首鲁拜的诗稿交给弗雷泽杂志，但迟迟没有发表。1859 年 1 月，他收回这 35 首，加上一直在修改的 40 首，编成一共 75 首的《欧玛尔 · 海亚姆的鲁拜集》交给出版商夸里奇，他自费印了 250 册，其中 50 册自用，200 册销售。销售情况很不好，最终从一先令（有的资料说是五先令）贱卖到一便士。名诗人罗塞蒂和斯文伯恩等人偶然买到，大加赞誉，才引起一些关注，但也没有太流行。直到 1866 年，夸里奇那里还剩 10 册，就开始准备再版。1868 年，第二版印行，增加到 110 首。查尔斯 · 艾略特 · 诺顿在 1869 年 10 月号的《北美评论》上写了一篇评论，《鲁拜集》才真正得到广泛关注，其诗句开始被频繁引用了。1872 年，菲茨杰拉德出版了第三版，确定为 101 首，编次看起来也很有讲究。1879 年，《鲁拜集》跟《萨拉曼和阿布萨尔》合刊，这就是第四版，也是菲茨杰拉德的生前定本。1889 年，赖特根据菲茨杰拉德自己的个别修改，将《鲁拜集》收入三卷本文集中，是为第五版。这时《鲁拜集》已经名声远振，各个国家都在争相翻译、出版。据说，迄今为止，《鲁拜集》的版本之多，仅次于《圣经》和莎士比亚的作品。

这五个版本，尤其前三版，都有繁复的修改，可以看出菲茨杰拉德的精心。为了便于对照，从赖特编辑的第五版开始，一般都会附有各版译诗的异文和编次对照表。其实不仅原诗，连序文和注释都有修改。第一版序文，到第二版时进行了不少增删，尤其是增加了一段针对尼古拉斯版本的评论。第三版对那段针对尼古拉斯版本的评论进行了删改。第四版又把这段删掉了。第五版按照第三版重新恢复，由于这是赖特编辑的，不知是否是菲茨杰拉德的本意了。第一版注释最少，但第十七首的注释中有一段详细介绍波斯波利斯城，后来各版都删略了。第二版续有增添。第三版基本确定。到第四版，只在第三版的基础上增加了一小段，见于第 87 首。第五版没有改动。

三

我相信，菲茨杰拉德选译的《鲁拜集》，更近于一个真实的海亚姆，他的翻译并未改变原诗的主题，甚至连原作的态度和情调也都如实地传达了出来。最大的改变在于诗集的结构，菲茨杰拉德并不满意原抄本按照入韵字母的次序进行编排，如他说，“这就看到死亡和欢乐被奇怪地连接在一起了”。其实，这只是抄本的编排方式，海亚姆大概只是随手写了，并没有进行特别的编集。但菲茨杰拉德却把他选出的诗歌，按照他的理解进行了有意的安排，从第三版开始，固定为 101 首，第 1 首写太阳出来，第 100 首写月亮升起，第 2 首写呼饮，第 101 首写奠酒，总的篇数，循环照应的编排，都体现着他的匠心。尤其是第 82 首到第 90 首，那一组关于酒罐的诗歌，把被造的人比作被造的陶罐，本是海亚姆反复讲的比喻，菲茨杰拉德却把它们组合成了一组诗剧，就显得更为生动了。

这本《鲁拜集》表现出对宇宙、对人生一个朴素的态度，不相信任何神意，也不相信任何来世，支配我们的是盲目的命运，愉悦我们的是当下的享乐。在第 29 首里，正是写命运的不可捉摸：

进入这个宇宙，不知道缘由
也不知源头，如水漫漫而流；
　再从它出离，像风沿着荒漠，
漫漫而吹，我也不知道尽头。

但写得很旷达，透着睿智，没有丝毫的困惑，而是镇定，乐观。也由此不再期待对命运的改变，如第 71 首：

移动的手指在写，写完，继续
移动；所有你的虔敬和智力
　不能引它回来把半行删除，
所有泪水不能将一字洗去。

“移动的手指”比喻命运不可更改的进程，面对它，你的虔诚，你的学问，你的苦痛，都没有丝毫作用。放弃了该放弃的，也就可能获得你该拥有的，第 57 首说：

啊，人们说，或许是我的算制，
简化了岁时更好测算？——不是，
　那只不过是从历书删去了
未生的明天，和已死的昨日。

这是一个绝妙的比喻，海亚姆是当时出色的历法学家，却让他表明，再好的学术也不过让你明白，当下才具有人生最重要的意义。对于朴素的人来说，当下所有不过感官的享受，宁可顺从它让心灵平静，也不为了任何目的去虚饰矫作。时时因了对抗世俗，激成一种乖张的情绪，刻意夸张那享受，最有刺激作用的美酒，最有安慰作用的美女，成为夸张的对象。这一心理似乎具有普遍性，我们最熟知者莫过于魏公子讲的“醇酒妇人”，在《鲁拜集》里，也同样地反复歌咏。但情调是健康的，在讲美酒时不是沉湎，而是傲俗，如第 93 首：

真的，我热爱了这么久的偶像
贻误了我在这个世界的声望：
　淹没我的光荣在浅浅的杯中，
还出卖我的体面为一声低唱。

在讲美女时不是色相，而是爱情，如第 12 首：

带着一卷诗集到大树枝底，
一壶红酒，一条面包，还有你
　荒野中偎傍在我身边放歌，
哦，荒野已跟天堂相差无几！

前者让我们想到柳永《鹤冲天》里的“忍把浮名，换了浅斟低唱”，那个形象，也曾是蔑世傲俗的一个寄托：“黄金榜上，偶失龙头望。明代暂遗贤，如何向？未遂风云便，争不恣狂荡？何须论得丧。才子词人，自是白衣卿相。”而后者，早成为歌咏爱情最出名的篇章之一了，但谁还记得，那背后对宇宙人生的反思，对现世虚伪的鄙弃？

现代以来，古典道德日益遭受冷遇，资本主义一面是“资本来到世间，从头到脚，每个毛孔都滴着血和肮脏的东西”（马克思《资本论》第一卷第 24 章，《马克思恩格斯选集》第二卷，人民出版社 2012 年版，第 297 页），一面又从市场利益的算计中大倡功利主义的现代道德观，势必趋向更为深刻的伪善。这是现代性不可避免的趋势，我们从巴尔扎克《红房子旅馆》（1831年）对资本主义原罪的追问，到王尔德《理想丈夫》（1895年）对相似追问进行的嘲弄，见得异常清楚。这段时期西方社会经历了最为彷徨的历程，菲茨杰拉德适时地翻译出《鲁拜集》，获得了意外的成功。潜入意识里的世纪末颓废，和原诗产生出奇特的融合，无论是译者，还是读者，不自觉地把带些玩世不恭的叛逆色彩增强了，使之倾倒无数的现代读者。它最先在美国得以流行，不是没有缘故。也许，古波斯的黄金幻景，象征了世纪末对古典道德的最后一丝留恋。

菲茨杰拉德译本的风行，除了时代的因素，还需要关注翻译自身的因素。一般认为，菲茨杰拉德大胆地将原作重新剪裁，加以天才地再创造，将海亚姆原作的艺术感染力大大增强了。但也有不同的看法。首先，精通波斯文的学者不会认可菲茨杰拉德的译文优于海亚姆的原文，如张鸿年先生在“乐园”本《鲁拜集》的译者序言里说：“海亚姆的鲁拜看似平易，但是字斟句酌，朴素的字句下含有深意。一般来说，译文超过原文似乎不大可能。”其次，直接否定菲茨杰拉德的翻译，包括英国的专家学者们，以一种狭隘的视角，认为菲茨杰拉德的《鲁拜集》并不算合格的译作。这样的争论，至今一直存在。

我认可伏鲁基的看法：“海亚姆的鲁拜由一位具有独特欣赏能力的英国诗人菲茨杰拉德译为英文。菲茨杰拉德的译法是取海亚姆的思想以英国诗的形式表达出来。他共译101首。他的这个译本堪称译事的杰作。凡是读到这些诗的英国人无不由衷欣赏，十分珍视。有人甚至说菲译优于原作，我们不敢苟同。但是译者的译文的确巧妙地传达了原诗的内容，符合欧洲人的情趣。”（张鸿年译伏鲁基编《鲁拜集》序言）不用说，将异国的语言译成母语，一定会出现抵触，因此归化、异化的纠结一直困扰着翻译学。菲茨杰拉德以天才的译法，将翻译过程里出现的哪怕一丁点儿抵触都完美地清除掉了，以爽俊流畅的译笔，把波斯文的美传达在英文里。那些抵触不清除，翻译最多维持在“信”和“达”的层面，根本不可能做到“雅”。可以说，菲茨杰拉德的翻译既忠实原诗的思想，又适应英诗的表达，才能够成为伏鲁基所说的“杰作”，也才让《鲁拜集》借助英语风靡世界。说菲译优于原作，自是不敢苟同，但说菲译优于一切对抵触不加消除的译作，那是毫无问题的。菲茨杰拉德在消除翻译的抵触时，当然也会有过有不及，这些都可以争论，但他译法的巨大成功不应该被忽视。

菲茨杰拉德译本《鲁拜集》的中译繁多，至今已有胡适、徐志摩、郭沫若、闻一多、成仿吾、林语堂、吴宓、朱湘、梁实秋、屠岸、李霁野、黄克孙、黄杲炘、孟祥森、陈次云、柏丽、木心、眭谦等上百人相继全译或选译过，使用白话和文言的都有。现在这个译本当然需要有自己的特色。

我根据菲茨杰拉德五版译本的影印本，做了一个详尽的校订本，这是中译的根据。这样全面的校订，在国内尚未有过。分别用白话和文言进行翻译，是以翻译实践反思菲茨杰拉德成功的经验，因为汉语白话具有非同一般的适应异国语言的能力，而汉语文言又具有非同一般的抗拒异国语言的强度，处在这种张力之间的尝试，别具吸引力。我的白话译文，努力做到语序、标点、音节、韵脚都和原文保持一致。音节稍放宽松一些，每行五顿对应原文的五音步，但有时用十一个字，有时用十二个字。韵脚过于严苛，遵循旧体诗的传统，平、上、去三声不通押。如此势必造成表达不够流畅，恳请读者对我、对白话多些宽容。文言译文，已在尽量忠实原意的可能下，服从着汉语自身的美学要求，由此必定造成对原文表达的背离。对此做出的指责，我援菲茨杰拉德为例，替自己辩护。如果指责者根本不具备文言的基本读写能力，我则认为无须置辩。

非常感谢爱德华·赫荣-艾伦，他逐首考证了菲茨杰拉德译作的波斯文来源，这对我们全面了解《鲁拜集》之美、思考菲译之美，十分重要。我将他考证出的波斯文原作，根据他自己的英译，全文译出写入解读里。他的译文对译得比较严格，但不押韵，也稍有生硬之嫌。我的译文保持了同样的风格，不考虑诗的形式，只求尽量忠实地反映内容。他的考证主要根据菲茨杰拉德提到的乌斯利抄本和加尔各答抄本，但我相信，菲译仍有别的来源。由于我不通波斯文，只能根据所读到的张鸿年先生翻译的 1207 年抄本和“乐园”本做些增补，为大家阅读提供一点儿方便。

我的英文、中文能力都很有限，在翻译中得到了很多朋友的帮助。眭谦、黄福海、蒋毅帮我校阅了译文，周兮吟、田争争帮我翻译了涉及的法文，艾博、顾家华提供了各种资料，另外，翻译中我还参考了郭沫若、梁实秋、黄杲炘、黄克孙、眭谦诸位先生的译本。尤其是，吴伟辛苦地选配插图，并写了介绍，熊琼精心地设计版式，让这本书真正体现了《鲁拜集》之美。在此一并致以真诚的谢意。但是，我相信，译文中的错误和不如人意之处必有很多，都应该由我自己负责，也真诚地希望得到读者朋友的指正和赐教。

序言

PREFACE

OMAR KHAYYÁM,
THE
ASTRONOMER-POET OF PERSIA.

Omar Khayyám was born at Naishápúr in Khorassán[1] in the latter half of our Eleventh, and died within the First Quarter of our Twelfth[2] Century. The slender Story of his Life is curiously twined about that of two other[3] very considerable Figures in their Time and Country: one of whom tells the Story of all Three. This was Nizám ul Mulk, Vizyr to Alp Arslan the Son, and Malik Shah the Grandson, of Toghrul Beg the Tartar, [4] who had wrested Persia from the feeble Successor of Mahmúd the Great, and founded that Seljukian Dynasty which finally roused Europe into the Crusades. This Nizám ul Mulk, [5]in his *Wasiyat* [6]—or *Testament*—which he wrote and left as a Memorial for future Statesmen—relates the following, as quoted in the *Calcutta Review*, [7]No. 59, from Mirkhond's History of the Assassins.

"'One of the greatest of the wise men of Khorassan was the Imám Mowaffak of Naishápúr[8], a man highly honored and reverenced, —may God rejoice his soul; his illustrious years exceeded eighty-five, and it was the universal belief that every boy who read the Koran or studied the traditions in his presence, would assuredly attain to honor and happiness. For this cause did my father send me from Tús to Naishápúr[9] with Abd-us-samad[10], the doctor of law, that I might employ myself in study and learning under the guidance of that illustrious teacher. Towards me he ever turned an eye of favor and kindness, and as his pupil I felt for him extreme affection and devotion, so that I passed four years in his service. When I first came there, I found two other pupils of mine own age newly arrived, Hakim Omar Khayyám, and the ill-fated Ben Sabbáh. Both were endowed with sharpness of wit and the highest natural powers; and we three formed a close friendship together. When the Imám rose from his lectures, they used to join me, and we repeated to each other the lessons we had heard. Now Omar was a native of Naishápúr[11], while Hasan Ben Sabbáh's father was one Ali, a man of austere life and practise, but heretical in his creed and doctrine. One day Hasan said to me and to Khayyám, 'It is a universal belief that the pupils of the Imám Mowaffak will attain to fortune. Now, even if we *all* do not attain thereto, without doubt one of us will; what then shall be our mutual pledge and bond? 'We answered, [12] 'Be it what you please. ' 'Well, 'he said, 'let us make a vow, that to whomsoever this fortune falls, he shall share it equally with the rest, and reserve no pre-eminence for himself. ' 'Be it so, ' we both replied, and on those terms we mutually pledged our words. Years rolled on, and I went from Khorassan to Transoxiana, and wandered to Ghazni and Cabul; and when I returned, I was invested with office, and rose to be administrator of affairs during the Sultanate of Sultan Alp Arslán. ' [13]

"He goes on to state, that years passed by, and both his old school-friends found him out, and came and claimed a share in his good fortune, according to the school-day vow. The Vizier was generous and kept his word. Hasan demanded a place in the government, which the Sultan granted at the Vizier's request; but discontented with a gradual rise, he plunged into the maze of intrigue of an oriental court, and, failing in a base attempt to supplant his benefactor, he was disgraced and fell. After many mishaps and wanderings, Hasan became the head of the Persian sect of the *Ismailians*, —a party of fanatics who had long murmured in obscurity, but rose to an evil eminence under the guidance of his strong and evil will. In A.D. 1090, [14]he seized the castle of Alamút, in the province of Rúdbar, which lies in the mountainous tract[15] south of the Caspian Sea; and it was from this mountain home he obtained that evil celebrity among the Crusaders as the OLD MAN OF THE MOUNTAINS, and spread terror through the Mohammedan world; and it is yet disputed whether the word *Assassin*, which they have left in the language of modern Europe as their dark memorial, is derived from the *hashish*, or opiate of hemp-leaves (the Indian *bhang*), [16]with which they maddened themselves to the sullen pitch of oriental desperation, or from the name of the founder of the dynasty, whom we have seen in his quiet collegiate days, at Naishápúr[17]. One of the countless victims of the Assassin's dagger was Nizám-ul-Mulk himself, the old school-boy friend ❶ .[18]

"Omar Khayyám also came to the Vizier to claim his [20] share; but not to ask for title or office. 'The greatest boon you can confer on me, ' he said, 'is to let me live in a corner under the shadow of your fortune, to spread wide the advantages of Science, and pray for your long life and prosperity. ' The Vizier tells us, that, when he found Omar was really sincere in his refusal, he pressed him no further, but granted him a yearly pension of 1200 [21] *mithkáls* of gold, from the treasury of Naishápúr. [22]

"At Naishápúr[23] thus lived and died Omar Khayyám, 'busied, 'adds the Vizier, 'in winning knowledge of every kind, and especially in Astronomy, wherein he attained to a very high pre-eminence. Under the Sultanate of Malik Shah, he came to Merv, and obtained great praise for his proficiency in science, and the Sultan showered favors upon him. '

"When the Malik Shah determined to reform the calendar, Omar was one of the eight learned men employed to do it; the result was the *Jaláli* era[24] (so called from *Jalál-ud-din*[25], one of the king's names) [26]—'a computation of time, 'says Gibbon, 'which surpasses the Julian, and approaches the accuracy of the Gregorian style. ' He is also the author of some astronomical tables, entitled Zíji-Malikshâhí," and the French have lately republished and translated an Arabic Treatise of his on Algebra. [27]

"His Takhallus or poetical name (Khayyám) signifies a Tent-maker, and he is said to have at one time exercised that trade, perhaps before Nizám-ul-Mulk's generosity raised him to independence. Many Persian poets similarly derive their names from their occupations; thus we have Attár, 'a druggist, ' [28] Assár [29], 'an oil presser, ' [30] &c. ❷ [31] Omar[32] himself alludes to his name in the following whimsical lines: —

'Khayyám, who stitched the tents of science,
Has fallen in grief's furnace and been suddenly burned;
The shears of Fate have cut the tent ropes of his life,
And the broker of Hope has sold him for nothing! '

❶ *Some of Omar's Rubáiyát warn us of the danger of Greatness, the instability of Fortune, and while advocating Charity to all Men, recommending us to be too intimate with none. Attár makes Nizám-ul-Mulk use the very words of his friend Omar [Rub. xxviii.],* [19] *"When Nizám-ul-Mulk was in the Agony (of Death) he said, 'Oh God! I am passing away in the hand of the Wind.'"*

❷ *Though all these, like our Smiths, Archers, Millers, Fletchers, &c., may simply retain the Surname of an hereditary calling.*

【校记】———

[1] 'Khorassán' ,二版、三版、四版作 'Khorassan'。
[2] 'Twelfth' ,一版、二版作 'Twelfth,'。
[3] 'other' ,一版作 'others'。
[4] 'one of whom tells the Story of all Three. This was Nizám ul Mulk, Vizyr to Alp Arslan the Son, and Malik Shah the Grandson, of Toghrul Beg the Tartar,' ,一版作 'one of them, Hasan al Sabbáh,whose very Name has lengthen' d down to us as a terrible Synonym for Murder: and the other (who also tells the Story of all Three) Nizám al Mulk, Vizyr to Alp the Lion and Malik Shah, Son and Grandson of Toghrul Beg the Tartar,'。
[5] 'Nizám ul Mulk' ,一版作 'Nizám al Mulk'。
[6] '*Wasiyat*' ,一版、二版作 '*Wasiýat*'。
[7] '*Calcutta Review*' ,一版、二版、三版作 'Calcutta Review'。
[8] 'Naishápúr' ,一版作 'Naishápur'。
[9] 'Naishápúr' ,一版作 'Naishápur'。
[10] 'Abd-us-samad' ,一版作 'Abd-u-samad'。
[11] 'Naishápúr' ,一版作 'Naishápur'。
[12] 'answered,' ,一版、三版作 'answered'。
[13] 一版段末有'" 号。
[14] 'In A.D. 1090,' ,一版作 'In A.B. 1090,'。
[15] 'tract' ,一版、二版、三版作 'tract,'。
[16] '(the Indian *bhang*),' ,一版作 '(the Indian *bhang*,)'。
[17] 'Naishápúr' ,一版作 'Naishápur'。
[18] 一版段末有" 号,无脚注。
[19] '[Rub. xxviii.]' ,二版作 '[Rub. xxxi.]'。
[20] 'his' ,二版、三版、四版作 'the'。
[21] '1200' ,一版作 '1,200'。
[22] 'Naishápúr' ,一版、四版作 'Naishápur'。
[23] 'Naishápúr' ,一版作 'Naishápur'。
[24] 'era' ,一版作 'era,'。
[25] '*Jalál-ud-din*' ,一版、二版、三版、四版作 '*Jalal-ud-din*'。
[26] 'names)' ,一版作 'names,)' ,二版作 'names) ,'。
[27] 此段后,一版尚有一段:'These severer Studies, and his Verses, which, though happily fewer than any Persian Poet' s, and, though perhaps fugitively composed, the Result of no fugitive Emotion or Thought, are probably the Work and Event of his Life, leaving little else to record. Perhaps he liked a little Farming too, so often as he speaks of the "Edge of the Tilth" on which he loved to rest with his Diwán of Verse, his Loaf — and his Wine.'
[28] ''a druggist, '' ,一版作 '"a druggist,"'。
[29] 'Assár' ,一版作 'Assar'。
[30] ''an oil presser,'' ,一版作 '"an oil presser,"'。
[31] 此脚注,一版置于正文,另加括号。'&c.,' 作 '&c.' , 'Surname' 作 'Sirname'。
[32] 'Omar' ,一版作 '"Omar'。

"We have only one more anecdote to give of his Life, and that relates to the close; it is told[33] in the anonymous preface which is sometimes prefixed to his poems; it has been printed in the Persian in the Appendix[34] to Hyde's *Veterum Persarum Religio*, p. 499[35]; and D'Herbelot alludes to it in his Bibliothèque[36], under *Khiam* 3 [37]—

"'It is written in the chronicles of the ancients that this King of the Wise, Omar Khayyám, died at Naishápúr[38] in the year of the Hegira, 517 (A.D. 1123); in science he was unrivalled, —the very paragon of his age. Khwájah Nizámi of Samarcand, who was one of his pupils, relates the following story: 'I often used to hold conversations with my teacher, Omar Khayyám, in a garden; and one day he said to me, 'My[39] tomb shall be in a spot where the north wind may scatter roses over it.' I wondered at the words he spake, but I knew that his were no idle words. 4 Years after, when I chanced to revisit Naishápúr[47], I went to his final resting-place[48], and lo! it was just outside a garden, and trees laden with fruit stretched their boughs over the garden wall, and dropped their flowers upon his tomb, so that[49] the stone was hidden under them. '"

Thus far—without fear of Trespass—from the *Calcutta Review*[50]. The writer of it, on reading in India this story of Omar's Grave, was reminded, he says, of Cicero's Account of finding Archimedes' Tomb at Syracuse, buried in grass and weeds. I think Thorwaldsen desired to have roses grow over him; a wish religiously fulfilled for him to the present day, I believe. However, to return to Omar.

Though the Sultan "shower'd Favours upon him," Omar's Epicurean Audacity of Thought and Speech caused him to be regarded askance in his own Time and Country. He is said to have been especially hated and dreaded by the Súfis, whose Practise he ridiculed, and whose Faith amounts to little more than his own, [51]when stript of the Mysticism and formal recognition of Islamism under which Omar would not hide[52]. Their Poets, including Háfiz, who are (with the exception of Firdausi[53]) the most considerable in Persia, borrowed largely, indeed, of Omar's material, but turning it to a mystical Use more convenient to Themselves and the People they addressed[54]; a People quite as quick of Doubt as of Belief; as[55] keen of Bodily Sense as of Intellectual; and delighting in a cloudy composition of both [56], in which they could float luxuriously between Heaven and Earth, and this World and the Next, on the wings of a poetical expression, that might serve indifferently for either[57]. Omar was too honest of Heart as well as of Head for this. Having failed (however mistakenly) [58] of finding any Providence but Destiny, and any World but This, he set about making the most of it; preferring rather to soothe the Soul through the Senses into Acquiescence with Things as he saw them[59], than to perplex it with vain disquietude[60] after what they *might* be[61]. It has been seen, however, that his Worldly Ambition was not exorbitant; and he very likely takes a humorous or perverse pleasure in exalting the gratification of Sense above that of the Intellect, in which he must have taken great delight, although it failed to answer the Questions in which he, in common with all men, was most vitally interested. [62]

For whatever Reason, however, Omar, as before said, has never been popular in his own Country, and therefore has been but scantily [63] transmitted abroad. The MSS. of his Poems, mutilated beyond the average Casualties of Oriental Transcription, are so rare in the East as scarce to have reacht Westward at all, in spite of all the acquisitions of [64] Arms and Science[65]. There is no copy[66] at the India House, none at the Bibliothèque Nationale[67] of Paris. We know but of one in England: No. 140 of the Ouseley MSS. at the Bodleian, written at Shiráz, A.D. 1460. This contains but 158 Rubáiyát. One in the Asiatic Society's Library at Calcutta (of which we have a Copy), [68]contains (and yet incomplete) 516, though swelled to that by all kinds of Repetition and Corruption. So Von Hammer speaks of *his* Copy as containing about 200, while Dr. Sprenger catalogues the Lucknow MS. at double that number[69]. 5 [70] The Scribes, too, of the Oxford and Calcutta MSS. seem to do their Work under a sort of Protest; each beginning with a Tetrastich (whether genuine or not), taken out of its alphabetical order; the Oxford

3 *"Philosophe Musulman qui a vécu en Odeur de Sainteté dans sa Religion, vers la Fin du premier et le Commencement du second Siècle," no part of which, except the "Philosophe," can apply to our Khayyám.*

4 *[40] The Rashness of the Words, according to D'Herbelot, consisted in being so opposed to those in the Korán: "No Man knows where he shall die." —This story of Omar reminds me of another[41] so naturally—and[42] when one remembers how wide of his humble mark the noble sailor aimed—so pathetically told by Captain Cook—not by Doctor Hawkesworth—in his Second Voyage (i. 374) [43]. When leaving Ulietea, "Oreo's last request was for me to return. When he saw he could not obtain that promise, he asked the name of my Marai (burying-place) [44]. As strange a question as this was, I hesitated not a moment to tell him 'Stepney'; the parish in which I live when in London. I was made to repeat it several times over till they could pronounce it; and then 'Stepney Marai no Toote' was echoed through an [45] hundred mouths at once. I afterwards found the same question had been put to Mr. Forster by a man on shore; but he gave a different, [46] and indeed more proper answer, by saying, 'No man who used the sea could say where he should be buried.'"*

5 *"Since this Paper was written [71] (adds the Reviewer in a note), "we have met with a Copy of a very rare Edition, printed at Calcutta in 1836. This contains 438 Tetrastichs, with an Appendix containing 54 others not found in some MSS."*

with one of Apology; the Calcutta with one of [72]Expostulation, supposed (says a Notice prefixed to the MS.) to have arisen[73] from a Dream, in which Omar's mother asked about his future fate. It may be rendered thus: —

"Oh Thou who burn'st in Heart for those who burn
"In Hell, whose fires thyself shall feed in turn;
"How long be crying, 'Mercy on them, God! '
"Why, who art Thou to teach, and He to learn"

The Bodleian Quatrain pleads Pantheism by way of Justification.

"If I myself upon a looser Creed
"Have loosely strung the Jewel of Good deed,
"Let this one thing for my Atonement plead:
"That One for Two I never did mis-read."

6 Professor Cowell.

The Reviewer,6 to whom I owe the Particulars of Omar's Life, concludes his Review by comparing him with Lucretius, both as to natural Temper and Genius, [74]and as acted

【校记】

[33] 'it is told',一版作 'related'。
[34] 'Appendix',一版、二版、三版、四版作 'appendix'。
[35] '*499*',四版作 '*529*'。
[36] 'Bibliothèque',一版、二版作 'Bibliothéque'。
[37] 此注,一版作 'Though *he* attributes the story to a Khiam, "Philosophe Musulman qui a vêcu en Odeur de Sainteté dans la Fin du premier et le Commencement du second Siècle," no part of which, except the "Philosophe," can apply to *our* Khayyám, who, however, may claim the Story as *his*, on the Score of Rubáiyát, *77* and *78* of the present Version. The Rashness of the Words, according to D'Herbelot, consisted in being so opposed to those in the Korán: "No Man knows where he shall die." '。二版、三版亦无 'sa Religion, vers', 'our' 亦作 '*our*'。三版 'vêcu' 作 'vécu'。四版无 'dans sa Religion,', 'our' 亦作 '*our*'。
[38] 'Naishápúr',一版作 'Naishápur'。
[39] 'My',一版作 'my'。
[40] 此注一版无。
[41] 'reminds me of another',二版作 'recalls a very different one'。
[42] 'and',二版、三版、四版作 'and,'。
[43] '(i. *374*)',二版、三版、四版无。
[44] '(burying-place)',二版、三版、四版作 '—Burying-place'。
[45] 'an',二版、三版、四版作 'a'。
[46] 'different,',三版作 'different'。
[47] 'Naishápúr',一版作 'Naishápur'。
[48] 'resting-place',一版作 'resting place'。
[49] 'that',一版、二版、三版、四版作 'as'。
[50] '*Calcutta Review*',一版、二版作 'Calcutta Review',一版此段至此结束,无以下数句。
[51] 'own,',一版、二版、三版、四版作 'own'。
[52] 'hide',一版作 'hide under'。
[53] 'Firdausi',一版作 'Firdaúsi'。
[54] 'addressed',一版作 'address'd'。
[55] 'as',一版作 'quite as'。
[56] 'composition of both',一版作 'Element compounded of all',二版作 'compound of both'。
[57] 'might serve indifferently for either',一版作 'could be recited indifferently whether at the Mosque or the Tavern'。
[58] '(however mistakenly)',四版作 'however mistakenly'。
[59] 'he saw them',一版作 'they were'。
[60] 'disquietude',一版作 'mortifications'。
[61] 'be',一版、二版、三版作 '*be*'。
[62] 'It has been seen, however, that his Worldly Ambition was not exorbitant; and he very likely takes a humorous or perverse pleasure in exalting the gratification of Sense above that of the Intellect, in which he must have taken great delight, although it failed to answer the Questions in which he, in common with all men, was most vitally interested.',一版作 'It has been seen that his Worldly Desires, however, were not exorbitant; and he very likely takes a humourous pleasure in exaggerating them above that Intellect in whose exercise he must have found great pleasure, tough not in a Theological direction. However this may be, his Worldly Pleasures are what they profess to be without auy Pretence at divine Allegory:his Wine is the veritable Juice of the Grape:his Tavern,where it was to be had:his Sáki, the Flesh and Blood that poured it out for him:all which, and where the Roses were in Bloom, was all he profess' d to want of this World or to expect of Paradise.
The Mathematic Faculty, too, which regulated his Fansy, and condensed his Verse to a Quality and Quantity un-known in Persian, perhaps in Oriental, Poetry, help' d by its very virtue perhaps to render him less popular with his countrymen. If the Greeks were Children in Gossip, what does Persian Literature imply but a *Second Childishness* of Garrulity ? And certainly if no *ungeometric* Greek was to enter Plato' s School of Philosopher, no so unchastised a Persian should enter on the Race of Persian Verse, with its "fatal Facility" of running on long after Thought is winded! But Omar was not only the single Mathematician of his Country' s Poets; he was also of that older Time and stouter Temper, before the native Soul of Persia was quite broke by a foreign Creed as well as foreign Conquest. Like his great Predecessor Firdúsi, who was as little of a *Mystic*; who scorned to use even a *Word* of the very language in which the New Faith came clothed; and who was suspected, not of Omar' s Irreligion indeed, but of secretly clinging to the ancient Fire-Religion of Zerdusht, of which so many of the Kings he sang were Worshippers.'。
[63] 'scantily',一版作 'charily'。
[64] 'the acquisitions of',一版作 'all that'。
[65] 'Science',一版作 'Science have brought us'。
[66] 'no copy',一版作 'none'。
[67] 'Bibliothèque Nationale',一版作 'Bibliothêque Imperiále',二版、三版作 'Bibliothèque Imperiále'。
[68] '),',一版作 ')'。
[69] 'number',一版、二版、三版作 'Number'。
[70] 此注,一版在段末。
[71] 'written',一版、二版作 'written"'。
[72] 此下至段末,一版作 'Execration too stupid for Omar' s, even had Omar been stupid enough to execrate himself.',又不引二诗。
[73] 'arisen',二版、三版作 'risen'。

upon by the Circumstances in which he lived. Both indeed were men of subtle, strong, and cultivated Intellect, fine Imagination, and *[75]* Hearts passionate for Truth and Justice; who justly revolted from their Country's false Religion, and false, or foolish, Devotion to it; but who *[76]* fell short of replacing what they subverted by *[77]* such better *Hope* as others, with no better Revelation to guide them, *[78]* had yet made a Law to themselves. Lucretius, indeed, with such material as Epicurus furnished, satisfied himself with the theory of a vast machine fortuitously constructed, *[79]*and acting by a Law that implied no Legislator*[80]*; and so composing himself into a Stoical rather than Epicurean severity of Attitude, sat down to contemplate the mechanical Drama of the Universe which he was part Actor in*[81]*; himself and all about him*[82]* (as in his own sublime description of the Roman Theater*[83]*) discoloured *[84]* with the lurid reflex of the Curtain suspended between the Spectator and the Sun. *[85]* Omar, more desperate, or more careless*[86]* of any so complicated System as resulted in nothing but hopeless Necessity*[87]*, flung his own Genius and Learning with a bitter or humorous*[88]* jest into the general Ruin which their insufficient glimpses only served to reveal; and, pretending sensual pleasure as the serious purpose of Life, only *diverted* himself with speculative problems of Deity, Destiny, Matter and Spirit, Good and Evil, and other such questions, easier to start than to run down, and the pursuit of which becomes a very weary sport at last! *[89]*

With regard to the present Translation. The original Rubáiyát (as, missing an Arabic Guttural, these *Tetrastichs* are more musically called) are independent Stanzas, consisting each of four Lines of equal, though varied, Prosody; sometimes *all* rhyming, but oftener (as here imitated *[90]*) the third line a blank. Somewhat*[91]* as in the Greek Alcaic, where the penultimate*[92]* line seems to lift and suspend the Wave that falls over in the last. As usual with such kind of Oriental Verse, the Rubáiyát follow one another according to Alphabetic Rhyme—a strange succession*[93]* of Grave and Gay. Those here selected are strung into something of an Eclogue, with perhaps a less than equal proportion of the "Drink and make-merry," which (genuine or not) recurs over-frequently in the Original. Either*[94]* way, the Result is sad enough: saddest perhaps when most ostentatiously merry: more apt *[95]* to move Sorrow than Anger toward the old Tentmaker, who, after vainly endeavoring to unshackle his Steps from Destiny, and to catch some authentic Glimpse of To-morrow*[96]*, fell back upon To-day*[97]* (which has out-lasted so many To-morrows*[98]*!) as the only Ground he had got to stand upon, however momentarily slipping from under his Feet.

While the second Edition of this version of Omar was preparing, *[99]* Monsieur Nicolas, French Consul at Resht, published a very careful and very good Edition of the Text, from a lithograph copy at Teheran, comprising 464 Rubáiyát, with translation and notes of his own.

Mons. Nicolas, whose Edition has reminded me of several things, and instructed me in others, does not consider Omar to be the material Epicurean that I have literally taken him for, but a Mystic, shadowing the Deity under the figure of Wine, Wine-bearer, &c., as Háfiz is supposed to do; in short, a Sufi Poet like Háfiz and the rest.

I cannot see reason to alter my opinion, formed as it was more than a dozen years ago[7] *[100]* when Omar was first shown me by one to whom I am indebted for all I know of Oriental, and very much of other, literature. He admired Omar's Genius so much, that he would gladly have adopted any such Interpretation of his meaning as Mons. Nicolas' if he could[8] .That he could not, *[101]* appears by his Paper in the Calcutta Review already so largely quoted; in which he argues from the Poems themselves, as well as from what records remain of the Poet's Life.

And if more were needed to disprove Mons. Nicolas' Theory, there is the Biographical Notice which he himself has drawn up in direct contradiction to the Interpretation of the Poems given in his Notes. (See pp. xiii-xiv of his Preface.)*[102]*Indeed I*[103]* hardly

[7] *[This was written in 1868. W.A.W.]*

[8] *Perhaps would have edited the Poems himself some years ago. He may now as little approve of my Version on one side, as of Mons. Nicolas' Theory on the other.*

knew poor Omar was so far gone till his Apologist informed me. For here we see that, whatever were the Wine that Háfiz drank and sang, the veritable Juice of the Grape it was which Omar used, *[104]*not only when carousing with his friends, but (says Mons. Nicolas) in order to excite himself to that pitch of Devotion which others reached by cries and "hurlemens." And yet, whenever Wine, Wine-bearer, &c., occur in the Text—which is often enough—Mons. Nicolas carefully annotates "Dieu," "La Divinité," &c.: so carefully indeed that one is tempted to think that he was indoctrinated by the Súfi

【校记】———

[74] 'The Reviewer, to whom I owe the Particulars of Omar' s Life, concludes his Review by comparing him with Lucretius, both as to natural Temper and Genius,' 一版作 'The Reviewer, who translates the foregoing Particulars of Omar' s Life, and some of his Verse into Prose, concludes by comparing him with Lucretius, both in natural Temper and Genius,'。'Reviewer'下,一版、二版、三版、四版无脚注。

[75] 'Both indeed were men of subtle, strong, and cultivated Intellect, fine Imagination, and',一版作 'Both indeed men of subtle Intellect and high Imagination, instructed in Learning beyond their day, and of Hearts'。

[76] 'who',一版、二版、三版作 'who yet'。

[77] 'by',一版作 'by any'。

[78] 'with no better Revelation to guide them,',一版作 'upon whom no better *Faith* had dawned,'。

[79] 'satisfied himself with the theory of a vast machine fortuitously constructed,',一版作 'consoled himself with the construction of a Machine that needed no Constructor,'。'a vast',二版、三版作 'so vast a'。

[80] 'Legislator',一版作 'Lawgiver'。

[81] 'Actor in',一版作 'Actor'。

[82] 'him',一版作 'him,'。

[83] 'Theater',一版作 'Theater,'。

[84] 'discoloured',一版作 'coloured'。

[85] 'suspended between the Spectator and the Sun',一版作 'that was suspended between them and the outer Sun.'。

[86] 'careless',一版作 'careless,'。

[87] 'so complicated System as resulted in nothing but hopeless Necessity',一版作 'such laborious System as resulted in nothing more than hopeless Necessity'。

[88] 'bitter or humorous',一版作 'bitter'。

[89] 'pretending sensual pleasure as the serious purpose of Life, only *diverted* himself with speculative problems of Deity, Destiny, Matter and Spirit, Good and Evil, and other such questions, easier to start than to run down, and the pursuit of which becomes a very weary sport at last!',一版作 'yielding his Senses to the actual Rose and Vine, only *diverted* his thoughts by balancing ideal possibilities of Fate, Freewill, Existence and Annihilation; with an oscillation so generally inclined to the negative and lower side, as to make such Stanzas as the following exceptions to his general Philosophy—

Oh, if my Soul can fling his Dust aside,
And naked on the Air of Heaven ride,
Is't not a Shame, is't not a Shame for Him
So long in this Clay Suburb to abide!

Or is *that* but a Tent, where rests anon
A Sultán to his Kingdom passing on,
And which the swarthy Chamberlain shall strike
Then when the Sultán rises to be gone'。

[90] 'imitated',一版、二版作 'attempted'。

[91] 'a blank. Somewhat',一版作 'suspending the Cadence by which the last atones with the former Two. Something',二版、三版、四版作 'a blank. Something'。

[92] 'penultimate',一版作 'third'。

[93] 'succession',一版作 'Farrago'。

[94] 'Either',一版作 'For Lucretian as Omar' s Genius might be, he cross' d that darker Mood with much of Oliver de Basaelin Humour. Any'。

[95] 'more apt',一版作 'any way,fitter to'。

[96] 'To-morrow',一版、二版、三版作 'Tomorrow'。

[97] 'To-day',一版、二版、三版作 'Today'。

[98] 'To-morrows',一版、二版、三版作 'Tomorrows'。

[99] 'While the second Edition of this version of Omar was preparing,',二版作 'While the present Edition of Omar was preparing,'。此下一版、四版无。

[100] 此注怀特后加,二版、三版俱无。

[101] 'not,',二版作 'not'。

[102] '(See pp. xiii-xiv of his Preface.)',二版作 'Here is one of the Anecdotes he produces. "Mais revenous à Khéyam, qui, resté étranger à toutes ces alternatives de guerres, d' intrigues, et de révoltes, dont cette époque fut si remplie, vivait tranquille dans son village natal, se livrant avec passion à l' étude de la philosophie des Soufis. Entouré de nombreux amis il cherchait avec eux dans le vin cette contemplation extatique que d' autres croient trouver dans des cris et des hurlemens," &c. "Les chroniqueurs persans racontent que Khéyam aimait surtout à s' entretenir et à boire avec ses amis, le soir au clair de la lune sur la terrasse de sa maison, entouré de chanteurs et musiciens, avec un échanson qui, la coupe à la main, la présentait à tour de rôle aux joyeux convives réunis.—Pendant une de ces soirées dont nons venons de parler, survient à l' improviste un coup de vent qui éteint les chandelles et renverse à terre la cruche de vin, placée imprudemment sur le bord de la terrasse. La cruche fut brisée et le vin repandu. Aussitot Khéyam, irrité, improvisa ce quatrain impie à l' addresse du Tout-Puissant: 'Tu as brisé ma cruche de vin, mon Dieu! tu as ainsi fermé sur moi la porte de la joie, mon Dieu! C' est moi qui bois, et c' est toi qui commets les désordres de l' ivresse! oh! (puisse ma bouche se remplir de la terre!) serais tu ivre, mon Dieu?'
"Le poète, après avoir prononcé ce blasphème, jetant les yeux sur une glace, se serait aperçu que son visage était noir comme du charbon. C' était une punition du ciel. Alors il fit cet autre quatrain non moins audacieux que le premier. 'Quel est l' homme ici-bas qui n' a point commis de péché, dis? Celui qui n' en aurait point commis, comment aurait-il vécu, dis? Si, parce que je fais du mal, tu me punis par le mal, quelle est donc la différence qui existe entre toi et moi, dis？' "' 三版 'pp. xiii-xiv' 作 'pp. 13-14'。

[103] 'Indeed I',二版作 'I really',此下另起一段。

[104] 'used,',二版作 'used'。

with whom he read the Poems. (Note to Rub. ii. p. 8.) A Persian would naturally wish to vindicate a distinguished Countryman; and a Súfi to enrol him in his own sect, which already comprises all the chief Poets of Persia.

What historical Authority has Mons. Nicolas to show that Omar gave himself up "avec passion à l'étude de la philosophie des Soufis"? (Preface, p. xiii.) The Doctrines of Pantheism, Materialism, Necessity, &c., were not peculiar to the Súfi; nor to Lucretius before them; nor to Epicurus before him; probably the very original Irreligion of Thinking men from the first; and very likely to be the spontaneous growth of a Philosopher living in an Age of social and political barbarism, under shadow *[105]* of one of the Two and Seventy Religions supposed to divide the world. Von Hammer (according to Sprenger's Oriental Catalogue) speaks of Omar as "a Free-thinker, and *a great opponent of Sufism*;" perhaps because, while holding much of their Doctrine, he would not pretend to any inconsistent severity of morals. Sir W. Ouseley has written a note *[106]* to something of the same effect on the fly-leaf of the Bodleian MS. And in two Rubáiyát of Mons. Nicolas' own Edition Súf and Súfi are both disparagingly named.

No doubt many of these Quatrains seem unaccountable unless mystically interpreted; but many more as unaccountable unless literally. Were the Wine spiritual, for instance, how wash the Body with it when dead? Why make cups of the dead clay to be filled with—"La Divinité [9]" —by some succeeding Mystic? Mons. Nicolas himself is puzzled by some "bizarres"and "trop Orientales"allusions and images—"d'une sensualité quelquefois révoltante" indeed—which"les convenances" do not permit him to translate; but still which the reader cannot but refer to "La Divinité ." No doubt also many of the Quatrains in the Teheran, as in the Calcutta, Copies, are spurious; such *Rubáiyát* being the common form of Epigram in Persia. But this, at best, tells as much one way as another; nay, the Súfi, who may be considered the Scholar and Man of Letters in Persia, would be far more likely than the careless Epicure to interpolate what favours his own view of the Poet. I observed that very few of the more mystical Quatrains are in the Bodleian MS. which must be one of the oldest, as dated at Shiraz, A.H. 865, A.D. 1460. And this, I think, especially distinguishes Omar (I cannot help calling him by his—no, not Christian—familiar name) from all other Persian Poets: That, whereas with them the Poet is lost in his Song, the Man in Allegory and Abstraction; we seem to have the Man—the *Bonhomme*—Omar himself, with all his Humours and Passions, as frankly before us as if we were really at Table with him, after the Wine had gone round.

I must say that I, for one, never wholly believed in the Mysticism of Háfiz. It does not appear there was any danger in holding and singing Súfi Pantheism, so long as the Poet made his Salaam to Mohammed at the beginning and end of his Song. Under such conditions Jeláluddín, Jámi, Attár, and others sang; using Wine and Beauty indeed as Images to illustrate, not as a Mask to hide, the Divinity they were celebrating. Perhaps some Allegory less liable to mistake or abuse had been better among so inflammable a People: much more so when, as some think with Háfiz and Omar, the abstract is not only likened to, but identified with, the sensual Image; hazardous, if not to the Devotee himself, yet to his weaker Brethren; and worse for the Profane in proportion as the Devotion of the Initiated grew warmer. And all for what? To be tantalized with Images of sensual enjoyment which must be renounced if one would approximate a God, who according to the Doctrine, *is* Sensual Matter as well as Spirit, and into whose Universe one expects unconsciously to merge after Death, without hope of any posthumous Beatitude in another world to compensate for all one's *[107]* self-denial in this. Lucretius' blind Divinity certainly merited, and probably got, as much self-sacrifice as this of the Súfi; and the burden of Omar's Song—if not "Let us eat"—is assuredly—"Let us drink, for To-morrow we die! " And if Háfiz meant quite otherwise by a similar language, he surely miscalculated when he devoted his Life and Genius to so equivocal a Psalmody as, from his Day to this, has been said and sung by any rather than Spiritual*[108]* Worshippers.

[9] *A note to Quatrain 234 admits that, however clear the mystical meaning of such Images must be to Europeans, they are not quoted without "rougissant" even by laymen in Persia—"Quant aux termes de tendresse qui commencent ce quatrain, comme tant d'autres dans ce recueil, nos lecteurs, habitués maintenant à 1'étrangete des expressions si souvent employés par Khéyam pour rendre ses pensées sur l'amour divin, et à la singularité des images trop orientales, d'une sensualité quelquefois révoltante, n'auront pas de peine à se persuader qu'il s'agit de la Divinité, bien que cette conviction soit vivement discutée par les moullahs musulmans et même par beaucoup de laïques, qui rougissent véritablement d'une pareille licence de leur compatriote à 1'égard des choses spirituelles."*

However, as there is some traditional presumption, and certainly the opinion of some learned men, in favour of Omar's being a Súfi—and even something of a Saint—those who please may so interpret his Wine and Cup-bearer. On the other hand, as there is far more historical certainty of his being a Philosopher, of scientific Insight and Ability far beyond that of the Age and Country he lived in; of such moderate worldly Ambition as becomes a Philosopher, and such moderate wants as rarely satisfy a Debauchee; other readers may be content to believe with me that, while the Wine Omar celebrates is simply the Juice of the Grape, he bragged [109] more than he drank of it, in very defiance perhaps of that Spiritual Wine which left its Votaries sunk in Hypocrisy or Disgust. [110]

【校记】———

[105] 'shadow',二版作 'sanction'。
[106] 'note',二版作 'Note'。
[107] 'one's',二版作 'the'。
[108] 'Spiritual',二版作 'spiritual'。
[109] 'bragged',二版作 'bragg'd'。
[110] 此段二版作 'However, it may remain an Open Question, both with regard to Háfiz and Omar: the reader may understand them either way, literally or mystically, as he chooses. Whenever Wine, Wine-bearer, Cypress, &c., are named, he has only to suppose "La Divinité;" and when he has done so with Omar, I really think he may proceed to the same Interpretation of Anacreon—and even Anacreon Moore.'

欧玛尔·海亚姆：波斯的天文学家诗人

欧玛尔·海亚姆在我们的十一世纪后半叶生于呼罗珊的内沙普尔，死在我们的十二世纪的头一个二十五年。他生平那一点儿的故事却跟他们那个时代和国家里两个相当重要的人物奇妙地联系在一起——其中一个讲述了他们三个的故事。这就是尼查木·乌尔·穆尔克，鞑靼人脱斡邻勒·伯克的儿子阿尔普·阿尔斯兰、孙子马立克·沙的维齐尔。[4]脱斡邻勒·伯克从马赫穆德大帝无能的继承人手里夺得波斯，建立了最终激起欧洲发动十字军东征的塞尔柱王朝。这个尼查木·乌尔·穆尔克，在他作为留给将来政治家的一个借鉴而写的《遗书》里，有下面的讲述。这里引自《加尔各答评论》第59号，源出米尔克洪的《阿萨辛史》。

"'呼罗珊智慧的人中最伟大的一个是内沙普尔的伊玛目·穆瓦法克，一个享有极高荣誉和受尊崇的人，——愿神使他的灵魂快乐，他光辉的年岁超过了八十五。人们普遍相信，在他眼前诵读《可兰经》和学习传统的孩子，确定能够得到荣耀和幸福。为了这个原因，我父亲把我从突斯送到内沙普尔，跟法学博士阿布德·乌斯·沙玛德一起，好让我在这位杰出老师的教导下全心学习。他对我特加垂青和慈爱，作为学生我对他无限尊敬和热爱，就这样在他那里我服侍了四年。刚到那儿时，我遇上另外两个新来的同龄学生，哈基姆·欧玛尔·海亚姆，和带着厄运的本·萨巴赫。两个人都赋有敏锐的才智和极高的天资，于是我们三个结下了亲密的友谊。每当伊玛目起身离开讲席，他们常常和我一起，彼此共同复习听过的课程。欧玛尔是内沙普尔本地人，哈桑·本·萨巴赫的父亲是个阿里，一个过着自我克制的生活且现实的人，但他的信仰和教条是异端的。一天哈桑对我和海亚姆说：'大家普遍相信伊玛目·穆瓦法克的学生将会获得幸运。就算我们不能都获得，无疑我们中的一个也会，那我们相互之间该有什么誓言和约定？'我们回答：'你喜欢的就是了。''好，'他说，'让我们起誓，不论这幸运降临到谁，他都要跟其他人相等地分享，不能给他自己留任何特别。''就这样。'我俩一起回答，于是照那个条款我们互相起誓。岁月如驰，我从呼罗珊去了中亚河中地区，又游历了伽兹尼和喀布尔。我返回时，被委以官职，后来在阿尔普·阿尔斯兰苏丹治下升任首相。'

"他继续叙述，几年过去了，他的老同学都找到了他，根据求学时代的誓言，前来要求共享他的好运。维齐尔慷慨大方，遵守誓言。哈桑要求在政府里有个位置，对此苏丹因维齐尔的请求同意了。但他不满足于渐次升迁，陷入一个东方宫廷阴谋的迷途，然而，未能实现取代他的恩人的卑鄙企图，他不光彩地落败了。在经过许多不幸和流离之后，哈桑成为亦思马因教波斯教派的首领。这是一群狂热分子，经历了长期的暗中酝酿，在哈桑强大而邪恶的意志引导下最终达致邪恶的巅峰。公元1090年，他占据鲁德巴省的阿剌模式堡，地处里海南面的山区。正是由于这个山中据点，他在十字军中获得了邪恶的名号：山中老人，并将恐怖遍布伊斯兰世界。现代欧洲语言中的暗杀一词，就是他们遗留下的黑色记忆。其字源仍有争论，有的说来自 hashish，即从大麻叶中提炼的麻醉剂（印度文 bhang），用这个东西他们使自己迷狂，达到东方人绝望时阴郁的极点。有的说来自集团创始者的名字，我们在他平静的内沙普尔求学时代看到过。暗杀之刃的无数牺牲者之一，就是尼查木·乌尔·穆尔克他自己，旧时的学友。**1**

"欧玛尔·海亚姆也来到维齐尔那里要求他的一份，但并不要名衔和官职。'你能给我的最大恩惠，'他说，'就是让我生活在你好运庇护的一隅，广播科学之益，同时为你的长寿和昌盛而祈祷。'维齐尔告诉我们，当他发现欧玛尔的谢绝确实是真诚的，就不再强劝，而从内沙普尔的国库中每年支给他1200金币作为年金。

1 欧玛尔《鲁拜集》的一些篇章警告我们盛时的危险，好运的无常，倡言对所有人友善的同时，劝告我们不要跟任何人过于密切。阿塔尔让尼查木·乌尔·穆尔克使用了他朋友欧玛尔的那句话（《鲁拜集》第28首），"当尼查木·乌尔·穆尔克处在死亡的痛苦中，他说：'哦，主啊，我正从风的手里消逝。'"

“在内沙普尔欧玛尔·海亚姆这样生活直至去世，维齐尔又说：‘忙于获取各种知识，特别是在天文学领域，他已登峰造极。当马立克·沙苏丹治下，他来到梅尔夫，因为学问的精深获致盛誉，苏丹对他颇示恩宠。’

“那时马立克·沙决定修订历法，欧玛尔是从事于此的八位学者之一。其成果就是哲拉里历（这个称呼来自国王的一个名字哲拉鲁丁）。‘在时间的推算上，’吉本说，‘超过了尤利安历，接近格里高利历式的精准。’他也是一些被命名为马立克·沙希星算表的天文图表的作者。”法国人近来曾有重版，并且翻译了他的一篇阿拉伯文代数论。[27]

“他写诗所用之名海亚姆，意思是帐篷制作者，据说他曾一度从事此业，大概是在尼查木·乌尔·穆尔克的慷慨使他生活独立之前。很多波斯诗人都同样地由他们的职业而得名，像我们知道的阿塔是‘药剂师’，阿萨是‘榨油匠’，等等。❷欧玛尔自己在下面诡异的诗行里隐指其名：

海亚姆，他缝制了科学的帐篷，
很快被焚烧在忧患的炉火中；
命运之剪剪断他人生的帐绳，
希望的商贩出卖他只为虚空。

“他的生平，我们只能再提供一件轶事，关系到他临终。这是在某个时期置于他诗集之前的一篇佚名序言里讲的。其波斯原文印在海德《波斯古教》的附录里，见第 499 页。戴波卢的《文库》，在海姆条下也提到过。❸ [37]

“它被记录在古代的编年史里，这位智慧的王者，欧玛尔·海亚姆，在海吉拉历 517 年（公元 1123 年）卒于内沙普尔。在科学上他无与伦比，是他那个时代的典范。撒马尔罕的尼札米和卓，是他的一个学生，讲述了下面这个故事：‘我经常跟我的老师，欧玛尔·海亚姆，在花园里谈话。一天他对我说：“我的坟墓要在那样一个地方，北风会把玫瑰吹落在它上面。”我很诧异他说出这样的话，但我知道他从不说空话。❹很多年过去，我有机会重访内沙普尔，我去了他最后的安息之地。看啊！它正好在一个花园外边，树上缀满果实，枝条伸过花园的围墙，把花朵撒在他的墓上，直到墓石被掩盖在花下。’”

我已不惮侵权从《加尔各答评论》大量征引。它的作者，在印度读了欧玛尔坟墓的故事，他说，让他想起西塞罗在叙拉古寻找到被杂草所掩埋的阿基米德坟墓的记述。我想到多瓦尔德森希

❷ 所有这些，就像我们的史密斯（铁匠）、阿切尔（射手）、米勒（磨工）、弗莱彻（箭工）等，只不过是从世代传袭的称呼取得了姓氏。

❸ “一世纪末二世纪初，这位伊斯兰教哲人有圣香的体验。”除了同为哲学家，没有其他任何一点，能够适合我们的海亚姆。

❹ 根据戴波卢，这段话的轻率在于跟《可兰经》里那个说法相抵牾：“没有人能知道他将死在哪里。”——欧玛尔这个故事，很自然地让我想起另外一个故事，特别是当一个人想起那位高贵的水手在设定自己卑微

【校记】

[4] 一版作：他们中的一个，哈桑·艾尔·萨巴赫，他那个名字已经到了我们沿用为谋杀的可怕同义词；另一个，讲述了他们三个的故事，尼查木·艾尔·穆尔克，鞑靼人脱斡邻勒·伯克的儿子和孙子——狮子王阿尔普和马立克·沙的维齐尔。

[27] 一版后尚有一段：这些更为严密的研究，以及他那些诗，虽然比任何波斯诗人的幸好都要少，而且，虽然可能是随便创作的，却也不是随意的情感或思想的结果，可能就是他一生的工作和事件，此外几乎没有留下任何记录。可能他也喜欢干点儿农活儿，他经常讲到“耕地的边缘”，他喜欢歇息在那儿，带着他的诗集，他的面包和他的酒。

[37] 此注，一版作：虽然他把这个故事归于海姆，“一世纪末二世纪初，这位伊斯兰教哲人有圣香的体验”，除了同为哲学家，没有其他任何一点，能够适合我们的海亚姆，然而，海亚姆可以宣称这故事是他的，根据目前这个《鲁拜集》版本第 77 和 78 首的痕迹。根据戴波卢，这段话的轻率在于跟《可兰经》里那个说法相抵牾：“没有人能知道他将死在哪里。”

【解读】

这里所引的诗，是考威尔教授根据乌斯利抄本第 22 首翻译的，亦见加尔各答抄本第 59 首，“乐园”本第 433首。

望种出玫瑰来掩盖他，我相信，他的愿望直到今天都被虔诚地满足着。好了，回到欧玛尔吧。

虽然苏丹“对他颇示恩宠”，但欧玛尔享乐主义思想和言论的大胆使他在自己的时代和国度为人侧目。相传苏菲派尤其痛恨和惧怕他，他们的行为是他所嘲笑的，他们的信仰也根本不比他自己的多一点儿，如果除去欧玛尔不愿用以掩饰的神秘主义及伊斯兰教义的形式认可。他们的诗人，包括哈菲兹，他是菲尔多西之外波斯最重要的诗人，确实都大量取资于欧玛尔，但转而用作神秘的用途以便于他们自己和他们对之诵读的民族。这个民族怀疑和信仰都很容易，感官和理智都很敏锐，喜欢在一起暧昧地结合，[56] 在其中他们可以纵情浮游于天国和尘世、今生和来生之间，凭着诗句的翅膀，不在乎地投身于任何一方。[57] 欧玛尔的心灵和头脑对此都太过诚实。他（不管多错误地）找不到任何神意除了命运，找不到任何世界除了此世，他就尽量抓住它，他宁肯使感官顺受他看到的事物 [59] 以愉悦心灵，也不肯困惑于它们以后将会如何以致徒然扰乱 [60]。我们也看到，他世俗的追求并不过度，他很像是在使人欣喜的感官满足中得到一种幽默、乖张的乐趣，将之置于理智之上。其实在理智中他得到了极大的愉悦，尽管理智不能回答他那些，和所有人都一样的，最受关切的问题。[62]

然而，不管什么原因，如之前所说，欧玛尔从未在他自己的国家广受欢迎，因此也很少传到国外。他的诗集稿本《东方散佚抄本集》未收，在东方已很少见，就根本传不到西方了，虽说在武器和科学方面东西方交流还是很充分的。其复制本印度学舍没有，巴黎国家图书馆也没有。我们知道只有一本在英国，就是牛津包德勒图书馆编号乌斯利第 140 号的写本，公元 1460 年写于设拉子。这里包括 158 首鲁拜。有一本在加尔各答亚洲协会图书馆，我们得到一个副本，包括仍不够完备的 516 首，还被各样的重出和劣制品种充斥。冯·海默尔说他的副本包括 200 首，施普伦格博士著录的鲁克诺稿本两倍于此。[5]看来，牛津和加尔各答写本的抄写者，都在一种抵触之下做着他们的工作。每一个都以一首四行诗（不论真伪）开始，将之从其字母次序的排列中抽出，牛津写本是一首忏悔诗，加尔各答写本是一首告诫诗。[72] 后者根据缀于稿本的说明被推测起因于一个梦，梦中欧玛尔的母亲询问他未来的命运。可以这样来译述：

哦你为那地狱被焚者心如焚，
你自己也得轮到那火里焚身；
**　你呼喊多久：“怜悯他们吧，上帝！”**
去教的汝何人？来学的彼何人？

包德勒写本的四行诗通过自证的方式为泛神论辩护。

如果我自己用那松散的信念，
松散地去把善行的珠宝贯串，
**　就让这件事为我的赎罪辩护：**
我从来都没有把一当二讲乱。

评论者[6]——欧玛尔生平的细节我都得益于他，[74] 在评述的结尾他比较了欧玛尔和卢克莱修，二人的自然性情和天赋都很相像，所遭遇的生存环境也很相像，都是敏锐、坚强的人，有经受训练的智力和良好的想象力，[75] 心灵渴求真理和正义。他们正当地反抗国家的虚伪宗教，和委身于此的虚伪或愚昧。不过，他们不能像别的人一样用更好的希望取代他们所推翻的，也没有更好的启示来引导他们，[78] 可也还是为自己订立了律法。卢克莱修的确是靠着伊壁鸠鲁提供的那些材料，满足于自己认为的宇宙是偶然形成的巨大机械这一理论，[79] 它的运动虽循法则却找不出立法者。他把自己塑造成斯多葛式的，而非伊壁鸠鲁式的严肃态度。他坐下来凝视着宇宙的机械戏剧，在其中他也扮演了一个角色，他自己和围绕他的一切（就像他自己对罗马剧场的壮观描写），都在悬挂于观众和太阳之间的幕布的可怕反射下褪尽颜色。对于任何这样的复杂体系，其结果只是没有希望的必然性，欧玛尔显得更悲观，或是更漫不在意。他把自己的天才和学问，伴以苦涩、幽默的玩笑，倾注在他们不充分的一瞥仅能揭示的普遍毁灭上。于是假装把俗欲之乐当成人生的严肃目的，只是用神、命运、物质和精神、善和恶等等这些理论问题让自己得到消遣，而这些问题开始要比继续下去

的目标时是多么茫然无绪——库克船长，而不是霍克沃斯博士，在他的《第二次航行》（第一卷第 374 页）一书里这样哀伤地写道。当离开乌列特亚时，奥瑞奥的最后一个请求是要我返回。当他看到他不能得到我的许诺时，就问我将来安葬地的名字。虽说这个问题很奇怪，我还是毫不犹豫地告诉他：“斯特普尼。”这是我在伦敦时居住的教区。他们要求我重复念了好几遍，直到他们可以发音读出来。这时“斯特普尼的安葬地里没有图特”的声音立刻回响在上百人的口中。我后来发现一个海岸上的人也对福斯特先生问了同样的问题，但是他给出了一个不同却更恰当的回答，是这样说：“一个经常在海上的人是不能说出他会葬在哪里的。”

[5] 评论者在注释里补充说：“写完这篇文章后，我们又碰上一个极其罕见版本的副本，1836 年在加尔各答印行。这里包括 438 首四行诗，附录中还包括另外不见于其他稿本的 54 首。”

[6] 考威尔教授。

更容易，对它们的探索最终成为令人倦怠的游戏。[89]

来看看现在的译本。原初的鲁拜（由于缺少一个阿拉伯语的喉音，这些四行诗念起来更具音乐性）是单独的诗节，每节由四行相等的诗句组成，其韵律大致相同也偶有变化，有时全部押韵，但经常是（像这里所模拟的）第三句不押韵。[91] 有些类似古希腊的阿尔凯奥斯诗体，倒数第二行像是被提起来，暂停一下再如波浪般落在最后一行。就像一般常见的这类东方诗集一样，鲁拜集按照入韵字母的次序编排，这就看到死亡和欢乐被奇怪地连接在一起了。那些被选出的诗歌恰好成为一组田园诗，这里相较于原文中经常出现的“饮酒和作乐”的内容（真实或不真实）在同样的比例上可能更少一些。不管如何，[94] 这结果是足够伤感的，最伤感的可能是最夸耀欢乐的时候，反使老帐篷匠更易于哀伤而非愤怒。他徒然努力

【校记】———

[56]“在一起暧昧地结合”，一版作：所有成分暧昧地结合。

[57]“不在乎地投身于任何一方”，一版作：不在乎地在清真寺或者酒店里诵读。

[59]“他看到的事物”，一版作：它们就是如此的事物。

[60]“徒然扰乱”一版作：徒然禁欲。

[62] 此句一版作：虽然没有在神学的方向上。然而是如此，他承认他的世俗快乐没有神圣的寓意，他的酒是真正的葡萄汁，他的酒肆就在那儿，他的行酒人是为他倒酒的血肉之躯，玫瑰是开着花的，所有这些他承认就是他今世的需求和来世的向往。

数学方面的才能也规范了他的想象，将他的诗歌凝成一种在波斯诗歌、也许在东方诗歌中都没有的质和量；也许就是这种质量，让他在本国人中不太受欢迎。如果说古希腊人是喜欢说三道四的孩子，那么我们是否可以说，波斯文学就是饶舌的“第二个童年”？如果说进入柏拉图哲学学院的人，都是懂得几何学的，那么参加波斯诗歌竞赛的人，也都是放纵其才的诗人，因为波斯诗歌“致命的能力”就是在缠绕地思想之后再作冗长地叙写。但是，欧玛尔不仅是本国诗人中唯一的数学家，他也继承了远古时代，以及波斯人本来的精神被外族信仰和外国侵略彻底摧垮之前的那种更刚毅的性格。这像他伟大的前辈菲尔多西，菲尔多西也不是个神秘主义者，他甚至不屑使用新信仰所赋予的那些词汇；他确实不是像欧玛尔那样的无宗教者，而是被猜测和古代琐罗亚斯德的拜火教有某些暗里的关联，他歌颂的许多国王都是拜火教的信仰者。

[72]“加尔各答写本是一首告诫诗”，一版作：加尔各答写本是一首对欧玛尔愚蠢的诫骂，欧玛尔也真是蠢得够一骂。

[74]“评论者”，一版作：评论者，他翻译了前引欧玛尔生平之详情，还把他的一些诗译成散文体。

[75]“有经受训练的智力和良好的想象力”，一版作：都有着敏锐的智力和超绝的想象力，受到逾越时代的学术训练。

[78]“也没有更好的启示来引导他们”，一版作：没有更好的信仰降临他们。

[79]“满足于自己认为的宇宙是偶然形成的巨大机械这一理论”，一版作：用一台不需要构建者的机械构造物来安慰自己。

[89] 一版作：就把他的感官委之于真正的玫瑰花和酒中，只是为了转移其思想以达致平衡命运、自由意志、存在、毁灭的理想可能。稍有扰乱，通常会走向负面和低层，于是就有了这样出其通常哲学之外的诗行——

我的灵魂如把躯壳丢一边，
哦，飘游在天空里无挂无牵，
能不羞愧，难道他能不羞愧
如此久地在这泥土内蹒跚！
那不过是短暂停息的帐篷，
在苏丹去往他的国土途中，
黑暗的侍卫不是会去打点
一旦等到那苏丹起身将行？

[91]“（像这里所模拟的）第三句不押韵”，一版作：（像这里所尝试的）中止第三行的韵脚，而在最后一行偿还前两行。

[94] 一版前有：卢克莱修大概和欧玛尔的天才很像，他把阴郁的情绪和更多的奥立弗·德·巴塞林的幽默交织在一起。

【解读】———

加尔各答抄本第 1 首根据赫荣 - 艾伦译文：

哦，烧掉被烧掉中（忍受的）一个！
注定轮到被烧掉，
哦，你！地狱之火将从他那里燃烧，
你还要说多久，“怜悯欧玛尔！”
你想成为上帝仁慈的老师吗？

“乐园”本第 17 首、第 32 首也有相近的内容。

包德勒图书馆的乌斯利抄本第 1 首（加尔各答抄本第 274 首，1207 年抄本第 159 首，“乐园”本第 2 首），根据赫荣 - 艾伦译文：

如果我从未串起你服侍的珍珠，
如果我从未从我脸上拭去罪过的尘土，
然而，对你的仁慈我没有绝望，
因为这个原因我从未把一说成二。

想让自己的脚步摆脱命运，能赶上真正瞥见明天，可还是跌回了今天（这今天比很多的明天都要长！）。那是他唯一可以立足的地方，尽管也很快会从他脚下溜走。

当欧玛尔这个译本的第二版正在准备时，法国驻雷什特总领事尼古拉斯先生也出版了一个非常仔细和完美的文本版本，底本是德黑兰的一个石印本，收有 464 首鲁拜，以及他自己的翻译和注释。

尼古拉斯先生，他的版本在一些地方提示了我，在另一些地方指导了我，他并不认为欧玛尔是个物质的伊壁鸠鲁主义者，而我倒是真这么看的。他认为欧玛尔是一个神秘主义者，在酒、担酒者等形象下隐喻着神，如同我们猜想哈菲兹所做的，简单说，是一个像哈菲兹和其他诗人一样的苏菲诗人。

我没能看出我改变观点的理由，它在十几年前就形成了，当时有个人第一次把欧玛尔拿给我看。我对东方的所有了解，以及大量其他的知识，包括文学，都受惠于这个人。他对欧玛尔那么赞赏，如果他能认可，一定会愉快地征引尼古拉斯先生那样的关于他的意义的阐释。[7] 然而他不能，我已大量引用的他发表在《加尔各答评论》上的文章能够表明，在那里他的论述或者来自诗本身，或者来自诗人生平的遗留记录。

[7] 大概多年前他自己也编辑了这部诗集。他现在可能很少会赞同我这一边的译文，对尼古拉斯先生那一边的理论也是一样。

如果需要进一步反驳尼古拉斯先生的理论，这有一条他自己所写的传记性附言（见他的序言第 13、14 页）[102]，和他在注释里给出的诗的解释直接相反。真的，我几乎不知道可怜的欧玛尔走到这么远，直到他的辩解者告诉我。在这里我们看到，不管哈菲兹喝的和歌唱的酒究竟是何物，欧玛尔用到的就是真正的葡萄汁。不仅在和朋友畅饮时，甚至（如尼古拉斯先生所说）在为了刺激他自己进入狂热的程度时，而这是别人通过哭喊叫骂达到的。然而，不管何时只要文本中出现酒、担酒者等等，这又是很经常的，尼古拉斯先生都小心地注解为“神”“神圣的”等等。如此小心的行为，会引起人猜想他是被一个一起读诗的苏菲时时在教导。(《鲁拜集》第 2 首的注释，见第 8 页）一个波斯人自然会希望维护一个杰出的本国人的声望，而一个苏菲也自然会把他纳入他自己的教派，那里已经包括了所有波斯的重要诗人。

尼古拉斯先生表示，欧玛尔“酷嗜苏菲派的学说”（序言第 8 页）而沉溺其中，这一点有什么历史性的权威根据？泛神论、唯物论、必然性等原则，并不是苏菲派独有的，也不是他们之前的卢克莱修和他之前的伊壁鸠鲁独有的。它可能属于最早的思想者那种非常原始的无神论，更可能是一个社会和政治野蛮时代，在七十二宗的每一个都想分裂世界的阴影下，生活于其中的哲学家自发产生的。冯·海默尔（根据施普伦格的《东方目录》）说欧玛尔是“自由思想者，苏菲派的伟大反对者”。大概是因为，当他掌握了很多他们的学说时，他就不会假装在道德上过分严苛，从而导致矛盾。乌斯利爵士在包德勒稿本的扉页上也写下了表示相同观点的题记。在尼古拉斯先生自己的版本里，也有两首鲁拜，苏弗和苏菲都是被贬抑地称呼的。

无疑很多这样的四行诗如果不做神秘解释看来无法理解，但更多的如果不是照字面解释也是无法理解的。比如，酒如果是精神性的，那一个人死后如何用它清洗身体？为什么用没有生命的泥土做酒杯，必须被一些后来的神秘主义者注入“神灵”？尼古拉斯先生自己看来被一些“奇异”和“过于东方”的暗示和形象所困扰，这些东西诚然“过于肉欲而有时使人起反感”，这样的“方便语”不允许他把它们翻译出来，而读者只有指向“神圣性”而别无他法了。[8] 无疑在德黑兰写本中也有一些四行诗，就像在加尔各答写本中，都是伪作，这样的鲁拜其实是波斯短诗的常见形式。但这里至少同时揭示了事情的两个方面。虽然苏菲被看作波斯的学者和文学家，但他们比漫不经心的伊壁鸠鲁主义者更可能挟带有利于自己的关于这位诗人的看法。我注意到，在包德勒抄本里很少有较为神秘的四行诗，它应该是最古老的抄本之一，在回历 865 年、公元 1460 年写于设拉子。这个，我认为，特别有助于将欧

[8] 在第 234 首的注释他承认了这一点，不管这些意象的神秘意义对于欧洲人是多么显而易见，但它们即使被波斯的平信徒所引述，也不会不“脸红”。“当读到这首四行诗开头的欢爱之情时，一如读这本诗集中其他篇章时那样，我们的读者如今早已习惯于这些奇异的表达——海亚姆经常用这种方式来表达他对神圣之爱的思索。而对于那些太过东方化的意象所具有的特点，那种有时过于叛逆的肉欲，我们的读者可以毫无困难地将它们看作是指向神圣性的。然而这种信念在穆斯林毛拉间引起了激烈的争论，而且不少世俗信徒对此也颇有非议——其同胞们对于这些指向精神的事物一视同仁的许可令他们确实为之感到脸红。”

玛尔（我忍不住用他，不，不是基督教的教名，是他为人熟知的名字称呼他）与其他波斯诗人区别开来。和他们不同，他是沉溺在他的歌中的诗人，在寓言和玄思中的人。我们看来面对着这个人——欧玛尔自己，和所有他的幽默和热情，坦率地在我们之前。好像我们真的跟他同桌共饮，那酒已经开始轮流倒上了。

我必须说，就个人而言，我从来没有完全相信哈菲兹的神秘主义。只要这位诗人在他的歌曲开头和结尾向穆罕默德行额手礼，即便他持有和歌唱苏菲的泛神论，也似乎不会有什么危险。哲拉鲁丁、贾米、阿塔，还有其他人，都是在这样的条件之下歌唱的，他们实际上是用酒和美人作为意象去阐明，而非作为面具去掩饰，他们赞颂的神明。也许用些不那么容易犯错或滥用的讽喻，对于容易激动的人民比较合适。更为严重的是，一些人认为对于哈菲兹和欧玛尔，那种抽象不只是与肉欲形象相似，而且与之相同。这些都是危险的，即便对于虔诚教徒自身而言不如此，对于他的较脆弱的兄弟们而言仍然如此。对于刚入会的新的教徒，敬拜越是热烈，相应的亵渎就越严重。这一切是因为什么呢？如果一个人想接近神，用感官愉悦的形象去诱惑，这是必须弃绝的。根据教义，这位神既是感官物质也是精神，人们不知不觉地期望进入他的宇宙并在死后与之相合，而不是去期望在此世的全部克己努力，可以从另一世界获得任何福祉的补偿。卢克莱修的盲目神性，显然值得而且很可能已经获得了跟苏菲一样多的自我牺牲。而欧玛尔的歌的主题，如果不是"让我们吃"，那一定是"让我们喝，因为明天我们就死了！"如果哈菲兹用相近的语言表达了完全不同的意思，那么当他把自己的生命和天才倾注在如此模棱两可的赞美诗时，他肯定失算了。因为从他那时候到现在，曾说过和唱过这些赞美诗的，都不是精神上的礼拜者。

然而，由于有一些传统的推测，当然还有一些有学问人的意见，赞成欧玛尔是苏菲派，甚至是某种意义上的圣徒，因此，有些人乐于如此解释他的酒和担酒者。可是另一方面，也有大量的历史事实证明他是一个哲学家，他具有远超他所生活的时代和国家的科学洞见和能力，证明他节制的世俗抱负使他只想做个哲学家，节制的欲望使他只想做个容易知足的享乐者。其他的读者会同意我，相信欧玛尔赞颂的酒只是葡萄的汁液，他的夸口远胜他的酒量，那也许只是他为了表示对精神上的酒的蔑视，这酒让它的徒众陷入了虚伪或令人嫌恶之中。[110]

【校记】

[102]"（见他的序言第13、14页）"，二版作：这是他提供的一个轶闻。"在那个充斥着战争、阴谋诡计和暴动的时代中，海亚姆一直如局外人般平静地生活在他出生的村庄里，热情地投入到苏菲哲学的学习。他与许多朋友一道，在酒里追寻这种狂喜的沉思，而其他人则认为应该在叫喊和呼号中去找。""波斯的编年史作者们记述道，海亚姆尤其喜欢与他的朋友们谈话、喝酒：夜晚，澄明的月光照亮他家中的露台，歌手与乐手环绕在身边。斟酒人手持酒盏，依次向欢聚一堂的宾客们敬酒。一夜，突如其来的一阵风吹灭了蜡烛，又将随意摆放在露台边上的酒罐打翻在地。酒罐被打碎，酒流了一地。恼怒的海亚姆立刻即兴写了这首渎神的四行诗，对全能的主说：'你打碎了我的酒罐，我主！你由是关闭了我的欢乐之门，我主！我只是喝酒，但醉酒之混乱则是你导致的！哦！（愿我的嘴里塞满泥土！）你会喝醉吗，我主？'

"诗人说了这些渎神的话之后，瞥见镜中自己的脸黑如木炭，以为这是上天的惩罚。他又作了另一首比前作更加放肆的四行诗：'人世间的哪一个从没有过罪孽，你说？从没有过罪的人又如何活着，你说？如果因为我作恶，而你又用这恶来惩罚我，那你我之间又有何差别呢，你说？'"

（此段法文由田争争译出，谨此致谢。）

[110]此段二版作：然而，对于哈菲兹和欧玛尔，这里都保持为一个开放的问题：读者可以根据他们的选择去理解任何一种，字面地或神秘地。当看到酒、担酒者、翠柏这些叫法，他可以只是去猜测神；也可以就像跟欧玛尔在一起，我真的觉得他可以延续和阿那克里翁，甚至阿那克里翁·穆尔一样的解释。

【解读】

"你打碎了我的酒罐"这首也见于1207年抄本第543首（"乐园"本第543首），第三句作："把我红色的酒浆泼洒在地。"（张鸿年译文）

"人世间的哪一个从没有过罪孽"这首也见于1207年抄本第212首（"乐园"本第8首）。

奥玛珈音者，呼罗珊省之纳霞堡城人也。生当公历十一世纪后期，卒在十二世纪初。生平甚略，独与当时国中二显人颇相纠葛。其一名尼查木·乌尔·穆尔克，尝述三人事。穆尔克历相鞑靼人脱斡邻勒·伯克子阿尔普·阿尔斯兰、孙马立克·沙。[4] 初，马赫穆德大帝之后继寡能，脱斡邻勒·伯克遂有波斯，是为塞尔柱朝，而终致欧人十字军之役。穆尔克之书曰《遗书》，盖遗后之为政者也，其言有云：今据《加尔各答评论》五九号转录米尔克洪之《阿萨辛史》。

纳霞堡有伊玛目曰莫瓦法克，呼罗珊之圣哲也。得人尊崇，受天眷顾，寿逾八十五。从之穷经考古，可信必致荣福。吾父乃遣余与法科博士阿布德·乌斯·沙玛德自突斯往纳霞堡，期从明师，沉潜于学。师于我特加垂青，而吾为弟子亦尽忠爱，亲侍讲席，四载于兹矣。吾初至此，即见年相仿者二人，哈基姆·奥玛·珈音与厄运之本·萨巴赫，皆新来从学。二人并捷才异禀，遂为至好。伊玛目讲席每罢，二人常共我游处，温故时习。奥玛固纳霞堡人也，哈桑·本·萨巴赫父为阿里，守约而务实，然所遵信多近异端。一日，哈桑语吾与珈音曰："皆信从伊玛目莫瓦法克学者必致嘉命。虽三人俱致，或有所疑，必有一人致焉。然则欲相约誓者何？"吾与珈音曰："从君所愿。"彼曰："善，请为此誓：嘉命天降，当与共之，毋得专！"吾与珈音曰："必如是。"誓遂定。日居月诸，吾自呼罗珊往河中，且游伽兹尼与喀布尔。既返，被命入宫，旋相阿尔普·阿尔斯兰王。

越数年，二同学循之至，因昔日之誓请共嘉命。相君践誓，无少吝。哈桑求一官，王因相君之请予之。然不餍于递迁，遂与东国之乱谋，拟代恩相之位。谋既不成，名丧身败。屡经困踬颠沛，终为波斯亦思马因教魁首。亦思马因教人皆狂信，阴蓄既久，得哈桑行其凶强之志，遂成极恶。公元之一千零九十年，哈桑竟取鲁德巴省之阿剌模忒堡，在里海之南，乱山之间。自是十字军竟传其号曰"山中老人"。其大行畏怖，几遍回教之地。今欧人语中行刺一词，疑其凶念之孑遗也。其字源或出哈石失，盖大麻叶所制之烟食也，印度谓之卜昂，服之能致人迷幻，阴郁颠倒，失志走险。或出彼魁首名，纳霞堡志学之日，固已识之矣。被行刺之刃者固多，其同学故交，尼查木·乌尔·穆尔克竟其一也。奥玛《鲁拜集》颇有诗警盛时之易倾，嘉命之不固，倡言与人人为善而莫与人密迩。阿特尝使尼查木·乌尔·穆尔克用其友奥玛语（《鲁拜集》其二十八）："尼查木·乌尔·穆尔克之垂死也，号曰：噫，主！吾方自风之手中逝。"

奥玛珈音亦往见相君，请其所有，然非名位也。曰："君所能惠莫若处我于一隅，为君嘉命所荫，广播学问之泽，吾兼为君之福寿祈。"相君告吾辈曰，既知奥玛之却名位实出其诚，乃不复强，即敕纳霞堡公库，年予之一千二百金。

奥玛珈音终其生居纳霞堡，相君言其汲汲乎博学，而于天学尤精，实造极焉。马立克·沙王时，尝至谋夫，以学问之湛深得盛誉，王甚致恩宠。

时马立克·沙王修历法，八人与其事，奥玛其一也。遂制哲拉里历，用王之一名哲拉鲁丁焉。吉本曰："其算精于儒略历，而近乎格列高里历。"又尝绘星图，题曰马立克·沙希星算表。近法人重印之，且译其回文代数论焉。[27]

珈音者，盖其赋诗之别号也，考其义，厥为制庐帐者，传其尝事此业，殆在尼查木·乌尔·穆尔克渥恩厚予使能自立前欤？波斯诗客例以所业为名，若阿特为方剂师、阿萨为榨油匠也。亦若吾英伦之史密斯（铁匠）、阿切尔（射手）、米勒（磨工）、弗莱彻（箭工）等，不过呼先世之业为姓氏耳。奥玛尝有奥句隐括其名，曰："珈音以智织穹庐，何事忽投忧患火？命绝其绳今世哀，望虚其报来生左。"

其轶事尚有一可述者，在其临终。见其诗集之序文，文出何人手、出何世，均莫能详。海德有书名《波斯古教》，附录之四百九十九页，有其波斯原文。戴波卢之《文库》，海音目下亦有之。“回教哲人，约当一世纪末二世纪初，专力精修，住于神圣之香境。”然珈音之与彼也，但同为哲人耳，外皆无所类。[37]

古之编年史有言，智之王者奥玛于海吉拉历五百一十七年，公元一千一百二十三年，卒于纳霞堡，学迈往古，范垂当世。撒马尔罕之长者尼札米，尝从其学，有言：“吾每与吾师奥玛珈音语于园中，一日，谓我：吾墓所在，当有北风扬玫瑰于其上。我固讶其言，然知非谩语也。戴波卢以为此语实率，盖与《可兰经》抵牾，经言“无人能知其将死何地”也。奥玛之轶事使吾忆及另一事，此库克而非霍克沃思之《再航记》第一卷三七四页所述者。彼尊贵之航者道其卑微之的，一何惘然也。“方辞乌列特亚，奥瑞奥惟欲吾返。知不可必，遂问吾葬所。虽所问甚诡，吾仍径告之曰斯特普尼，盖吾居伦敦所隶之教区也。彼众乞吾数言之，俾彼亦能言，顷时百人齐呼：‘斯特普尼墓间无图特。’吾后知福斯特亦在水滨遭此问，彼所答异，然尤当也。彼云：‘无长在海上者能言其将葬何地也。’”数年后，吾重过纳霞堡，吊其葬处，正邻一园，园中横枝逾墙，结实累累，而倾其朵墓上，墓石为尽覆焉。”

吾不惮剽夺之嫌繁录《加尔各答评论》之文如右。其作者在天竺读奥玛墓事，言令彼忆及西塞罗述访叙拉古之阿基米德墓，墓正掩于草丛间。而吾则念多瓦尔德森，彼欲所植玫瑰得覆其身，吾信至今仍敬从其愿也。然请再言奥玛。

虽王甚致恩宠，而奥玛于逸乐之坦然根于思、形诸言，多为时人侧目。皆云诸苏菲于奥玛惧恨交并，盖彼辈之践行，常为奥玛所嘲；彼辈之信仰，若去其为奥玛不屑之玄秘与虚饰，又实无以过之也。彼国诗客多取资奥玛，虽哈菲兹亦犹是也，盖自菲尔多西外，哈菲兹为波斯最可瞩目者。然尽转作玄秘之用，俾其诗于己于众俱有所便。盖彼众轻于疑信，敏于感智，愉于诸者之冥合，[56] 遂藉诗句为羽翼，恣游乎天国凡尘、今世来生，而不执一端。[57] 惟奥玛知命而疑天，重生而轻死，虽云过，想思尽出乎诚。故宁于今世极其所有，用所遇[59]诸物娱六欲而抚一心，不徒扰扰于将来之忧也。[60] 然吾人亦见其于俗世之求实不逾度。于感官之娱也，得滑稽乖张之趣，用以尚心智。虽其于心智也，亦颇有足乐者。然心智不足解其惑，其惑正人人所同者，攸关甚大。[62]

无问何故，前已言奥玛之诗向未驰声国中，亦眇传海外。其诗集稿本，支离不全，通行《东方散佚抄本集》中未录。虽在东国犹称罕觏，况传乎西海耶？然西人每能尽得东国之兵械与技巧也。其副本，印度学舍无有也，巴黎之国家图书馆亦无有也。吾知英伦存一写本，在牛津饱蠹楼，标识号

【校记】

[4] 此句一版作：一名哈桑·乌尔·萨巴赫，其名久同刺客之恶称，一名尼查木·乌尔·穆尔克，尝述三人事。穆尔克历相鞑靼人脱斡邻勒·伯克子狮王阿尔普、孙马立克·沙。

[27] 一版后尚有一段：其终生之业或即此精严之学与其诗，余无闻耳。其诗较波斯他诗客殊少，若出无意，然非游情谩想也。或亦喜稍事农作，每言耕田之畔，乐携其诗卷、箪食与酒而息焉。

[37] 此注，一版作：虽彼将此事系之海音，“回教哲人，约当一世纪末二世纪初，专力精修，住于神圣之香境”，然珈音之与彼也，但同为哲人耳，外皆无所类。而珈音或可言此其事也，是本《鲁拜集》其七十七、七十八，倘能踪迹之。戴波卢以为此语实率，盖与《可兰经》抵牾，经言“无人能知其将死何地”也。

[56] 一版作：愉于全幅之冥合。

[57] 一版作：诵之寺庙耶酒肆耶，皆无问。

[59] 一版作：所是。

[60] 一版作：不徒为将来之忧而苦行也。

[62] 一版作：然心智不足指其信仰之津。故其所言俗世之娱必非妄托神道，酒也实出葡萄之浆，酒肆也实有其处，行觞者也实为血肉之躯，玫瑰也实花，凡此皆其今世所欲来生所期。

且算学之才，制其逸思，遂令诗成别体，盖奥句深义，无多赘词，殊非波斯及东国之诗格也，为是湮其名于故国。如言希腊之文犹童子饶舌，则波斯之文无乃又成一童子耶？不晓几何学之希腊人无得入柏拉图哲学之宫，而无异思奇彩之波斯人亦无得竞于波斯诗域，盖其视驰想繁言为决定之力也。波斯诗人精算学者惟奥玛，能持异族异教败波斯族魂前之古风毅性者亦惟奥玛。颇类其先辈大家菲尔多西，略无玄思，虽有一字为新信仰所被犹不屑用也。然彼非若奥玛之不信教，疑其潜附往古苏鲁支之袄教，盖彼所歌列王皆信奉焉。

乌斯利一四零，公元一千四百六十年写于设拉子，凡鲁拜一百五十八章。加尔各答之亚洲协会图书馆藏一本，吾得录副焉，存五百一十六章，亦非完本，然重见与妄拟者已充斥其间。而冯·海默尔言其有副本约存二百章，施普伦格著录之鲁克诺写本又倍其数。评论者附言曰：“写此文竟，吾等又遇一极罕版本之副本，一千八百三十六年加尔各答刊行。凡四行诗四百三十八章，附录中尚有五十四章不见诸他写本。”牛津与加尔各答写本之抄手，其写此也，似俱先以声言。卷首皆有四行诗一章，可毋问其真赝，实自原字母排序中别出。牛津写本为忏辞。加尔各答写本为诫辞，[72] 依是本前缀之语，诗盖肇因于一梦，梦中奥玛母氏询其将来之运命。可如是译：“火生地狱每焚心，说到焚身汝亦临。上帝枉呼垂悯念，递相教授遣谁任？”饱蠹楼写本之诗，质以自证，申白泛神。诗云：“我如约束不坚牢，善行成珠竟散绦。幸是一元无二读，即逢天谴可相逃。”

评论者考威尔教授，奥玛生平尽从之而得也。[74] 于文末以卢克莱修譬奥玛，盖二人不但气禀与天才相近，即所遭亦相近也。皆敏于见，勇于行，学深才富，[75] 求是慕义。国有伪信，愚者竭诚，俱能以正相斥。既败伪信，虽无能正之，亦无能得真信，[78] 然犹有则守。卢克莱修得伊壁鸠鲁之学，视宇宙为偶成之机械，[79] 虽循法度，而无制之者。然其处身也，严苛殊近斯多葛而远伊壁鸠鲁。独坐凝视，观宇宙之运行，如机械之戏剧，自身亦在戏剧中，并相环者，一若其壮词所赋之罗马歌台，俱为帷幕惨色之映而黯然，彼帷悬诸天日与观剧者间。奥玛并此繁琐之统系亦无所踐，或直漠视之，盖此统系惟无望之定命也。乃倾其深学富才，杂以苦涩、滑稽之谈笑，付之其匆遽一瞥中仅见之万有遍坏。聊作玩世之态，嬉言生惟逸乐，但为遣兴故，而语神语命，判物灵，辨善恶，然始则易，继则难，终则殆矣。[89]

厥述今之所译。鲁拜之名，夺回文之一音，增英言之摇曳。本一一孑立之短章，章四句，皆律句，时有变化，而格律略同。四句或皆入韵，然第三句多不入韵，若此所拟者是也。[91] 此略似希腊阿尔凯奥斯之体，不入韵处逆挽其韵，令其稍止，复坠于末句也。东国之诗卷，胥依入韵字母次序，《鲁拜集》亦是也。故死与乐竟成诡列，为其韵字之同也。今所选者，适成一田园诗集。“醇酒妇人”，本原作屡爱言之者，虽未知果出其诚否，而今所删余者于比率则殊少矣。然 [94] 此终为悲怀诗也。悲之甚者，无过于故矜逸乐，而实则令彼老庐帐工能伤不能怒也。盖徒然欲步出定命，往瞥明朝，然复堕今日，又将无尽迟明朝也。彼惟能于今日立足，而今日又转瞬从足下逝矣。

吾方预此奥玛译本之再版，法国驻腊什特总领事尼古拉斯君刊一校勘甚备之善本，影德黑兰钞本为底本，凡鲁拜四百六十四章，并其所译与所注。

尼古拉斯版，或以发我，或以益我。然吾诚视奥玛为耽耳目之伊壁鸠鲁辈，而尼君必欲归之玄门，其言酒也提壶也皆隐指神，一若哈菲兹之所素行者。盖视奥玛为苏菲诗客，与哈菲兹诸人等也。吾未见有以易吾说之由也。吾说之成，肇在十数年前，时有人初以奥玛示我。吾于东国及其文学故实所知独多，皆得是人之惠。彼激赏奥玛之才，若能有所与，必乐援引若尼君之义诠也。数年间，彼或亦编订此集竟，恐今于吾译与尼古拉斯之说皆少有所许矣。然不能与也。其刊于《加尔各答评论》之文，吾尝备引者，可以为征。其所述皆据诗作及诗客生平之遗录也。

倘更须一证以攻尼君之说，彼序之第十三、十四页有类传记之附笔一则，其自写者也，决与其诠诗之说龃龉。[102] 非有辩说者相晓，吾诚不知不幸之奥玛至于此极也。兹须识之，无论哈菲兹所饮所歌之酒竟为何物，惟奥玛所言之酒实出葡萄之浆者无虚。非但与诸友酣乐时如是也，即如尼君所言，赴身幻信之境时亦如是也，而他人则徒赖呼号耳。然尼君一俟见诗中有酒与提壶字，即以“神”“神属”释之。其如是之谨也，颇疑有一苏菲辈人从其共读，时训导之。若《鲁拜集》第二章注，第八页。一波斯人必与其同族之杰出者，一苏菲亦必党之，而况波斯名诗客固多入其彀中欤？

尼君言奥玛之溺陷于苏菲也，见序文第八页，果以何文献征之？泛神之则、唯物之论、必然之法，非苏菲辈独有也，亦非彼辈所从之卢克莱修、奥玛所从之伊壁鸠鲁独有也。或太始冥想者初无崇信，或立政生民犹在蒙昧、七十二宗欲裂天下，遂令哲人神机潜运，自然而萌耶？冯·海默尔之言奥玛，据施普伦格之《东方目录》，“独行之士，苏菲辈雠对之雄也。”盖因所知教义既多，未得伪持不合之峻德也。乌西利爵士于饱蠹楼写本之扉页，亦题识类似之辞。即尼君自刊本，亦有鲁拜二章，直以贬抑之辞气呼彼苏菲辈也。

确有诗章，非作玄释，似无可解。然更多者，非依文释，亦无可解。今且试问，酒诚为精魄，命终之际将何能以之浴体？何故以无生之陶土作杯，必由后来玄家注以神灵？盖尼君每为诸庾辞意象所扰，彼皆极异而着东国之色彩，诚色欲泰甚而每致人厌者，故临其文踌躇不敢译。无已，乃为读之者委诸神灵也。第二百三十四章之注可征，彼言其诗意象之玄义虽于欧人也昭然，而彼文辞之征述即于波斯之俗人也犹不免乎赧然。“此章开端述浓情之语，集中甚多，读之者亦已习之。虽珈音繁言以喻慕神之思者极异，虽其意象过着东国色彩而时因色欲致人非议，然使吾人信其事涉神圣固无难也。此固每为回教贤哲所辩，亦偶为俗人所议，盖其侪辈于此俱无间言，虽事涉神思，实足令之色赧也。”德黑兰钞本中诸多诗章，一如加尔各答钞本，显为赝作，貌若鲁拜，实则波斯剌诗习见之短章耳。然吾从此赝作中实有所窥，见尼君之说误也。盖在波斯，苏菲辈虽多为学者文人，而实较漠然之伊壁鸠鲁辈更易窜乱原意以成其说也。吾见饱蠹楼写本中罕有稍涉玄秘之诗章，盖最古钞本之一也，回历八百六十五年，公元一千四百六十年写于设拉子。吾以此足别奥玛与波斯他诗客。吾尤喜以奥玛呼之，此固非教名，而人皆熟知之名也。不则其诗于歌吟间、其人于玄隐间乱于彼也。我辈遂宛若与奥玛同坐，彼坦然席前，令睹其人，习其滑稽，会其高兴，而酒已巡矣。

自我言之，固未尽信哈菲兹之玄义妙蕴也。诗客但于始歌终曲之际额手颂穆罕默德，纵以泛神持论而咏歌之，殊无伤也。类是者，哲拉鲁丁、贾米、阿特与他歌者，诚以醇酒妇人为意象，用昭其所赞之神明，非故为覆幂以掩蔽之也。然恐置诸血气贲张者前，以不易致误致滥之譬说为较善也。或有视哈菲兹与奥玛之玄思，非仅拟喻，正为身欲，方此之时尤若是也。兹虽于持信者无伤，然于弱信之民胞或恐有害。甚者新徒愈激，亵玩愈剧。何者？必欲近神，而以身欲之乐诱之，此决须弃者。盖依教义，神即灵即肉者也，身终入其宇宙可期潜相契合，而毋得用他世之福祉偿此间之克己。卢克莱修之瞽神，诚堪甚或已得若苏菲辈之自厉。然奥玛所歌者，非使吾食，必使吾饮，盖为明日之定死也。若哈菲兹以相类之辞述相异之义，彼之所度必误矣。彼倾其生与才付诸若此隐微之颂诗，自其生之日至于今，言之歌之者恐多非纯信者也。

然颇有博学之鸿儒持成见、采新说，许奥玛为一苏菲，甚乃一圣徒，故乐由是而诠其酒与提壶之辞也。而有更多之史事足征彼哲人也，具学力，逾世代，但谦谦乎欲为一世间之智者、一知足之纵乐者耳。故必有人也同乎吾，以奥玛所颂者实出葡萄之酒浆也，而其所夸实过所饮，盖欲蔑弃酒之神明，以其驱彼徒众沦胥于伪善与嫌恶也。[110]

【校记】

[72] 一版作：加尔各答写本为诫辞，盖诫奥玛之愚，其愚也亦适足骂之。

[74] 一版作：彼译前引奥玛生平详目，又以无韵之笔译述其诗若干首。

[75] 一版作：皆敏于智，神于思，学迈当时。

[78] 一版作：亦无能临真信。

[79] 一版作：以宇宙为无设计者之机械。

[89] 一版作：嗣委其觉知于玫瑰与酒之间，但为移其思以得调适乎命志存灭之际也。稍一扰乱，每反其正，遂有若此二章，实出其恒言之外也。诗云：君若去为尸解仙，御风直上自泠然。多惭客养千金体，长在齐州九点烟。又云：大行途上见穹庐，只是匆匆暂驻舆。冥侍自来收拾了，君王一去肯重居？

[91] 一版作：然常于第三句令韵一阙，而以末句还诸前二句，若此所尝试者是也。

[94] 一版前有：卢克莱修盖似奥玛之才，使愁郁与奥立弗 · 德 · 巴塞林之滑稽交并。

[102] 二版后有：此其相示轶闻之一也。“其时世乱兵荒，诡诈间作，惟珈音避身乡土，乐学苏菲。每与诸友饮，酒佐其思，如颠如乐。而他人每以为在呼号时始能有此境耳。”“波斯编年史家言，珈音尤喜宴饮，夜中，月华如水，流照露台，歌乐方作，行觞已巡。忽有风至，堂中烛灭，台前缶倾，酒浆遍地。珈音微愠，即席赋诗，未免渎神之过也。其诗曰：‘碎我壶罂绝我欢，威仪抑抑谅无端。不妨泥土填吾口，问主真曾到醉阑？’”

[110] 此段二版作：然则究当如何诠哈菲兹与奥玛之诗，吾无断语焉，玄释文解，惟读者自择之。睹酒、提壶、翠柏之辞，以为其语神可也。即如亲见奥玛而事之，吾诚以为继阿那克里翁，抑阿那克里翁 · 穆尔而作同解亦可也。

RUBÁIYÁT
OF
OMAR KHAYYÁM OF NAISHÁPÚR

纳霞堡人奥玛珈音

《波斯短歌行》

内沙普尔人欧玛尔·海亚姆

《鲁拜集》

正

集

RUBÁIYÁT

1

菲译第二版第 1 首，
1910 年版
174 mm × 223 mm

埃德蒙·杜拉克（Edmund Dulac，1882—1953），英籍法裔插画家。画面展示了诗里的意象。衣袂飘飘、驾着祥云而来的天使，象征着太阳的升起，新的一天开始了。

I

WAKE! For the Sun, who scatter'd into flight
The Stars before him from the Field of Night,
  Drives Night along with them from Heav'n, and strikes
The Sultán's Turret with a Shaft of Light.

【校记】——
●一版、二版异文较多,皆别出。
●三版、四版:首行'Sun,'作'Sun'。

I-I(V- I)

AWAKE! for Morning in the Bowl of Night
Has flung the Stone that puts the Stars to Flight:
  And Lo! the Hunter of the East has caught
The Sultán's Turret in a Noose of Light.

【注释】——
Flinging a Stone into the Cup was the Signal for *"To Horse!"* in the Desert.

【注释校记】——
此注唯见一版。

II-I(V- I)

WAKE! For the Sun behind yon Eastern height
Has chased the Session of the Stars from Night;
  And, to the field of Heav'n ascending, strikes
The Sultán's Turret with a Shaft of Light.

III - I (the first draught)(V- I)

Wake! For the Sun before him into Night
A Signal flung that put the Stars to flight,
  Drives Night along with them from Heav'n, and strikes
The Sultán's Turret with a Shaft of Light.

【校记】——
● 此三版初稿,见五版末怀特所作校记引,仅前二行与五版不同。

其一

东君长矢举遥空，
直迫星芒夜色穷。
为唤人间新睡觉，
金光正射素檀宫。

二版其一

日出东山夜色澄，
尽驱星斗转高升。
金光长矢中天举，
遥射宫楼最上层。

一版其一

夜天如碗日如璆，
星斗纷纷避一投。
起看东君遥出猎，
金光长索罥宫楼。

【注】——大漠中，投石于杯，以示 上马 也。

三版其一 初稿

金光长矢掷遥空，
直迫星芒夜色穷。
唤得华胥春梦醒，
辉煌齐指大明宫。

1

醒来吧！太阳，已经让他前面
那些群星从夜的领域飞散。
连夜也一起驱出天空，再把
光芒之箭射上苏丹的塔殿。

1-1（5-1）

醒来吧！早晨已把石子投入
夜天之碗让群星飞遁四处：
看啊！那位东方猎手用一道
光绳正把苏丹的塔殿套住。

【注释】——

在沙漠里，把石子投入杯中是“上马”的信号。

2-1（5-1）

醒来！太阳自那东山的后面
已把集会之星从夜里驱散。
然后，上升到了天域中，再向
苏丹的塔殿射出光芒之箭。

3-1（初稿）（5-1）

醒来吧！太阳腾跃到他前面
那夜空之中，迫使群星飞散，
连夜也一起驱出天空，再把
光芒之箭射上苏丹的塔殿。

【解读】——

第 1 首，菲茨杰拉德第一版的来源，见于加尔各答亚洲协会图书馆藏抄本第 134 首（1207 年抄本第 66 首，“乐园”本第 346 首），原文是：

太阳把黎明的套索抛上屋顶，
掌管白日的凯·霍斯鲁，他把石子投进碗里：
喝酒！晨光的使者，起身了，
朝白天里叫出“你们喝！”的喊声。

“喝酒”的意象被移到第 2、第 3 首里了。原文“太阳”和“晨光的使者”被译文结合为“东方猎手”，这样抛出“套索”就显得很自然。“石子投进碗里”，在原文中很晦涩，菲茨杰拉德把它的喻义点明了，于是成为非常著名的比喻。尽管这个比喻在以后诸版里都没有了，却令人念念不忘，可以说，很多读者对第一版的喜爱，这个比喻是很重要的原因。

我们无法得知菲茨杰拉德去掉这个比喻的原因。在温菲尔德和佩恩的译本里，“石子”被译作“酒”。尽管菲茨杰拉德注出：“在沙漠里，把石子投入杯中是‘上马’的信号。”他是否仍然心存疑虑？或者，他想尽力去除这个过于异域化的意象？然而，他尽力修改了三次，效果都不及原来比喻的新颖、奇丽。

无论从前后文、还是从形象来看，“光芒之箭”都比“套索”更合适，这是第四版定型后的名句。全诗如此写起，给带着颓废味道的及时行乐，预先铺垫了一个黄金幻景，那样精力弥满，那样天真烂漫，也许正符合西方人对东方情调的想往。放在第 1 首的位置，自有特别的匠心。只是，从第二版的修改开始，就完全成了菲茨杰拉德自己的创作，虽说原文的精神仍然保留着。

第三版初稿的译文，效仿菲茨杰拉德的放纵，添上了中国的古典。既然用到“华胥春梦”，似乎再用“素檀宫”就不很协调，直接写作“大明宫”，在字面和实指之间闪烁其词。

2

菲译第一版第 2 首，
1930 年版
128 mm × 191 mm

匈牙利插画家威利·波加尼（Willy Pogány，1882—1955）绘制的 1930 年版《鲁拜集》，有三个版本。所选插图源自 1930 年美国纽约出版的普通版，共有 12 幅贴片式彩色插图。1930 年英国伦敦版，有一幅与此类似的插图。波加尼在此展示了一个东方式的场景：黎明时分一对恋人还沉醉未醒。

II

Before the phantom of False morning died,
Methought a Voice within the Tavern cried,
"When all the Temple is prepared within,
"Why nods the drowsy Worshipper outside?"

【校记】

●一版异文较多,别出。
●二版:四行 'nods' 作 'lags'。

【注释】

The "*False Dawn;*" *Subhi Kázib*[1], a transient Light on the Horizon about an hour before the *Subhi sádik* [2], or True Dawn; a well-known Phenomenon in the East. [3]

【注释校记】

[1] '*Subhi Kázib*',一版作 '*Subhi Kházib*'。
[2] '*Subhi sádik*',一版、二版作 '*Subhi sâdhik*'。
[3] 一版后尚有 'The Persians call the Morning Gray, or Dusk, "*Wolf-and-Sheep-While.*" "Almost at odds with, which is which."'。

I-II(V- II)

Dreaming when Dawn's Left Hand was in the Sky
I heard a Voice within the Tavern cry,
"Awake, my Little ones, and fill the Cup
"Before Life's Liquor in its Cup be dry."

【校记】

●注释见前。

其二

朝曦尚自掩虚烟，
客舍先闻高语传：
『早向堂前歌乐圣，
何为枕上梦游仙？』

【注】——
所谓「幻曙」者，真曙前约一小时，天际顷刻之光芒也。此天象在东国人皆能详。

【注校记】——
一版文末尚有：波斯人谓之晨灰色时，昏昧时，「亦狼亦羊时」，彼是相持时」。

一版其二

天外朝曦左手临，
酒翁喝破梦沉沉：
『几生未似杯常满，
莫负及时来一斟。』

2

虚假晨光的幻色还没消退，
我想有个声音喊自酒店内，
　“寺里的一切全都准备好了，
怎么礼拜者还在外头昏睡？”

【校记】———
●二版：四行“瞌睡”作“落后”。

【注释】———
“虚假黎明”（*Subbi Kázib*），在真正的黎明（*Subbi sádik*）前大约一个小时，地平线上短暂的光芒。在东方是个很常见的现象。[3]

【注释校记】———
[3] 一版后尚有：波斯人叫早晨灰色，尘昏，“狼和羊相共时”，“几乎不一致者”。

1-2（5-2）

睡梦里黎明左手已在天空，
我听见酒店里面传来喊声，
　“醒醒，我的孩子们，倒满杯子，
别等到生命之酒干涸杯中。”

【解读】———
第 2 首，菲茨杰拉德的第一版，见于加尔各答抄本第 5 首：
一个早晨从我们的酒馆里传来喊声：
“呵！我们的疯子，常在酒馆晃荡的浪子，
“起来！我们要把量器里装满酒，
“直到它们装满我们（生命的）量器。”
“乐园”本第 203 首，以及第 202 首、204 首、205 首的内容也很类似。从第二版以后，却没有找到相应的波斯文字。但我疑心菲茨杰拉德有所根据，否则，第一版的“黎明左手”，第二版的“虚假黎明”“寺里”“礼拜者”这些意象，就是为了给“及时痛饮”这个普遍的意思增添些东方色彩。这些特别的色彩在汉语里都挺难表达的，因此，黄克孙先生本是根据第四版翻译的，这一首却用了第一版的文字——“生涯莫放金尊懒，人易凋零酒易晞”。这里的译文把“虚假黎明”拿“虚烟”做了点儿渲染，“礼拜者”用上了徐邈以嗜酒为“乐圣”的典故，总是想更符合汉语文言的语境。

紧接着第 1 首的日出人起，立刻点醒“及时痛饮”的主题，为整部诗集定下了基调。

3

菲译第二版第 3 首，
1898 年版
89 mm × 122 mm

英国插画家吉尔伯特·詹姆斯（Gilbert James，1865—1941）为菲译《鲁拜集》画的插图，在英国多种杂志上刊登过。詹姆斯插图版《鲁拜集》版本众多，大致可以分为 1898 年、1907 年和 1909 年三个系列，有黑白插图、手工上色插图和彩色插图三种。

III

And, as the Cock crew, those who stood before
The Tavern shouted—"Open then the Door!
　"You know how little while we have to stay,
"And, once departed, may return no more."

其三

雄鸡一叫客来呼，
直到门前索酒沽：
『万岁千秋君莫问，
此回归去更来无？』

3

雄鸡刚叫，他们在门外徘徊
对着酒店大喊——“快把门开开！
**　你知道我们只能待上一会儿，**
一旦离去，也许就不再回来。”

【解读】———

这一首菲茨杰拉德熔铸了好几首的内容，相近的内容见于加尔各答抄本第 641 首：

这是晨风和鸡鸣的时刻，哦萨吉，
这里有我们，和酒，和酒馆街，哦萨吉，
这是供奉的时间吗？别出声，哦萨吉，
保持传统吧，喝干，哦萨吉。

和第 207 首的后两行：

你一定要喝酒，满足你心里的快乐，
这很清楚在这个世界你能待多久（就不再）。

还有第 273 首（1207 年抄本第 169 首，“乐园”本第 430 首）：

啊，快乐的本质！起来，黎明了！
悠然地，悠然地喝着酒，弹着琴，
那些睡着的人发现不了这些，
那些要离去的没有一个会再回来。

以及第 247 首（1207 年抄本第 99 首，“乐园”本第 427 首）：

这是黎明了！起来，哦奇怪的孩子！
在水晶般的杯里倒满红宝石般的酒。
因为（存在的）时分里借给你在这有限生命的一角，
你不论要去寻找多久，你也不会再找到它。

另外，“乐园”本第 61 首（1207 年抄本第 186 首）也很接近。

在这首里，酒徒打门的急促，把生命一去不返的紧迫感特别地突出了，态度更豁达，情调更豪放。这是菲茨杰拉德熔裁能力一个显著的体现，同时，也做到了不犯第 2 首的内容。

4

菲译第一版第 4 首，
1901 年版
102 mm × 120 mm

美国作家、画家布兰奇·麦克马纳斯（Blanche McManus，1870—1935）出版了近 60 本插图书。她配插图的菲译《鲁拜集》有好几版。画面中穿波斯服装的男士倚靠在树枝上，凝视着远方。新开的花朵象征着新的一年的来临。插图中的部分彩色属于手工上色，使作品具有了独特性。

IV

Now the New Year reviving old Desires,
The thoughtful Soul to Solitude retires,
Where the White Hand of Moses on the Bough
Puts out, and Jesus from the Ground suspires.

【注释】

New Year. Beginning with the Vernal Equinox, it must be remembered; and (howsoever the old Solar Year is practically superseded by the clumsy *Lunar* Year that dates from the Mohammedan Hijra) still commemorated by a Festival that is said to have been appointed by the very Jamshyd whom Omar so often talks of, and whose yearly Calendar he helped to rectify.

"The sudden approach and rapid advance of the Spring," says Mr. Binning *,[1]"are very striking. Before the Snow is well off the Ground, the Trees burst into Blossom, and the Flowers start forth[2] from the Soil. At *Now*[3]*Rooz* [*their* New Year's Day] [4]the Snow was lying in patches on the Hills and in the shaded Vallies, while the Fruit-trees in the Gardens were budding beautifully, and green Plants and Flowers springing up on[5] the Plains on every side—

'And on old Hyems' Chin and icy Crown
'An odorous Chaplet of sweet Summer buds
'Is, as in mockery, set. [6]'—

Among the Plants newly appeared[7] I recognised[8] some old[9] Acquaintances I had not seen for many a Year: [10] among these, two varieties of the Thistle—[11] a coarse species of Daisy[12] like the 'Horse-gowan' —[13] red and white Clover—[14] the Dock—[15]the blue Corn-flower—[16]and that vulgar Herb the Dandelion rearing its yellow crest on the Banks of the Watercourses." The Nightingale was not yet heard, for the Rose was not yet blown: but an almost identical Blackbird and Woodpecker helped to make up something of a North-country Spring.

"The White Hand of Moses." [17]Exodus iv. 6; where Moses draws forth his Hand—not, according to the Persians, *"leprous as Snow,"* —but *white*, [18]as our May-Blossom in Spring perhaps. [19]According to them also the Healing Power of Jesus resided in his Breath.

* *Two Years' Travel in Persia, &c.*i.165.

【注释校记】

[1] 'says Mr. Binning,',一版作 '(says a late Traveller in Persia) *',二版、三版、四版无脚注。
[2] 一版、二版、三版、四版无 'forth'。
[3] '*Now*',二版、三版、四版作 '*Naw*'。
[4] '[ ]',一版、二版、三版、四版作 '()'。
[5] 'up on',一版、二版、三版、四版作 'upon'。
[6] 'set.',一版、二版、三版、四版作 'set—'。
[7] 'appeared',一版、二版、三版、四版作 'appear' d'。
[8] 'recognised',一版、二版、三版、四版作 'recognized'。
[9] 'old',三版、四版无。
[10] ':',三版作 ';'。
[11] '—',一版、二版、三版、四版作 ';'。
[12] 'Daisy',一版、二版、三版、四版作 'Daisy,'。
[13] ''Horse-gowan' —',一版、二版、三版、四版作 'Horse-gowan;'。
[14] '—',一版、二版、三版、四版作 ';'。
[15] '—',一版、二版、三版、四版作 ';'。
[16] '—',一版、二版、三版、四版作 ';'。
[17] 一版、二版、三版另作一注,无 '"The White Hand of Moses."'。
[18] '*white,*',一版作 '*white*'。
[19] 'perhaps.',一版作 'perhaps!'。

其四

万象更新始一元，
幽人观化到无言。
白华如手缀枝遍，
淑气发春生物繁。

【注】——

必知此新岁之始为春分。盖旧有之太阳历久为陋劣之太阴历所替，彼计日起自穆罕默德之改邑。以春分为元日佳节，杰姆西王之命也。奥玛每言彼王，且尝与其历之修订。

宾宁言[一]《波斯二岁游历》卷一第一六五页：『春色忽来，顷时渐满，殊动人也。冰雪方解，已见杂花生树，新芽破土矣。元日之雪点缀山际，明灭谷间，园树萌蘖，郊青处处。「冰雪浅作冠，夏荣繁作饰。斯观一何谑……」译注：此出莎士比亚《仲夏夜梦》第二出，盖谓冬神耄耋，着浅冰冠，而缀夏荣以为花环，谑饰其上也。群植新生者中，吾犹识数种，而频年未睹矣。有蓟一种，野春菊，颇类马头兰，红白之苜蓿，阔叶之酸模，蓝矢车菊。而沿水岸，遍蒲公英，黄华采采。』夜莺未闻，玫瑰未放，然画眉与啄木鸟固能唤北鄙之春矣。

『摩西白色之手』，见《出埃及记》四章六节。彼处言，摩西方出其手云云，而波斯人固未言麻风如雪，惟言色白耳，殆类吾地春日之山楂花耶？彼又云，耶稣愈病之力存乎其息中。

【注校记】——

[一]『宾宁言』，一版作：『近有游波斯者言』，无下注文。

4

这时新年把旧愿重新唤起，
沉思的灵魂返归幽独，那里
　有摩西白色的手伸在枝头，
还有耶稣的呼息吹来地底。

【注释】———

“新年”。必须记得这里新年的开始是春分（无论如何旧太阳历实际上已经被极不方便的太阴历取代了，它的计日从穆罕默德迁居算起）。这个日子据说是由杰姆西王指定为纪念节日的。杰姆西王是欧玛尔经常提到的，其历法他也参与过修订。

宾宁说* [1]：“春色突然到来，很快遍布，非常吸引人。田野才开始解冻，树木抽芽，花朵从土壤里发出。他们的元旦（*Now Rooz*）时，雪在山上如补丁，在谷间像阴影，园中果树的新枝已很美丽，绿草杂花在平原到处都是。

‘老迈的冬日之神戴着冰冠
夏天的蓓蕾做成一个芬芳的花环
嘲讽似的，放在—’

在新生的各种植物中我又认出一些多年未见的熟悉品种，有两种蓟；野雏菊，很像马头兰；红白三叶草；酸模；蓝色的矢车菊；水岸两边的野生草药蒲公英生出黄色的顶冠。”还听不到夜莺，看不到玫瑰，但是画眉鸟和啄木鸟已经唤起了北方乡村的春天。

“摩西的白色之手”，见《出埃及记》第四章第六节。那里说，摩西抽出他的手—根据波斯人，没有说“大麻风像雪”，只说“白”—大概类似我们春天的山茶花。也是据他们说，耶稣的治愈能力就在他的气息中。

*《波斯二年游记》，第一卷第165页。

【注释校记】———

[1]“宾宁说”，一版作：“一个近时的波斯旅行者说”，无脚注。

【解读】———

这一首的意思，在牛津包德勒图书馆的乌斯利第140号抄本里有两首，第13首：

既然这世界有个幸福的可能，
每一颗活跃的心都渴望荒漠，
每一条树枝上都有摩西的手出现，
每一阵轻风都是耶稣气息的呼吸。

第80首（加尔各答抄本第204首）：

现在是世界让春风装扮的时候，
在对雨水的企盼里它睁开了眼，
摩西的手像白泡般出现在树枝，
耶稣的气息从大地传来。

也见于“乐园”本第135首。乌斯利抄本第80首的意思很容易理解，春天来了，似乎神圣的感应也遍布世界。可是乌斯利抄本第13首，第二句若有深意，却显得违背常理：春天来了，万象更新，反倒去渴望荒漠。菲茨杰拉德把这个意思表达得更有哲理，一面是唤醒的旧欲望，一面是孤独中的沉思，于是在两者张力中，神圣的感应便不是泛泛说起了。

5

菲译第一版第 5 首，
1904 年版
100 mm × 143 mm

这幅插图最早出现在 1898 年版《鲁拜集》中，属于英国插画家吉尔伯特·詹姆斯（Gilbert James，1865—1941）的黑白插图系列。这幅插图中，詹姆斯重点表现了诗中所说的依傍水际的花园。“诗人”虽悠闲地坐着，但略有愁容，美姬捧着一朵玫瑰，似乎正沉醉在芳香中。画面中的酒罐、葡萄和玫瑰，是诗中反复出现的意象。

V

Iram indeed is gone with all his Rose,
And Jamshyd's Sev'n-ring'd Cup where no one knows;
But still a Ruby kindles in the Vine,
And many a Garden by the Water blows.

【校记】——

●一版：首行 'Iram' 作 'Irám'，'his' 作 'its'；
二行 'Jamshyd's' 作 'Jamshýd's'；
三行 'a Ruby kindles in the Vine' 作 'the Vine her ancient Ruby yields'；
四行 'many' 作 'still'。
●二版：二行 'Jamshyd's' 作 'Jamshýd's'；
三行 'kindles in' 作 'gushes from'。
●三版：三行同二版。

【注释】——

Iram[1], planted by King Shaddád[2], and now sunk somewhere in the Sands of Arabia. Jamshyd's Seven-ring'd Cup was typical of the 7[3] Heavens, 7 Planets, 7 Seas, &c.,[4] and was a *Divining Cup*.

【注释校记】——

[1] 'Iram'，一版作 'Irám'。
[2] 'Schaddád'，一版作 'Schedad'。
[3] '7'，一版作 'Seven'。
[4] '&c.,'，一版作 '&c.'。

其五

碛中帝苑逐时穷，
海外神杯照世空。
惟有年年溪水畔，
等闲红紫尽春风。

【注】——

伊兰园，夏达德王之所建也，今湮于大食国沙碛中。杰姆西王之七环杯，以象七重天海、七耀星宿诸事，神杯也。

5

伊兰园和他的玫瑰都无踪迹，
杰姆西王的七环杯没处寻觅；
**　只有藤间的红宝石依然闪耀，**
和许多花开的园子依傍水际。

【校记】

●一版：三行“藤间的红宝石依然闪耀”作“藤间自古以来红色的葡萄仍在结实”；四行“许多”作“依然”。

●二版：三行“闪耀”作“迸出”。

●三版：三行同二版。

【注释】

伊兰园，为夏达德王所建，现在已经湮没在阿拉伯沙漠的某个位置。杰姆西王的七环杯象征七重天、七大行星、七个海等，是一只神杯。

【解读】

第 5 首抒发“茂陵刘郎秋风客”（李贺《金铜仙人辞汉歌》）般的悲哀，这是东西方常见的主题，也是人类对权势、命运之无常的共同体悟。菲茨杰拉德拿波斯的名物、风光作了点染。在波斯文诗歌里，杰姆西王出现过（加尔各答抄本第 254 首），“藤间的红宝石”（乌斯利抄本第 39、87、149 首，加尔各答抄本第 296、304、413、460 首）和“水边的园子”（乌斯利抄本第 151 首，加尔各答抄本的第 415 首大致相近；加尔各答抄本第 44、417 首）更是经常出现的意象，但并没有任何一首与之相合。也许菲茨杰拉德另有底本，也许就是他受了感发后的仿作——那更加纯粹的精神之译。

6

菲译第五版第 6 首，
1942 年版
103 mm × 145 mm

匈牙利插画家威利·波加尼（Willy Pogány，1882—1955）在德国、法国和英国都享有很大名望，他在美国好莱坞曾做过艺术指导的工作。一般认为，波加尼插图版《鲁拜集》有三个系列，主要是 1909 年版、1930 年版和 1942 年版。1942 年版的作品，被命名为“情色与幻想”，共有 20 幅全页黑白插图。这幅插图描绘了第三行和第四行诗中的意象。

VI

And David's lips are lockt; but in divine
High-piping Pehleví, with "Wine! Wine! Wine!
"Red Wine!"—the Nightingale cries to the Rose
That sallow cheek of hers to' incarnadine.

【校记】

●一版：首行 'lockt' 作 'lock't'；
二行 'High-piping' 作 'High piping'，'Pehleví' 作 'Péhlevi'；
三行 'Red' 作 '*Red*'；
四行 'sallow cheek' 作 'yellow Cheek'，'hers' 作 'her's'。
●二版：二行 'Pehleví' 作 'Péhlevi'；
四行 'hers' 作 'her's'，'to'' 作 'to'。
●三版：二行同二版；
四行 'hers' 作 'her's'。
●四版：四行 'hers' 作 'her's'。

【注释】

Pehlevi [1], the old Heroic *Sanskrit* of Persia. Háfiz also speaks of the Nightingale's *Pehlevi* [2], which did not change with the People's.

I am not sure if the fourth line, [3] refers to the Red Rose looking sickly, or to the Yellow Rose that ought to be Red; Red, White, and Yellow Roses all common in Persia. [4] I think that Southey, in his Common-Place Book, quotes from some Spanish author about the [5] Rose being White till 10 o'clock; "Rosa Perfecta" at 2; and "perfecta incarnada" at 5.

【注释校记】

[1] '*Pehlevi*',一版、二版、三版作 '*Péhlevi*'。
[2] '*Pehlevi*',一版、二版、三版作 '*Péhlevi*'。
[3] 此注一版、二版、三版另作一条，'the fourth line' 作 'this'。
[4] 此句以下,一版无。
[5] 'the',二版作 'a',三版无。

其六

诗律长喑似冻乌，
殷勤谁解劝提壶？
不辞唱尽春风媚，
添与蔷薇一点朱。

【注】——
巴列维语，古波斯雅言也。哈菲兹亦言夜莺之巴列维语，未与吾人之语偕易。
吾不能决四行中所言，究为红玫瑰带惨色耶，抑彼黄玫瑰实应为红耶？盖红、白、黄之玫瑰，在波斯均常见者。索西之《类纂》征诸西班牙著述，云玫瑰十时为白，二时为黄，五时为红。

6

大卫的唇紧锁；而绝世稀有
高亮的巴列维语调，“酒！酒！酒！
殷红的酒！”——是夜莺叫向玫瑰
让鲜红将她颊边蔫黄驱走。

【注释】———

巴列维语，波斯古代英雄时代类似梵语的古老语言。哈菲兹也讲过夜莺的巴列维语，没跟着人类的一起改变。

我不能确定第四行所指，究竟是看起来很惨黄的红玫瑰，还是黄玫瑰本该为红色？红色、白色、黄色的玫瑰在波斯都很普遍。我想索西在他的《类纂》里，引用了一些西班牙作者的说法，说玫瑰在十点是白色，两点是黄色，五点是红色。

【解读】———

第 6 首译自乌斯利抄本的第 67 首（1207 年抄本第 211 首，“乐园”本第 220 首）：

这是快乐的一天，天气不热不冷；
雨水洗去了玫瑰脸上的尘土；
夜莺用巴列维语调向蔫黄的玫瑰
一直在喊：“你要喝酒！”

大卫是古代以色列的国王，善于歌唱，又能作诗，据说《圣经》里的诗篇就出自他的手笔。菲茨杰拉德把他拿来作了陪衬，让夜莺劝酒的巴列维古调更加突出了悠远和美好。在中国，虽然没有如此浓重的渲染，但提葫芦的叫声同样令人神往。

7

菲译第一版第 7 首，
1920 年版
158 mm × 186 mm

英国插画家罗纳德·鲍尔弗（Ronald Balfour，1896—1941）为《鲁拜集》画的作品，具有早期“装饰艺术”的风格，原作藏于维多利亚和阿尔伯特博物馆。插图中的美女像是20世纪20年代的时髦女郎。画面中的绿树繁花喻指春天。显然，憩息在女郎手上的小鸟就是诗中提到的“时光之鸟”。

VII

Come, fill the Cup, and in the fire of Spring
Your Winter-garment of Repentance fling:
The Bird of Time has but a little way
To flutter—and the Bird is on the Wing.

【校记】——

●一版：首行 'fire' 作 'Fire'；
二行 'Your Winter-garment' 作 'The Winter Garment'；
四行 'To flutter—and' 作 'To fly—and Lo!'。

其七

春火先燔冬日衣，
杯中问甚去年非。
好知万古无多路，
过眼长空一鸟飞。

7

来吧，倒满杯子，就在这春日
火中把你悔恨的冬衣抛掷，
　时光之鸟只有短短的路程
要去飞过——而那鸟已经展翅。

【校记】———
●一版：四行“去飞过—而”作“去飞—而看！”

【解读】———
第 7 首，头两行据赫荣 - 艾伦的说法，融合了加尔各答抄本的第 431 首：

每一天我都决心在晚上忏悔，
忏悔那满满的高杯，和浅盏；
（但是）现在玫瑰的季节来了，我不能悲伤，
在玫瑰的季节把后悔给了忏悔，哦我主！

和第 460 首的头两行：

花开了，带上酒，哦萨吉，
扔掉狂信者的修行，哦萨吉。

不过，我认为这和菲茨杰拉德的第 94 首更相似，赫荣 - 艾伦也提到，这两首有些难于区别。但让我们注意到，这里的“悔恨”应该和忏悔是相关的。

后两行很像来自阿塔尔《鸟会》里的一个对句：

天空的鸟儿沿着它被指定的路线飞行。

我相信，这不会是菲茨杰拉德偶然的疏忽。

8

菲译第一版前言，
1901 年版
78 mm × 47 mm

英国画家赫伯特 · 科尔（Herbert Cole，1867—1930）善于运用线条，作品形象地体现了诗中的意象和韵味。画面中的老海亚姆正手捻长须，举杯欲饮。桌子上的仪器、鹅毛笔、圆规、三角板等表明了其学者身份。玫瑰、孔雀是诗中反复出现的意象。“不管杯里是酸苦还是甘醇”，生命之酒不会停止渗沥。

VIII

Whether at Naishápúr or Babylon,
Whether the Cup with sweet or bitter run,
The Wine of Life keeps oozing drop by drop,
The Leaves of Life keep falling one by one.

【校记】

●一版：无此首。

其八

朝野未应妨性殊，
苦甘一例得心娱。
莫辞浅把涓涓酒，
便好深怜叶叶梧。

8

不管内沙布尔或者巴比伦，
不管杯里是酸苦还是甘醇。
生命之酒在一滴一滴渗沥，
生命之叶在一片一片飘沦。

【解读】———

第 8 首主要来自乌斯利抄本第 47 首（加尔各答抄本第 123 首，1207 年抄本第 136 首，“乐园”本第 74 首）：

因为生命过往；巴格达怎样巴尔赫怎样？
当杯子斟满，它是甜是苦又有何干？
喝酒啊，在你和我过后，这月亮还会继续过往
从一个月的最后一天到第一天，再从第一天到最后一天。

第三句可能出于尼古拉斯校订本第 18 首的后两行：

不管是我们的萨吉用手抓住瓶颈，
还是酒之魂溢出杯沿。

第四句“生命之叶”经常出现，或指树叶，或指书页，这应该来自加尔各答抄本第 377 首的头两行：

我在逃脱定命的那一刻，
像葡萄叶一样，从枝上坠落。

这一首在菲茨杰拉德第一版里是没有的，赫荣 - 艾伦认为，他显然受到尼古拉斯版的提示，因为只有尼古拉斯本用“内沙布尔”替掉了“巴尔赫”。在波斯文学中，“巴尔赫”和“巴比伦”是经常互换的。内沙布尔，是海亚姆出生的地方。

菲茨杰拉德将这些零散在波斯文中的意象加以重组，写成了《鲁拜集》中的名句，把生命的飘逝感表达得更加形象，更加动人心魄。生命一刻一刻，不停地趋向死亡，面对这个冷酷的现实，处身何处，生活的滋味如何，都没有实际的区别了。这带些恐吓，但更多的是催人反省。

9

菲译第一版第 8 首，
1921 年版
154 mm × 222 mm

这幅插图的作者是英国女插画家多丽丝 · M. 帕尔默（Doris M. Palmer，1896—？）。关于她的去世时间，一说 1931 年，一说 1977 年。她绘的《鲁拜集》插图共有 12 幅彩图，色彩艳丽。画面中神秘男子伫立在河畔的花园里，凝视着远方，若有所思。他的装扮表明了这是炎热的“夏月”。多丽丝以华丽的装饰艺术风格展示了诗中所说的“千朵花”。

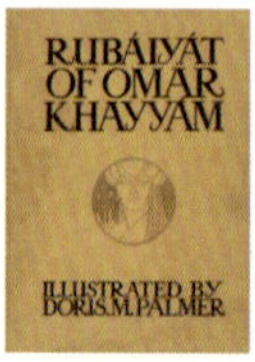

IX

Each Morn a thousand Roses brings, you say;
Yes, but where leaves the Rose of Yesterday?
　And this first Summer month that brings the Rose
Shall take Jamshyd and Kaikobád away.

【校记】——

●一版：列其八；
首行作‘And look—a thousand Blossoms with the Day’；
二行作‘Woke—and a thousand scatter’d into Clay:’；
三行‘month’作‘Month’；
四行‘Jamshyd’作‘Jamshýd’。
●二版：首行‘Each Morn’作‘Morning’；
二行‘Yesterday’作‘yesterday’；
四行同一版。

其九

朝来千朵一时开，
零落谁将昨日哀？
同是催花风信在，
无端也把哲王催。

9

你说，每个早晨带来千朵花，
不错，可昨日玫瑰落去谁家？
**　带来这些玫瑰的首个夏月**
还会带走杰姆西和凯柯巴。

【校记】———

●一版：首二行可译作："看啊——每天醒来了一千朵花，/——一千朵花又要飘落在泥沙。"

【解读】———

第 9 首来自三个片断，乌斯利抄本第 135 首的后两行：

坐在玫瑰花荫里，因为，被风吹，许多玫瑰
散落在地变成了尘土。

加尔各答抄本第 500 首的头两行：

随着春天的到来和十二月的回归
我们生命的叶子持续地卷折。

加尔各答抄本第 481 首的后两行：

它把十万个杰姆和凯扔在地上，
这第一个夏月的到来和十二月的离去。

我们从中可以看到菲茨杰拉德的裁剪功夫：只把玫瑰和雄主点出来，再不着一字。玫瑰美好而短暂，这是我们容易看到的，雄主显赫一时，却也一样终归零落，往往让人忘记。二者一联系，人生飘逝的普遍哀叹更显得深沉了。这时，苏轼"大江东去，浪淘尽、千古风流人物"（《念奴娇·赤壁怀古》）的高旷之句，不知不觉就让我们想起。

10

菲译第一版第 9 首，
1910 年版
40 mm × 100 mm

这是英国插画家莫里斯·格莱芬哈根（Maurice Greiffenhagen，1862—1931）的作品。第一版中这首诗提到了海亚姆。画面中老海亚姆的白胡子，近处的书卷、长颈酒瓶、碗，远处的星空，均表明了海亚姆诗人、学者的形象和身份。玫瑰花、葡萄藤和英文字体是典型的新艺术运动风格。这幅插图的清晰度表明，彼时的彩色印刷技术与现在的技术不同。

X

Well, let it take them! What have we to do
With Kaikobád the Great, or Kaikhosrú?
  Let Zál and Rustum bluster as they will,
Or Hátim call to Supper—heed not you.

【校记】

●一版：列其九，异文较多，别出。
●二版：三行作 'Let Rustum cry "To Battle!" as he likes,'；四行作 'Or Hátim Tai "To Supper!" —heed not you.'。
●三版：三行 'bluster' 作 'thunder'。

【注释】

Rustum, the "Hercules" of Persia, and Zál his Father, [1]whose exploits are among the most celebrated in the Sháh-náma[2]. Hátim Tai, a well-known type of Oriental Generosity.

【注释校记】

[1] 'and Zál his Father,'，一版、二版无。
[2] 'Sháh-náma'，一版作 'Shah-náma'。

I-IX(V- X)

But come with old Khayyám, and leave the Lot
Of Kaikobád and Kaikhosrú forgot:
  Let Rustum lay about him as he will,
Or Hátim Tai cry Supper—heed them not.

【校记】

●注释见前。

其十

哲王催老只由他，
天地徒劳涕泪多。
谁见大人龙战怒？
谁听小雅鹿鸣歌？

【注】——
鲁斯塔姆，波斯之赫拉克勒斯也，扎尔其父。《王书》盛称其绩。哈蒂姆，以豪爽疏财闻名东国。

10

让它把他们带走！凯柯巴大帝，
凯霍斯鲁跟我们有什么干系？
　让扎尔和鲁斯图姆纵情叫战，
或是哈蒂姆命宴——你不用留意。

【校记】——
●二版：三行作“让鲁斯塔姆像他喜欢的那样喊‘去作战！’”。

【注释】——
鲁斯塔姆，波斯的“赫拉克利特”，扎尔是他的父亲，《列王纪》里高度颂扬了他的功绩。哈蒂姆·泰，东方式慷慨的闻名典范。

1-9（5-10）

只须跟着我老海亚姆，忘尽
凯柯巴和凯霍斯鲁的命运。
　让鲁斯图姆自去为所欲为，
哈蒂姆·泰命宴——他们不用问。

【解读】——
第10首，头两行来自乌斯利抄本第139首（1207年抄本第236首，“乐园”本第337首）的后两行：
酒杯胜过法里东的王国一百倍，
盖酒坛的瓦片胜过凯霍斯鲁的王冠。
以及加尔各答抄本第57首（1207年抄本第70首，“乐园”本第279首）的头两行：
一口酒胜过卡乌斯的帝国
也胜过柯巴的王座和图斯的帝国。
后两行来自加尔各答抄本第503首的后两行：
即使扎尔的儿子鲁斯塔姆是你的敌人也别低头，
即使哈蒂姆·泰是你的朋友也别庆幸。
但是，前两句似乎没有波斯原文惊警，后两句的意思也不够显豁，需要看了原文才明白起来。译文逊色于原文的情况，也绝非没有。

不过，菲茨杰拉德把这些内容和前一首勾连在一起，同样的意思再加唱叹，着重点并不在对权势的傲视。既然生命同样短暂易逝，雄主和你是平等的，权势不值艳羡，盛衰无须关心。

11

菲译第二版第 11 首，
1910 年版
174 mm × 223 mm

法裔英籍插画家埃德蒙·杜拉克（Edmund Dulac，1882—1953）是欧美插图黄金时期的著名插画家。1909 年，他为菲译《鲁拜集》第二版配了 20 幅彩色插图。1910 年，他配图的《鲁拜集》法文版出版。画面中的马穆德安坐在富丽堂皇的宫殿宝座上，身边席地而坐的宫女正在演奏音乐，地毯上散落着卷帙。插画家形象地表达了第三行和第四行诗的意蕴。

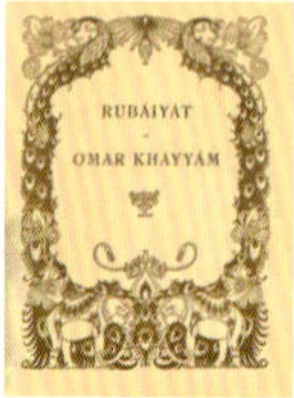

XI

With me along the strip of Herbage strown
That just divides the desert from the sown,
　Where name of Slave and Sultán is forgot—
And Peace to Mahmúd on his golden Throne!

【校记】

●一版：列其十；
首行 ‘the strip’ 作 ‘some Strip’；
三行 ‘is forgot—’ 作 ‘scarce is known,’；
四行作 ‘And pity Sultán Máhmúd on his Throne.’。
●二版：四行 ‘Mahmúd’ 作 ‘Máhmúd’。
●三版：四行同二版。

其十一

牧草逶迤一带青，
恰分穷壤与新町。
偕来肯较君王业？
聊祝承平到帝廷。

11

跟我沿着狭长的牧草地带
那里正把荒地隔出田亩外，
　在这儿忘了奴隶和苏丹之名——
且祝金座之上马穆德安泰！

【校记】———
●一版：三行“尽忘”作“很少知道”；
四行作“而同情他的宝座上的马穆德苏丹”。

【解读】———
第 11 首，赫荣 - 艾伦没有找到相应的波斯原文，但他提醒我们和第 12 首一起考虑。或许，菲茨杰拉德为了那著名的第 12 首，在这里预先勾画了一个背景。

需要提到的是，Mahmúd 应该译作马穆德，是加兹尼王朝苏丹，公元 998 年到 1030 年在位，以强权著称，统治了波斯的呼罗珊地区，并多次入侵印度。郭沫若译为穆罕默德，容易引起和 Muhammad 的混淆，似乎不甚妥当。

12

菲译第二版第 12 首，
1910 年版
174 mm × 223 mm

法裔英籍插画家埃德蒙·杜拉克（Edmund Dulac，1882—1953）的这一幅插图在众多知名插画家的同题材作品中是佼佼者。整个画面弥漫着浓郁的东方情调。弯月挂在蓝色的星空中，一对身着波斯服装的情侣在树下乘凉，男士一手执书悠闲地斜靠在坡地上，草地上还有面包和一壶酒，美人倚树而歌，姿态娇媚。

XII

A Book of Verses underneath the Bough,
A Jug of Wine, a Loaf of Bread—and Thou
　Beside me singing in the Wilderness—
Oh, Wilderness were Paradise enow!

【校记】——

●一版：列其十一；
首行作‘Here with a Loaf of Bread beneath the Bough,’；
二行作‘A Flask of Wine, a Book of Verse—and Thou’；
四行作‘And Wilderness is Paradise enow.’。
●二版：首行作‘Here with a little Bread beneath the Bough,’；
二行同一版。

其十二

袖诗一卷傍高株，
食一箪兮酒一壶。
得汝清歌相媚妩，
荒郊那与乐郊殊？

12

带着一卷诗集到大树枝底，
一壶红酒，一条面包，还有你
**　荒野中偎傍在我身边放歌，**
哦，荒野已跟天堂相差无几！

【校记】——

●一版：首行作“这儿有一条面包在大树枝底”；二行作“一瓶红酒，一卷诗集，还有你”。

●二版：首行作“这儿有一点儿面包在大树枝底”。

【解读】——

第 12 首是歌颂爱情至上的名篇，遍传人口，据说是菲茨杰拉德被人引用最多的诗句，甚至说是《圣经》之外最为熟知的英语译文。来自乌斯利抄本第 155 首（加尔各答抄本第 474 首，1207 年抄本第 161 首，“乐园”本第 126 首）：

如果现有一个麦粉大饼，
一葫芦酒，一块羊腿，
而且，如果我和你坐在旷野中，——
那种快乐不是任何苏丹的权力能企及的。

还有第 149 首（“乐园”本第 282 首）：

我想要一瓶红酒和一本诗集
只是足够让我活着，还有半个饼也是需要的，
那时，我和你就坐在旷野中，
胜过了苏丹的王国。

值得提到的是，在“乐园”本第 210 首里讲到“天堂”：

与美女、萨吉畅饮在原野之上，
我愿享受当今，任你梦想天堂。
不要听信天堂火狱的痴言妄语，
谁到过地狱，又有谁来自天堂？

（张鸿年、宋丕方译文）

或许菲茨杰拉德在翻译时，还参考了乌斯利抄本和加尔各答抄本之外的波斯文本，只是我们无从考据了。

这首也是菲茨杰拉德善于熔铸的著名例子，引起了钱锺书的注意，在《槐聚诗存》一首诗的诗题里，他说：

Edward Fitzgerald 英译波斯《醹醅雅》（*Rubáiyát*），颂酒之名篇也。第十二章云：“坐树荫下，得少面包，酒一瓯、诗一卷、有美一人如卿者为侣（and thou），虽旷野乎，可作天堂观。”为世传诵。比有波斯人 A.G.E'Tessam-Zadeh 译此雅为法语，颇称信达，初无英译本尔许语。一章云：“倘得少酒，一清歌妙舞者，一女便娟，席草临流，便作极乐园主想，不畏地狱诸苦恼耳。”又一章云：“有面包一方，羊一肩，酒一瓯，更得美姝偕焉，即处荒烟蔓草间而南面王不与易也（Vaux mieuxque d`un empire être le Souverain）。”乃知英译剪裁二章为一，反胜原作。

这里所谓一章，即“乐园”本第 210 首；又一章，即乌斯利抄本第 155 首。赫荣 - 艾伦和钱锺书各漏掉了一首波斯原诗，也就都没有看到，菲茨杰拉德的第 12 首中每一句其实都是有来源的。

这首的中译，黄克孙先生无可超越——“一箪疏食一壶浆，一卷诗书树下凉。卿为阿侬歌瀚海，茫茫瀚海即天堂。”译文质朴无华，却雅韵盎然，尤其难得的是朗朗上口，所以一下子就传开了。

13

菲译第五版第 13 首，
1898 年版
143 mm × 207 mm

英国插画家吉尔伯特·詹姆斯（Gilbert James，1865—1941）的这幅插图以军队占据画面的主体，用行进的军队来喻指远方嗵嗵的鼓声，用穿盔甲的指挥官喻指人间的权力。画面前景中的人物在专注地倒酒，“且典春衣拼一醉”，对外界的喧嚣置若罔闻，与中景中的老人形成了鲜明的对比。

XIII

Some for the Glories of This World; and some
Sigh for the Prophet's Paradise to come;
　Ah, take the Cash, and let the Credit go,
Nor heed the rumble of a distant Drum!

【校记】——

●一版：列其十二，异文较多，别出。
●二版：三行 'Credit' 作 'Promise'；四行 'rumble' 作 'music'。

【注释】——

A Drum—beaten outside a Palace.

I-XII(V- XIII)

"How sweet is mortal Sovranty!"—think some:
Others—"How blest the Paradise to come!"
　Ah, take the Cash in hand and wave the Rest;
Oh, the brave Music of a *distant* Drum!

【注释】——

同上。

其十三

人间天上说荣华，
笑尔区区计已差。
且典春衣拼一醉，
晨钟暮鼓两俱遐。

【注】——
是鼓，宫外所击者也。

13

有人为了此世的荣光；有人
渴慕先知所说天堂的来临；
**　啊，拿了现钱，不要理会债券，**
远方嗵嗵的鼓声别挂在心！

【校记】———
●二版：三行“债券”作“承诺”；
四行“嗵嗵声”作“音乐”。

【注释】———
这个鼓，是在宫外敲击的。

1-12（5-13）

“人间权力何等惬意！”——有人想，
另有人——“天堂来临何样赐享！”
**　啊，把现钱攥在手丢开其余，**
哦，那远方的鼓乐声威震响。

【解读】———
第13首的波斯原文，是乌斯利抄本第34首（加尔各答抄本第51首，1207年抄本第147首，“乐园”本第414首）：
他们说跟神女在伊甸园是让人快乐的；
我说葡萄的汁液是让人快乐的。
紧牢这现金别动那支票，
兄弟，远方传来的鼓声是让人快乐的。
加尔各答抄本第156首也有相近的意思：
他们说那里会有天堂和考萨尔泉，
那里，那里会有纯净的酒和蜜和糖，
倒满酒杯把它放在我手里，
（因为）现成的金钱比支票好过千倍。
在波斯神话里，考萨尔泉是天堂所有河流的上游，据《可兰经》说，穆罕默德的女婿阿里在那里作萨吉。《可兰经》许诺了河边的花园，还有宫殿，加尔各答抄本第288首的头两行（第225首的头两行意思也相近）说到了宫殿：
人类从虚妄的想象中沦入傲慢，
在寻找神女和宫殿中耗尽。
乌斯利抄本第40首（加尔各答抄本第107首）也讲到“当前”和“许诺”：

我不知道造我的他是否
指定我住在天堂或是可怕的地狱，
（但是）一些吃的，一个可爱慕的，还有酒在绿野边上——
这三样是我当前的金钱：你的是许诺的天堂！

菲茨杰拉德把“神女”拿掉，以适应基督教的天堂景象；把葡萄酒换成“此世的荣光”，更具普遍性的意义。后两句几乎做了直译，但波斯原文里鼓声是“让人快乐的”，所以菲氏前两版都以“鼓乐”来译，三版后放弃了，直接改用“嗵嗵声”，就把光阴易逝的紧迫感更突出了。在脱离波斯文语境后，这样的改译应该说表达更为忠实。就全诗看，菲译显得凝练紧凑，但似乎失去了一种萧散疏狂的风致。毫无疑问的是，改变后的诗句更为适合英国绅士的气质，这就把翻译从媒介提升为文学本体了。

这里的旧体诗译文，第一句考虑到俗世和天堂的对比在中国传统语境中并不常见，改作了“人间天上”，以“说荣华”总括，反倒跟波斯文的趣味相近。菲氏所着力的第三、四句，置换了中国的意象语汇，但仍然突出了光阴易逝的急迫中及时行乐的态度，算得是“换骨法”。第三句借用了杜甫的《曲江二首》之一“朝回日日典春衣，每日江头尽醉归”，第四句则是以寺院的“晨钟暮鼓”显示超然时间之外，而将急迫感全都移入“且典春衣拼一醉”一句。

14

菲译第五版第 14 首，
1956 年版
78 mm × 127 mm

杰夫·希尔（Jeff Hill，生平不详）为菲译《鲁拜集》第五版配了 8 幅插图。除了这个版本，同样的插图还有蓝色、黑色等版本。这幅插图紧扣诗意，以简洁流畅的线条来强调玫瑰的造型。男子专注的表情透出些许怅惘。左边的图案也不仅仅是插图边框，其作用是丰富画面，也使得整个画面更贴近诗意。

15

菲译第一版第 15 首，
1941 年版
89 mm × 131 mm

出生于苏格兰的画家戈登·罗斯（Gordon Ross，1872—1946）后来移民到美国。他为菲译《鲁拜集》第一版配了 75 幅黑白插图。第 15 首诗告诉我们：有人将金钱看得很重，吝惜如命，而有的人却挥霍无度，然而人生最终结局都相同，人人都会成为尘土而不会变成黄金。戈登·罗斯用死神来收命的寓意形象地表达了诗意。

第十四首

XIV

Look to the blowing Rose about us—“Lo,
“Laughing,” she says, “into the world I blow,
    “At once the silken tassel of my Purse
“Tear, and its Treasure on the Garden throw.”

【校记】——

●一版：列其十三；
首行 ‘blowing Rose’ 作 ‘Rose that blows’；
二行句末作冒号；
三行 ‘tassel’ 作 ‘Tassel’。
●二版：列其十五。
●三版：首行 ‘“Lo’ 作 ‘Lo’。

【注释】——

That is, the Rose's Golden Centre.

第十五首

XV

And those who husbanded the Golden grain,
And those who flung it to the winds like Rain,
    Alike to no such aureate Earth are turn'd
As, buried once, Men want dug up again.

【校记】——

●一版：一行 ‘grain’ 作 ‘Grain’；
二行 ‘winds’ 作 ‘Winds’。
●二版：列其十六；首行 ‘And’ 作 ‘For’。

其十四

玫瑰开遍绕吾身，
道是嫣然同世尘。
囊里珍奇应不惜，
倾来为续满园春。

【注】——
彼处，玫瑰最盛地也。

其十五

瓦缶黄钟一例沉，
当时枉自费行吟。
江头谁问怀沙恨？
淘尽江沙只见金。

第十四首

14

看那绽放的玫瑰缭绕身边——
“看啊，”她说，“我含笑绽放世间，
　很快我的锦囊丝穗被扯掉，
把它里头的珍宝撒落花园。”

【注释】——

那里是玫瑰的黄金中心。

【解读】——

第 14 首译自加尔各答抄本第 383 首：

玫瑰说：我有抛撒金子的手，
笑着，笑着，我绽放在世间，
我扯下我钱袋顶上缠着的丝绳就离去！
我把我所有的金钱抛向世间。

但菲茨杰拉德使比喻更加显豁了。玫瑰花开放的时间虽然不久，但在最美好的季节，把自己最美好的都绽放出来了，甚至凋零之后也在所不惜。这是面对无常世界，乐观、健康的态度，尽管没有主动奉献的意思，还是让我们想到龚自珍的“落红不是无情物，化作春泥更护花”。（《己亥杂诗》其五）

第十五首

15

那一些耕耘出了金色的稻米，
那一些把它如雨般抛在风里，
　他们都不会变成这样的金沙，
一旦沉埋，还会被人们再掘起。

【解读】——

第 15 首的意思来自乌斯利抄本第 68 首（加尔各答抄本第 151 首，1207 年抄本第 116 首，“乐园”本第 382 首）：

在命运袭击你的头颅之前
命令他们带给你玫瑰色的酒；
你不是财宝，哦不留心的笨蛋！你
让他们埋进地里就不会再挖出。

据说，在东方，当预先觉察到土匪和劫犯要来夜袭时，人们就会把财宝埋在地里隐藏。这个比喻的地域性太强，我们中国人也很陌生，菲茨杰拉德把它改变了，就能得到更广泛的理解。菲茨杰拉德很多改易的例子，都表明波斯不少说法对于西方人和对于我们是同样陌生的，经他改变之后我们都更容易理解了。似乎菲茨杰拉德特别注意表达的普遍性，并非只是一味照顾英伦的习惯。他增添的前两句的内容，也使主题更加深刻。

16

菲译第一版第 14 首，
1925 年版
72 mm × 90 mm

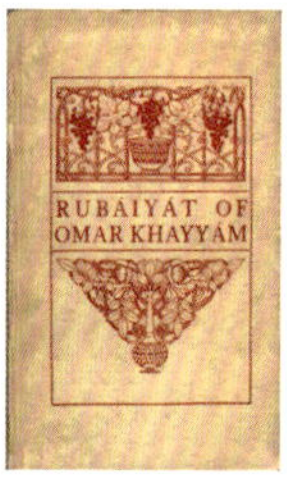

这是美国作家、画家布兰奇·麦克马纳斯（Blanche McManus，1870—1935）的作品。画面中穿波斯服装的男士，垂垂老矣，正低头沉思。韶华易逝，名利、富贵终究是过往云烟，或如大漠沙面上的雪虽明亮一时，但会迅速消逝。人生得意须尽欢？人生的意义究竟何在？

17

菲译第一版第 16 首，
1913 年版
130 mm × 130 mm

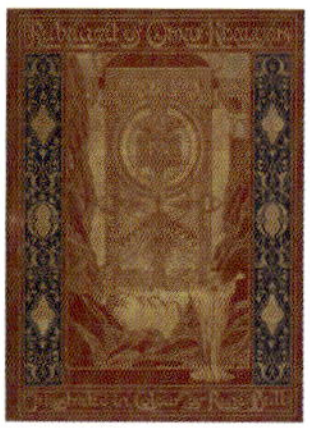

英国插画家、摄影家雷恩·布尔（René Bull，1872—1942）为菲译《鲁拜集》第一版配的插图，除了彩色的之外，还有 58 幅深蓝色插图。画面中展示了一位声势显赫的苏丹形象。这是一位享受人间荣华富贵的苏丹。这首诗告诉我们，再风光的帝王，也只不过是人世间的匆匆过客而已。

第十六首

XVI

The Worldly Hope men set their Hearts upon
Turns Ashes—or it prospers; and anon,
Like Snow upon the Desert's dusty Face,
Lighting a little hour or two—is gone.

【校记】——

●一版：列其十四；
四行 'Lighting' 作 'Lightning'，五版末附一版文亦作 'Lighting'；'hour' 作 'Hour'。
●二版：列其十七；
四行 'is gone' 作 'was gone'。
●三版、四版：四行同二版。

第十七首

XVII

Think, in this batter'd Caravanserai
Whose Portals are alternate Night and Day,
How Sultán after Sultán with his Pomp
Abode his destined Hour, and went his way.

【校记】——

●一版：列其十六；
二行 'Portals' 作 'Doorways'；
四行 'his destined Hour' 作 'his Hour or two'。
●二版：列其十八；
四行 'destined' 作 'destin'd'。
●三版、四版：四行同二版。

其十六

一世浮华幻乐哀，
炽于炎火冷于灰。
消除终似龙沙雪，
谁见当时明灭来？

其十七

天地何妨逆旅看？
门前日月转双丸。
荣华多少逢迎尽，
一样匆匆遣素檀。

第十六首

16

人们置心其上的俗世希望
变成灰烬——或者，它变得兴旺；
很快，就像大漠沙面上的雪，
消逝了——只是一时半刻明亮。

【解读】———

第 16 首来自加尔各答抄本第 266 首：

哦心！料想所有的俗世事务都在你的能力之内，
并且整个世间从头到尾一如你所愿望，
既如此，像沙漠上的雪，在它的表面
待个两三天，明白你自己就该消失了！

菲茨杰拉德增加了相反的一面——“变成灰烬”，两相比照，俗世的虚幻被揭示得更淋漓尽致。不过，这里的态度也许并非消极绝望，而是冷静睿智。《鲁拜集》里常有这样的冷静睿智，应该来自海亚姆的哲人气质，郭沫若认为海亚姆是波斯的李白，其实更近于道家，或者介于道家和李白之间，不全是放纵，也不只是睿智。《兰亭序》里所说：“向之所欣，俯仰之间，已为陈迹，犹不能不以之兴怀，况修短随化，终期于尽！古人云：死生亦大矣。岂不痛哉！”大概最合于海亚姆。由此冷静反显出的及时行乐，便具有对执着于虚幻的批判态度了。然而行乐之后，仍是无法抹去的痛。菲茨杰拉德序言里说：“最伤感的可能是最夸耀欢乐的时候，反使老帐篷匠容易哀伤过于愤怒。”这确实是很正确的看法。

第十七首

17

想想，这商队旅舍破败凋敝
它的大门是昼夜轮番开闭，
苏丹一个个如何擅其声势
留到命定的时刻，便自离去。

【校记】———

●一版：四行“命定的时刻”作“一两个小时”。

【解读】———

第 17 首译自加尔各答抄本第 95 首（1207 年抄本第 34 首，“乐园”本第 58 首）：

这个破败的商队旅舍就叫世界
是夜和日这两匹黑白之马的停居处；
它是被上百个贾姆希德弃用的帐篷，
它是上百个巴拉姆的停居之所。

波斯原文“黑白相间色”之马的比喻，在中文里也显得稍隔膜，倒是菲茨杰拉德的讲法更亲切，和“日月双丸跳”（白玉蟾）或“日月双转毂”（苏轼）都很谐调。

郭沫若认为：“此首宜与李白《春夜宴桃李园序》并读。”自然是指开篇的两句：“夫天地者，万物之逆旅也；光阴者，百代之过客也。”并且用到了他自己的译文里：“天地是飘摇的逆旅，昼夜是逆旅的门户。”

18

菲译第一版第 17 首，
1922 年版
146 mm × 190 mm

英国插画家安妮 · 哈丽特 · 菲胥（Anne Harriet Fish，1890—1964）为许多杂志画过漫画和插图。安妮为《鲁拜集》绘制的插图具有“装饰艺术”的风格，人物形象类似她画的讽刺漫画。这幅插图以黑色和银色为主，加了少量紫色、蓝灰色，在狮子身上和少部分地方用了金色。画面整体是灰冷的，符合苍凉的诗境。

XVIII

They say the Lion and the Lizard keep
The Courts where Jamshyd gloried and drank deep:
    And Bahrám, that great Hunter—the Wild Ass
Stamps o'er his Head, but cannot break his Sleep.

【校记】

●一版：列其十七；
二行 'Jamshyd' 作 'Jamshýd',五版末附一版文句末冒号作分号；
四行 'but cannot break his Sleep' 作 'and he lies fast asleep'。
●二版：列其十九；
二行同一版。

【注释】

[1]Persepolis: call'd also *Takht-i-Jamshyd*[2]—The Throne Of Jamshyd, *"King Splendid,"* of the mythical *Peshdàdian* Dynasty, and supposed (according to the Sháh-náma) to have been founded and built by him. Others refer it to the Work of the Genie King, Ján Ibn Ján—who also built the Pyramids—before the time of Adam.

BAHRÁM GÚR.—*Bahram*[3] *of the Wild Ass*—a Sassanian Sovereign—had also his Seven Castles (like the King of Bohemia!) each of a different Colour: each with a Royal Mistress within; each of whom tells him a Story, as told in one of the most famous Poems of Persia, written by Amír Khusraw: all these Sevens also figuring (according to Eastern Mysticism) the Seven Heavens; and perhaps the Book itself that Eighth, into which the mystical Seven transcend, and within which they revolve. The Ruins of Three of those[4] Towers are yet shown by the Peasantry; as also the Swamp in which Bahrám sunk, like the Master of Ravenswood, while pursuing his *Gúr*.

The Palace that to Heav'n his pillars threw,
And Kings the forehead on his threshold drew—
    I saw the solitary Ringdove there,
And "Coo, coo, coo, " she cried; and "Coo, coo, coo. " [5]

This Quatrain Mr. Binning found, among several of Háfiz and others, inscribed by some stray hand among the ruins of Persepolis. The Ringdove's ancient *Pehlevi*[6] *Coo, Coo, Coo,* signifies also in Persian *"Where? Where? Where?"* In Attár's "Bird-parliament" she is reproved by the Leader of the Birds for sitting still, and for ever harping on that one note of lamentation for her lost Yúsuf.

【注释校记】

[1] 一版注异文较多,别出。
[2] '*Takht-i-Jamshyd*',二版、三版作 '*Takht* 'I *Jamshyd*'。
[3] '*Bahram*',二版作 '*Bahrám*'。
[4] 'those',二版、三版作 'these'。
[5] 此首二版列入正文第 20 首,诗后文字即作注文。
[6] '*Pehlevi*',二版作 '*Péhlevi*,',三版作 '*Péhlevi*'。

【注释（一版）】

Persepolis: call'd also *Takht'i Jamshyd*—The Throne Of Jamshyd, "*King-Splendid*," of the mythical *Peeshdádian* Dynasty, and supposed (with Shah-náma Authority) to have been founded and built by him, though others refer it to the Work of the Genie King, Ján Ibn Jann, who also built the Pyramids before the time of Adam. It is also called *Chehl-minar*—*Forty-column*; which is Persian, probably, for *Column-countless*; the Hall they adorned or supported with their Lotus Base and taurine Capital indicating double that Number, though now counted down to less than half by Earthquake and other Inroad. By whomsoever built, unquestionably the Monument of a long extinguished Dynasty and Mythology; its Halls, Chambers and Galleries, inscribed with Arrow-head Characters, and sculptured with colossal, wing'd, half human Figures like those of Nimroud; Processions of Priests and Warriors —(doubtful if any where a Woman) —and Kings sitting on Thrones or in Chariots, Staff or Lotus-flower in hand, and the *Ferooher*—Symbol of Existence—with his wing'd Globe, common also to Assyria and Ægypt—over their heads.
All this, together with Aqueduct and Cistern, and other Appurtenance of a Royal Palace, upon a Terrace-platform, ascended by a double Flight of Stairs that may be gallop'd up, and cut out of and into the Rock-side of the *Koh'i Ráhmet*, *Mountain of Mercy*, where the old Fire-Worshiping Sovereigns are buried, and overlooking the Plain of Merdasht.

Persians, like some other People, it seems, love to write their own Names, with sometimes a Verse or two, on their Country's Monuments. Mr. Binning (from whose sensible Travels the foregoing Account is mainly condens't) found several such in Persepolis; in one Place a fine Line of Háfiz: in another "an original, no doubt," he says, "by no great Poet," however "right in his Sentiment." The Words somehow looked to us, and the "halting metre" sounded, familiar; and on looking back at last among the 500 Rubáyiát of the Calcutta Omar MS.—there it is: old Omar quoted by *one* of his Countrymen, and here turned into hasty Rhyme, at any rate—

"This Palace that its Top to Heaven threw,
And Kings their Forehead on its Threshold drew—
I saw a Ring-dove sitting there alone,
And 'Coo, Coo, Coo,' she cried, and 'Coo, Coo, Coo.'"

So as it seems the Persian speaks the English Ring-dove's *Péhlevi*, which is also articulate Persian for "Where?"
BAHRÁM GÚR—*Bahrám of the Wild Ass*, from his Fame in hunting it—a Sassanian Sovereign, had also his Seven Castles (like the King of Bohemia!) each of a different Colour: each with a Royal Mistress within side; each of whom recounts to Bahrám a Romance, according to one of the most famous Poems of Persia, written by Amír Khusraw: these Sevens also figuring (according to Eastern Mysticism) the Seven Heavens, and perhaps the Book itself that Eighth, into which the mystical Seven transcend, and within which they revolve. The Ruins of Three of these Towers are yet shown by the Peasantry; as also the Swamp in which Bahrám sunk, like the Master of Ravenswood, while pursuing his *Gúr*.

其十八

狮据蜥盘天地穷，
宫陵芜没宴歌空。
野驴踏得骷髅破，
不遇君王射虎弓。

【注】

波斯波利斯城，有杰姆西王御座之名。神古俾什达迪朝“荣耀之王”，即杰姆西王也。依《王书》说，是城即王所兴筑。又说为精怪之迹，在生人之先，其遗迹尚有金字塔云。

巴拉姆，有野驴之号，萨珊朝帝君，亦有七城，若波希米亚王，而每城异彩，城居一妃，妃为说一传奇。此据阿米尔·霍斯陆所作之波斯名诗也。东国小说家云七城等俱象七重天，霍斯陆之诗故名《八重天》也，既凌彼七重，遂使环而潜运。今尚遗废址三，乡人以为名胜。亦有废沼，巴拉姆王逐驴时陷焉，一若雷文斯伍德之主家。

“废宫遗柱上凌空，日角龙颜想象中。惟有斑鸠偏称意，自来自去叫春风。”在尼古拉斯版《鲁拜集》，列第三百五十章，亦在温菲尔德之译本。此章宾宁所得，为荡子刻诸波斯波利斯废址，杂之哈菲兹诸人所作间。斑鸠声若古巴列维语“咕，咕，咕”，近波斯语“何处，何处，何处”之意也。阿特《鸟会》亦言斑鸠，伊为鸟首所责，盖自失彼优素福，停而不飞，喃喃无休，恒作一悲调也。

【一版注】

波斯波利斯城，有杰姆西王御座之名。神古俾什达迪朝“荣耀之王”，即杰姆西王也。依《王书》说，是城即王所兴筑。又说为精怪之迹，在生人之先，其遗迹尚有金字塔云。又有四十柱之名，波斯语或亦为无央数柱。盖以柱支殿堂，兼为饰焉，柱有莲础与牛首，数即倍之，而今太半为地震兵燹所毁。无问谁作此者，必一湮灭旧朝或鬼斧神工之遗迹也。其殿堂、房室、回廊，皆镌文字，若楔形之状。亦刻像焉，有半人形类尼姆鲁德者，甚伟而挟翼；有祭司与兵士成列者，中疑无女子焉；有王者，或踞座，或御车，执杖或莲华；有法拉瓦什者，盖存在之征，并其飞翼圆球，此于亚述、埃及亦常有之，踞其顶焉。与夫飞渠蓄池，及宫室之诸附着。又有两侧飞梯攀露台而上，交互岩侧，履之可直凌慈山。山瞰美尔达什平原，旧日之祆教君主尽葬于此。

波斯人，亦如他国人，喜于国中遗址留其姓氏，偶亦题一二诗句。宾宁言，自前揭游历纪撮述，于波斯波利斯得如是者若干，一为哈菲兹之佳句，另一显出无闻之诗客，然哀情颇合。而吾人觉其辞句音节似曾相识，竟于加尔各答写本之奥玛《鲁拜集》五百章中检得。盖老奥玛为其乡党引述也，然其协韵颇率易。诗云：“废宫遗柱上凌空，日角龙颜想象中。惟有斑鸠偏称意，自来自去叫春风。”似波斯人操英伦斑鸠之巴列维语，其声亦确同波斯语之“何处”也。

巴拉姆，有野驴之号，为其猎驴之名也，萨珊朝帝君，亦有七城，若波希米亚王，而每城异彩，城居一妃，妃为说一传奇。此据阿米尔·霍斯陆所作之波斯名诗也。东国小说家云七城等俱象七重天，霍斯陆之诗故名《八重天》也，既凌彼七重，遂使环而潜运。今尚遗废址三，乡人以为名胜。亦有废沼，巴拉姆王逐驴时陷焉，一若雷文斯伍德之主家。

18

他们说是狮子蜥蜴正侵占
杰姆西王壮丽豪饮的宫殿；
**　巴拉姆王——伟大的猎手，野驴**
踏在他头顶，他仍睡梦难唤。

【校记】——

●一版：四行“睡梦难唤”作“长眠沉睡”。

【注释】——

波斯波利斯，也被叫作杰姆西王的宝座。杰姆西王是神话时代的俾什达迪王朝的“辉煌国王”，根据《列王纪》的说法，他被认为兴建了这座城。也有人说是妖王詹·伊卜·詹在亚当时代之前的工程，这位妖王也建造过金字塔。

巴拉姆·古尔，有野驴巴拉姆之称，是萨珊王朝君主。像波西米亚王一样，也有他的七座城堡，每个城堡有不同的颜色，住着一位皇家公主，每个公主给他讲一个故事。这是一首波斯最著名的诗歌所讲，它的作者是阿米尔·霍斯陆。根据东方的神话，这些七个都象征七重天，大概这部诗自己就是八重天，它凌驾在神秘的七重之上，被它们围绕。那些塔楼还有三座遗址，乡民们将之开放以供参观。还有一个沼泽，像那个雷文斯伍德的主人，巴拉姆追猎野驴时曾经陷入。

宫殿把他的柱子向天空投出，
宫门曾悬着国王容貌的画图。
　我看到一只鸽子孤零零飞落，
“咕咕咕”，她在那儿叫着，“咕咕咕”。

这首四行诗是宾宁发现的，和哈菲兹等人的一些诗，被游人刻在波斯波利斯的遗址上。鸽子的“咕咕咕”像古代巴列维语，在波斯语里的意思也是“哪里？哪里？哪里？”。在阿塔尔的《鸟会》里，也提到鸽子被群鸟领袖责备，她一直落着不动，因为失去的优素福永远弹着忧伤的曲调。

【注释（一版）】——

波斯波利斯，也被叫作杰姆西王的宝座。杰姆西王是神话时代的俾什达迪王朝的“辉煌国王”，根据《列王纪》的说法，他被认为兴建了这座城。也有人说是妖王詹·伊卜·詹在亚当时代之前的工程，这位妖王也建造过金字塔。它也被叫作四十柱，波斯语可能是指无数柱。殿堂被两倍数目的带有莲花柱础和牛头柱头的柱子所装饰和支撑。今天只剩了不到一半，大部分毁于地震和入侵。不管是谁建造的，无疑是一个消逝很久的王朝或神话的遗迹。它的殿堂、房室、回廊，都刻有楔形文字，还雕着浮雕像，有巨大的、带翅膀的、半人形的，像是尼姆鲁德的那些，有祭司和战士队伍（是否有女人值得怀疑），有坐在宝座或战车上，手持令牌或莲花的国王，有法拉瓦什——存在的象征——和他那带着翅膀的圆球，这在亚述人和埃及人那里也很常见——在他们的头顶。所有这些外，还有渡槽、蓄水池和皇宫的其他附属设施，从露台通过可以急驰直上的两重飞梯，便捷地进出于慈山悬崖，那里是往日拜火教君主的埋骨处，俯瞰着美尔达什平原。

波斯人，也像其他人民，看起来喜欢在他们国家的遗址上写下自己的名字和一两首诗。宾宁说，（主要根据之前提及的他那实用的旅行记撮述）在波斯波利斯发现了几首这样的，在一处是哈菲兹的佳句，在另一处是“一首原创的，无疑，”他说，“出自一个不伟大的诗人，”但“他的感情很合适”。这些句子对我们来说，停顿的节奏听起来很熟悉，最后在加尔各答欧玛尔写本的五百首鲁拜里找到。那就是，老欧玛尔被他的一个同乡引用了，无论如何，这里的押韵显得匆促草率——

宫殿把他的柱子向天空投出，
宫门曾悬着国王容貌的画图。
　我看到一只鸽子孤零零飞落，
“咕咕咕”，她在那儿叫着，“咕咕咕”。

因而似乎波斯人说的是英国斑鸠的巴列维语，那也分明是波斯语“哪里”的意思。

巴拉姆·古尔，有野驴巴拉姆之称，因为他猎驴的名声，是萨珊王朝君主。像波西米亚王一样，也有他的七座城堡，每个城堡有不同的颜色，住着一位皇家公主，每个公主给他讲一个故事。这是一首波斯最著名的诗歌所讲，它的作者是阿米尔·霍斯陆。根据东方的神话，这些七个都象征七重天，大概这部诗自己就是八重天，它凌驾在神秘的七重之上，被它们围绕。那些塔楼还有三座遗址，乡民们将之开放以供参观。还有一个沼泽，像那个雷文斯伍德的主人，巴拉姆追猎野驴时曾经陷入。

【解读】————

第 18 首译自加尔各答抄本第 99 首（“乐园”本第 151 首）：

在那巴拉姆握着酒杯的宫殿；

狐狸产崽，狮子栖息；

巴拉姆总爱抓野驴——

今日却见墓上（野驴）在抓巴拉姆。

菲茨杰拉德译本将狐狸换成了巨蜥，增添蛮荒之感，更符合欧洲人对东方遗址的想象。平添出杰姆西王，以东方的豪奢加强对比。后两句写野驴在巴拉姆墓上踩踏，画面感更强，盛衰之感也更深刻。很显然，菲译比波斯原文更精警，允称名作。

注释中所引的一首，在第二版列为正文第 20 首，出自加尔各答抄本第 419 首（“乐园”本第 66 首）：

宫殿把它的柱子竖向天空，

国王匍匐在它的门槛；

我看到一只鸽子，在它的墙垛上，

发出叫喊：“哪儿，哪儿，哪儿，哪儿？”

虽然菲茨杰拉德讲了它的毛病，但诗境还是蛮苍凉的。

19

菲译第一版第 18 首,
1907 年版
90 mm × 144 mm

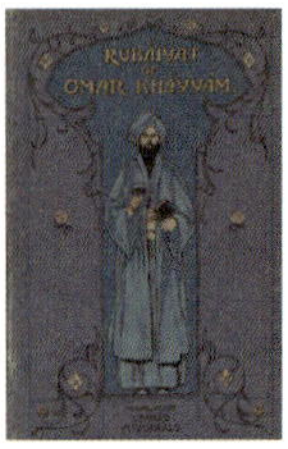

这是英国插画家托马斯 · 希思 · 鲁宾逊(Thomas Heath Robinson,约 1869—1950)的作品。他的弟弟查尔斯 · 鲁宾逊和威廉 · 希思 · 鲁宾逊也是插画家。这幅插图重点突出了美人和红玫瑰。人生无常,英雄、美人往往也可能成为权力争斗中的牺牲品。殷红的玫瑰花像帝王流淌的鲜血,美丽的风信子像被砍落的嫔妃的头颅。

20

菲译第五版第 20 首,
1898 年版
143 mm × 205 mm

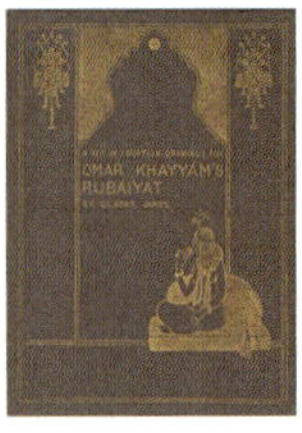

英国插画家吉尔伯特 · 詹姆斯(Gilbert James,1865—1941)为菲译《鲁拜集》第五版配了 14 幅黑白插图,这是唯一全面展示整首诗歌意象的插图。芳草如茵的河滨,一对恋人似乎在安详宁静地沉思。一位被捆绑着的女人如飘落的花瓣,在河水里的树根之间沉浮。

XIX

I sometimes think that never blows so red
The Rose as where some buried Cæsar bled;
That every Hyacinth the Garden wears
Dropt in her Lap from some once lovely Head.

【校记】

●一版：列其十八；
四行 'her' 作 'its'。
●二版：列其二十四。

【注释】

[1]Apropos of Omar's Red Roses in Stanza xix, I am reminded of an old English Superstition, that our Anemone Pulsatilla, or purple "Pasque Flower[2]" (which grows plentifully about the Fleam Dyke, near Cambridge), grows only where Danish Blood has been spilt.

【注释校记】

[1] 一版、二版无此注。
[2] 'Flower',三版、四版作 'Flower,'。

XX

And this reviving Herb whose tender Green
Fledges the River-Lip on which we lean—
Ah, lean upon it lightly! for who knows
From what once lovely Lip it springs unseen!

【校记】

●一版：列其十九；
首行 'reviving' 作 'delightful'；
二行 'River-Lip' 作 'River's Lip'。
●二版：列其二十五；
首行 'reviving' 作 'delightful'，'tender' 作 'living'；
二行同一版；
四行 'it' 作 't'。

其十九

玫瑰红艳世难偕，
开处君王碧血埋。
一一园中风信子，
料应先在美人钗。

【注】——奥玛十九章之红玫瑰，余忆一英伦旧日异谈，吾国之紫白头翁，近剑桥之富利姆渠多有焉，惟生于丹麦人喋血处。

其二十

春来河畔草如茵，
携得同心缓倚身。
爱惜一弯真媚态，
多应忆着美人唇。

第十九首

19

我常想，没有哪儿的玫瑰花丛
开得能似恺撒埋血处一样红；
**　每一朵花园绽放出的风信子**
都是落自昔时的美人头上风。

【注释】———
关于欧玛尔第 *19* 首里的红玫瑰，我想起一个英格兰的老迷信说法，我们的紫色白头翁（靠近剑桥的富利姆渠生长很多），只生长在丹麦人洒血之地。

【解读】———
第 19 首译自乌斯利抄本第 43 首（加尔各答抄本第 47 首，1207 年抄本第 247 首，“乐园”本第 439 首）：

每一处生长玫瑰和郁金香的地方，
它都来自君王血色的殷红；
每枝从土中长出的紫罗兰嫩芽
都是（曾）在美人颊上的痣。

菲茨杰拉德用欧洲人熟悉的“恺撒”代替了君主，中译还是平实地用“君王”译出，没敢径用“苌虹”化碧的字面。美人痣的意象大概太东方化了，菲译改为风信子从美人头上落下，让人想到周邦彦的名句“钗钿堕处遗香泽”。（《六丑 · 蔷薇谢后作》）

第二十首

20

这新草青嫩像是毛羽铺垫
在那我们斜躺的如唇河畔——
**　啊，躺下时轻些，因为谁知它**
悄然生自昔时的娇唇哪片？

【校记】———
●一版：首行“新生”作“喜人”。
●二版：首行“新生”作“喜人”，“嫩”作“生机”。

【解读】———
第 20 首译自加尔各答抄本第 44 首（1207 年抄本第 125 首，“乐园”本第 82 首）：

生长在溪边的所有青葱草木，
你可以说，都是从一个天使般的人儿唇边生出；
小心不要把脚轻蔑地踏上青葱草木，
因为那青葱草木是从一个郁金香般脸颊的美人化成的泥土中生出。

这种描写在“乐园”本里经常出现，比如，第 76 首（1207 年抄本第 179 首）的后两行，和这里几乎一样，而第 84 首写得更惊心动魄：

地上生灵脚下的每一片黄土，
都覆盖着美人面颊，情人的发肤。
楼台殿阁上的每块青砖，
都来自大臣的手臂、国王的头颅。

（张鸿年、宋丕方译文）
菲茨杰拉德译得很浪漫，而且巧妙地关联了 the River-Lip 和 lovely Lip，成为出名的修辞。

21

菲译第一版第 20 首，
1944 年版
143 mm × 192 mm

英国插画家以利亚·艾伯特·考克斯（Elijah Albert Cox，1876—1955）为菲译《鲁拜集》第一版配了 8 幅全页彩色插图。这幅插图中有亮丽的绿色和红色，诗人正与美人饮酒作乐，这是一个欢愉的时刻。人生苦短，犹如一日。今朝有酒今朝醉，就用今天的酒驱走以往的悔恨和将来的忧烦吧。

22

菲译第一版第 21 首，
1922 年版
146 mm × 190 mm

这是英国插画家安妮·哈丽特·菲茜（Anne Harriet Fish，1890—1964）的作品。画面中三位女士的服装具有装饰性，画面以黑、银等冷色调为主，线条流畅，人物形象的重复出现，表达了诗句中“持酒数行依次去，一眠泉下不来逢”的无奈和怅惘。

XXI

Ah, my Belovéd, fill the Cup that clears
To-day of past Regrets and future Fears:
To-morrow!—Why, To-morrow I may be
Myself with Yesterday's Sev'n thousand Years.

【校记】——

●一版：列其二十；
二行 'Fears:' 作 'Fears—'；
三行 '*To-morrow!*' 作 '*To-morrow*？'。
●二版、三版、四版：二行 'Regrets' 作 'Regret'。

【注释】——

A thousand years[1] to each Planet.

【注释校记】——

[1] 'thousand years'，一版作 'Thousand Years'。

XXII

For some we loved, the loveliest and the best
That from his Vintage rolling Time hath prest,
Have drunk their Cup a Round or two before,
And one by one crept silently to rest.

【校记】——

●一版：列其二十一；
首行 'For' 作 'Lo!'；
二行作 'That Time and Fate of all their Vintage prest,'；
四行 'rest' 作 'Rest'。
●二版、三版：二行 'hath' 作 'has'。

其二十一

殷勤把酒劝卿卿，
来日须同去日倾。
万一明朝天地改，
劫灰飞尽古今平。

【注】——一行星为一千年也。

其二十二

年华酝酿出醇浓，
同是精英世所钟。
持酒数行依次去，
一眠泉下不来逢。

21

啊，我亲爱的，倒满杯子，让今天
驱走以往的悔恨将来的忧烦：
**　明天！——什么，到了明天我也许**
自己也进入了昨天的七千年。

【注释】———

每一个行星一千年。

【解读】———

第 21 首译自加尔各答抄本第 348 首（1207 年抄本第 60 首，“乐园”本第 133 首）：

来吧，哦朋友！让我们别为明天忍受痛苦，
让我们好好利用这几个现钱在手的时刻，
当，明天，我们离开大地的表面
我们将和那些七千年前离去的人等同。

菲茨杰拉德去掉了那个用过的“现钱”比喻，拿以往和将来作衬托，更突出了当前的紧迫感。但在 1207 年抄本第 234 首诗里，明确提到美酒和情人，意思也颇有关联。我们没有证据，说菲茨杰拉德看到过 1207 年抄本和“乐园”本，但经常发现他的意思出现在这两个本子里，应该是他还参考了乌斯利抄本和加尔各答抄本以外的本子，译文恰好跟这两个本子有相合的地方，而赫荣 - 艾伦并没有关注到。

郭沫若注释说：“依波特逊夫人解说，我默时代波斯以地球的年龄为七千岁。”这和菲茨杰拉德的注释说法不同，但好像符合波斯文原诗的意思。

22

那些人为我们热爱，最是珍稀
如滚动时光压榨的陈酿之奇。
**　在此前也不过喝得一巡两转，**
就一个跟一个默默进去安息。

【校记】———

●一版：二行作“时光和命运自它们的葡萄压榨出的”。

【解读】———

第 22 首译自加尔各答抄本第 185 首（“乐园”本第 372 首）：

我所有的同心挚友都离开了我，
一个接一个他们在死神脚下沦没。
在灵魂的交谊上他们是同杯共盏人，
喝了一两圈他们就先我醉倒了。

“乐园”本第 232 首第一行：“喂，你是世界上精英中的精英，”（张鸿年、宋丕方译文）不知道这是不是波斯文里常用的说法，菲茨杰拉德应该是看到的，把这个意思也加了进去，并且用了很巧妙的一个比喻——“滚动时光压榨的陈酿”。第 8 首也说“生命之酒在一滴一滴渗沥”，都是用酒比生命，似乎暗示生命最快乐的时刻就是在酒之中，只是，即使在快乐中生命也不知不觉地逝去了，真可谓“死生亦大矣”！

23

菲译第一版第 22 首，
1913 年版
126 mm × 153 mm

英国插画家埃德蒙·约瑟夫·沙利文（Edmund Joseph Sullivan，1869—1933）为菲译《鲁拜集》第一版诗配了 75 幅插图。这幅插图展示的是一位女士即将离世，天使和死神都来到她的床前。诗人告诉我们，世人终将眠于尘土下，成为一抔黄土，人世也只是人们离去的房间。

XXIII

And we, that now make merry in the Room
They left, and Summer dresses in new bloom,
　Ourselves must we beneath the Couch of Earth
Descend—ourselves to make a Couch—for whom?

【校记】——

●一版：列其二十二；
二行 'bloom' 作 'Bloom'；
四行 'Descend—' 作 'Descend,'。
●二版：四行同一版。

其二十三

昔人别馆作欢场，
仍看熏风新弄妆。
我自将眠尘土下，
为谁身亦是眠床？

【注】——

一行星为一千年也。

23

我们，作乐在他们留下的空房，
夏日又穿起时新的鲜花衣裳。
**　我们必躺到大地之床的底下——**
为了谁？——也把自己变成一张床。

【解读】———

第 23 首的意思，和加尔各答抄本第 388 首一致：

起来，不要为这个流逝的世界悲伤，
要平和地，伴着幸福经历这世界。
如果世界的本质是持续不断的，
他人的命运也不会落到你自己身上。

使用的比拟，见于加尔各答抄本第 82 首后两行：

这片青葱草木，是我当前的欢乐之地
直到——从我变成的土中（长出）的青葱草木变成欢乐之地——为谁？

还有乌斯利抄本第 129 首（加尔各答抄本第 416 首）后两行：

坐在草坪上，哦我的偶像，因为已经没有太多时间
在我的和你的尘土中长出草坪之前。

在"乐园"本第 98 首（1207 年抄本第 162 首）里，又说用尸土作墓砖，"乐园"本第 73 首（1207 年抄本第 148 首）还说用尸土做盖楼的砖，更为惊耸。

黄克孙先生这首的译文："醉眠陵上草芊芊，草下长埋古圣贤。借问他年陵上客，阿谁枕我骨头眠？"深得菲茨杰拉德译法之神，尽管表述颇有改变，但意思都传达了出来，尤其是那旷达里略带感喟的语调，竟然惟妙惟肖。

24

菲译第一版第 23 首，
1909 年版
103 mm × 152 mm

英国插画家吉尔伯特·詹姆斯（Gilbert James，1865—1941）为菲译《鲁拜集》第一版画了 16 幅全页彩色插图。诗中说“明朝黄土垄中卧，无酒无歌无再晨”，詹姆斯反诗意而作，在画面中展示了人间的美色、美酒和花朵。但是在美人的不远处，死神已经靠近，所以人生得意须尽欢，否则归为尘土后一切都是枉然。

XXIV

Ah, make the most of what we yet may spend,
Before we too into the Dust descend;
    Dust into Dust, and under Dust to lie,
Sans Wine, sans Song, sans Singer, and—sans End!

【校记】——

●一版：列其二十三；
三行‘under Dust’作‘under Dust,’。
●二版：列其二十六；
三行同一版。
●三版、四版：三行同一版。

其二十四

且斗樽前见在身，
一钱犹剩莫辞贫。
明朝黄土垄中卧，
无酒无歌无再晨。

24

啊，把我们还能花费的用完，
在我们也要沦入尘下之前；
**　尘土进入尘土，尘土下入睡，**
无酒，无歌，无歌者，也——无终端！

【解读】———

和第 24 首相近的，有乌斯利抄本的第 76 首（加尔各答抄本第 173 首）：

不要让悲哀环抱住你，
也不要让无聊的忧虑占据了你的日子，
不要放弃书本和恋人的唇和田地的绿沿，
在大地拥你入怀之前。

和第 35 首（加尔各答抄本第 80 首，“乐园”本第 273 首）前两行：

喝酒，你将长眠泥土之下
没有一个亲人、朋友、同道，或伴侣。

但都不及菲茨杰拉德来得旷达洒脱。

他那尽情花费的豪情，冲决了一切表面的虚饰，愈质朴，愈深入人心。所有的大诗人，在写到及时行乐时，无不坦率真诚，以见出对世俗的别样批判态度。尽管风格各异，如李白是浪漫的——“天生我身必有财，千金散尽还复来。烹羊宰牛且为乐，会须一饮三百杯。”（《将进酒》）杜甫是写实的——“街头酒价常苦贵，方外酒徒稀醉眠。径须相就饮一斗，恰有三百青铜钱。”（《偪仄行赠毕曜》）这里则是哲思的。

25

菲译第一版第 24 首，
1940 年版
116 mm × 167 mm

波兰犹太艺术家亚瑟·西克（Arthur Szyk，1894—1951），以创作书籍插图和政治讽刺画而闻名。他继承了欧洲中世纪和文艺复兴时期的传统，比较重视作品的色彩和细节。在这幅插图中，西克突出了盛装打扮的报时人，画面的装饰繁复，具有华丽的东方风格，局部涂有金色。

XXV

Alike for those who for To-day prepare,
And those that after some To-morrow stare,
　A Muezzín from the Tower of Darkness cries,
"Fools! your Reward is neither Here nor There."

【校记】——

●一版：列其二十四；
二行'some To-morrow'作'a To-morrow'；
三行句末无逗点；
四行'There.'作'There!'。
●二版：列其二十七；
四行同一版。

其二十五

他生未卜此生劳，
空仰森森殿塔高。
上有鸡人呼一语：
『愚夫去住总无褒。』

25

就像那些人为了今天从事，
和那些人向明天之后注视，
唤礼者从那黑暗之塔高喊，
“愚人！这儿和那儿你的报偿莫致。”

【解读】———

第 25 首译自加尔各答抄本第 396 首（“乐园”本第 41 首）：

有些人陷入教义和信仰的深思，
另一些则在怀疑和确信之间惊愕，
突然那唤礼者，从他隐身之处，呼叫
“哦愚人，那路既不在这里也不在那里。”

这首诗除了更加突出今生和来世的对立，基本意思没有太多的改变。

Muezzín 是清真寺塔楼上的呼唤者，每天在固定的时刻呼唤信徒祈祷。鸡人，据《周礼·春官》：“鸡人掌共鸡牲，辨其物。大祭祀，夜呼旦以叫百官。凡国之大宾客、会同、军旅、丧纪，亦如之。凡国事为期，则告之时。凡祭祀，面禳衅，共其鸡牲。”后来专指宫廷的值漏者，陆倕《新刻漏铭》：“坐朝晏罢，每旦晨兴，属传漏之音，听鸡人之响。”两者并不一样，但古典的表达有时正是从不一致里透出某种一致来，从而引起惊奇的美感。

世俗的努力，神学的信仰，无一不是他律的约束，越是谨守，越远离自我。这一喊声，不正为唤回自我吗？康德竭力扭转神学的道德为道德的神学，也出于同样的目的。

26

菲译第一版第 25 首，
1913 年版
112 mm × 116 mm

英国插画家雷恩・布尔（René Bull，1872—1942）在这幅插图中展示了“三人行”的情景。从衣着打扮和手执的书卷可知他们是学者。插画家为我们描述了他熟悉的东方建筑。作为摄影家的布尔，注重透视和细节，画面具有纵深感，人物总是被置于合适的场景中。

XXVI

Why, all the Saints and Sages who discuss'd
Of the Two Worlds so wisely—they are thrust
Like foolish Prophets forth; their Words to Scorn
Are scatter'd, and their Mouths are stopt with Dust.

【校记】——

●一版：列其二十五；
二行作 'Of the Two Worlds so learnedly, are thrust'。
●二版：列其二十九；
二行同一版。
●三版：二行作 'Of the Two Worlds so learnedly are thrust'。

其二十六

圣徒雄辩究天人，
谁谓愚同术士伦？
土掩尘封终不语，
至今贻笑说通神。

26

为什么，所有那些圣徒和哲人
智慧地就两个世界议论纷纭——
却像愚蠢先知般被推翻；他们
话语遭唾弃，他们嘴让封了尘。

【校记】———

●一版：二行“智慧地”作“有学问地”。

●二版、三版：二行同一版。

【解读】———

第 26 首相近的意思，出自乌斯利抄本第 140 首（加尔各答抄本第 453 首）：

那些人，哦萨吉，在我们之前走了的，
已经沉睡，哦萨吉，在自大的尘土（或睡梦）中，
你去喝酒，从我这里听到真理，
任何他们所说的，哦萨吉，只是风！

还有加尔各答抄本第 236 首：

那些人是人类存在的精华，
激励着他们思想的布拉卡升上最高的天堂，
研究你的存在，就像天堂本身
他们的头被扭转，被倒竖，并急旋着。

布拉卡，是一匹飞骡，传说穆罕默德跨着它从耶路撒冷直上天堂。“乐园”本第 160 首（1207 年抄本第 1 首）也有相近的叙写。

理智一旦超越了经验，进入玄虚世界，也就超越了知识的界限。所以佛教的《箭喻经》里，佛陀禁止追问类似的问题：“世间有常，世间无常，世间有边，世间无边，命是身，命异身异，有如此命终，无有命终，有此无有此，无有命终。”但是，这时的理智丝毫不缺乏知识的形态，诱使我们竭尽心力去研究，由于丧失了知识的内容，这样的研究沦为徒劳。亚里士多德对第一推动力的探求，不过如此。这里的讽刺，正是针对研究类似问题的哲人。

27

菲译第一版 27 首，
1911 年版
112 mm × 81 mm

英国画家弗兰克·威廉·布朗温（Frank William Brangwyn，1867—1956）出生在比利时。他为《鲁拜集》配的彩色插图是油画，有明显的印象主义风格。1911 年菲译《鲁拜集》版本中有 8 幅彩色插图，1919 年版增加到 15 幅。这幅插图主要描绘了学者和圣人围在一起高谈阔论的情景。

XXVII

Myself when young did eagerly frequent
Doctor and Saint, and heard great argument
　About it and about: but evermore
Came out by the same door where in I went.

【校记】——

●一版：二行‘argument’作‘Argument’；
四行‘door where’作‘Door as’。
●二版：列其三十；
四行‘where’作‘as’。

其二十七

玄谈圣论昔能尊，
直欲因之穷道根。
其我独芒终未达，
出时仍在入时门。

27

自己年轻时经常热切造访
学者和圣人，听到高论宏讲
关于这个和那个；然而始终
只是从同一个门来而复往。

【解读】———

第 27 首的措辞，融合了乌斯利抄本第 121 首（“乐园”本第 408 首）：

一段时间里，在年轻时，我们常去见一位老师，
一段时间里我们满意我们的精熟；
看看讲论的结果：——在我们发生了什么？
我们来如水我们去如风。

还有加尔各答抄本第 281 首：

（有一次）作为猎鹰，我飞出神秘世界，
从下面我可以飞到上面的高度；
但是，没有发现那儿有任何亲密的朋友，
我从进入的同一道门出来。

乌斯利抄本第 121 首的后两句，被用到了第 28 首里。

一切超越界限的理智，都不能给我们任何真正的知识，无论如何热情地渴求，勤奋地学习，获得的只是无知。自无知始，以无知终，当然是“从同一个门来而复往”。

28

菲译第一版第 28 首，
1938 年版
106 mm × 208 mm

这是英国插画家、版画家约翰·巴克兰·莱特（John Buckland Wright，1897—1954）的作品。1938 年版《鲁拜集》普通版有 8 幅铜版画，1944 年版荷兰文《鲁拜集》有 11 幅珂罗版插图。这些插图线条流畅，格调高雅。书中某一幅插图一般不是严格对应菲译的某首诗。莱特在一封信中谈到这幅插图，说其背景是“来如水去如风”。

XXVIII

With them the seed of Wisdom did I sow,
And with mine own hand wrought to make it grow
    And this was all the Harvest that I reap'd—
"I came like Water, and like Wind I go."

【校记】——

●一版：首行‘seed’作‘Seed’；
二行作‘And with my own hand labour' d it to grow:’。
●二版：列其三十一；
二行‘mine’作‘my’，‘grow；’作‘grow：’。
●三版：二行‘mine’作‘my’。

其二十八

相从植慧待其丰，
手自浇培久用功。
竟至获时惟是此，
我来如水去如风。

28

随他们我把智慧之种播土中，
用自己亲手的劳作让它长成；
**　而这就是我得到的所有收获——**
我到来如水，并且我离去如风。

【解读】——

第 27、28 首的末句，菲茨杰拉德撷取了两个形象的比喻，这里讲述的意思，在波斯原文里经常出现，如乌斯利抄本第 72 首（加尔各答抄本第 176 首）：

没有人解开过永恒的纷乱秘密，
没有人踏出过（人类理智的）轨道，
因为，就我所见，从初学者到老师，
所有妇人所生之人的手都是乏力的。

还有“乐园”本第 54 首，都在讲求知的落空。这一首利用了乌斯利抄本第 121 首的后两句，菲茨杰拉德又配了一个非常生动的比喻——智慧种子的播种和培植，全诗顿时精彩。尤其是最后一句，形容人生的流逝空幻，已成为《鲁拜集》最广泛传诵的名句之一。

如果说，上两首讲理智进入玄虚世界后的诞妄，这一首进而讲，理智解决不了人生的根本问题。《箭喻经》禁止追问那些问题，也出于同样的理由——都和人生的解脱无关。

29

菲译第三版第 29、30 首，
1884 年版
214 mm × 285 mm

1884 年，美国画家伊莱休·维德（Elihu Vedder，1836—1923）为菲译《鲁拜集》画了 56 幅全页插图，此图乃其中之一。维德按照自己的理解，将菲译第三版诗做了重新组合，并在大部分插图里镶嵌了文本框。他以旋转的飘带和飘扬的头发来增加画面的动感，以此诠释水漫漫地流和风漫漫地吹的诗意。

XXIX

Into this Universe, and *Why* not knowing
Nor *Whence*, like Water willy-nilly flowing;
　And out of it, as Wind along the Waste,
I know not *Whither*, willy-nilly blowing.

【校记】——

●一版：首行‘*Why*’作‘*why*’,句末有逗点；
二行‘*Whence*’作‘*whence*’,句末作冒号；
四行‘*Whither*’作‘*whither*’。
●二版：列其三十二；
首行句末有逗点；
二行句末作冒号。
●三版：首行句末有逗点。

其二十九

来时无故亦无方，
一水悠悠天地长。
莫问泠然安所适，
如风吹过碛沙旁。

29

进入这个宇宙，不知道缘由
也不知源头，如水漫漫而流；
再从它出离，像风沿着荒漠，
漫漫而吹，我也不知道尽头。

【解读】

第 29 首，根据赫荣 – 艾伦的考证，出自加尔各答抄本第 235 首：

他首先把我在混乱中带入存在，
我能从我的生命获得什么，除了我对它的惊诧？
我们违背自己的意志离开了，我们不知道什么是
这次来，去，和存在的目的。

以及乌斯利抄本第 20 首（加尔各答抄本第 23 首）头两行：

像大河之水像沙漠之风，
我存在的时日里又一天过去。

加尔各答抄本第 23 首是这样写的：

我存在时日里这样的两三天过去了，
它们过去像风吹过沙漠。

但“乐园”本第 45 首（1207 年抄本第 142 首）似乎更接近：

我们来去匆匆的宇宙，
上不见渊源，下不见尽头。
从来无人道出个中隐秘，
我们从何处来，向何处走。（张鸿年、宋丕方译文）

看来这是波斯文里常有的说法，因了“渊源”和“尽头”把“大河之水”的比喻拉了进来，再把“沙漠之风”来对应，就更自然、更形象了。

我们应该特别注意，这是一首音韵极美的英文诗，轻吟低诵，仿佛水流风过就在耳畔。音韵带来的轻快感，和诗人坦然、平静的态度相合，很有匠心。遗憾的是，我的中文不足以将之传达出来。

30

菲译第一版第 30 首，
1922 年版
147 mm × 190 mm

这是英国插画家安妮·哈丽特·菲胥（Anne Harriet Fish，1890—1964）的作品。占据画面主体的是高举双手向苍天的人物形象，主要表现了第一行和第二行诗的诗意。背景中由曲线和不同颜色构成的云层增加了画面的纵深感。这幅插图除了少部分金色，主要由黑白灰构成，体现了安妮插图的特色。

31

菲译第一版第 31 首，
1920 年版
140 mm × 190 mm

英国插画家罗纳德·鲍尔弗（Ronald Balfour，1896—1941）的这幅插图表达了第一行和第二行诗的意思。整个画面具有装饰艺术的风格，似乎充斥着天使和各类怪人、魔鬼，展示了如梦如幻的场景。美女膨胀起来的黑袍上布满曲线，而天使翅膀上都有孔雀翎，这表明作品受到了奥伯利·比亚兹莱的影响。

XXX

What, without asking, hither hurried *Whence*?
And, without asking, *Whither* hurried hence!
Oh, many a Cup of this forbidden Wine
Must drown the memory of that insolence!

【校记】——

●一版：首行 'Whence' 作 'whence'；
二行 'Whither' 作 'whither'；
三行作 'Another and another Cup to drown'；
四行作 'The Memory of this Impertinence!'。
●二版：列其三十三；
三行作 'Ah, contrite Heav' n endowed us with the Vine'；
四行 'Must drown' 作 'To drug'。

XXXI

Up from Earth's Centre through the Seventh Gate
I rose, and on the Throne of Saturn sate,
And many a Knot unravel'd by the Road;
But not the Master-knot of Human Fate.

【校记】——

●一版：三行 'many a Knot' 作 'many Knots'；
四行作 'But not the Knot of Human Death and Fate.'。
●二版：列其三十四；
三行同一版。

【注释】——

Saturn, Lord of the Seventh Heaven.

其三十

长疑何事不先询，
遣作匆匆来去身。
持酒连杯须莫禁，
湎淫那复忆狂嗔？

【校记】——

二版：后二句作：『应是天公深悔在，解忧为赐万藤春。』

其三十一

人间眇眇镇星尊，
寻入遥天第七门。
终是命途难借问，
群疑破尽一疑存。

【注】——

镇星，第七重天之君也。

30

为何，没问问，从哪儿匆忙到这里？
也没问问，又从这儿匆忙去哪里！
哦，得用很多杯这被禁绝的酒
淹没那个追问的记忆太无礼！

【校记】———

●一版：三行、四行作“又一杯接着又一杯去淹没 / 关于这个鲁莽的记忆！”。

●二版：三行作“啊，悔恨的上天赐给我们酒”；四行“淹没”作“麻醉”。

【解读】———

第 30 首，赫荣－艾伦认为出自乌斯利抄本第 21 首（加尔各答抄本第 49 首）：

看在创世之日我的到来不是我的能力，
和我不希望的离开（对我来说）是固定的结局，
起来束好你的腰身，哦机敏的持杯人，
我要在酒中洗去这世界的悲苦。

以及乌斯利抄本第 157 首（加尔各答抄本第 494 首）：

如果这事由我，我不会来，
同样，我要能支配我的去，我如何去？
在这个世界上不是没有什么比这更好
我没有来，没有去，没有生活？

我认为，这与“乐园”本第 90 首的后两行也很像。菲茨杰拉德在这些困扰之外，增添了以酒浇愁的意思，再用反跌的语气来加重，感慨极深。

31

从地心直上将第七门穿过
我飞升，稳踞在了土星宝座。
许多疑惑都已在路上解开；
除了人类命运的最大之惑。

【校记】———

●一版：四行作“除了人类死亡和命运之惑”。

【注释】———

土星，第七重天的主宰。

【解读】———

第 31 首译自加尔各答抄本第 314 首（“乐园”本第 18 首）：

从地球的最低点，升至土星的最高点
我解决了所有天上的问题；
我逃脱了所有骗局和诡计的约束，
所有的障碍都被清除，只除了命运的制约。

根据波斯的旧说，最高的一层天是第七重天，土星是这里的主宰，可能因为土星是当时所知太阳系最远的一颗行星。这里仍然透露出，理智和科学无法解决人生问题的怀疑，让我们想起庄子“吾生也有涯，而知也无涯，以有涯随无涯，殆已！”（《庄子·养生主》）那样的感慨。对菲茨杰拉德来说，这首诗就算是很忠实的翻译了，尽管他的巡天之行描绘得更加生动形象。

全诗极强的波斯风格的意象，译成中文实在困难。黄克孙先生的译文：“骑鹤神游阿母台，七重天阙拂云来。玉皇仙籍偷观尽，司命天书揭不开。”潜用了江西派的“换骨法”，十分成功。

32

菲译第一版第 16 首，
1913 年版
75 mm × 130 mm

这是英国插画家、摄影家雷恩·布尔（René Bull，1872—1942）的作品。画面中展示了山谷里一道装饰繁复的坚固大门，这也是隔在阳间和阴世之间的帷幕。人在山谷中举手大叫，“这有门户我不能找到钥匙，这有帷幕里面我不能窥知”。生死、人神之谜的确很难参透。人神之论也只是片刻的谈论，只能是人活着时的话题。

XXXII

There was the Door to which I found no Key;
There was the Veil through which I might not see:
　Some little talk awhile of Me and Thee
There was—and then no more of Thee and Me.

【校记】

●一版：首行‘the Door’作‘a Door’,句末作冒号；
二行作‘There was a Veil past which I could not see:’；
三行‘talk’作‘Talk’；
四行‘There was’作‘There seemed’,五版末附一版文作‘There seem’d’。
●二版：列其三十五；
首行句末作冒号；
二行‘might’作‘could’。
●三版：二行同二版。

【注释】

Me-and-Thee: some dividual Existence or Personality distinct from the Whole. [1]

【注释校记】

[1] 此注一版作‘Me and Thee; that is, some Dividual Existence or Personality apart from the Whole.’。

其三十二

高门扃闭钥难寻，
望极空愁帘幕深。
片语微闻及吾汝，
那知倏忽已同沉？

【注】——

吾汝，别于全之独、一也。

32

这有门户我不能找到钥匙；
这有帷幕里面我不能窥知：
些许话语片时谈到我和你
这有——此后你和我再无存时。

【注释】——
我和你，某些不同于全体的独立存在或单一体。

【解读】——
第 32 首来自加尔各答抄本第 387 首（1207 年抄本第 36 首，“乐园”本第 30 首）：

你和我都不知道永恒的秘密，
你和我都不能猜出这个谜；
有一些交谈在我和你的幕后，
但幕落之时你我都不在那里。

赫荣 - 艾伦翻译的第三句很费解，菲茨杰拉德似乎也是如此理解的，然而张鸿年、宋丕方的译文却很明白：

大幕未落，你我尽可交谈言笑，
大幕落时，你我都无影无踪。

“幕”的比喻也出现在乌斯利抄本第 29 首的头两行（加尔各答抄本第 56 首，1207 年抄本第 108 首，“乐园”本第 81 首）：

没有人能够进入遮蔽着秘密的帷幕，
没有人的心智认识那里是什么。

以及加尔各答抄本第 193 首的头两行：

没有人能进入命运之幕
没有人是命运之谜的行家。

这首诗从神秘中透出无奈，毕竟是人身，也没有可能永远冷静睿智，感慨和叹息总要有的。

33

菲译第五版第 33 首，
1898 年版
145 mm × 206 mm

这是英国插画家吉尔伯特·詹姆斯（Gilbert James，1865—1941）的作品。画面中一位男子伫立在海边，望着茫茫大海，天空和海洋都弥漫着荒凉和沧桑。诗中出现“Purple”这个词，在 1901 年版中，男子的衣服被涂成紫色。波斯人以紫衣为丧服，强调的是哀悼之情。关于人与神的问题，大地、天空和海洋都无法给出答案。

XXXIII

Earth could not answer; nor the Seas that mourn
In flowing Purple, of their Lord forlorn;
　Nor rolling Heaven, with all his Signs reveal'd
And hidden by the sleeve of Night and Morn.

【校记】

●一版：无此首。

●二版：列其三十六；

三行作‘Nor Heaven, with those eternal Signs reveal’d’，

五版末附二版文‘Heaven’作‘Heav’n’。

其三十三

地惟渊默海鞶呻，
遥失沧波旧主人。
天自频翻晨夕袖，
星躔显晦与同循。

33

地不回答；海也不，而只悼咽
他们渺茫的主，紫色中漂曳；
**　旋转的天也不，只把他所有**
星象隐现在如袖的晨和夜。

【校记】———
●二版：三行作“天也不，只把那些永恒的星象”。

【解读】———
第 33 首极有玄理，是菲茨杰拉德的名篇，也是黄克孙先生的名译：“遍访乾坤总惘然，天垂日月寂无言。海涛悲涌深蓝色，不答凡夫问太玄。”但是在《鲁拜集》的波斯原文中却没有相近的表述，只有那关于海的一句半，来自阿塔尔的《鸟会》，开始于第 972 个对句：

一个灵性事物的观察者走近大海
说“哦大海，你为什么是蓝色的？
你为什么穿着哀悼的长袍？
这里没有火，你为什么沸腾？”
大海对那个好心人做出回答，
“我哭泣是为了跟我朋友的分离，
因为我无能的缘故我配不上他，
只为我对他的悲伤我把自己的长袍染成蓝色。”

足见菲茨杰拉德的翻译何样的自由奔放了。不过，那冷静中透出的悲凉，借了阿塔尔这段来表达却十分合适。

34

菲译第一版第 33 首，
1909 年版
114 mm × 172 mm

1909 年版《鲁拜集》插图是匈牙利插画家威利 · 波加尼（Willy Pogány，1882—1955）为菲译《鲁拜集》绘制的第一个插图系列。书中除了插图还有装饰图案和手写字母，色彩绚丽。这幅插图的画面以不同人物造型和分布着大量骷髅头的山坡构成坚实的金字塔形状。这首诗告诉我们，从身外去盲目找寻神祇，只是徒然。

XXXIV

Then of the THEE IN ME who works behind
The Veil, I lifted up my hands to find
　A Lamp amid the Darkness; and I heard,
As from Without—"THE ME WITHIN THEE BLIND!"

【校记】———

●一版：列其三十三；异文甚多，别出。
●二版：列其三十七；
二行作 'The Veil of Universe I cried to find'；
三行作 'A Lamp to guide me through the darkness; and'；
四行作 'Something then said— "An Understanding blind."'。

I-XXXIII(V- XXXIV)

Then to the rolling Heav'n itself I cried,
Asking, "What Lamp had Destiny to guide
　"Her little Children stumbling in the Dark?"
And—"A blind Understanding!" Heav'n replied.

其三十四

祈向帷间汝在吾，
冥行能得一灯无？
似闻天外遥相语：
『吾在汝兮盲且愚。』

一版其三十三

潜运高天一任呼，
更无灯火指明途。
婴孩匍匐原非惜，
直日智兮盲且愚。

34

面对那支配着的我中之你
在幕后，我把我的双手举起
　寻找暗中之灯；于是我听到，
似来自外部——“你中之我盲矣！”

【校记】———
●二版：后三行作“在宇宙之幕后面我呼喊着寻找 / 指引我穿过黑暗的一盏灯；而 / 有什么在说——‘一个盲目的理智’”。

1-33（5-34）

我就向着旋转的上天呼喊，
问道，“命运是用何样的灯盏
　把她暗里摸爬的孩童引领？”
上天回答——“一种理智是瞎眼！”

【解读】———
第 34 首从第一版到第三版，改变不小，因此我猜想这首诗不会出自特定的一首。所谓“我中之你”，出自苏菲派的一种学说，认为凡俗的生物是从造物主流射，再被重新吸收回去。勒克瑙石印本第 641 首、Bankipur 公共图书馆藏抄本第 457 首，列为温菲尔德译本的第 400 首：

我身体的生命和力量来自你！
我内在的灵魂和灵魂属于你！
我的存在属于你，你是我的，
我是你的，因为我迷失在你之中！

有类似的说法。但赫荣 - 艾伦认为菲茨杰拉德并不知道这些文本，他确认这一首出自阿塔尔《鸟会》的两段，第一段从第 3090 个对句开始：

世界的创造者从秘密之幕的后面对大卫这样说：“世界上的任何事物，好的或坏的，可见的或不可见的，你都可以找到替代者，但我，你找不到替代者，也找不到同样的。因为没有东西可以替代我，不要停止留在我之中。我是你的灵魂，不要毁灭你的灵魂；我对你是必要的，哦你，我的仆人。别试图离开我存在。”

第二段从第 3735 个对句开始：

“从很久以前，真的，我是你，你是我；我俩只是一。你是我，或我是你？在这事里有二元性？或者我是你，或者你是我，或者你，你是你自己。因为你永远是我和我永远是你，我们两个身体是一：致意！”

显然，菲茨杰拉德这一首并未把“我”和“你”的玄思作为主题，他强调的是：造物主是盲目的！

也许英文比起中文来，更长于表现思辨性较强的内容，所以，在前两版里只说到理智的盲目不足以认识命运，但从第三版开始就加入了“我”和“你”的玄思，显得更有思辨味道。但在中文里，无论白话和文言，表达起来都不够顺畅。

35

菲译第一版第 34 首，
1921 年版
153 mm × 222 mm

这幅插图的作者是英国女插画家多丽丝 · M. 帕尔默（Doris M. Palmer，1896—？）。她的去世时间一说 1931 年，一说 1977 年。这幅插图色彩艳丽。画面中的男子在装饰华丽的房间里悠闲地欢饮。他的头巾、衣着，桌子和长颈瓶都具有东方风格。这首诗延续前三首的意思，既然生死、人神的问题难觅答案，不如借酒浇愁，不经意间陶罐述说了人生的秘诀：及时畅饮，酒是灵药。

XXXV

Then to the Lip of this poor earthen Urn
I lean'd, the Secret of my Life to learn:
　And Lip to Lip it murmur'd—"While you live,
"Drink!—for, once dead, you never shall return."

【校记】

●一版：列其三十四；
首行作 'Then to this earthen Bowl did I adjourn'；
二行作 'My Lip the secret Well of Life to learn:'；
三行句末无逗点；
四行 'for, once dead, you' 作 'for once dead you'。
●二版：列其三十八；
二行 'the Secret of my Life' 作 'the secret Well of Life'。

其三十五

侧身试就紫泥杯，
待问吾生大惑来。
相接如言及时饮，
一朝归去不能回。

35

我向这个粗制陶罐的唇边
俯身，请教我的生命之幽玄。
**　唇接唇时它咕哝——“当你活着，**
喝啊！——你一旦死去，再不能还。”

【校记】——

●一版：首行、二行作“朝着这陶土的碗我移近 / 我的唇请教那生命的神秘之泉”。

●二版：二行“生命之幽玄”作“生命的神秘之泉”。

【解读】——

第 35 首译自乌斯利抄本第 100 首（加尔各答抄本第 283 首）:

在极大的欲望中我把我的唇压在陶壶的唇上，
要从中问出生命能达到多长；
它把它的唇接上我的且咕哝着，
“喝酒！因为你不能重返这个世界。”

加尔各答抄本第 489 首的后两行也有同样的表达：

喝酒！我告诉了你一千次
你没有归途；当你离开了，你就离开了！

其实，在波斯原文里，这个接吻的比喻很常见，比如，1207 年抄本第 114 首（“乐园”本第 13 首）和第 127 首就都用到了。咕哝出的声音，当然是想象的酒的话语，并非夜莺那种叫声一如巴列维语的“酒，酒，酒”。原文很质朴，但对生命只有一次的感慨写得极为感人，菲茨杰拉德虽然只是做了轻微的改变，质朴却成了玄妙，这跟作者的气质、诗体的要求都有关，但仍然让我们有些文胜质的感觉。

36

菲译第一版第 35 首，
1920 年版
138 mm × 194 mm

不同的画家对诗中 Vessel 的理解是不同的，有的将之画成酒瓮，有的画成酒碗。英国插画家罗纳德·鲍尔弗（Ronald Balfour，1896—1941）的这幅插图犹如一幕舞台剧，画面富有装饰性，男女主角手持酒碗，美人似乎羞涩地转过脸去。画家突出了诗中的主题。诗人相信这个酒器是有灵性的，前世也曾风流。

XXXVI

I think the Vessel, that with fugitive
Articulation answer'd, once did live,
　And drink; and Ah! the passive Lip I kiss'd,
How many Kisses might it take—and give!

【校记】——

●一版：列其三十五；
三行作‘And merry-make; and the cold Lip I kiss' d'。
●二版：列其三十九；
三行作‘And drink; and that impassive Lip I kiss' d,'。

其三十六

器物喁喁若起予，
恋生嗜酒必其初。
唇间授受应无度，
今更接时情已疏。

36

我想这酒器，用那咕哝话语
回答的，有过生命，饮过酒醴；
**　啊，我吻着的顺从被动的唇，**
会有多少吻接受——并且给与！

【校记】———

●一版：三行作“做过乐；我吻着的冰冷的唇”。
●二版：三行“顺从被动”作“冷漠”。

【解读】———

第 36 首译自乌斯利抄本第 9 首（加尔各答抄本第 48 首，1207 年抄本第 239 首，“乐园”本第 107 首）：

这陶壶也曾是哀伤的情人，如我一般，
追求着一张美丽的脸；
你在它脖子上看到的这个把手，
曾是揽着他朋友脖子的手臂。

第二句，加尔各答抄本第 48 首作：“为情人的卷发所奴役。”这更形象地把葡萄作为情人的意思表达出来。菲茨杰拉德放弃了把手如手臂的比喻，利用上一首唇的比喻让两首诗联结到了一起，而且形成一个对比：上一首的酒杯显得关心，这一首却变得冷漠。在对比中，透出无限的苍凉：面对不可抗拒的命运，你可以放纵，可以取乐，却不可动情，你只是被动顺从就好。“雕栏玉砌应犹在，只是朱颜改。”（李煜《虞美人》）在宇宙中，多情者先凋谢，无情者近于常在。

37

菲译第一版第 36 首，
1910 年版
152 mm × 213 mm

英国插画家查尔斯 · 鲁宾逊（Charles Robinson，1870—1937）的兄长托马斯·希思·鲁宾逊在 1907 年版的《鲁拜集》中也为这首诗配了插图。查尔斯的这幅插图在构图上类似托马斯的作品。画面呈现的是室内场景，诗人正专注地看着陶工干活。诗中的陶土称陶工“兄弟”，喻指生命来自尘土，又复归尘土。

XXXVII

For I remember stopping by the way
To watch a Potter thumping his wet Clay:
    And with its all-obliterated Tongue
It murmur'd—"Gently, Brother, gently, pray!"

【校记】

●一版：列其三十六；
首行作 'For in the Market-place, one Dusk of Day,'；
二行 'To watch a Potter' 作 'I watch' d the Potter'；
三行 'all-obliterated' 作 'all obliterated'。
●二版：列其四十。
●三版：二行句末作逗点；
四行句末作问号。

【注释】

[1]One of the Persian Poets—Attár, I think—has a pretty story about this. A thirsty Traveller dips his hand into a Spring of Water to drink from. By-and-by[2] comes another who draws up and drinks from an earthen Bowl, and then departs, leaving his Bowl behind him. The first Traveller takes it up for another draught; but is surprised to find that the same Water which had tasted sweet from his own hand tastes bitter from the earthen Bowl. But a Voice—from Heaven, I think—tells him the clay[3] from which the Bowl is made was once *Man*; and, into whatever shape renewed[4], can never lose the bitter flavour of Mortality.

【注释校记】

[1] 一版、二版无此注。
[2] 'By-and-by'，三版作 'By and by'。
[3] 'clay'，三版作 'Clay'。
[4] 'renewed'，三版、四版作 'renew' d'。

其三十七

记驻行途看治陶，
冶中陶土作悲号：
『君当太古原吾与，
今日君工且缓操。』

【注】——

一波斯诗客，吾忆为阿特，尝述小说，可资比观。一游子渴，掬泉而饮。旋来一人，依次就饮，以陶碗取水。饮毕，留其碗而去。游子遂执碗再饮，颇讶同一水也，手掬之则甘，碗取之则苦。时有声来，吾度之或自天也，语之曰：制碗之土尝抟为人，今虽易其形，无易其促命之苦也。

37

我记得曾在道路边上停留
看一个陶匠将其湿泥捣揉：
用着全已失传的方言语调
它咕哝——“轻点儿，兄弟，轻点儿，求求。”

【校记】———
●一版：首行作“一天黄昏，我在市场上逗留”。

【注释】———
一个波斯诗人，我想是阿塔尔，讲过一个与此相关的美丽故事。一个口渴的旅人从泉水里捧水喝。跟着又来了另一个，他用陶碗舀水喝，然后把碗留在身后就离开了。第一个旅人拿起碗来再舀，他吃惊地发现，同样的水从他手里喝的是甜的，从陶碗里喝的就是苦的。这时有个声音，我想是从天上传来的，告诉他：制碗的陶土一度被做成人，尽管形状改变，但是必死者的苦味再不能去掉了。

【解读】———
第 37 首译自乌斯利抄本第 89 首（加尔各答抄本第 261 首，“乐园”本第 402 首）：
昨天在集市上我看见一个陶匠，
他猛烈捶打着一些新鲜的陶土，
陶土用神秘的语言对他说，
“我曾经跟你一样——所以待我好些。”
1207 年抄本第 17 首（“乐园”本第 104 首）也与此近似，只是把陶土比作了父辈的骨殖。这里把陶泥被捶打的声音，当作失传的方言语调，并模拟成语言，既巧妙又形象。其实，和那酒的咕哝声一样，语言不是拟声，只是想象。

菲茨杰拉德在第 87 首的注释里，详细讲述了历史上人和造物主跟陶罐和人的对应比喻。这里的说法也类似，但偏重于体现支配者缺乏爱惜之心。

38

菲译第四版第 38 首，
1930 年版
114 mm × 163 mm

匈牙利插画家威利·波加尼（Willy Pogány，1882—1955）配插图的《鲁拜集》1930 年纽约版，包括菲译第一版和第四版。这幅插图是菲译第四版中的，没有严格对应哪一首诗。画中美人正在弹琴，她的面前摆着一个陶罐。从诗意中可知，人与陶罐或许没有本质的区别，都是由造物主用饱含水分的泥土做成的。

XXXVIII

And has not such a Story from of Old
Down Man's successive generations roll'd
    Of such a clod of saturated Earth
Cast by the Maker into Human mould?

【校记】———
●一版：无此首。
●二版：列其四十一；
首行'And'作'For'。
●三版异文甚多,别出。

III -XXXVIII(IV- XXXVIII)

Listen—a moment listen!—Of the same
Poor Earth from which that Human Whisper came
    The luckless Mould in which Mankind was cast
They did compose, and call'd him by the name.

【校记】———
●五版末怀特所作校记引三版初稿,
首行作'For, in your Ear a moment—of the same'。

其三十八

此说孰云非是焉？
古人以降代相传。
即斯泥土成生类，
塑作功由造化全。

三版其三十八

同为尘土更伶俜，
若有微言谁肯听。
一入模间真铸错，
以人呼我岂叨荣？

38

不就是这样一个故事承继
远世人们代代相传的遗绪
　就是这样饱含水分的泥土
被造物者投进人形的模具？

3-38（5-38）

听——听一会儿——同样可怜的泥巴
人类的低语也是从中生发
　人形被投入这个不幸铸模
他们去塑造，用这名字叫他。

【校记】———
●五版末怀特所作校记引三版初稿，首行作“那，你倾耳听一会儿——同样”。

【解读】———
第 38 首是对前面三首的一个总结，表达了一个在《鲁拜集》中不断重复的思想：人和陶土是同源的。比如，加尔各答抄本第 475 首（“乐园”本第 106 首）：

我对着陶匠的作坊思考，
在旋轮的影中我看见巧匠，和他的双脚，
他给杯子和罐子做把手和盖子，
用的国王的头骨和乞丐的脚。

和加尔各答抄本第 488 首（“乐园”本第 105 首）：

我走入当时陶匠（的居处），
每时每刻都在陶土上展示出新的技艺；
我看到，虽然缺乏眼力的人看不见，
我祖先的尘土粘在每个陶匠的手上。

只是因为，陶器由泥土做成，传说人也是泥土做的，所以两者同源。

菲茨杰拉德在这首里，更突出了造物主之“不仁”。（《老子》第五章：“天地不仁，以万物为刍狗。”）人偏偏还是情识最盛者，就比别的被造物更显得不幸，这层意思在第三版里有，但第四版又恢复了第二版的内容。其实那是个挺好的讲法，不知道为什么放弃了。

39

菲译第一版第 18 首，
1907 年版
58 mm × 123 mm

这幅插图虽然是英国插画家吉尔伯特·詹姆斯（Gilbert James，1865—1941）为菲译第一版第 18 首诗绘制的，但表现的是诗人在繁花似锦、绿草如茵的山畔“酹酒于地”的情景。

XXXIX

And not a drop that from our Cups we throw
For Earth to drink of, but may steal below
　To quench the fire of Anguish in some Eye
There hidden—far beneath, and long ago.

【校记】

●一版：无此首。
●二版：列其四十二；
二行 'For Earth to drink of,' 作 'On the parcht herbage'。

【注释】

The custom of throwing a little Wine on the ground before drinking still continues in Persia, and perhaps generally in the East. Mons. Nicolas considers it "un signe de libéralité[1], et en même temps un avertissement que le buveur doit vider sa coupe jusqu'à la dernière goutte." Is it not more likely an ancient Superstition; a Libation to propitiate Earth, or make her an Accomplice in the illicit Revel?Or, perhaps, to divert the Jealous Eye by some sacrifice of superfluity, as with the Ancients of the West? With Omar we see something more is signified; the precious Liquor is not lost, but sinks into the ground to refresh the dust of some poor Wine-worshipper foregone.

Thus Háfiz, copying Omar in so many ways: "When thou drinkest Wine pour a draught on the ground. Wherefore fear the Sin which brings to another Gain?"

【注释校记】

[1] 'libéralité', 二版作 'liberalité'。

其三十九

满引休辞金叶蕉，
持来一酹泯然消。
土中埋眼忧如火，
长在冥昏待酒浇。

【注】——

饮前酹酒于地之俗，今波斯犹是也，东方盖皆如是。尼古拉斯以为：『以示慷慨豁达，兼劝饮者饮必尽也。』不殊类古俗，奠酒以媚地神，且使伊同此逸乐耶？抑或意同西方之古民，以祭余移人妒羡眼目耶？而吾人见奥玛尚别有意在，盖酒为菁华，殊不能弃，将以渗之地下，欲使古昔之饮者复苏也。

哈菲兹多方拟奥玛，其有诗曰：『惟汝倾此最佳酿，罪其增益慎勿忘。』

39

从那我们酹向大地的杯中
不是每滴都渗下无息无声
　去熄灭那些眼中愁苦之火
在很久以前，那里深埋——重重。

【校记】———

●二版：二行“大地”作“干草”。

【注释】———

饮酒前在地面洒一点儿酒的习俗在波斯还保留着，可能在东方普遍如此。尼古拉斯先生认为这是“表示慷慨豁达，同时劝说喝酒者应当一饮而尽，直到最后一滴”。这不是很像古代的迷信观点，奠酒以取悦地神，或使她一起参与这违禁的狂欢？或者，可能是用多余的祭品转移那些嫉妒的目光，就像西方的古代人？而我们看到欧玛尔还有另外的用意，珍贵的酒不能丢弃，让它渗入地下好使那些从前可怜的好酒者重新振作。

哈菲兹在很多方面都模仿欧玛尔，他说：“当你喝酒时把一杯倾倒地上，难道不怕罪孽又添了分量？”

【解读】———

第39首译自乌斯利抄本第81首（加尔各答抄本第180首）的头两行：

持酒者洒落在地上的每一滴
都能浇灭那些燃烧的眼中的苦痛之火。

而菲茨杰拉德那悠长的节奏里，尤见唱叹之工。

注释里提到海亚姆把酒洒向地面的独特用意，并用哈菲兹的诗作证明，其实珍惜酒的意思倒在其次，更重要的是重新振作地下的好酒者。借着这个意思，说出酒对于生者、死者都一样重要，也暗示了生和死没有差别。

40

菲译第一版卷首插图，
1907 年版
58 mm × 123 mm

这幅插图是英国插画家吉尔伯特·詹姆斯（Gilbert James，1865—1941）的作品。画面中诗人手持书卷，正凝视远方，而身旁的美人则在专注地倒酒。画家将他们置身于山脚下的墓园中，暗示生命无常，当及时行乐，痛饮美酒。

XL

As then the Tulip for her morning sup
Of Heav'nly Vintage from the soil looks up,
　Do you devoutly do the like, till Heav'n
To Earth invert you—like an empty Cup.

【校记】——

●一版：无此首。

●二版：列其四十三；
首行'morning'作'wonted'；
二行作'Of Heavenly Vintage lifts her chalice up,'；
三行作'Do you, twin offspring of the soil, till Heav' n'；
四行'you—like'作'you like'。

●三版：二行，五版末怀特所作校记引三版初稿，作'Of Wine from Heav' n her little Tass lifts up.'；
四行同二版。

其四十

擎杯当学郁金香，
朝露擎来作酒浆。
身不覆时杯不覆，
百年三万六千场。

40

郁金香从那尘间仰沐朝晖
仰起头来渴望天赐的新醅，
**　你可愿真心效仿？直到上天**
把你翻倒地上——像一只空杯。

【校记】———

●二版：首行“早晨的”作“习惯的”；

二行“从尘间仰头”作“举起她的圣餐杯”；

三行作“你，尘土的孪生子孙，直到上天”。

●三版：二行，五版末怀特所作校记引三版初稿，

作“举起她的小杯从上天之酒”。

【解读】———

第 40 首译自加尔各答抄本第 37 首（1207 年抄本第 128 首）：

像春天里的郁金香举起你的杯子；
如果你得到一个（幸福）的机会伴随面如满月的一位，
开心地喝酒，因为这旧敝的天空
会突然把你翻倒在地面。

1207 年抄本第 143 首（“乐园”本第 294 首）的头两行，也把郁金香和酒杯并提，但没有点明其间的比喻关系。

原文很质朴，菲茨杰拉德把里面提到的美女去掉了，把人完全比作了郁金香，沉浸在痛饮之中，显得更具豁达爽朗的神采，让人想到李白，如“百年三万六千日，一日须倾三百杯”。（《襄阳歌》）郭沫若说，海亚姆是波斯李白，大概就是看到了这一类诗。

41

菲译第四版第 39—41 首，
1900 年版
114 mm × 138 mm

美国插画家佛罗伦萨·兰德贝格（Florence Lundborge，1871—1949）采用将诗歌嵌入画面的形式，作品整体属于典型的“新艺术运动”风格。这幅插图主要是表现第 41 首诗的内容，画面中苗条的长发美人正倾倒长颈瓶往杯中倒酒。柏树和苗条的酒姬形象体现的正是诗中“身修如柏的行觞侍女”的意象。

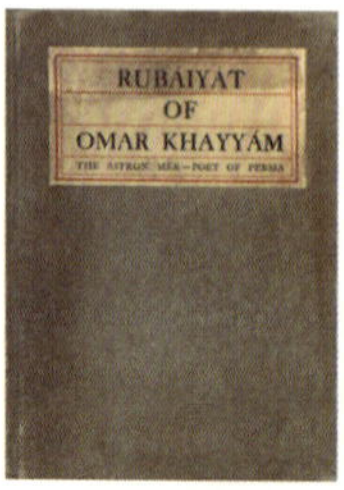

XLI

Perplext no more with Human or Divine,
To-morrow's tangle to the winds resign,
　And lose your fingers in the tresses of
The Cypress-slender Minister of Wine.

【校记】

●一版：无此首。
●二版：列其五十五；
首行‘Perplext’作‘Oh, plagued’；
二行‘the winds’作‘itself’。

其四十一

人天有惑再无忧，
明日风前万事休。
为唤酒姬修若柏，
青丝一握恋温柔。

41

莫再于人天之际困惑不已，
明天的纠结丢弃到了风里，
**　让你的手指在她发间放纵**
那样身修如柏的行觞侍女。

【解读】———

第 41 首来自乌斯利抄本第 73 首（加尔各答抄本第 179 首；“乐园”本第 426 首意思相近，尤其是后两行）：

要限制你对世俗事物的欲望知足生活，
割断依附在生命善恶之上的关联，
把酒拿在手（抚弄）你所爱的那个的鬈发，因为很快
一切都会过去——这不多的日子不会留下。

那个抚弄鬈发的描写，也见于乌斯利抄本第 118 首的后两行：

让我们停止奋斗在长久延宕的希望之后
去抚弄长长的鬈发和琵琶的手柄。

还有乌斯利抄本第 131 首（加尔各答抄本第 443 首）的头两行：

逃离一切科学研究——这样更好，
把你的手指缠在你所爱的那个的鬈发里——这样更好。

因为菲茨杰拉德从第二版开始才有这一首，因此，赫荣 - 艾伦猜想他受了尼古拉斯本第 48 首、第 155 首和第 359 首（加尔各答抄本第 443 首）的提示。

跟上一首紧接，都是写醇酒妇人，这首侧重在妇人，我们也许明白那首为什么只写饮酒了，否则会显得内容重叠。不仅如此，菲茨杰拉德还照顾到一种错落感，那首只写饮酒，写得痛快淋漓，这首写劝酒的女子，是纠缠于天人之际时的宽慰，透出一丝颓废。

42

菲译第一版第 47 首，
1938 年版
136 mm × 192 mm

这幅插图的作者是卡尔（H.A.-U.Karr，生平不详）。画面色彩丰富。插画家描绘了苏丹和妻子、嫔妃们饮酒的欢乐场面。虽然背景中的柳枝有中国画的特点，但总体风格类似波斯的细密画。

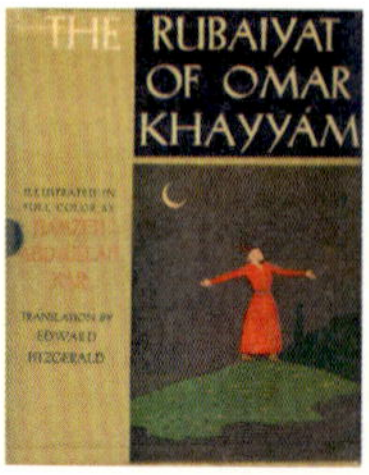

XLII

And if the Wine you drink, the Lip you press,
End in what All begins and ends in—Yes;
　Think then you are To-day what Yesterday
You were—To-morrow you shall not be less.

【校记】

●一版：列其四十七，异文甚多，别出。
●二版：列其四十五；
首行‘Wine’作‘Cup’；
三行作‘Imagine then you *are* what heretofore’；
四行作‘You *were*—hereafter you shall not be less.’。
●三版：首行，五版末怀特所作校记引三版初稿，作‘And if the Cup,and if the Lip you press’。

I-XLVII(V- XLII)

And if the Wine you drink, the Lip you press,
End in the Nothing all Things end in—Yes—
　Then fancy while Thou art, Thou art but what
Thou shalt be—Nothing—Thou shalt not be less.

其四十二

醇酒妇人安所终，
从来终始只为空。
计今之汝诚如昨，
何事长忧明日穷？

一版其四十七

酒有竭时唇有枯，
不疑万物尽归无。
汝今倘在终难在，
那见其间得丧殊？

42

如果你喝的酒，你吻的唇，
终结之处与所有终始俱存——
　是，想想今天的你既是昨天
的你——明天的你不会减一分。

【校记】———
●二版：首行“酒”作“杯子”；
三行“想象你既是从前的”作；
四行作“你还是——此后你将不会变少”。
●三版：首行，五版末怀特所作校记引三版初稿，作“如果杯子，和唇你压上的”。

1-47（5-42）

而如果唇你曾吻，酒你曾喝，
终结在万物终结之无——是的——
　那就想想当你在，你在只是
你会——无——你将只会不失不得。

【解读】———
第 42 首来自乌斯利抄本第 102 首（加尔各答抄本第 291 首）：
海亚姆，如果你陶醉于酒，要开心，
如果你和郁金香般脸颊的一个相倚，要开心，
因为万事的结局是你将成为空无；
当你在时，想想你不在——要开心！
还有加尔各答抄本第 412 首：
忘记从你身边逝去的日子，
别太在意还未到来的明天，
不要想你自己的到来和离去，
现在喝酒，莫把你的生命抛入长风。

菲茨杰拉德进一步指出空无也就是不增不减，无得无丧，更增添了玄思。这种玄思是人类所共有，波斯如此，印度如此，中国也如此，欧洲人也一样会心不远。

43

菲译第二版第 46 首，
1910 年版
174 mm × 223 mm

法裔英籍插画家埃德蒙·杜拉克（Edmund Dulac，1882—1953）依据诗意，描述了一个悲伤的场面。男人侧依在地上，接过“黑酒天使”递给他的黑酒。他身旁的女人痛心疾首，露出绝望的神态。天使穿着黑色斗篷，显得冷漠绝情。这幅插图和杜拉克为《鲁拜集》绘制的其他插图一样，为画面配了新艺术风格的花边。

XLIII

So when that Angel of the darker Drink
At last shall find you by the river-brink,
　　And, offering his Cup, invite your Soul
Forth to your Lips to quaff—you shall not shrink.

【校记】

●一版：列其四十八，异文甚多，别出。
●二版：列其四十六；
首行作 'So when at last the Angel of the drink'；
二行 'At last shall find you' 作 'Of Darkness finds you'；
三行作 'And, proffering his Cup, invites your Soul'；
四行 'quaff—you shall not shrink.' 作 'quaff it—do not shrink.'。
●三版：首行 'that Angel' 作 'the Angel'；
三行，五版末怀特所作校记引三版初稿，'offering' 作 'proffering'。
●四版：首行同三版。

【注释】

[1] According to one beautiful Oriental Legend, Azräel accomplishes his mission by holding to the nostril an Apple from the Tree of Life.

[2] This, and the two following Stanzas would have been withdrawn, as somewhat *de trop*, from the Text, [3] but for advice which I least like to disregard.

【注释校记】

[1] 一版无此注。
[2] 后段二版无。
[3] 'Text,'，三版作 'Text'。

I-XLVIII (V- XLIII)

While the Rose blows along the River Brink,
With old Khayyám the Ruby Vintage drink:
　　And when the Angel with his darker Draught
Draws up to Thee—take that, and do not shrink.

其四十三

逢迎终自在河滨，
黑酒高持俨若神。
满引向前邀汝魄，
径须欢饮莫逡巡。

【注】——

东国有传奇言，亚兹拉尔以生死树之实置人鼻下，用践其命。或言此章及下一章宜删，盖未当之辞也，然吾殊不为意。

一版其四十八

江边共我老珈音，
花下尊前兴不禁。
莫畏他年逢帝使，
持来黑酒径须斟。

43

当那位天使手持浓黑的酒
最终发现了你沿着河边走，
　举起他的杯子，送到你唇边
邀请你灵魂痛饮——你别颤抖。

【注释】———
根据一个美丽的东方传说，亚兹拉尔把生命之树的苹果放在鼻孔下面，就完成了他的使命。
这一首，和之后的两首，稍嫌不大合适，应该从文本中删去，但我对此建议宁可忽视。

1-48（5-43）

正当这玫瑰沿着河边开遍，
喝起红酒跟老海亚姆相伴：
　等到天使手持浓黑的药液
走近了你——接过来，不要发颤。

【解读】———
第 43 首来自加尔各答抄本第 256 首：
在苍穹的圆周中，它的深远是看不见的，
有一个杯子，定时的，他们让所有人来喝；
当轮到你时，不要哀叹，
开心地喝因为轮到了你。
菲茨杰拉德在注释里提到的那个删去此下三首的建议，赫荣 - 艾伦说出自考威尔教授，但大家都不知道为什么会有这样的建议。这一首以及下面两首都很好，也都有根据。

这一首，波斯文原诗和菲茨杰拉德译作所说的酒，未必跟中国讲的孟婆汤有关联，但总会让人自然地联想到。中国那个故事也很美丽，说是将要去的黄泉路上，有一条忘川河，河上有一座奈何桥，走过奈何桥有一个土台叫望乡台，在望乡台上向人间看上最后一眼，喝下旁边老妇人孟婆在卖的茶汤。那就是用忘川河水煮的孟婆汤，喝下去就忘记掉了人间的一切记忆，不论是爱，还是恨，是欢喜，还是烦恼。

44

菲译第五版第 44 首，
1942 年版
125 mm × 180 mm

这是匈牙利插画家威利・波加尼（Willy Pogány，1882—1955）的作品。这幅插图中的两个人物形象犹如雕塑，将美与丑作对比，似乎是将一个形象比作灵魂，一个形象比作肉体。灵魂正从肉体中超脱，欲升腾而上。

45

菲译第一版第 16 首，
1901 年版
77 mm × 120 mm

虽然这幅插图是英国画家赫伯特・科尔（Herbert Cole，1867—1930）为菲译第一版第 16 首（对应第五版第 17 首）绘制的，但从画面表现的内容来看，更符合第五版第 45 首的内容。第 45 首明确讲到“黑暗侍者收起帐篷”。科尔依据对诗意的理解为这位“黑暗侍者”添加了一双巨大的翅膀。

XLIV

Why, if the Soul can fling the Dust aside,
And naked on the Air of Heaven ride,
    Were't not a Shame—were't not a Shame for him
In this clay carcase crippled to abide?

【校记】

●一版：无此首，序文引之，
首行作 'Oh, if my Soul can fling his Dust aside,'；
三行作 'Is't not a Shame, is't not a Shame for Him'；
四行作 'So long in this Clay Suburb to abide!'。
●二版：列其六十九；
三行作 'Is't not a shame—is't not a shame for him'；
四行作 'So long in this Clay suburb to abide!'。
●三版、四版：三行 'Were't' 作 'Wer't'，'were't' 作 'wer't'。

XLV

'Tis but a Tent where takes his one day's rest
A Sultán to the realm of Death addrest;
    The Sultán rises, and the dark Ferrásh
Strikes, and prepares it for another Guest.

【校记】

●一版：无此首，序文引之，首行作 'Or is *that* but a Tent, where rests anon'；
二行作 "A Sultán to his Kingdom passing on,"；
三行作 'And which the swarthy Chamberlain shall strike'；
四行作 'Then when the Sultán rises to be gone?'。
●二版：列其七十；
首行作 'But that is but a Tent wherein may rest'；
二行、三行 'Sultán' 作 'Sultan'；
四行 'Guest' 作 'guest'。
●三版：一行 'one day's' 作 'one-day's'；
二行、三行 'Sultán' 作 'Sultan'。

其四十四

君若去为尸解仙，
御风直上自泠然。
多惭客养千金体，
长在齐州九点烟。

其四十五

大行途上一穹庐，
冥侍迎王暂驻舆。
王去自将收拾起，
明朝过客尚堪居。

44

什么，灵魂如把躯壳丢一边，
飘游在那天空里无挂无牵，
　能不羞愧——难道他能不羞愧
在这泥土遗骸里忍耐蹒跚？

【校记】——

●二版：四行作“如此长久地在这尘间逗留！”。

【解读】——

第 44 首译自乌斯利抄本第 145 首（加尔各答抄本第 447 首，“乐园”本第 103 首）：

哦灵魂！如果你能从肉体的尘土中净化自己，
你，赤条条的灵魂，能在天空翱翔，
最高天是你的领域——让它成为你的羞耻，
就是你来到并成为大地界内的栖身者。

菲茨杰拉德并未改变波斯原文的基本意思，但应该注意他文字的表达、韵脚的安顿，如此自然洎凑，大概是可遇不可求的。

王充《论衡·道虚》里讲到“尸解”：“所谓尸解者，何等也？谓身死精神去。”从这首诗来看，这样的想法似乎是人类共有的，异域的诗人也表达得如此自然。

45

这只作为一日逗留的帐篷
苏丹去往死亡之域的途中，
　一俟苏丹起驾，黑暗侍者就
收起，准备另一个客人居停。

【解读】——

第 45 首译自加尔各答抄本第 110 首：

海亚姆！你的肉体就像个帐篷，
灵魂是苏丹而停留之处是易逝的世界，
命运的侍者，为下一个停留之处做准备，
将要收起帐篷当苏丹动身的时候。

菲茨杰拉德只是把明喻变作了暗喻。

Ferrásh 是指管理帐篷的侍者，帐篷就是所谓“万物之逆旅”，那个侍者的工作就是在辅助命运了。郭沫若的注释在这里引用了《诗经·唐风·山有枢》：“宛其死矣，他人入室！”这让人很费解，两者之间是没有联系的。《山有枢》这两句，和第 23 首是同样的意思。

46

菲译第五版第 46 首，
1898 年版
149 mm × 205 mm

英国插画家吉尔伯特·詹姆斯（Gilbert James，1865—1941）将这首诗中的 Sákí 描画为一位美女，她正饮下一杯酒。坐在河畔的天使一手搂着她，一手牵着她的手。画家用《鲁拜集》中提到的“黑酒天使”来喻指这首诗中说的生死。

XLVI

And fear not lest Existence closing your
Account, and mine, should know the like no more;
The Eternal Sákí from that Bowl has pour'd
Millions of Bubbles like us, and will pour.

【校记】——

●一版：无此首。

●二版：列其四十七；
首行'your'用斜体；
二行作'Account, should lose, or know the type no more;'。

其四十六

百年有死若为惊？
天地无穷德曰生。
君看碗中千万沫，
神姬长在宴前倾。

46

不要怕存在把你的账目销掉，
还有我的，如许事就不再知道；
　不死的酒侍从碗里倒出像是
我们这样的千万酒沫，还会倒。

【校记】——

●二版：二行作“就会丢失，或者这类就不再知道，”。

【解读】——

第 46 首，赫荣 - 艾伦认为，不在乌斯利抄本和加尔各答抄本之内，应该来自尼古拉斯本第 137 首：

海亚姆！虽然天堂的看台
已经展开它的帐篷又关闭所有讨论的大门，
在生存之杯中，像是酒的泡沫
永恒的萨吉倒出来一千个海亚姆。

后两行那个比喻，可能让菲茨杰拉德很喜欢。

Sákí 是波斯语音译，在《鲁拜集》里经常出现，汉语音译作“萨吉”，意思是持杯劝酒者，郭沫若译作“醽客”，性别有男有女。这里不死的萨吉，比喻造化。全诗说，无数人像酒沫一样，来而又去，永恒不绝，一人的生死丝毫不重要。

47

菲译第一版第 52 首，
1913 年版
126 mm × 178 mm

这幅插图是英国插画家、摄影家雷恩 · 布尔（René Bull，1872—1942）为菲译第一版第 52 首绘制的，但是画面表现了天地苍茫、海浪翻腾，人如投入大海的一粒石子般渺小的意境。个体的呼告和吁请、存在和消失对这个世界并无影响，这正是第五版第 47 首所表达的意思。

XLVII

When You and I behind the Veil are past,
Oh, but the long, long while the World shall last,
Which of our Coming and Departure heeds
As the Sea's self should heed a pebble-cast.

【校记】——

●一版：无此首。
●二版：列其四十八；
二行‘Oh, but the long, long’作‘Oh but the long long’；
四行作‘As much as Ocean of a pebble-cast.’。
●三版：二行同二版；
四行‘Sea' s self’作‘SEV' N SEAS’。

其四十七

灵帷偕入渺无痕，
空见绵绵天地存。
来去但如投一石，
微澜不改海波翻。

47

当你和我在那个幕后消失，
哦，很久很久，世界仍会维持，
**　而它对待我们到来和离去**
像大海自身对待一块投石。

【校记】———

●二版：四行作“和海洋对一块投石一样”。
●三版：四行“大海自己”作“七海”。

【解读】———

第 47 首的意思，见于乌斯利抄本第 26 首（加尔各答抄本第 83 首）的头两行：

知道这个——你将和你的灵魂分离，
你将到那上帝秘密之幕的后面。

和乌斯利抄本第 51 首（加尔各答抄本第 129 首）的头两行：

我的来到对天界没有益处，
我的离去也不增加它的美丽和神圣。

因为从第二版开始才有这首，所以赫荣－艾伦认为此首诗受到了尼古拉斯本第 137 首的提示：

哦！多久我们将不再生存，世界将继续存在，
它将继续存在，不用我们的名望和迹象，
很久之前我们不存在，（世界）并没更糟，
此后，当我们已不存在，它还将是一样。

这一首和上面那首意思一样，也许，菲茨杰拉德很喜欢那首的“酒沫”和这首的“投石”两个比喻，故写成了两首。这首添加的比喻，的确远为鲜明形象。

黄杲炘先生曾经根据马修·阿诺德的名作《多佛海滩》的两句：

pebbles which the waves drew back, and flung
At their return, up the high strand
鹅卵石随着海浪退去，转盼
又被扔回来，向着高高的河岸

把最后一句译作：“就像大海对潮汐裹挟的石头。”但后来又改成“投石”了。不过，他的想法很有启发，阿诺德的诗句正好和菲茨杰拉德的相映成趣。

48

菲译第四版第 48 首，
1930 年版
126 mm × 183 mm

这幅插图是匈牙利插画家威利·波加尼（Willy Pogány，1882—1955）所绘。画面前景中的美人正在甘泉旁跪地掬水欲饮，她是如此专注，根本没注意她后身幻影般的商队。画家运用色彩和形象的对比来表达对生命虚无的理解。

XLVIII

A Moment's Halt—a momentary taste
Of Being from the Well amid the Waste—
And Lo!—the phantom Caravan has reach'd
The Nothing it set out from—Oh, make haste!

【校记】

●一版：列其三十八，二版列其四十九，异文甚多，别出。

●三版：三行，五版末怀特所作校记引三版初稿，作 'Before the starting Caravan has reach' d'。

●四版：三行 'reach' d' 作 'reacht'。

I-XXXVIII(V- XLVIII)

One Moment in Annihilation's Waste,
One Moment, of the Well of Life to taste—
The Stars are setting and the Caravan
Starts for the Dawn of Nothing—Oh, make haste!

【校记】

●二版：列其四十九；
三行 'setting' 作 'setting,'；
四行 'Starts for' 作 'Draws to'。

【注释】

The Caravan travelling by Night (after their New Year's Day of the Vernal Equinox) by command of Mohammed, I believe. [1]

【注释校记】

[1] 三版、四版、五版无此注。二版作 'The Caravan travelling by Night, after the Vernal Equinox—their New Year' s Day .This was ordered by Mohammed himself, I believe.'。

其四十八

沙碛清泉甘有余，
暂留遽饮信非虚。
起看商队遥如幻，
直往无中复太初。

一版其三十八

一脉沙间司命泉，
相呼速饮在穷边。
即催商队虚无去，
星斗离披曙色悬。

【注】——商队在元日即春分日后夜行，吾以为穆罕默德之命也。

48

一霎时的停留——一霎时存在
之饮从那荒漠中清泉一脉——
　看！——幻影般的商队已经到达
出发其中的那虚无——哦，赶快！

【校记】———
●三版：三行，五版末怀特所作校记引三版初稿，作“在出发的商队到达之前”。

1-38（5-48）

等片刻在那荒沙废碛中间，
等片刻，去尝一口生命之泉——
　群星正在沉没，商队已启程
向着虚无之晨——哦，不要拖延！

【校记】———
●二版：四行“出发”作“拽入”。

【注释】———
商队在元旦，即春分，之后夜行，我相信是穆罕默德的命令。

【解读】———
第 48 首来自乌斯利抄本第 60 首（加尔各答抄本第 135 首，1207 年抄本第 64 首，“乐园”本第 492 首）：
生命的商队神秘地经过；
愿你抓住快乐地经过的瞬间！
持杯者，为什么悲哀你主顾的明天？
给我们一杯酒，因为此夜已阑。
还有加尔各答抄本第 368 首的后两行：
人是苦难的存在，在受折磨的陶土中成形，
他尝了尝泥土然后离去。

在菲茨杰拉德的不断修改下，人生的虚无感就写得极富玄理了。在向着虚无的无穷来而复往中，人生的匆促根本也是虚无。

49

菲译第四版插图，
1912 年版
116 mm × 169 mm

美国画家、摄影师阿德莱德·汉斯科姆（Adelaide Hanscom，1875—1931）在画面中展示了一位身着半透明薄纱般长裙的美貌女子。面对青春，诗人、画家也要慨叹：韶华流尽而玄机难解，光阴易逝而人生有何所依?

50

菲译第一版第 31 首，
1913 年版
127 mm ×104 mm

菲译第一版无此首诗，对应的是第二版第 51 首诗。这幅插图是英国插画家雷恩·布尔（René Bull，1872—1942）为菲译第一版第 31 首诗绘制的作品。宇宙浩渺无垠，没有慧眼怎能觅得宝库，识得真主呢?

XLIX

Would you that spangle of Existence spend
About THE SECRET—quick about it, Friend!
A Hair perhaps divides the False and True—
And upon what, prithee, may life depend?

【校记】——

●一版：无此首。
●二版：列其五十；
三行‘A Hair perhaps divides’作‘A Hair, they say, divides’；
四行‘may’作‘does’。
●三版、四版：四行同二版。

L

A Hair perhaps divides the False and True;
Yes; and a single Alif were the clue—
Could you but find it—to the Treasure-house,
And peradventure to THE MASTER too;

【校记】——

●一版：无此首。
●二版：列其五十一；
首行‘A Hair perhaps divides’作‘A Hair, they say, divides’；
二行‘clue—’作‘clue,’；
三行‘it—’作‘it,’。

其四十九

君如不惜掷韶华，
径指玄关道路赊。
性命空余百年在，
是非唯间一毫差。

其五十

是非惟间一毫差，
直借神名引路遐。
若过宝山无妄喜，
许能径造主人家。

49

你如果想把生存的珠片耗败
为了去探求那秘密——朋友，赶快！
　一丝头发就隔开谬误和真理——
在什么上头，请问，人生能依赖？

50

一丝头发就隔开谬误和真理；
是的，只一个阿里夫就是开启——
　只要你能找到它——就直达宝库，
或许也能够就直达真主那里。

【解读】———

第 49 首和第 50 首，按照赫荣 - 艾伦的说法，应该放在一起来看。相关的意思出自加尔各答抄本第 482 首：

哦孩子！因为所有的秘密你已学会，
为什么在徒然的关注之后还如此忧伤？
如果事物不能按照你的愿望塑造它们自己，
不管怎样要快乐在你存在的这个时刻。

和加尔各答抄本第 19 首：

从背叛到信仰只是一息，
从怀疑到确信只是一息，
你珍重这一个宝贵的瞬间，
因为我们存在的结果只是一个瞬间。

还有乌斯利抄本第 28 首：

我的心对我说："我渴望灵智知识，
如果你会就教给我，"
我说是阿里夫。我的心说："别再说了。
如果全一在房间，一个字母足够了。"

在菲茨杰拉德的熔铸之下，相近的用语表达出迥异的理境。

这两首共有的一句："一丝头发就隔开谬误和真理。"全靠了加尔各答抄本第 19 首才让我们能够理解。第 49 首写得消极，在这一丝之际，人生难得找到依赖，往往就走向了谬误，因此耗败。而耗败的过程有着奋斗的光彩，让人误解为意义所在，其实那只是个幻象，因此用了"珠片"的比喻。珠片是装饰服饰的，很光亮，却很廉价。第 50 首就积极了，在那一丝之际，一个字母能够把我们引向真主。不过，在波斯原诗里更可能是指灵智知识，在菲茨杰拉德译文里就是指当下行乐吧。

51

菲译第四版插图，
1912 年版
116 mm × 169 mm

美国画家、摄影师阿德莱德·汉斯科姆（Adelaide Hanscom，1875—1931）的这幅摄影作品展现了低头沉思的诗人形象。诗人或许在探寻玄理：永恒的主宰化身为万物，有鱼儿也有月亮，万物变幻、消亡，他却常在。

LI

Whose secret Presence, through Creation's veins
Running Quicksilver-like eludes your pains;
Taking all shapes from Máh to Máhi; and
They change and perish all—but He remains;

【校记】

●一版：无此首。

●二版：列其五十二；

二行‘Running’作‘Running,’,句末作冒号。

【注释】

From Máh to Máhi ; from Fish to Moon.

其五十一

象外环中动不居，
退藏冥宰莫仁予。
鱼而至月形俱赋，
变灭由之但自如。

【注】——波斯文意，始乎鱼终乎月也。

51

隐秘的出场,通过宇宙之脉
水银般避于你的痛苦以外;
赋予从鱼到月所有的形状;
他们皆变化消亡——但他常在。

【注释】——

From Máh to Máhi,从鱼到月。

【解读】——

第 51 首,赫荣 - 艾伦找到了两个意象,"变形的月亮"在加尔各答抄本第 72 首:

月亮从本性说娴于变形
时而是牲畜时而是蔬菜,
不要想象它会变成不存在——离开了思想!
即使它的质不在了它总还有它的本质。

"水银"在加尔各答抄本第 40 首:

把酒放在我手里因为我的心在燃烧,
这捷足的存在像是水银。
起来!因为好运的觉醒要变成沉睡,
你知道青春之火像水一般(流逝)。

也许菲茨杰拉德的意思更接近"乐园"本第 478 首:

你永不消亡,是绝对的存在,
你处处都不在,又无处不在。
居无定处是你的本质,
你究竟何在?你何所不在?(张鸿年、宋丕方译文)

而"乐园"本第 406 首的最后一句更应该被指出:

一口酒胜过从鱼到月的宇宙。(张鸿年、宋丕方译文)

根据古波斯的说法,万物从鱼开始,到月结束。

这仍是和上面几首相关联的玄理:世界无穷的变化消亡,背后却隐然有永恒的主宰在,隐秘的出场,敏捷的规避。

52

卷首插图，
1958 年版
116 mm × 169 mm

约翰·扬·贝特曼（John Yung Bateman，活跃期 1946—1958 年）的这幅插图，描绘的是美人在音乐伴奏下跳舞的瞬间。我们或许可以把这个画面理解为真宰自编自导自演自看的一场戏。

53

第一版第 41 首，
1913 年版
125 mm × 125 mm

这幅插图是英国插画家雷恩·布尔（René Bull，1872—1942）为菲译第一版第 41 首诗绘制的作品，但画中情景也符合第五版第 53 首的诗意。画面中的男士举着酒杯，正向前凝视，若有所思："今天你还是你时，尚能瞩目——明天，你不再是你，那怎么办？"

LII

A moment guess'd—then back behind the Fold
Immerst of Darkness round the Drama roll'd
    Which, for the Pastime of Eternity,
He doth Himself contrive, enact, behold.

【校记】——

●一版：无此首。
●二版：列其五十三；
四行 'doth' 作 'does'。
●三版：四行同二版。

LIII

But if in vain, down on the stubborn floor
Of Earth, and up to Heav'n's unopening Door,
    You gaze To-day, while You are You—how then
To-morrow, You when shall be You no more?

【校记】——

●一版：无此首。
●二版：列其五十四；
三行 'To-day' 作 'To-day'；
四行 'To-morrow' 作 'To-morrow'。
●三版：四行，五版未怀特所作校记引三版初稿，作 'To-morrow, when You shall be You no more.'

其五十二

半晌登场解意无？
退身还自隐堂隅。
也知真宰闲游戏，
一本传奇终古娱。

其五十三

地锢天遥愿已违，
汝能为汝日常稀。
莫辞上下穷瞻顾，
待得明朝事尽非。

52

霎时被猜出——就退回到幕后面
隐入了围绕上演戏剧的黑暗
　那戏剧，只是为了永恒之消磨，
他让他自己去编导，演出，观看。

【解读】———

第 52 首译自加尔各答抄本第 479 首：

有时你藏匿，没人能见你的面，
有时你出现，以被造生命的样子，
你展示这个景观给你自己。
你自己同时是观看的真实之物和观众。

原文的意思被菲茨杰拉德说得更为显豁了。

这首把主宰形象化了，比作一个自编、自演、自己看戏的导演兼观众，在用戏剧点出世界的虚幻之时，也暗示了主宰的无聊。那个神秘的“幕”的背后，其实不过如此。

53

如果徒然，下是永锢的地面，
向上天堂的大门也被锁断，
　今天你还是你时，尚能瞩目——
明天，你不再是你，那怎么办？

【解读】———

第 53 首的意思近于加尔各答抄本第 24 首（“乐园”本第 93 首）：

如果心明白了存在如其所是的秘密，
在死亡里它能知道上帝所有的秘密：
如果今天你什么都不懂，你还和你自己在一起，
那么明天你能懂什么当你离弃了你自己？

菲茨杰拉德大概从“秘密”的探求，联想出类似“上穷碧落下黄泉”般的寻找，又都归徒然，因此有了头两行的句子。

54

菲译第一版第 39 首，
1921 年版
156 mm × 221 mm

这幅插图的作者是英国女插画家多丽丝 · M. 帕尔默（Doris M. Palmer，1896—？）。她用舞台上的表演者和舞台下的观众形成鲜明对比，以此诠释自己对这首诗的理解。台上的人欢呼雀跃，被众人抬着的人一手拿着酒杯一手拿着葡萄，而台下的人在观赏表演的同时也喝着杯中之酒。人生如戏，为何要寻找意义？不如喝酒。

55

菲译第二版第 57 首，
1947 年版
150 mm × 210 mm

R.S. 谢里夫斯（R.S. Sherriffs，1906—1960）插图版《鲁拜集》收入菲译第一版、第二版和第五版诗，共有 12 幅彩色插图。这幅插图主要表现的是“迎来了葡萄的女儿缔结良缘”的诗意，“葡萄的女儿”指的是葡萄酒。插画家以一对相恋的男女来诠释诗句，将人物至于前景中，画面色彩鲜明。

LIV

Waste not your Hour, nor in the vain pursuit
Of This and That endeavour and dispute;
　Better be jocund with the fruitful Grape
Than sadden after none, or bitter, Fruit.

【校记】———

●一版：列其三十九；
首行作‘How long, how long, in infinite Pursuit’；
二行句末作问号；
三行‘jocund’作‘merry’。
●二版：列其五十六；
三行同一版。

LV

You know, my Friends, with what a brave Carouse
I made a Second Marriage in my house;
　Divorced old barren Reason from my Bed,
And took the Daughter of the Vine to Spouse.

【校记】———

●一版：列其四十；
首行作‘You know, my Friends, how long since in my House’；
二行作‘For a new Marriage I did make Carouse:’。
●二版：列其五十七；
首行作‘You know, my Friends, how bravely in my House’；
二行同一版。

其五十四

此攻彼守漫徒劳，
有限生涯偶值遭。
结实非空即为苦，
何如欢压万葡萄？

其五十五

何期再赴合欢宫，
宾客喧阗高兴同。
虚廓天成离妇恨，
蒲桃酒是女儿红。

第五十四首

54

别浪费时间，也别徒劳驱驰
于这里那里的努力和争执；
欢享繁实累累的葡萄，胜似
苦寻虚无，或是涩口的，果实。

【校记】———

●一版：首行作“多么久，多么久，无尽地追寻”。

【解读】———

第54首的意思来自乌斯利抄本第50首：

那些人成了理智和苛察的奴隶，
在关于存在和不存在的争吵中毁掉；
走开，傻瓜！（宁肯）选择葡萄汁，
吃葡萄干的无知者（自己）变得（像是）生葡萄。

在苏菲派的词汇里，葡萄酒是生命或神性的象征，而生和熟隐喻修行的境界，这里应该是说，不懂得饮酒境界不够。还有乌斯利抄本第107首（加尔各答抄本第312首，“乐园”本第93首）：

关于未来的永恒和过去的永恒谈了多久？
现在是快乐之时，酒也不能替代！
理论和实践全超出了我的理解力，
（但是）酒解开了所有困难之结。

但菲茨杰拉德表达得更精炼，也更明晰。

经过了上面几首的反思，我们认识到，寻找固是徒劳，甚至所寻找的意义本来就是虚无，这时酒的意义就凸显了。

第五十五首

55

你知道，我的朋友，盛大的狂欢
是我第二次婚礼在我的房间；
老迈不育的理性休离我的床，
迎来了葡萄的女儿缔结良缘。

【校记】———

●一版：首行作“你知道，我的朋友，很久之前在我的房间”；二行作“为了一次新的婚姻我举行了狂欢”。

●二版：首行作“你知道，我的朋友，何等盛大在我的房间”；二行同一版。

【解读】———

第55首译自加尔各答抄本第175首（1207年抄本第63首，“乐园”本第347首）：

我要在一莫恩德的高足杯中倒满酒，
我要用两次半莫恩德的酒满足自己：
首先我要三次宣布跟学问和信仰离异，
然后我要娶葡萄的女儿做配偶。

在波斯男人可以两次宣布离婚，然后两次把妻子再娶回，但第三次就无法改变了。所以，加尔各答抄本里说三次宣布。

波斯诗歌善于比喻。我们在之前已经看到，很多诗的主旨其实是相同的，但不同的比喻方式仍然带给我们新颖的感受。在讲到理智不及行乐这点上，大概没有比这里的比喻更有趣的了，也难怪成为《鲁拜集》屡屡被提到的名篇。

56

菲译第一版第 41 首，
1956 年版
78 mm ×127 mm

杰夫·希尔（Jeff Hill，生平不详）的这幅插图与大多数插画家的作品不同，画面中没有人物形象。这首诗的思想是象征性的，画家描绘酒瓶、书册和地球仪 / 星盘。画中意象是东方式的，尤其是背景窗户的形状和图案。

LVI

For "Is" and "Is-not" though with Rule and Line
And "Up-and-down" by Logic I define,
　Of all that one should care to fathom, I
Was never deep in anything but—Wine.

【校记】

●一版：列其四十一；
首行 'with' 作 '*with*'，句末有逗点；
二行作 'And "Up-and-down" *Without*, I could define,'；
三行作 'I yet in all I only cared to know,'。
●二版：列其五十八，首行句末有逗点。
●三版：首行同二版，二行句末无逗点。
●四版：首行同二版。

【注释】

[1] A Jest, of course, at his Studies. A curious mathematical Quatrain of Omar's has been pointed out to me; the more curious because almost exactly parallel'd by some Verses of Doctor Donne's, that are quoted in Izaak Walton's Lives! Here is Omar: "You and I are the image of a pair of compasses; though we have two heads (sc. our *feet*) we have one body; when we have fixed the centre for our circle, we bring our heads (sc. feet) together at the end." Dr. Donne:

If we be two, we two are so
　As stiff twin-compasses are two;
Thy Soul, the fixt foot, makes no show
　To move, but does if the other do.

And though thine in the centre sit,
　Yet when my other far does roam,
Thine leans and hearkens after it,
　And grows erect as mine comes home.

Such thou must be to me, who must
　Like the other foot obliquely run;
Thy firmness makes my circle just,
　And me to end where I begun.

【注释校记】

[1] 此注一版作 "A Laugh at his Mathematics perhaps."。

其五十六

尺墨须能绳是非，
形名亦得测沉飞。
一生苦恨钩玄客，
不解杯中妙理微。

【注】——

此固言其学之滑稽语也。奥玛有诗以算学为喻，吾以为奇，而更奇者，彼诗乃与多恩博士之诗意堪并行，见艾萨克·沃尔顿所撰之本传。奥玛诗曰：『规如吾汝形同有，共一身兮分二首。圆径圆周果取中，相循终到长相守。』多恩诗曰：『身异何妨同挽携？如规二足正相齐。汝心贞似圆心定，辗转徒缘踪迹睽。正似闺中晏坐安，闺心长把远行牵。倾身听到归来日，始得相迎直起看。汝心相待感吾心，一样倾身忆念深。直使圆周贞固在，不辞终始誓相寻。』

【注校记】——

一版文曰：或自嘲其算学也。

56

为了是和非而用直尺和墨线
那升和降我依靠逻辑来判断，
于一个人想要探求的一切中，
除了——酒，我没在任何事上深陷。

【校记】———
●一版：二行作“那升和降不用，我能够判断”；
三行作“然而在我只想知道的一切中”。

【注释】———
这当然是关于他学问的一个玩笑。欧玛尔有一首让人好奇的数学四行诗被指出给我，更让人好奇的是它跟多恩博士的一些诗几乎完全可以对应，这些诗被艾萨克·沃尔顿的传记引用过！这是欧玛尔的诗：

我和你能跟圆规的形象相比；
我们虽有两个头是一个身体；
每当我们固定了圆周的中心，
到最终我们的头合在了一起。

多恩博士：
如果我们是两个，我们两个
也像直直的圆规两脚相并。
你的灵魂，是固定的脚，不过，
只是看来不动，另一个动你就动。

虽然你在中心稳坐，
但当我，那另一个去远行，
你就倾听着我，把身斜侧，
等到我回家你才直起身形。

对我你正是这样，我也像
另外那只脚，跑时身子也斜着。
你的坚定使我的圆恰当，
我的终点与起点相合。

【注释校记】———
一版此注作：“可能是关于他的数学的一个玩笑。”

【解读】———
第 56 首译自乌斯利抄本第 120 首（1207 年抄本第 113 首，“乐园”本第 268 首）：
我知道存在和不存在的外在，
我知道一切高和低的本质；
不过让我为自己的知识羞愧
如果我认识到任何高过沉醉的品级。
菲茨杰拉德后两句的意思表达得更为醒豁。尽管海亚姆具有极高的理智，但在人生问题上，他似乎根本不信任理智。色诺芬记述苏格拉底，说：“他并不像其他大多数哲学家那样，辩论事物的本性，推想智者们所称的宇宙是怎样产生的，天上所有的物体是通过什么必然规律而形成的。相反，他总是力图证明那些宁愿思考这类题目的人是愚妄的。”（《回忆苏格拉底》）两人虽然很像，但苏格拉底严肃地思考人如何正义生活，海亚姆却乖张地声称及时行乐。

注释里所引欧玛尔的诗，“乐园”本第 25 首基本相同。

57

菲译第四版插图，
1912 年版
116 mm × 169 mm

这幅插图是美国画家、摄影师阿德莱德·汉斯科姆（Adelaide Hanscom，1875—1931）的摄影作品，展示了画家心目中的海亚姆的形象，没有对应具体某首诗。诗人海亚姆是数学家、天文学家，曾受塞尔柱王朝第三代苏丹的邀请，到都城伊斯法罕主持天文学观测并进行历法改革。

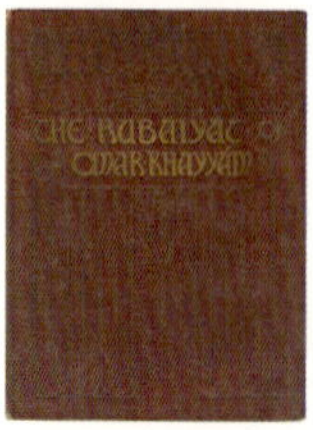

LVII

Ah, but my Computations, People say,
Reduced the Year to better reckoning?—Nay,
  'Twas only striking from the Calendar
Unborn To-morrow, and dead Yesterday.

【校记】

●一版：无此首。

●二版：列其五十九；

二行作‘Have squared the Year to human compass, eh?’；

三行‘'Twas only’作‘If so, by’。

其五十七

岁时不赘始称佳，
推算工夫以简夸。
后日未生前日死，
那须更向历书加？

57

啊，人们说，或许是我的算制，
简化了岁时更好测算？——不是，
**　那只不过是从历书删去了**
未生的明天，和已死的昨日。

【校记】———

●二版：二行作“修正了岁时使人理解，嗯？”；三行“那只不过是”作“若是如此，那是”。

【解读】———

第 57 首，赫荣 - 艾伦指出，其灵感来自加尔各答抄本第 381 首：

我的对手错误地称我哲学家，
主知道我并不是他们所称的；
但是，当我来到这个悲哀的蔽身地，
最终我却在更糟的处境，因为我不知道我是谁。

但我们并未看到其间的真正联系。他又指出了乌斯利抄本第 20 首的后两行（加尔各答抄本第 23 首，“乐园”本第 140 首）：

忧虑从不逗留在我心中，为了两个日子，
那还没到来的日子，和过去的日子。

倒是确有意思上的关联。

海亚姆是数学家、天文学家，菲茨杰拉德也就很自然地想到用数学和天文学来比方，上一首是数学，这一首是天文学。不过，这里天文学的比喻纯粹是菲茨杰拉德增添的，但表达更生动，格调也更符合海亚姆，可谓神来之译。

58

菲译第五版第 58 首，
1942 年版
127 mm × 178 mm

匈牙利插画家威利·波加尼（Willy Pogány，1882—1955）描绘了一位肩扛罐子的天使在暮色中闪闪而降。天使的腰带上画着葡萄和葡萄叶子，暗示罐子里装的是葡萄酒。

LVIII

And lately, by the Tavern Door agape,
Came shining through the Dusk an Angel Shape
　Bearing a Vessel on his Shoulder; and
He bid me taste of it; and 'twas—the Grape!

【校记】

●一版：列其四十二；
二行‘shining’作‘stealing’。
●二版：列其六十。

其五十八

曾记前时暮色青，
长天遥坠酒旗星。
蓬门未入先呼饮，
自向肩头解玉瓶。

58

不久前，门户大开的酒店边上，
一天使身影暮色中闪闪而降
**　一个罐子扛在他肩上；于是他**
请我尝尝它；那竟是——葡萄佳酿！

【校记】———
●一版：二行"闪闪"作"悄悄"。

【解读】———
第 58 首，赫荣 - 艾伦认为出自加尔各答抄本第 297 首（1207 年抄本第 106 首，"乐园"本第 276 首）：

昨天，正当醉时，我路过一家酒馆，
我看见一个喝酒的老人肩上扛着盛酒的东西。
我说："老人，主不让你羞愧吗？"
他回答："主是仁慈的，走，喝酒！"

可是，除了"肩上扛着罐子"的形象，差不多没有多少相同之处了。

郭沫若说，歌德的《掘宝者》一诗，内容与此相类。根据郭沫若的译文录出原诗的第三节：

我在远处得见一点光明，
好像是从无边的天际
来了一颗明星，
那时候正是子夜时分。
一个优美的童男
送了我满杯光晶，
突然地更加光明；
我想这绝不是人能前定。

我们知道歌德晚年的诗集《西东合集》，受到波斯诗人，尤其是哈菲兹，很多影响。不知道菲茨杰拉德有没有可能读了歌德的诗，觉得和东方情调相近，直接用了过来？

这首以天使爱酒讽刺人间禁酒，颇像孔融对曹操的调侃。"太祖制酒禁，而融书嘲之曰：'天有酒旗之星，地列酒泉之郡，人有旨酒之德。故尧不饮千钟，无以成其圣。'"（《三国志·魏书·崔琰传》裴松之注引张璠《汉纪》）因此，七绝译文把天使译作了酒旗星。

59

菲译第一版第 43 首，
1910 年版
129 mm × 183 mm

英国画家尤恩·盖迪斯（Ewan Geddes，1866—1935）的这幅作品描绘了一位年老的炼金术师和美貌的天使，表现的是“那至尊的炼金术士顷刻间，就把生命的铅块变成黄金”一句的诗意。画面以葡萄、葡萄叶和葡萄藤作为边框，富有装饰性。

LIX

The Grape that can with Logic absolute
The Two-and-Seventy jarring Sects confute:
　The sovereign Alchemist that in a trice
Life's leaden metal into Gold transmute:

【校记】

●一版：列其四十三；
三行'sovereign'作'subtle'，'trice'作'Trice'；
四行'metal'作'Metal'，句末作句号。
●二版：列其六十一。

【注释】

[1] The Seventy-two Religions supposed to divide the World, [2] *including* Islamism, as some think: but others not.

【注释校记】

[1] 此注一版作"The 72 Sects into which Islamism so soon split."。
[2] 'World,'，二版作'World:'。

其五十九

辩尽无涯辩有涯，
不如全付酒仙家。
能收君泪如铅水，
炼作黄金买岁华。

【注】——

七十二宗所分之世界，或言回教在其内，或言非也。

【注校记】——

二版文曰：回教旋为七十二宗所分。

59

葡萄酒能以逻辑的绝对真
辩破七十二家教派的纷纭。
**　那至尊的炼金术士顷刻间**
就把生命的铅块变成黄金。

【校记】———
●一版：列其四十三；
三行“至尊”作“巧妙”。

【注释】———
七十二教派据说分裂了世界，包括伊斯兰教，有些人认为，但有些人不这么认为。

【注释校记】———
此注一版作：“伊斯兰教不久分裂成七十二教派。”

【解读】———
第 59 首来自乌斯利抄本第 77 首（加尔各答抄本第 165 首，“乐园”本第 350 首）：
喝酒，将会驱散你无尽的忧烦，
也会驱散七十二宗的思考。
不要躲开那炼金术士，从他
你喝上一口，他能驱散一千种灾祸。
只是，菲茨杰拉德增添了一个很巧妙的比喻。

江西派有个诗法：“窥入其意而形容之，谓之夺胎法。”利用古典翻进一层，似乎就是“窥入”的要义。我们看看黄庭坚自己的例子。《寄黄几复》的第一句“我居北海君南海”，说他和黄几复离得遥远，第二句“寄雁传书谢不能”，说远到连封信都很难寄到。第二句的意思太普通了，但黄庭坚偏要表达得迂曲不同寻常。他只说托大雁带个信，但大雁推辞了。可实际用了两个典故在里面，并且“窥入其意而形容之”。头一个据《汉书·苏武传》：“得雁，足有系帛书。”第二个据陆玑《毛诗草木鸟兽虫鱼疏》：“旧说，鸿雁南翔不过衡山。”两个典故大家太熟知了，但黄庭坚这样一用就新奇了。我想让大雁替我寄个信，大雁推辞：“我飞不过衡山，怎么能带到广州四会呢？”那遥远，那信难寄到，就全在“窥入其意而形容之”里头了。在中国的古典里，实在找不到炼金术士把生命的铅水变作黄金这样的表述，如果直译，难免过于异化，和旧体诗的格调不合。于是从“生命的铅水”联想到李贺《金铜仙人辞汉歌》里“忆君清泪如铅水”的句子，就借用过来“窥入其意而形容之”了。

60

菲译第一版第 44 首，
1913 年版
128 mm × 185 mm

这幅插图中，英国插画家埃德蒙·约瑟夫·沙利文（Edmund Joseph Sullivan，1869—1933）描绘了鳄鱼、蛇、章鱼、猴子、年轻美女和老妪等形象，画面比较混乱，以此来表现“灵魂已被恐惧和悲伤扰乱”的诗意。

LX

The mighty Mahmúd, Allah-breathing Lord,
That all the misbelieving and black Horde
　Of Fears and Sorrows that infest the Soul
Scatters before him with his whirlwind Sword.

【校记】

●一版：列其四十四：
首行‘Allah-breathing’作‘the victorious’；
四行作‘Scatters and slays with his enchanted Sword.’。
●二版：列其六十二。

【注释】

[1] Alluding to Sultan Mahmúd's Conquest of India and its dark people.

【注释校记】

[1] 此注一版作‘This alludes to Mahmúd's Conquest of India and its swarthy Idolaters.’。

其六十

君王赫赫俨如神，惊走玄肤外道民。魂魄未怜忧惧在，剑锋四运剧风轮。

【注】——

隐指马穆德王征印度而役其黑民。

【注校记】——

一版文曰：隐指马穆德征印度而役其黑种降民。

60

强大的马穆德，如真主降临，
让所有邪教和黑色的族群
　灵魂已被恐惧和悲伤扰乱
在他和他的旋风剑前溃奔。

【校记】———

●一版：列其四十四：

首行“真主呼吸的”作“胜利的”；

四行作“溃散和被杀用他的魔法之剑”。

【注释】———

暗指马穆德苏丹征服印度和它的黑种人。

【注释校记】———

一版作：“暗指马穆德征服印度和它的黑种皈依者。”

【解读】———

第 60 首讲到的马穆德征服印度及其黑种人，在阿塔尔《鸟会》里有记述，见于第 3117 个对句开始的段落。赫荣 - 艾伦认为，这首诗的后两句出自乌斯利抄本第 81 首（加尔各答抄本第 180 首）的后两行：

感谢主！你认识到酒
是使你的心从百种苦痛中得以自由的汁液。

那么，菲茨杰拉德在这里是以马穆德苏丹的威力来比喻酒。这样的比喻我们并不陌生，与黄庭坚的名句“攻许愁城终不开，青州从事斩关来”（《行次巫山宋懋宗遣骑送折花厨酝》），意思非常接近。青州从事，指酒，这是《世说新语·术解》里的著名典故：“桓公有主簿善别酒，有酒则令先尝，好者谓‘青州从事’，恶者谓‘平原督邮’。”

61

菲译第三版第 65、66 首，
1884 年版
214 mm ×285 mm

这幅插图是美国画家伊莱休·维德（Elihu Vedder，1836—1923）的作品。菲译第五版第 61 首，在维德的插图中被编为第 65 首。画家在这里展示的是神态安详的酒姬持酒罐的形象，背景有葡萄、葡萄叶和葡萄藤。

62

菲译第四版第 60—62 首，
1900 年版
115 mm × 140 mm

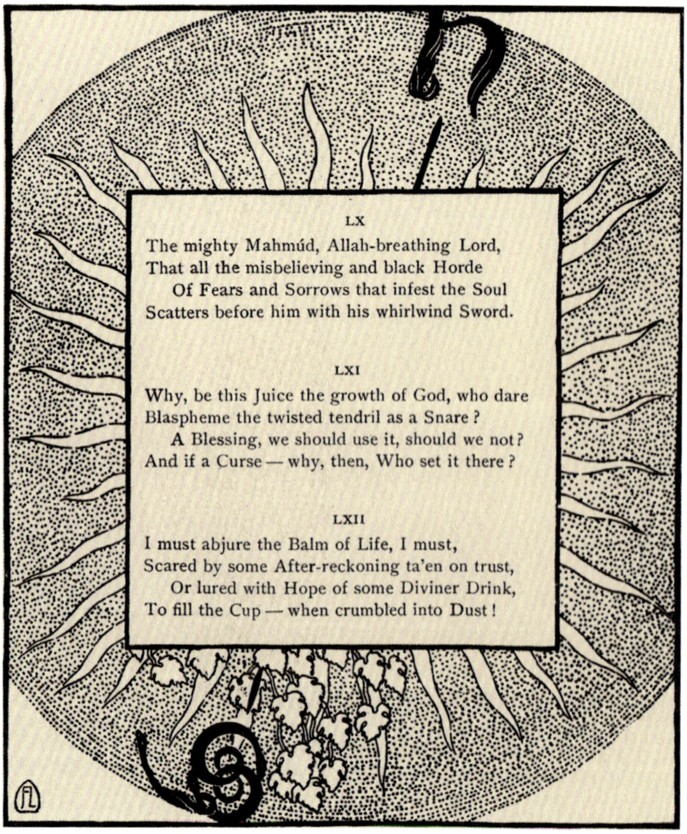

这幅插图是美国插画家佛罗伦萨·兰德贝格（Florence Lundborge，1871—1949）的作品。她将第 60 首、61 首和 62 首置入一个画面中。画面中有藤蔓、葡萄叶，还有类似火焰、圆盘的造型，总体比较抽象，可以任君想象。

LXI

Why, be this Juice the growth of God, who dare
Blaspheme the twisted tendril as a Snare?
　A Blessing, we should use it, should we not?
And if a Curse—why, then, Who set it there?

【校记】——

●一版：无此首。

●二版：列其六十三。

LXII

I must abjure the Balm of Life, I must,
Scared by some After-reckoning ta'en on trust,
　Or lured with Hope of some Diviner Drink,
To fill the Cup—when crumbled into Dust!

【校记】——

●一版：无此首。

●二版：列其六十四；

四行作‘When the frail Cup is crumbled into Dust!’。

其六十一

既云酒醴作由神，
敢指葡萄藤蔓嗔？
苦说陷人谁设置，
如为天赐正须亲。

其六十二

人生沉湎禁无难，
说到天刑惨不欢。
仍待长承神液满，
粉身碎骨化杯盘。

61

什么,这酒浆若是上帝的产物,
谁敢咒骂缠绕的卷须如网布?
　是赐福,我们就该受用,为何不?
若是诅咒——那,是谁,把它置此处?

【解读】———

第 61 首,赫荣 - 艾伦说出自乌斯利抄本第 75 首(加尔各答抄本第 202 首):

我喝酒,每一个喝酒的,如我,是值得的;
我喝酒对他来说只是个小事;
主在创世之日知道,我将会喝酒;
如果我不喝酒,主的知识成了无知。

但我们不敢断定,大概他把菲茨杰拉德的翻译想得过分自由了。不过,这个意思在波斯文本里倒是常出现,尽管表达并不同,如 1207 年抄本第 214 首。其实,上帝如果是一切的主宰,为什么造出了恶,不是一直有的疑惑吗?何况酒本身并非就是恶呢。这样的讲法并不亵渎。

62

我必须绝此人生之慰,我必须,
为相信那些身后清算而惊疑,
　或是为期待那些神酒而眩惑,
去注满那杯子——只待碎落尘泥!

【校记】———

●二版:四行作“当脆弱的杯子碎落尘泥!”。

【解读】———

第 62 首的来源,赫荣 - 艾伦指出了两处,一是加尔各答抄本第 505 首:

他们说:“不要喝酒因为你将为此受罚,
在报赎之日你会被扔进火里。”
那就是如此;但配得上两个世界的
是你因酒而兴奋快乐的时刻。

另一是乌斯利抄本第 143 首(加尔各答抄本第 495 首)的后两行:

用酒和杯为自己在这儿做出天堂,
因为天堂所在之处,你可能到达,也可能到不了。

也许,波斯原诗把酒看成现世天堂的说法,比菲茨杰拉德的翻译更打动人。菲译用了反激的说法,从中透露出无奈,甚至绝望,原诗却是傲然的。

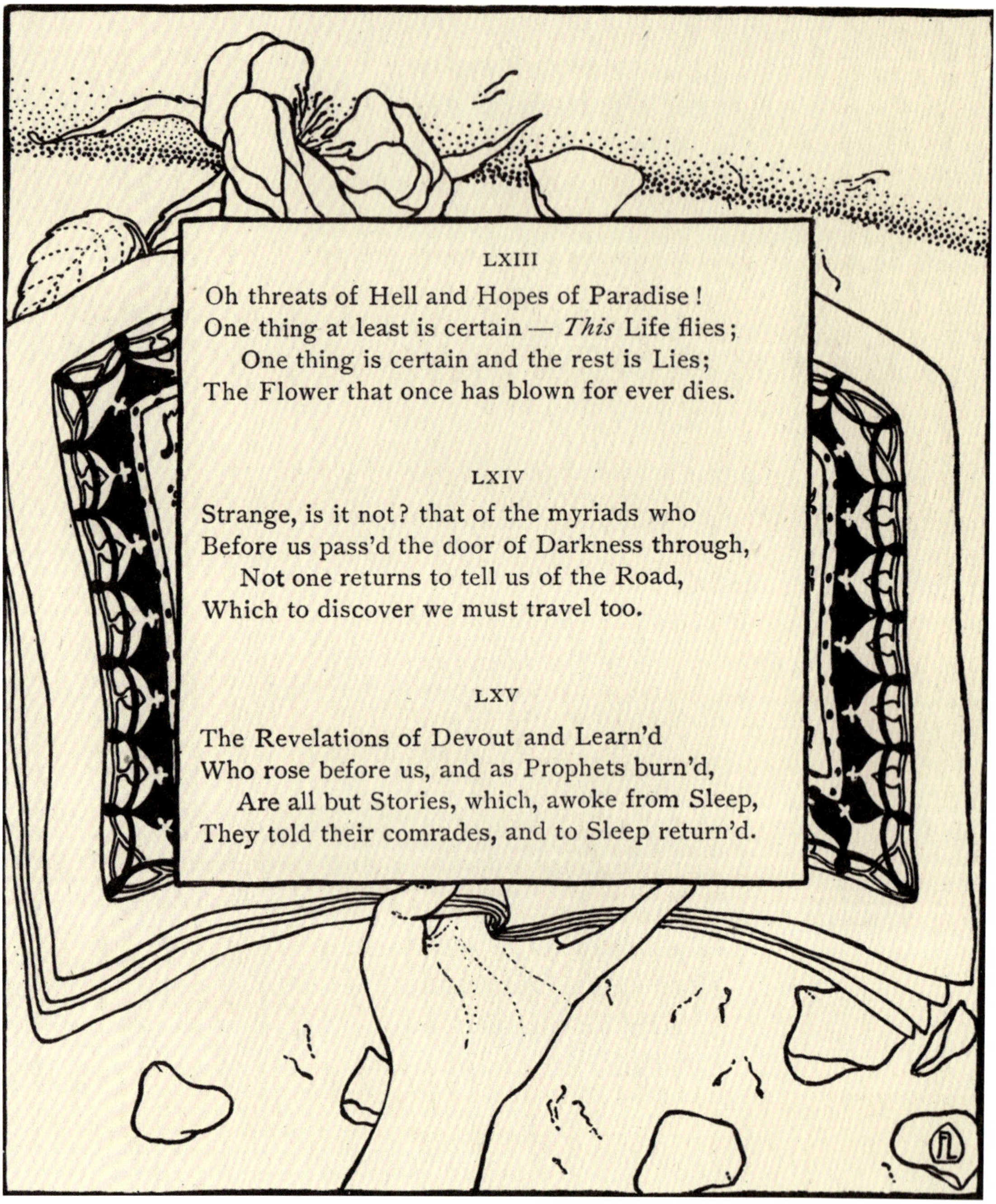

LXIII

Oh threats of Hell and Hopes of Paradise!
One thing at least is certain — *This* Life flies;
One thing is certain and the rest is Lies;
The Flower that once has blown for ever dies.

LXIV

Strange, is it not? that of the myriads who
Before us pass'd the door of Darkness through,
Not one returns to tell us of the Road,
Which to discover we must travel too.

LXV

The Revelations of Devout and Learn'd
Who rose before us, and as Prophets burn'd,
Are all but Stories, which, awoke from Sleep,
They told their comrades, and to Sleep return'd.

63

菲译第四版第 63—65 首，
1900 年版
115 mm × 140 mm

这是美国插画家佛罗伦萨·兰德贝格（Florence Lundborge，1871—1949）的作品。画面中有敞开的书籍、盛开的花朵和凋落的花瓣。地狱和天堂是怎样的，没有人确切知道，但花朵盛开一次后却永远凋丧，这是肯定的。

LXIII

Oh threats of Hell and Hopes of Paradise!
One thing at least is certain—*This* Life flies;
One thing is certain and the rest is Lies;
The Flower that once has blown for ever dies.

【校记】——

●一版：列其二十六，异文甚多，别出。
●二版：列其六十六；四行 'has' 作 'is'。

I-XXVI(V- LXIII)

Oh, come with old Khayyám, and leave the Wise
To talk; one thing is certain, that Life flies;
One thing is certain, and the Rest is Lies;
The Flower that once has blown for ever dies.

其六十三

上穷碧落下黄泉，
惟此常迁是不迁。
好记万花开顷刻，
休教赚作一生颠。

63

哦地狱的威胁和天堂的期望!
一事至少确定——这生命如飞样;
**　一事确定而其他都是些谎言;**
花朵只一次盛开却永远凋丧。

1-26(5-63)

哦,跟着老海亚姆,让智者高谈
阔论;一事确定,这生命如飞般;
**　一事确定,而其他都是些谎话;**
花朵只一次盛开却永远凋残。

【解读】———

第 63 首,用到了乌斯利抄本第 35 首(加尔各答抄本第 80 首,“乐园”本第 273 首)的后两行:

小心,你别把这隐藏的秘密告诉任何人:

郁金香枯萎了就不会再开。

前两行已经用在第 24 首里了。看来,菲茨杰拉德有时会把相同的说法,用到不太相同的意思上。那首劝告当下的挥霍,为了死亡的恐惧,这首珍惜眼前的光阴,为了信仰的虚无。但是,诗文总要做到文辞整体的妥帖,翻译的准则置于美学的要求之下。

64

第一版第 26 首，
1913 年版
98 mm ×132 mm

这幅插图是英国插画家雷恩·布尔（René Bull，1872—1942）的作品。整个画面显得比较神秘。一对男女伫立在星空之下，又似在云雾缥缈的山巅，他们身后又好像是黑黢黢的无底深渊。去过鬼门关的人至今没有一位回来告诉我们那里的秘密，每个人都要自己摸索。

65

菲译第一版结尾插图，
1914 年版
167 mm × 60 mm

这是印度画家梅拉·塞特（Mara Sett）为菲译第一版诗结尾画的插图。那些虔诚博学的先知遭到火焚，他们传下来的启示只不过是一些故事。梦醒之后诗人将这些故事讲给同道听听，然后又进入梦乡。地狱和天堂真实存在吗？这需要诗人自己去探寻。

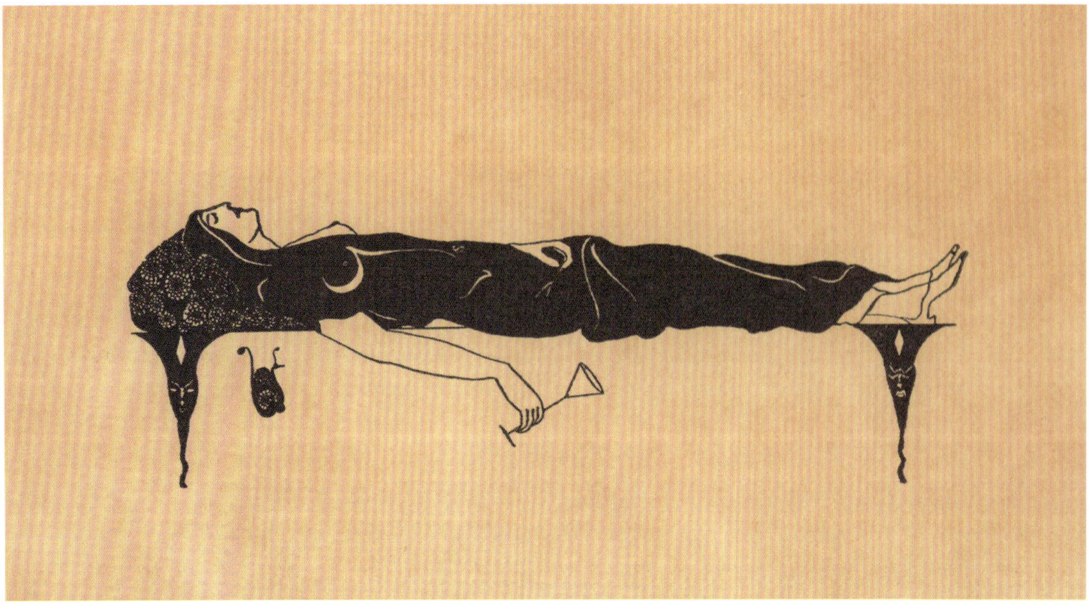

LXIV

Strange, is it not? that of the myriads who
Before us pass'd the door of Darkness through,
    Not one returns to tell us of the Road,
Which to discover we must travel too.

【校记】——

●一版：无此首。
●二版：列其六十七；二行句末无逗点。
●三版：二行同二版。

LXV

The Revelations of Devout and Learn'd
Who rose before us, and as Prophets burn'd,
    Are all but Stories, which, awoke from Sleep
They told their comrades, and to Sleep return'd.

【校记】——

●一版：无此首。
●二版：列其六十八；
四行 'comrades' 作 'fellows'。
●三版：四行同二版。

其六十四

异哉先我入冥关，
过者憧憧无一还。
前路悬知终要赴，
不来相告尔何悭？

其六十五

先知焚死士何期？
虐智空传开示词。
不过都将枕中记，
篝灯夜话赚痴儿。

第六十四首

64

奇怪，不是吗？那有无数的人
先我们穿过那扇黑暗之门，
**　没一个回来告诉我们那路，**
须知那也是我们所必追循。

【解读】

第 64 首里“没一个回来告诉我们那路”的说法，见于加尔各答抄本第 36 首：

我走出了很远漂泊在山谷和荒漠，
最后我漂泊到了世界的所有地方。
我没有从来自那条路的任何人听说，
那条路他走过，没有旅行人再去旅行。

和加尔各答抄本第 270 首（1207 年抄本第 120 首，“乐园”本第 119 首）：

在这条漫长路上的所有旅行人，
他会从那里回来，他会告诉我们那秘密吗？
注意在这宅第里（用隐喻的方式）
你留不下什么，你也不会回来。

“乐园”本第 89 首（1207 年抄本第 23 首）和第 398 首也都有类似的叙述。

这里既有对来世的疑惑，也有对复活的失望，应该说，此诗具有强烈的异端思想，这大概是海亚姆本来的意思。至于不少波斯原诗有着明显的信仰，以及苏菲式的寓意，大半不会是海亚姆的手笔。当然，也不排除海亚姆有时候会有挣扎。

第六十五首

65

那些虔诚和博学的人像是
被焚先知，对我们讲的启示，
**　只是，睡梦刚醒又重入睡梦**
之时，他们讲给同伴的，故事。

【解读】

第 65 首译自加尔各答抄本第 127 首（1207 年抄本第 55 首，“乐园”本第 52 首）：

那些人很多成了卓越和有教养的，
他们出色的一群成了他们同伴的明灯，
没有找出一条路走出这暗夜，
他们讲了一个寓言就睡着了。

菲茨杰拉德的改变，也许是因为英诗遣词和声律的要求，就和七绝译文的后两句一样，但比原诗的轻蔑意味强多了。博学，虔诚，都会用错方向，那走得越远也就越离奇了。

66

菲译第四版第 66—68 首，
1900 年版
115 mm × 140 mm

LXVI

I sent my Soul through the Invisible,
Some letter of that After-life to spell:
And by and by my Soul return'd to me,
And answer'd "I Myself am Heav'n and Hell:"

LXVII

Heav'n but the Vision of fulfill'd Desire,
And Hell the Shadow from a Soul on fire
Cast on the Darkness into which Ourselves,
So late emerg'd from, shall so soon expire.

LXVIII

We are no other than a moving row
Of Magic Shadow-shapes that come and go
Round with the Sun-illumin'd Lantern held
In Midnight by the Master of the Show;

美国插画家佛罗伦萨·兰德贝格（Florence Lundborge，1871—1949）的这幅插图寓意令人费解。画面右上角似乎是飘浮在空中的灯笼。S 形线条给整个画面增加了动感，难道是暗示穿越幽冥之境的灵魂？

67

菲译第二版第 72 首，
1942 年版
127 mm ×185 mm

这幅插图是匈牙利插画家威利·波加尼（Willy Pogány，1882—1955）的作品。画面中占主体的是美女昂头举手向天，而男子低头趴在地上。这首诗是诗人在探究天堂、地狱之后，表达了自己对天堂和地狱的认识：天堂只不过是满足欲望的幻象，而地狱是火中灵魂的影像。

LXVI

I sent my Soul through the Invisible,
Some letter of that After-life to spell:
And by and by my Soul return'd to me,
And answer'd "I Myself am Heav'n and Hell:"

【校记】——

●一版：无此首。

●二版：列其七十一；

三行作 'And after many days my Soul return'd'；

四行作 'And said, "Behold, Myself am Heav'n and Hell："'。

LXVII

Heav'n but the Vision of fulfill'd Desire,
And Hell the Shadow from a Soul on fire,
Cast on the Darkness into which Ourselves,
So late emerged from, shall so soon expire.

【校记】——

●一版：无此首。

●二版：列其七十二；

二行 'from' 作 'of'；

四行 'emerged' 作 'emerg'd'。

●三版：二行、四行同二版。

●四版：二行句末无逗点；

四行同二版。

其六十六

遣教魂魄往幽途，
异世书文辨得无？
魂魄顷时还报语：
『天堂地狱正为吾。』

其六十七

心足神劳幻妄生，
天堂地狱本虚名。
暗投莫怨浮沉在，
但遣人间嗜欲平。

66

我派灵魂先通过不可见之地，
去拼读生命之后的那些字句：
不久我的灵魂回到我这里，
回答“我自己就是天堂和地狱”。

【校记】———

●二版：三行、四行作“很多天后我的灵魂回来 / 说，‘看，我自己就是天堂和地狱’”。

【解读】———

第 66 首译自乌斯利抄本第 15 首（“乐园”本第 57 首）：

在创世之日，诸天之外，我的灵魂已经
求索板和笔，天堂和地狱；
最后老师用他有识见的判断跟我说，
“板和笔，天堂和地狱，在你自己之内。”

伊本·阿拉比《麦加的启示》里说：“最高之笔在法版上书写，就产生了万有。”菲茨杰拉德大概因为这个说法在英语里过于生僻，就忽略了。“乐园”本第 515 首，也有一个更生动的讲法：

心灵自语：我是卑微的水滴，
一生一世也无缘汇入海里。
它正说着此话居然汇入大海，
不禁惊呼：原来大海就是自己。（张鸿年、宋丕方译文）

“乐园”本第 513 首，更把这个意思提高到心性与神一致的哲思高度上了。当心性显示出普遍性的时候，往往会将之引向神性，如《中庸》所说“天命之谓性”。而当神性沦为伪善的法则时，又会重新走向心性，如这里的讲法，正好形成了自然的对应。

67

天堂只是满足欲望的幻象，
而地狱是火中灵魂的影像，
投射在黑暗之上，我们自己
才从那黑暗浮现，很快又泯丧。

【解读】———

第 67 首来自乌斯利抄本第 33 首（加尔各答抄本第 90 首）：

天穹是我疲惫身体的腰带。
吉洪河是我滤过的泪水的水流，
地狱是我无用的忧虑中的火花，
天堂是我宁静的片刻时间。

该诗也很明显地受了《鸟会》第 1866 个对句的影响：

天堂和地狱是影像，一个是你的善良，另一个是你的愤怒。

然后加倍写出人间的虚幻。

这首延续上一首，从神性，到天堂、地狱的信仰，全都返归于心性。这样的思想出现在有今生来世的宗教氛围中，也许同样是自然的。

68

菲译第一版第 46 首，
1914 年版
168 mm × 220 mm

印度画家梅拉·塞特（Mara Sett）在这幅插图中描绘了一些奇异的形象，有裸女、面具、烛火、花朵、孔雀、蝴蝶等，如梦幻一般。诗人在这首诗中将人比作跟着灯笼转来转去的幻化影像。

LXVIII

We are no other than a moving row
Of Magic Shadow-shapes that come and go
Round with the Sun-illumined Lantern held
In Midnight by the Master of the Show;

【校记】

●一版：列其四十六，异文甚多，别出。
●二版：列其七十三；
二行 ‘Magic Shadow-shapes’ 作 ‘visionary Shapes’；
三行 ‘the Sun-illumined’ 作 ‘this Sun-illumin’d’。
●三版：三行同二版。
●四版：三行 ‘Sun-illumined’ 作 ‘Sun-illumin’d’。

【注释】

Fánúsi[1] *khiyál*, a Magic-lantern[2] still used in India; the cylindrical Interior being painted with various Figures, and so lightly poised and ventilated as to revolve round the lighted Candle[3] within.

【注释校记】

[1] ‘*Fánúsi*’，一版作 ‘*Fanúsi*’。
[2] ‘Magic-lantern’，一版、二版、三版、四版作 ‘Magic-lanthorn’。
[3] ‘ighted Candle’，一版作 ‘Candle lighted’。

I-XLVI(V- LXVIII)

For in and out, above, about, below,
'Tis nothing but a Magic Shadow-show,
Play'd in a Box whose Candle is the Sun,
Round which we Phantom Figures come and go.

一版其四十六

马骑灯里影回旋，
尽自纷纷幻大千。
一点孤明阳燧火，
是谁取向正中悬？

其六十八

何人夜半力无双，
提得纱笼日作釭。
环以往来虚幻相，
大千世界看幢幢。

【注】——
幻灯今犹用之印度也，内置一柱筒，绘诸色人物于其上，巧使平稳，兼令风生，环其内之烛火旋焉。

68

我们只不过是移动的一排
幻化影像旋转着去去来来
**　跟着太阳点亮的灯笼它在**
半夜被提着由那演出主裁。

【注释】———
魔灯（*Fánúsi khiyál*）在印度仍在使用，一个圆筒形内芯上画着各种人物，小心地使之平稳和通风，围绕着里面点燃的蜡烛旋转。

1-46（5-68）

在那儿，进出不停，上下匆遽，
这其实不过就是幻化影戏，
**　演在灯笼里蜡烛就是太阳，**
周围任我们这些虚形来去。

【解读】———
第 68 首译自乌斯利抄本第 108 首（加尔各答抄本第 332 首，“乐园”本第 380 首）：
天穹之下我们困惑地站立，
我们知道就是走马灯的一类：
你知道太阳是火宇宙是那灯，
我们就像在里面旋转的影子。
这既是个绝妙的比喻，也透露出太阳是被围绕的中心的意思，或许和海亚姆先进的天文学思想相关，或许只是个偶合——太阳和蜡烛都是发光的。

此下三首，菲茨杰拉德把三个不同来源的比喻放在一起，说明人生的盲目、虚假，这些比喻既有波斯特色，又生动鲜明，都成为《鲁拜集》里著名的意象。

69

菲译第一版第 49 首，
1913 年版
127 mm × 145 mm

这是英国插画家埃德蒙·约瑟夫·沙利文（Edmund Joseph Sullivan，1869—1933）的作品。画面中表现的是下国际象棋的情景。这首诗以棋局比喻人世，将人比作无法自己做主的棋子。国际象棋的棋盘由黑白相间的格子组成，故诗中“日夜成格的棋盘”正如白昼黑夜的交替。

LXIX

But helpless Pieces of the Game He plays
Upon this Chequer-board of Nights and Days;
    Hither and thither moves, and checks, and slays,
And one by one back in the Closet lays.

【校记】——

●一版：列其四十九；
首行作 ‘’Tis all a Chequer-board of Nights and Days’；
二行作 ‘Where Destiny with Men for Pieces plays:’；
三行 ‘checks’ 作 ‘mates’。
●二版：列其七十四；
首行 ‘But helpless’ 作 ‘Impotent’；
三行句末作分号。
●三版：首行同二版。

其六十九

身如戏弄在围棋，
昼夜为枰安所之？
任尔推移争劫罢，
无过一一笥中遗。

69

那是无助的棋子供他消磨
在这棋盘那上面日夜成格；
**　任由他到处走子，将子，吃子，**
随后一个跟一个放回棋盒。

【校记】———

●一版：首行、二行作“这是昼和夜相间的棋盘 / 那儿神把人当成棋子玩”。

●二版：首行“无助的”作“无力的”。

●三版：首行同二版。

【解读】———

第 69 首译自乌斯利抄本第 94 首（加尔各答抄本第 280 首）：

说平实的话，不用寓意，
我们是棋子而上天在玩游戏
我们在存在的棋盘上一起玩着儿童游戏，
然后一个跟一个我们被放回虚无的盒子。

用棋局比喻人世，是很普遍的。苏轼《和李太白》“世道如弈棋，变化不容覆”，跟这里很接近，是从总体着眼，杜甫《秋兴》第 4 首“闻道长安似弈棋，百年世事不胜悲”，那是写政局，邵雍淋漓尽致的《观棋大吟》，那是历史哲学的思考，各诗就各有侧重了。

70

菲译第五版第 70 首，
1898 年版
146 mm × 203 mm

这是英国插画家吉尔伯特·詹姆斯（Gilbert James，1865—1941）的作品。画面中景展示的是打球的场面，诠释了第一和第二句诗。前景中的诗人伫立一旁，正专注地看着球赛，若有所思。

LXX

The Ball no question makes of Ayes and Noes,
But Here or There as strikes the Player goes;
And He that toss'd you down into the Field,
He knows about it all—HE knows—HE knows!

【校记】

●一版：列其五十；
首行 'question' 作 'Question'；
二行 'Here or There' 作 'Right or Left'，五版末附一版文作 'Right or Left,'；
三行 'you' 作 'Thee'；
四行 'HE' 作 'He'。
●二版：列其七十五；
二行同一版。
●三版：二行同一版。

【注释】

A very mysterious Line in the Original: [1]

O dánad O dánad O dánad O —[2]

breaking off something like our Wood-pigeon's Note, which she is said to take up just where she left off.

【注释校记】

[1] 'Original:'，一版作 'Original;'。
[2] 'O dánad O dánad O dánad O —'，一版作 'U dánad u dánad u dánad u —'。

其七十

玉勒金鞍笑打球，
一杆击处看星流。
偶然堕地真游戏，
怨甚君身不自由？

【注】——

原文有一句甚诡，辞之断续颇类吾国《木鸽记》，言伊每从中断处重操也。

70

球没有去问是和否那个必要，
这儿或那儿都由着打球的人打到；
**　是他把你打落在地，他知道**
关于它的一切——他知道——他知道！

【校记】———

●一版：二行“这儿或那儿”作“右或左”。

●二版、三版：二行同一版。

【注释】———

原文有一句很奇怪，文词断续有些像我们的《木鸽笔记》，据说她总是从停止的地方再开始。

【解读】———

第 70 首译自加尔各答抄本第 422 首（1207 年抄本第 40 首，“乐园”本第 144 首）：

哦你像球一样被命运之杆驱使，
向右或朝左，却说不了什么；
是他那个让你滚动和飞驰的人，
他知道，他知道，他知道，他——

最后一句就是菲茨杰拉德在注释里提到的奇怪的断续文词，我怀疑是模拟球滚动的声音，又传达出波斯语“他知道”的意思。钱锺书先生谈到过这种“拟声达意”的修辞：

象物之声，而即若传物之意，达意正亦拟声，声意相宜（the sound as echo to the sense），斯始难能见巧。《高僧传》卷九佛图澄言相轮铃语：“替戾冈、劬秃当”，在“羯语”可因声达意，而在汉语则有声无意，聆音而难察理，故澄译告大众。敦煌卷子刘丘子写《启颜录·嘲诮》门记一僧欲弟子温酒，悬铃作“号语”云：“荡荡朗朗铛铛”，申之曰：“依铃语荡朗铛子，温酒待我”；苏轼《大风留金山两日》：“塔上一铃独自语，明日颠风当断渡”，冯应榴《合注》卷一八引查慎行曰：“下句即铃音也。”此二者声意参印，铃不仅作响，抑且能“语”：既异于有声无意，如“卢令令”；亦别于中国人只知其出声，外国人方辨其示意，如“替戾冈”；又非只言意而不传声，如“遥听风铃语，兴亡话六朝”（唐彦谦《过三山寺》）。唐玄宗入蜀，雨中闻铃，问黄幡绰：“铃语云何？”黄答：“似谓：‘三郎郎当’”；窦巩《忆妓东东》：“惟有侧轮车上铎，耳边长似叫‘东东’”；皆拟声达意之“号语”也。（《管锥编·毛诗正义·三八伐檀》）

“卢令令”，见《诗经·齐风》，是猎犬挂着铃铛的声音，有声无意。佛图澄的故事，《晋书》有记载：“石勒将攻刘曜，群下咸谏以为不可。勒问佛图澄，澄曰：‘相轮铃音云：秀支替戾冈，仆谷劬秃当。此羯语也。秀支，军也。替戾冈，出也。仆谷，刘曜胡位也。劬秃当，捉也。此言军出捉得曜也。”这个铃声，模拟的是羯语，得翻译成中文我们才明白。这首诗里球的声音模拟波斯语，菲茨杰拉德的英译没有办法表达出来，汉语也一样无奈。

这种修辞在第 6 首，那里夜莺的叫声像是巴列维语“酒”，还有第 18 首注释里引到的一首，那里鸽子的叫声像是巴列维语“何处”，都使用过。不过，这一首更容易引起注意。

71

菲译第四版插图，
1912 年版
119 mm ×130 mm

这是美国画家、摄影师阿德莱德·汉斯科姆（Adelaide Hanscom，1875—1931）的作品。画面中主要表现的是第一行诗的诗意。命运之手写下人生的案卷，人的命运自己无法决定，也无法改变。

72

菲译第一版第 51 首，
1920 年版
138 mm × 179 mm

从画面内容看，英国画家罗纳德·鲍尔弗（R. Balfour，1896—1941）的这幅插图更符合菲译第一版第 52 首（第四版或第五版第 72 首）的诗意，表现的是第一行和第二行诗的诗意："那个倒扣的碗他们叫作天，被扣的我们匍匐生死其间。"

LXXI

The Moving Finger writes; and, having writ,
Moves on: nor all your Piety nor Wit
　Shall lure it back to cancel half a Line,
Nor all your Tears wash out a Word of it.

【校记】——

●一版：列其五十一；
二行、四行‘your’作‘thy’。
●二版：列其七十六。

LXXII

And that inverted Bowl they call the Sky,
Whereunder crawling coop'd we live and die,
　Lift not your hands to It for help—for It
As impotently moves as you or I.

【校记】——

●一版：列其五十二；
首行‘they’作‘we’，‘the’作‘The’；
二行‘coop'd’作‘coop't’；
三行‘your’作‘thy’；
四行作‘Rolls impotently on as Thou or I.’。
●二版：列其七十八；
首行同一版；
四行‘moves’作‘rolls’。
●三版：四行同二版。

其七十一

神指常书更不居，
空劳虔智挽其徂。
半行一字挥毫定，
倾泪休期得湔除。

其七十二

苍然覆碗指为天，
下者芸芸剧可怜。
举手遥呼休乞援，
一般无奈自回旋。

71

移动的手指在写，写完，继续
移动；所有你的虔敬和智力
**　不能引它回来把半行删除，**
所有泪水不能将一字洗去。

【解读】——

第 71 首来自乌斯利抄本第 31 首（加尔各答抄本第 87 首）：

从开始将是什么就已经写定；
笔毫不犹豫地（书写）并不顾及善恶；
在第一天他指定了一切必是如此——
我们的悲伤和我们的努力是徒然。

菲茨杰拉德只是发挥波斯原文第二行和第四行的意思，剩下的用在了第 73 首里。这种把命运的不移，比作写定的案卷，和我们俗说的“生死簿”之类很相似。

72

那个倒扣的碗他们叫作天，
被扣的我们匍匐生死其间，
**　不必举手向它求助——因为它**
无助地运转，也像你我一般。

【解读】——

第 72 首来自乌斯利抄本第 134 首的头两行（加尔各答抄本第 435 首，1207 年抄本第 191 首，第 166 首）：

天穹像一只倒扣下来的碗，
其下所有的智者都无助地被扣着。

和乌斯利抄本第 41 首（加尔各答抄本第 62 首，1207 年抄本第 190 首，“乐园”本第 100 首）：

善和恶都在人本性之内，
幸福和不幸于我们都已注定，
不要把它们归罪于天，因为，在智慧的道路上，
那些天比你更无助千倍。

从后者仅仅采用了天也是无助的这个意思。1207 年抄本第 2 首也有相近的意思。

海亚姆天文学家的洞见，窥破了宇宙也不过是机械地运动，并无自由。似乎波斯并没有推论那个不动的推动者的思辨学说，在失去信仰之际，宇宙也就失去了超越的因果性。

73

菲译第三版第 77 首，
1884 年版
214 mm × 285 mm

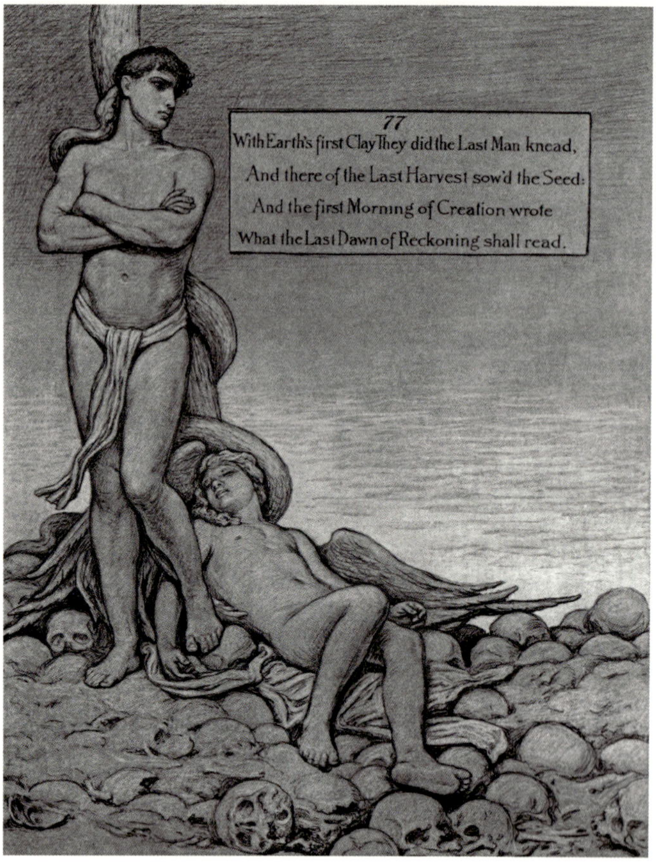

这是美国画家伊莱休·维德（Elihu Vedder，1836—1923）的作品。菲译第五版第 73 首，在维德的插图中被编为第 77 首。在维德的注释中，将这幅插图称为“最后的人”：孤立于族群的尸骸中，爱在脚下逝去，邪恶的灵魂在低语，痛恨“这个可悲的设计”。

74

第一版第 69 首，
1941 年版
90 mm × 126 mm

戈登·罗斯（Gordon Ross，1872—1946）的这幅插图，主要表现的是饮酒的情景。前景中的人物似乎已经喝光一瓶酒，又举起一瓶酒，喻指“今朝有酒今朝醉”。背景中的两组人，或许可以代表昨日和明日。生前死后均不可知，唯有今生可靠，“莫问去来挥汝觞”。

LXXIII

With Earth's first Clay They did the Last Man knead,
And there of the Last Harvest sow'd the Seed:
　And the first Morning of Creation wrote
What the Last Dawn of Reckoning shall read.

【校记】

●一版：列其五十三；
首行 'Last Man' 作 'Last Man's'；
二行 'there' 作 'then'；
三行 'And' 作 'Yea,'。
●二版：列其七十九。

LXXIV

Yesterday *This* Day's Madness did prepare;
To-morrow's Silence, Triumph, or Despair:
　Drink! for you know not whence you came, nor why:
Drink! for you know not why you go, nor where.

【校记】

●一版：无此首。
●二版：列其八十；
首行 'Yesterday' 作 'Yesterday'；
二行 'To-morrow's' 作 'To-morrow's'。

其七十三

太初抟土尽成人，
便是浮生代代尘。
笑尔身终忧会计，
不知注定在兹晨

其七十四

昨日预为今日狂，
明朝得丧转茫茫。
人生自是无根蒂，
莫问去来挥汝觞。

73

用第一块泥把最后一人抟出，
他们为最后的收获下种耕除：
　在创世的第一个早晨写下的
要在清算的最后日拂晓宣读。

【解读】

第 73 首用到乌斯利抄本第 31 首的第一行和第三行（第 71 首的解读里已经引过），赫荣 - 艾伦认为，还有乌斯利抄本第 95 首（1207 年抄本第 153 首，“乐园”本第 78 首）：

哦，心！因为，在这个世界，
真理自身就是虚夸的，
你为什么带着这烦恼和屈辱如此担忧？
把你的身体交给命运，让你自己顺应时间，
因为，笔一旦写下，它不会为你重写。

不过，就字面来看，还是和第 71 首更像一些，当然是因为最后一句。而“乐园”本第 21 首(1207 年抄本第 5 首)：

主啊，我此身是你用泥土塑造，
一经一纬由你纺织，我能如何？
我一生善恶早在头上写就，
对此，我只有徒唤奈何。（张鸿年、宋丕方译文）

其实在意思上更接近。

相比第 71 首，这首不仅慨叹命运，还质疑造物主。一旦造物主把一切都变作了不可更改的定命，世界也就和机械的一样没有区别了。

74

昨天预备出了今天的疯狂；
明天的沉默，失望，或者辉煌：
　喝！你不知你从何来，为何来：
喝！你不知你为何去，去何方。

【解读】

第 74 首的前半来自乌斯利抄本第 152 首（加尔各答抄本第 473 首）：

要开心！他们昨天已经确定了你的事务，
昨天已是你所有渴望无法企及的；
开心生活，昨天对你没有任何强求，
他们已经安排定了你明天要做的——在昨天！

后半来自乌斯利抄本第 26 首（加尔各答抄本第 83 首）的后两行：

要开心！——你不知道你从哪里来，
喝酒！——你不知道你会到哪里去。

在经过上面的反思后，再一次回到当下，回到饮酒。然而定命给了及时行乐合法性，既然将来已经注定，今日也就没有不疯狂的理由了。这是以逻辑表现出的冷静和镇定。

75

菲译第一版第 54 首，
1913 年版
100 mm × 124 mm

英国插画家、摄影家雷恩·布尔（René Bull，1872—1942）的这幅插图在菲译第一版第 50 首、第 54 首和第 73 首中均有出现，但最符合第 75 首诗的诗意。诗中的“天驹”或可如画家所理解的太阳。人生无常，生命虚无，我的宿命就是爱人世间的美酒。

76

第一版第 55 首，
1941 年版
90 mm ×134 mm

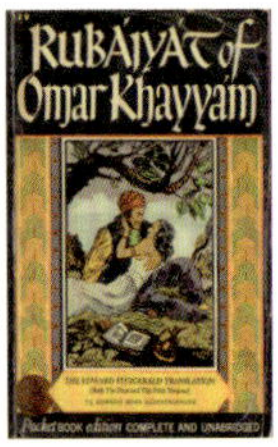

戈登·罗斯（Gordon Ross，1872—1946）的这幅插图，描绘了一位放浪形骸、如乞丐般的人正敲打一扇大门，这可能是宝库之门，也可能是去往天堂之门。远处那些伫立着的木讷僧人与此情景形成了鲜明的对比。

LXXV

I tell you this—When, started from the Goal,
Over the flaming shoulders of the Foal
Of Heav'n Parwín and Mushtarí they flung,
In my predestined Plot of Dust and Soul

【校记】

●一版：列其五十四；
首行 'you' 作 'Thee'，'started' 作 'starting'；
二行作 'Over the shoulders of the flaming Foal'；
三行 'Mushtarí' 作 'Mushtara'；
四行 'predestined' 作 'predestin'd'。
●二版：列其八十一；
三行 'Mushtarí' 作 'Mushtari'；
四行同一版。
●三版：三行同二版；
四行同一版，但句末有句号。
●四版：四行同一版。

【注释】

Parwín and Mushtarí[1]—The Pleiads and Jupiter.

【注释校记】

[1] 'Mushtarí'，一版作 'Mushtara'，二版、三版作 'Mushtari'。

LXXVI

The Vine had struck a fibre: which about
If clings my Being—let the Dervish flout;
Of my Base metal may be filed a Key,
That shall unlock the Door he howls without.

【校记】

●一版：列其五十五；
首行 'fibre:' 作 'Fibre;'；
二行 'Dervish' 作 'Súfi'；
三行 'metal' 作 'Metal'。
●二版：列其八十二。

其七十五

直掠乌鸢火色肩，
旄头太岁落长天。
黄尘定命轻抛掷，
枉说初行泰始前。

【注】——波斯语二辞即昴宿与木星也。

其七十六

葡萄藤蔓结吾生，
身贱那忧修士轻？
能启玄关为管钥，
外边留尔起嚣声。

75

我告诉你这个——那时，始自终末，
从天驹那火焰般的肩头越过
是他们把天上昴星和木星抛出，
在我尘骸和灵魂的定局坠落

【注释】———
Parwín and Mushtarí，就是昴宿和木星。

【解读】———
第 75 首译自加尔各答抄本第 147 首：
在那天当他们给太阳的野马备好鞍鞯，
定下了昴星和木星的律条，
这是命运之吏给我拈定的；
我怎能犯罪？（我的罪）是命运分配给我的一份。

菲茨杰拉德给诗添上了奇瑰的形象，连那无奈也显得浪漫、美丽。这大概是对星相学的反动，其方式和之前对造物主是一致的，仅仅对象改变了。由此也可见出，海亚姆的思考虽然单纯，但是涉及各个方面，还是严肃认真的。

76

葡萄藤生出须根：我的存在
如果被缠上——让托钵僧嗔怪；
用我这低贱材质锉把钥匙，
会打开那门，他正叫嚣在外。

【校记】———
●一版：二行“托钵僧”作“苏菲”。

【解读】———
第 76 首的描述包含在加尔各答抄本第 143 首里（“乐园”本第 50 首）：
因为永恒自身就是创造我的他，
从开始，他就给我讲授了爱的课程，
在那时我心上的些许尘屑，
他做成了物质宝库的钥匙。
菲茨杰拉德用了钥匙的比喻，把“爱的课程”换成了“葡萄藤”，——更多地用美酒取代美女，是菲译的一个特色。但本诗增添了对修士的反讽，从中表现的仍然是，及时的行乐胜过对将来的信仰。

77

菲译第一版第 56 首，
1913 年版
95 mm × 145 mm

英国插画家、摄影家雷恩·布尔（René Bull，1872—1942）的这幅插图，表现的是第一行和第二行诗的诗意。一对恋人在繁花之中，美女背后的心形喻指爱情。

78

菲译第一版第 68 首，
1941 年版
90 mm × 120 mm

戈登·罗斯（Gordon Ross，1872—1946）这幅插图中落在花朵上的蝴蝶正被一个网兜罩住。生命总是受到各种束缚，人生处处有枷轭，而破戒行乐又会遭受苦毒的刑罚，造物主对人真是不公啊。

第七十七首

LXXVII

And this I know: whether the one True Light
Kindle to Love, or Wrath-consume me quite,
　One Flash of It within the Tavern caught
Better than in the Temple lost outright.

【校记】——

●一版：列其五十六；
首行句末有逗点；
二行‘Wrath-consume’作‘Wrathconsume’；
三行‘Flash’作‘Glimpse’。
●二版：列其八十三；
首行同一版。

第七十八首

LXXVIII

What! out of senseless Nothing to provoke
A conscious Something to resent the yoke
　Of unpermitted Pleasure, under pain
Of Everlasting Penalties, if broke!

【校记】——

●一版：无此首。
●二版：列其八十四。

其七十七

灵光烛起遍生春，
失计无忧天殛身。
过眼旗亭才一瞥，
绝胜礼拜久迷真。

其七十八

莫向虚无怨不仁，
化生人物具形神。
禁欢一轭休思脱，
若被天刑长苦辛。

77

这我知道：不管是真实的光
点燃爱，还是怒火将我毁亡，
**　能在酒店里看到它的一闪**
也好过彻底迷失在那殿堂。

【解读】———

第 77 首译自乌斯利抄本第 2 首（加尔各答抄本第 272 首，1207 年抄本第 87 首，“乐园”本第 5 首）：

如果我和你在酒肆谈论神秘，
胜过我在朝龛前祷告而你并不在场。
哦你，一切被造物的初始和终极，
一个你将焚毁我，一个你将慈怜我。

在这一首里，原诗的质朴和玄思，译作的绚烂和热情，对比得十分强烈。然而这种风格上的差异，并不影响内容上的真实，翻译跟阅读一样，也应该允许接受上的差异性。

78

什么！从那没有感觉的虚无
一个有情感的东西会生出
**　会去怨恨禁绝快乐的枷轭，**
如果打破，必遭永罚之苦毒！

【解读】———

第 78 首和以下的三首不容易被分开，四首的意思都很接近。应该有不少波斯文原诗提供了翻译的材料，这一首主要来自加尔各答抄本第 85 首：

主，当他用泥土塑造我的身体时，
造我之中就知道会造出什么来；
（因为）没有他的命令就没有我的罪
他为何想在复活之日焚烧我？

还有尼古拉斯版的第 226 首：

你知道禁止犯（罪）是不可能的，
（尽管如此）已命令并规定禁止它；
如此在命令和禁令之间我们无助地站立，
我们凡夫是无助的在允许倾斜（杯子）却不让倾倒（它里面的东西）时。

但菲茨杰拉德把人的无助表达得更强烈，生而有不可遏抑的情识，却又不允许放纵，而限制者，不是为了强者的利益，就是被强者所戏弄。

郭沫若将头两句译作：

甚么话哟！从没感觉的“无”中
激发出一种有意识的“有”，

还特别注出：“有意识的‘有’”指宗教家所奉仰的有受想行识的人格神。但和下两句似乎很难衔接，未敢遵用。

79

菲译第一版第 52 首，
1913 年版
113 mm × 130 mm

英国插画家、摄影家雷恩·布尔（René Bull，1872—1942）的这幅插图，表现了人在荒野中向天祈求的情景。造物主对人不公平，人受到的限制犹如不公平的交易。

80

菲译第一版第 57 首，
1913 年版
127 mm × 196 mm

这首诗的大意是造物主给人布下了陷阱和罗网，人受到不公和暗算，但却要自己背负咎由自取的污名。英国插画家埃德蒙·约瑟夫·沙利文（Edmund Joseph Sullivan，1869—1933）在这幅插图中描绘了身受限制之人的无奈、困苦和呼告。

LXXIX

What! from his helpless Creature be repaid
Pure Gold for what he lent him dross-allay'd—
　Sue for a Debt he never did contract,
And cannot answer—Oh the sorry trade!

【校记】

●一版：无此首。
●二版：列其八十五；
二行 'him' 作 'us'；
三行 'he' 作 'we'。
●三版：二行、三行同二版。
●四版：三行同二版。

LXXX

Oh Thou, who didst with pitfall and with gin
Beset the Road I was to wander in,
　Thou wilt not with Predestined Evil round
Enmesh, and then impute my Fall to Sin!

【校记】

●一版：列其五十七；
首行 'pitfall' 作 'Pitfall'，'gin' 作 'Gin'；
三行 'Predestined Evil' 作 'Predestination'；
四行 'Enmesh, and then impute' 作 'Enmesh me, and impute'，句末作问号。
●二版：列其八十七；
三行 'Predestined' 作 'Predestin'd'；
四行句末作问号。
●三版、四版：三行同二版。

其七十九

大钧造物信难任，
予以泥沙索以金。
此责不闻相约束，
悲哉那肯更来寻？

其八十

客行辛苦共沾巾，
网罟犹多性肯驯？
直待一身罹罪日，
始知定命本无亲。

79

什么！他那无助的生物竟该
用纯金偿还他借出的废材——
**　责求的这债务他从未签订，**
不能答应——哦，这交易太悲哀！

【解读】———
第 79 首来自加尔各答抄本第 201 首：
当他们混合着我的形状的模具里的土，
他们从我这里创造了一百个奇迹；
我不能比我更好了，
因为我如何从熔炉脱出就是这样。
还有加尔各答抄本第 433 首，两者内容基本相同。但菲茨杰拉德把那限制的意思再陈述了一遍，从另一个角度指出，这限制犹如不公平的交易。如果我们把宗教那层撇开，庄子感慨的“诸侯之门而仁义存焉”（《庄子・胠箧》），不是同样的不公平吗？

80

哦你，你把陷阱和网罗置放
在我要去行游的那条路上，
**　你岂非先用注定的恶缭绕**
绊陷，再来咎责我堕入罪障！

【解读】———
第 80 首译自乌斯利抄本第 148 首：
在我经过路上的一千个地方，你布下罗网，
你说“如果你踏上它们我会抓住你，”
在最小的事物中也没有独立于你的世界，
你定下了一切事物，（然而）还叫我叛逆！
这首似乎回应了第 78 首，从虚无中因何生出有情感的东西，仍然在造物主。他布下的陷阱和罗网，正是为了捕捉有情感的。于是恶也是注定的。

菲茨杰拉德因为英文的修辞和格律要求，跟波斯原文各具风格，也许，原文的明快更为我们喜爱，但我们必须考虑到菲茨杰拉德受到的约束。任何语言的转换，都必须面对这样的约束，不予处理就是硬译。似乎硬译在现在格外流行，菲译给了我们值得反思的经验。

81

菲译第二版第 88 首，
1909 年版
175 mm × 225 mm

法裔英籍插画家埃德蒙·杜拉克（Edmund Dulac，1882—1953）在此描绘的是一位老者悲哀地望着年轻女孩的情景。女孩似乎已经香消玉殒。这首诗谴责造物主用烂泥造人且善恶不分，奉劝造物主赋予人宽容的禀赋，这样也会得到人的宽恕。

LXXXI

Oh Thou, who Man of baser Earth didst make,
And ev'n with Paradise devise the Snake:
For all the Sin wherewith the Face of Man
Is blacken'd—Man's forgiveness give—and take!

【校记】

●一版：列其五十八；
一行 'Oh' 作 'Oh,'；
二行作 'And who with Eden didst devise the Snake;'；
四行 'Is blacken'd—Man's forgiveness' 作 'Is blacken'd, Man's Forgiveness'。
●二版：列其八十八；
三行作 'For all the Sin the Face of wretched Man'；
四行 'Is blacken'd—Man's forgiveness' 作 'Is black with—Man's Forgiveness'。
●三版：四行 'forgiveness' 作 'Forgiveness'。
●诸版诗后俱有分隔号。

其八十一

抟土绳泥意已差，
力穷竟未拔其蛇。
人神从此交相怨，
黥面诛心漫正邪。

81

哦你，用低贱泥土把人来塑，
竟把蛇也安排在乐园深处：
所有的罪用来把人脸抹黑——
给予人类宽恕——也得到宽恕！

【校记】———
●一版：二行"乐园"作"伊甸园"。
●二版：三行"人脸"作"可怜人的脸"。

【解读】———
第 81 首混合了多个来源，围绕它的争论也很激烈。考威尔教授说："关于蛇那行没有来源。"但在菲茨杰拉德经常用到的阿塔尔《鸟会》的开始，起于第 3229 个对句，我们看到蛇出现在乐园里，在造亚当时，撒旦对上帝说：

如果有诅咒来自你，也会有宽恕，
被造的万物依赖你，因为命运在你手；
如果诅咒是我的命，我不怕，
这里必有毒药，一切俱非解药。

和这首诗类似的意思出现在加尔各答抄本第 115 首：

我是一个违命的奴隶，你的宽恕在哪里？
我的心是黑暗的，你的光明和清朗在哪里？
如果，因为侍奉你，你给我天堂，
这是回报，但是你的荣宠和恩赐——它们在哪里？

和加尔各答抄本第 286 首（尼古拉斯版第 236 首）：

哦！你知道所有人心中的秘密，
保护所有人在他们无助的时分：
哦，主！让我悔悟接受我的悔过，
哦！你让所有人悔悟接受所有人的悔过。

还有加尔各答抄本第 510 首：

死者和活人事务的管理者是你，
你是莫测天堂的守护者；
虽然我是邪恶的，你是我的主人，
明白你是（一切）创造者，谁又能犯罪？

考威尔教授认为菲茨杰拉德这首出自加尔各答抄本第 286 首，也就是尼古拉斯版第 236 首，可以参看本书后赖特的第五版编者增注。

黄杲炘先生在这一首的注释里说："这首诗中的'你'已不再是中世纪波斯的伊斯兰真主，而是维多利亚时代英国的基督教上帝。这首柔巴依极受托马斯·哈代喜爱。据说他临终时还请人把此诗念给他听。"

82

菲译第一版第 82 首，
1898 年版
147 mm × 207 mm

英国插画家吉尔伯特·詹姆斯（Gilbert James，1865—1941）的这幅插图表现的是第三行和第四行诗的诗意：“我又一次独自站在那陶匠屋中，被各色的陶坯围住。”诗以陶工和陶器的关系喻指造物主和人的关系。

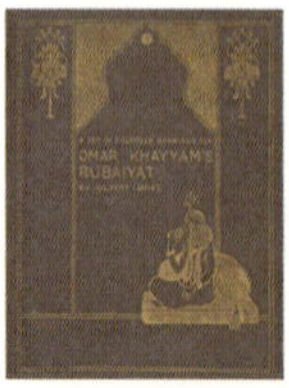

LXXXII

As under cover of departing Day
Slunk hunger-stricken Ramazán away,
　Once more within the Potter's house alone
I stood, surrounded by the Shapes of Clay.

【校记】———

●一版：列其五十九，其上题‘KÚZA-NÁMA.’，意为“壶罐章”，二版以后无此题，唯以分隔号标识，异文甚多，别出。

●二版：列其八十九。

I-LIX(V- LXXXII)

Listen again. One Evening at the Close
Of Ramazán, ere the better Moon arose,
　In that old Potter's Shop I stood alone
With the clay Population round in Rows.

其八十二　下九首为《瓮歌行》

斋月久为饥馁劳，
蔽诸去日得潜逃。
我来又向陶坊立，
百状胚輝拥四遭。

一版其五十九

临夕全非禁食天，
陶家旧肆月初悬。
独来侧耳重相觅，
一众成行绕我前。

82

像是被离去的白天所掩护
饥饿摧残的斋月找到逃路，
　又一次独自在那陶匠屋中
我站着，被各色的陶坯围住。

1-59（5-82）

再听。斋月结束的那个晚天，
更加美好的月亮升起之前，
　那个老陶坊里我独自站立
和那一排一排的泥众成员。

【解读】

从第 82 首到第 90 首，形成了一组关于陶罐的诗歌，第一版题名 KÚZA-NÁMA.，意为“陶罐章”。我们注意到，在这组诗中菲茨杰拉德的创作成分更多些，他从很多零散的篇章里撷取素材，编辑出情节完整的一组诗来，很像一幕剧作。不过，把被造的人比作被造的陶罐，这在海亚姆名下的《鲁拜集》中是经常出现的。菲茨杰拉德在第 87 首的注释中，详细讲述了文学中的这个比喻。这组诗可以看作鲁拜哲学的一个诗意形象的体现。这一首算是这组诗剧的序幕。

关于“斋月”，加尔各答抄本第 198 首中也有描述（“乐园”本第 409 首）：

他们说斋月的月亮又亮了
此后人不能再流连于酒；
在分离月的月末我要喝很多酒
斋月中我会被发现一直沉醉直到节日（到来）。

这个意思也见于 1207 年抄本第 18 首（“乐园”本第 183 首）。回历八月叫舍尔邦月，意为“分离月”；九月叫赖买丹月，意为“斋月”，这个月全月斋戒。

83

菲译第一版第 64 首，
1913 年版
145 mm × 205 mm

英国插画家、摄影家雷恩 · 布尔（René Bull，1872—1942）的这幅插图主要描绘的是“种种式样和尺寸，大小各异”的陶瓮。插画家以室内的繁花与窗外的台阶、建筑物、弯月丰富了画面。

LXXXIII

Shapes of all Sorts and Sizes, great and small,
That stood along the floor and by the wall;
  And some loquacious Vessels were; and some
Listen'd perhaps, but never talk'd at all.

【校记】——

●一版：无此首。
●二版：列其九十,异文甚多,别出。

II-XC(V- LXXXIII)

And once again there gather'd a scarce heard
Whisper among them; as it were, the stirr'd
  Ashes of some all but extinguisht Tongue,
Which mine ear kindled into living Word.

【校记】——

●三行：五版末怀特所作校记引二版文,句末无逗点；再附于仅见二版诗,此首又重出,句末亦有逗点。

其八十三

坛瓮瓶壶色样齐，
沿墙匝地各高低。
彼方饶舌此倾耳，
妙理沉浮何易稽？

二版其九十

相与私言微若摧，
譬之声熄冷于灰。
我今闻语明如在，
疑是银缸故照来。

83

种种式样和尺寸，大小各异，
全都沿着地靠着墙来站立；
　有些是爱唠叨的器皿，有些
也许一直在听，却绝不吭气。

2-90（5-83）

他们之中又一次聚起呢喃
几乎不能听到；它像是，轻煽
　一些几乎熄灭话语的灰烬，
被我耳朵点亮成活的语言。

【解读】——

第 83 首，以及第 82 首、第 87 首，都和乌斯利抄本第 103 首（加尔各答抄本第 301 首，1207 年抄本第 105 首，“乐园”本第 108 首）有关联：

我昨晚走进陶匠的作坊，
我看见两千个陶罐，一些说话，一些沉默；
突然陶罐的一个激烈地喊叫——
“做陶罐的，买陶罐的，卖陶罐的在哪儿？”

菲茨杰拉德大约是看到这首后，决定将之展开为一幕陶罐的诗剧，这首基本保留了下来，作为序幕后的一个总述。

84

菲译第一版第 34 首
1907 年版
80 mm × 126 mm

这幅插图是英国插画家托马斯·希思·鲁宾逊（Thomas Heath Robinson，约 1869—1950）的作品。画面表现的是诗人正在观赏年老的陶工塑造陶器的情景。

85

菲译第一版第 62 首，
1913 年版
129 mm × 152 mm

英国插画家埃德蒙·约瑟夫·沙利文（Edmund Joseph Sullivan，1869—1933）的这幅插图没有单纯描绘陶罐，而是表现了一位男子举起酒罐开怀畅饮的情景，表现的是第二行诗的诗意。

LXXXIV

Said one among them—"Surely not in vain
"My substance of the common Earth was ta'en
"And to this Figure moulded, to be broke,
"Or trampled back to shapeless Earth again."

【校记】——

●一版：列其六十一；
首行'Said one among them'作'Then said another'；
二行'substance of'作'Substance from',句末有逗点；
三行作'"That He who subtly wrought me into Shape'；
四行作'"Should stamp me back to common Earth again."'。
●二版：列其九十一；
二行同一版；
三行同一版；
四行作'"Should stamp me back to shapeless Earth again?"'。
●三版、四版：二行、三行、四行前均无引号。

LXXXV

Then said a Second—"Ne'er a peevish Boy
"Would break the Bowl from which he drank in joy;
"And He that with his hand the Vessel made
"Will surely not in after Wrath destroy."

【校记】——

●一版：列其六十二；
首行作'Another said— "Why, ne' er a peevish Boy,'；
三行作'"Shall He that *made* the Vessel in pure Love.'；
四行作'"And Fansy, in an after Rage destroy!"'。
●二版：列其九十二；
首行同一版；
二行'Bowl'作'Cup'；
三行作'"Shall He that of his own free Fancy made'；
四行作'"The Vessel, in an after-rage destroy!"'。

其八十四

一云制作岂无功，
拔我凡常泥土中。
旋复成形旋复毁，
蹴回泥土亦何忡？

其八十五

次云彼自手亲为，
孰谓怒来将毁之？
虽是狡童贪渴饮，
一杯犹解缓相持。

84

他们中的一个说——“实非徒然
我那泥土的材质本是平凡
**　选来塑成这样子，再被毁掉，**
或又踩回没有形状的泥团。”

【校记】———
●一版：三行、四行作“他巧妙地把我做成这个形状 / 还会再把我踩回普通的泥团”。
●二版：四行作“还会把我又踩回没有形状的泥团吗？”。

【解读】———
第 84 首出于加尔各答抄本第 293 首（“乐园”本第 13 首）：
这有个杯子它的智慧大声张扬，
为它的美丽在额上给了一百个吻，
这样可爱的杯子，这世界之陶匠
造好了，又把它摔碎在地上。
意思在此前的诗里多次提到，讲造物主并无一个善的目的，一切都是偶然机遇。棋子、马球那些比喻已经很精彩了，如果菲茨杰拉德不拿这首作为诗剧的一个情节，就会减少很多趣味。

从这首开始，借用陶罐之口，真正思考造物主和造物间的问题了。

85

第二个就说——“绝没一个拗怪
孩子会把他欢饮的碗摔坏；
**　他用他的双手做出这器皿**
必不会发怒之后把它毁败。”

【校记】———
●一版：三行、四行作“他做出的器皿出于纯粹的喜爱 / 和迷恋，之后怎会暴怒地毁坏！”。
●二版：二行“碗”作“杯子”；
三行、四行作“他出于自由的迷恋做出的 / 器皿，之后怎会暴怒地毁坏！”。

【解读】———
第 85 首出于乌斯利抄本第 19 首（加尔各答抄本第 64 首）：
他把杯子的元素混合在一起，
喝酒的人不能允许他们打碎，
所有这些头和脚——用他的指尖，
为爱谁他造出它们？——为恨谁他打碎它们？

另外，1207 年抄本第 114 首（“乐园”本第 13 首）后两行、第 135 首（“乐园”本第 182 首）都有类似的说法。很明显，菲茨杰拉德为了写这幕陶罐的诗句，撷取了各种相关材料放入他的场景中，但有时只是利用材料，意思却服从场景的需要。这首跟上一首联结，反驳说，造物者不会随意毁坏他的造物，因此跟原诗的意思就不一致了。

86

菲译第一版第 63 首，
1930 年版
85 mm × 115 mm

匈牙利插画家威利·波加尼（Willy Pogány，1882—1955）的这幅插图描绘了一只丑陋的陶器，它的身形歪歪斜斜。为什么会这样呢？难道是“当时陶匠的手在发抖？”

LXXXVI

After a momentary silence spake
Some Vessel of a more ungainly Make;
    "They sneer at me for leaning all awry:
"What! did the Hand then of the Potter shake?"

【校记】——

●一版：列其六十三；
首行作 'None answer'd this; but after Silence spake'；
二行 'Some' 作 'A',句末作冒号；
三行句末作分号。
●二版：列其九十三；
首行同一版,唯 'Silence' 作 'silence'；
三行句末作分号。

其八十六

时则诸壶默不言，
忽闻窳器苦鸣冤：
『人皆笑我形枯槁，
失手谁于大匠论？』

86

片刻沉静之后一个开了口
那些陶器里它算做得挺丑；
“他们笑我歪歪斜斜地立着；
怎么！当时陶匠的手在发抖？”

【校记】———
●一版：首行之前多“没一个回答这”。

【解读】———
第 86 首，赫荣 - 艾伦说，在加尔各答抄本和乌斯利抄本中，无法找到直接的来源。但他认为，这一首必须和第 88 首放在一起考虑。加尔各答抄本第 69 首有相关的意思：

因为负责者已经安排好自然的元素，
为了什么原因他又分散了他们以致缺失？
如果他们是好的，为什么他要打碎他们？
如果他们变坏了，那好，为什么对这些形式指责？

1207 年抄本第 188 首，虽然没有用陶罐做比喻，但意思和这首及其他几首都很相似。但菲茨杰拉德似乎为了场景的需要，自己添入了这个内容。这里在造物主有无目的的争论间隙中，以造物偶然的美丑，或者放远些说——善恶，再次提出对目的的质疑。

87

菲译第四版第 82 首，
1930 年版
110 mm × 107 mm

匈牙利插画家威利·波加尼（Willy Pogány，1882—1955）绘制插图的 1930 年版《鲁拜集》，是其三个系列之一。这个版本以彩色插图为主，但有许多黑白人像和拟人化的陶器，还有不少装饰图案。对应菲译第四版第 87 首诗的是以花叶为主的装饰图案。这幅陶器插图装饰性强，迥异于其他插图中的陶器形象。

LXXXVII

Whereat some one of the loquacious Lot—
I think a Súfi pipkin—waxing hot—
　“All this of Pot and Potter—Tell me then,
“Who is the Potter, pray, and who the Pot?”

【校记】

●一版：列其六十，异文甚多，别出。
●二版：列其九十四，异文甚多，别出。
●三版：四行作 ‘“Who makes—Who sells—Who buys—Who *is* the Pot? ”’。

【注释】

[1]This Relation of Pot and Potter to Man and his Maker figures far and wide in the Literature of the World, from the time of the Hebrew Prophets to the present; when it may finally take the name of “Pot theism,” by which Mr. Carlyle ridiculed Sterling’s “Pantheism.” My Sheikh, whose knowledge flows in from all quarters, writes to me—

“Apropos of old Omar’s Pots, did I ever tell you the sentence I found in ‘Bishop Pearson on the Creed’? ‘[2]Thus are we wholly at the disposal of His will, and our present and future condition framed and ordered by His free, but wise and just, decrees. *Hath not the potter power over the clay, of the same lump to make one vessel unto honour, and another unto dishonour?* [3] (Rom. ix. 21.) [4]And can that earth-artificer have a freer power over his *brother potsherd* (both being made of the same metal), than God hath over him, who, by the strange fecundity of His omnipotent power, first made the clay out of nothing, and then him out of that?’” [5]

And again—from a very different quarter—“I had to refer the other day to Aristophanes, and came by chance on a curious Speaking-pot story in the Vespæ, which I had quite forgotten.

Φιλοκλέων. Ἄκουε, μὴ φεῦγ᾽ · ἐν Συβάρει γυνή ποτε
l.1435
　　　　κατέαξ᾽ ἐχῖνον.
Κατήγορος.　　　Ταῦτ᾽ ἐγὼ μαρτύρομαι.
Φι.　Οὑχῖνος οὖν ἔχων τιν᾽ ἐπεμαρτύρατο ·
　　Εἶθ᾽ ἡ Συβαρῖτις εἶπεν, εἰ ναὶ τὰν κόραν
　　τὴν μαρτυρίαν ταύτην ἐάσας, ἐν τάχει
　　ἐπίδεσμον ἐπρίω, νοῦν ἂν εἶχες πλείονα.

“The Pot calls a bystander to be a witness to his bad treatment. The woman says, ‘If, by Proserpine, instead of all this ‘testifying’ (comp. Cuddie and his mother in ‘Old Mortality! ’) you would buy yourself a rivet[6], it would show more sense in you! ’ The Scholiast explains *echinus* as ἄγγος τι ἐκ κεράμου.”

One more illustration for the oddity’s sake from the “Autobiography of a Cornish Rector,” by the late James Hamley Tregenna. 1871.

“There was one old Fellow in our Company—he was so like a Figure in the ‘Pilgrim’s Progress’ that Richard always called him the ‘ALLEGORY,’ with a long white beard—a rare Appendage in those days—and a Face the colour of which seemed to have been baked in, like the Faces one used to see on Earthenware Jugs. In our Country-dialect Earthenware is called ‘*Clome*’; so the Boys of the Village used to shout out after him—‘Go back to the Potter, Old Clome-face, and get baked over again.’For the ‘Allegory,’though shrewd enough in most things, had the reputation of being ‘*saift-baked*,’ i.e., of weak intellect.”

【注释校记】

[1] 一版、二版无此注。三版无后二段。
[2] ‘“,三版作 ““”。
[3] 斜体文字,三版加 ““ ””, 四版加 “‘ ’”。
[4] ‘(Rom. ix. 21.)’,三版作 ‘(Rom. ix. 21).’。
[5] ‘”’”,三版作 ‘”’。
[6] ‘rivet’,三版作 ‘trivet’。

I-LX(V- LXXXVII)

And, strange to tell, among that Earthen Lot
Some could articulate, while others not:
    And suddenly one more impatient cried—
"Who *is* the Potter, pray, and who the Pot?"

【校记】

●注释见前。

II-XCIV(V- LXXXVII)

Thus with the Dead as with the Living, *What*?
And *Why*? so ready, but the *Wherefor* not,
    One on a sudden peevishly exclaim'd,
"Which is the Potter, pray, and which the Pot?"

其八十七

时有能言小缶来，
善齐物论语相开：
『若知天下无同异，
窳器何输大匠才？』

【注】——

陶罐、陶匠之与吾人，造物者相媲也，自希伯来先知以来至于今日，见之天下文辞中既久且广也。终有『罐神论』之名，而卡莱尔以之讥斯特林之『泛神论』也。吾之教长，其学博通，尝致吾书云：

『若老奥玛之陶罐，吾未尝示汝吾得之《皮尔森主教信仰论》中者耶？「故吾人全由其志处置，吾当今与将来境况之缔构悉付其独运而睿智、公正之裁。陶匠岂无权柄？于同一土也，或以为贵器或以为贱器。《罗马书》九章二十一节。彼抟土者之于同产之碎陶，盖皆自同质出者，岂不亦有独运之权柄，一若神之于彼？神擅全能之权柄，妙于创作，方自虚无造泥土，复自泥土造彼也。」』

又有得自绝不同之域中者。『他日吾将言阿里斯托芬，偶忆彼《马蜂》剧中有能言陶罐之奇事，而吾久忘之矣。』

陶罐为其恶遇请旁人证。有妇言，以冥后为誓，尔如不与其证，一若《清教徒》中卡迪并其母，市一钉，尤智。注疏者言其罐，是陶匠所制之碗也。

尚有一例尤奇，见已故詹姆斯·哈姆雷·特雷格纳《康沃尔郡教士自传》一八七一页。

『吾同侪中有老者，颇似《天路历程》中一人，故理查德每呼之「寓言」』，蓄长须，尽白，时人中罕有，面色如经焙，盖若吾人常见陶瓯所绘人面也。在吾乡之方言，呼陶器为「克娄」，故村童常逐其后，嬉闹曰：「老克娄面，往陶匠所，再焙之！」是「寓言」虽行事颇狡，而于待焙之名殊乏智数。

一版其六十

颇怪其间语默殊，
一坯不耐奋相呼：
『孰为工匠孰为器，
辨得环中同异无？』

二版其九十四

曰死曰生常有言，
谈因谈果竟无门。
一坯不耐语多躁：
『匠器区区何待论？』

87

在这儿有个话挺多的家伙——
我想是个苏菲小罐——发了火——
“所有这些个陶罐以及陶工——
谁是陶工，谁是陶罐？告诉我。”

【校记】———

●三版：四行作“‘谁做——谁卖——谁买——谁是陶罐？’”。

【注释】———

陶罐和陶匠跟人和造物主的比较关系，从希伯来先知时代到今天，在世界文学中流传既久且广。最后出现了“罐神论”这个名称，卡莱尔还用这个词揶揄斯特林的泛神论。我的教长，具有淹通的学问，写信给我：

“至于老欧玛尔的陶罐，我有没有告诉你我在《皮尔森主教论信仰》一文中发现的那句话？‘我们全由他的意志处置，我们当前和将来境况的缔构和安排全靠他自由却智慧、公正的决裁。陶匠难道没有对陶土的权力，同一块土，或者做出一个高贵的器皿，或者做出一个低贱的？（《罗马书》第9章第21节）制陶者对于他的陶片兄弟（他们都由同样的材料做成）不是有任意的权力，就像神对他？神用无所不能的权力去做奇妙的创造，先从虚无造出泥土，又从泥土造出他。’”

还有个收获，来自很不同的地方。“我在以后的时候会提到阿里斯托芬，偶然想起他的《马蜂》一剧中有个令人惊奇的说话陶罐的故事，但现在完全忘记了。”

陶罐请旁观者给他不幸的遭遇作证。一个妇人说：“以普洛塞尔皮娜起誓，你如果不去作证，（像《清教徒》里卡迪和他的母亲！）就去买个铆钉，在我看来倒是显得更聪明。”学者解释说，那个罐子就是陶匠做的碗。

为了猎奇可以再举个例子，见已故詹姆斯·哈姆雷·特雷格纳之《康沃尔郡教士自传》，第1871页。

在我的朋友里有个老家伙，他那么像《天路历程》里的一个人物，所以理查德总是叫他“寓言”。他留着长长的白胡子，那个年代这是少见的附加物，脸的颜色像经过烘焙，像我们常在陶罐上看到的面孔。在我们的方言里，把陶器叫“克娄”，所以村里的孩子常常在他后面喊叫：“赶快回到陶匠那儿，老克娄脸，再烤一下。”“寓言”在很多事上足够精明，就是对于这个“再烤一下”的名声显得颇乏智数。

1-60（5-87）

说来奇怪，在那堆土罐子中，
有一些能讲，另外一些不能：
**　忽然一个更性急的大声喊：**
“请说说，谁是陶罐，谁是陶工？”

2-94（5-87）

如此对死者一似对生者，什么？
为什么？这样容易，对它却难说，
**　忽然有个暴躁地叫嚷，“请回答，**
哪个是陶匠，哪个又是陶罐呢？”

【解读】———

第 87 首，和第 83 首应该放在一起看，前面已经提到了。这一首的注释很重要，对理解这一组陶罐的诗歌，提供了相当多的参考。

这首诗经过了反复修改，从这些修改痕迹我们看到，这个后来被定性为“苏菲派”的小罐，持一种类似庄子的“齐物论”，美丑、善恶、造的被造的，在它那里都齐同一致了。苏菲派是伊斯兰教的一个神秘主义派别，主张泛神论，认为通过隐修、沉思和禁欲能够达致与神合一。与神合一，那一切也就没有差等了。从这组诗看来，在问题的思考中，苏菲派的主张和那对立的两派都不一样，很难说更接近哪一派。

88

菲译第一版第 64 首，
1941 年版
128 mm × 90 mm

画家戈登·罗斯（Gordon Ross，1872—1946）在这幅插图中主要描绘了一个相貌丑陋的男人。他就是第一行诗中提到的“怪酒保”。陶罐也被做了拟人化的描绘。

LXXXVIII

"Why," said another, "Some there are who tell
"Of one who threatens he will toss to Hell
　"The luckless Pots he marr'd in making—Pish!
"He's a Good Fellow, and 't will all be well."

【校记】

●一版：列其六十四，异文甚多，别出。
●二版：列其九十五，文近一版。
●三版：四行 "t will' 作 "twill'。

I-LXIV、II- XCV(V- LXXXVIII)

Said one—"Folks of a surly Tapster tell,
"And daub his Visage with the Smoke of Hell;
　"They talk of some strict Testing of us—Pish!
"He's a Good Fellow, and 'twill all be well."

【校记】

●二版：首行 'Tapster' 作 'Master'；
三行 'strict Testing' 作 'sharp Trial'。

其八十八

又一前云莫妄疑，
物无美恶不相遗。
谁言地狱将投畀？
直以仁心翊化基。

一版其六十四、二版其九十五

一云地狱取烟尘，
污面来为恶主人。
大任于斯忧不识，
劳其筋骨显诸仁。

88

"什么，"又有一个讲，"一些人说道
有个恐吓说他要往地狱丢掉
　那被他做坏了的不幸陶罐——哼！
他是一个好伙伴，绝不会胡闹。"

1-64、2-95（5-88）

一个说——"人们提起个怪酒保，
用地狱的烟灰把容貌瞎搞；
　都说是要严酷考验我们——哼！
他是一个好伙伴，一切会好。"

【校记】———
●二版：首行"酒保"作"主人"。

【解读】———
第 88 首，赫荣 - 艾伦认为，必须和第 86 首一起看。这一首跟加尔各答抄本第 159 首似有关联：

他们说在复活时会有很多考查，
那位出色的朋友会很忙碌；
来自纯粹善良的只是善，
要开心！因为结局都会很好。

我们大概可以猜测，菲茨杰拉德为了完成这组诗，从各种材料中寻找相近的意思，但都在他的场景里改变了。这首是造物主仁与不仁的争论，只是用到加尔各答抄本讲仁善的内容。

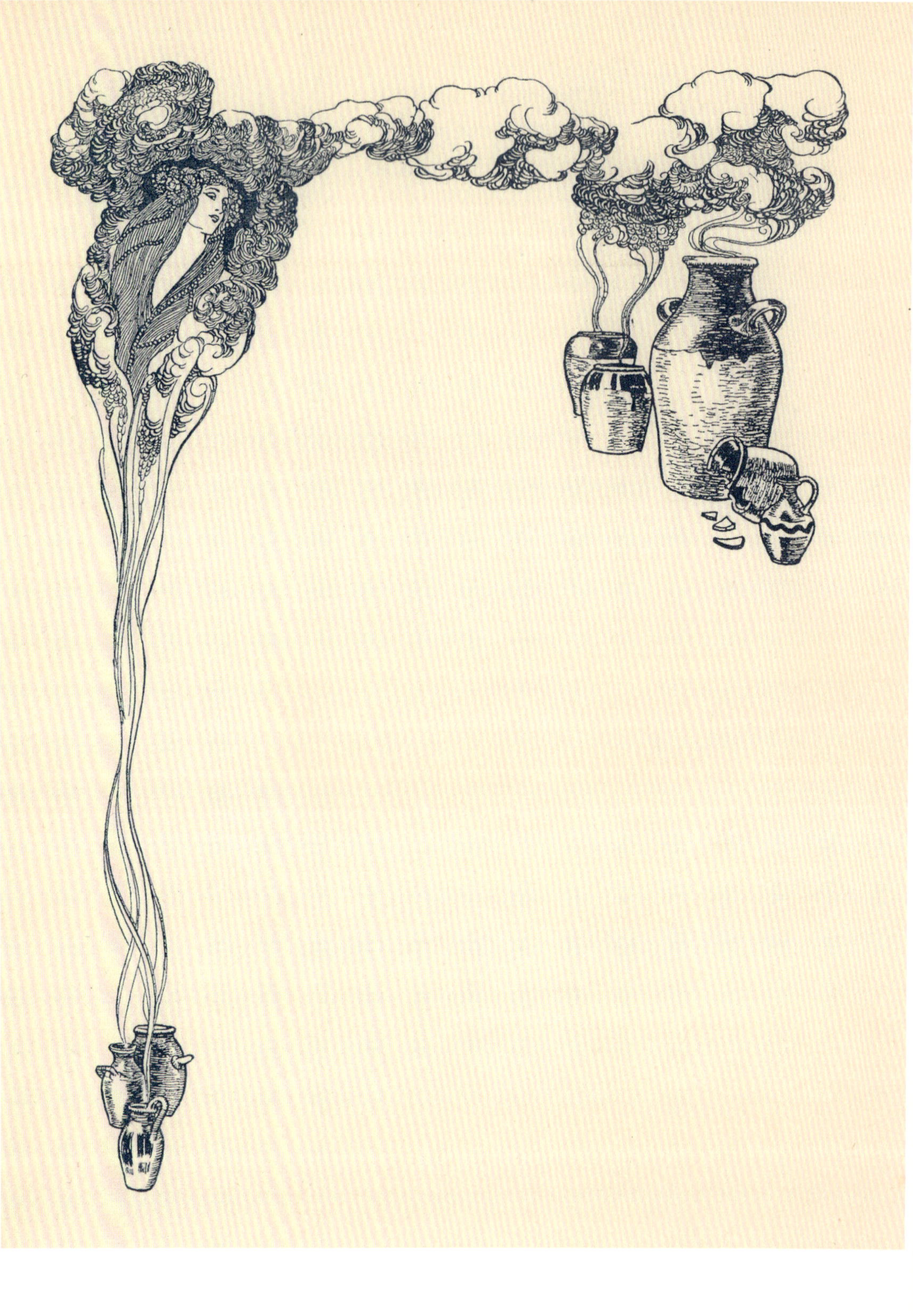

89

菲译第一版第 65 首，
1913 年版
145 mm × 205 mm

英国插画家、摄影家雷恩·布尔（René Bull，1872—1942）在这幅插图中将酒罐里冒出的热气幻化为美女的形象，或许也可以这样理解：画家按诗意描绘了酒罐获得酒浆的滋润而恢复了生命力。

LXXXIX

"Well," murmur'd one, "Let whoso make or buy,
"My Clay with long Oblivion is gone dry:
"But fill me with the old familiar Juice,
"Methinks I might recover by and by."

【校记】

●一版：列其六十五；
首行作 'Then said another with a long-drawn Sigh,'；
二行 'Oblivion' 作 'oblivion'；
三行 'But' 作 'But,'；
四行 'by and by.' 作 'by-and-bye!'。
●二版：列其九十六；
首行作 '"Well," said another, "Whoso will, let try,'；
二行、三行、四行同一版。

其八十九

孰陶孰市一长吁，
久置尘间身欲枯。
但取旧家陈酿到，
顷时沾润得全苏。

89

“好了，”一个嘟囔，“任谁造谁购，
长久弃置，我的土都已干透：
不过，倒进过去熟悉的酒浆，
我想我很快就能恢复如旧。”

【校记】———

●一版：首行作“另一个长叹一声说”。

●二版：首行作“‘好吧，’另一个说，‘谁想，就试，’”。

【解读】———

第 89 首，意思近于加尔各答抄本第 188 首：

在那时我生存的植物被连根拔起，
它的枝条散落在各个方向；
如果他们拿来我尸土做的大酒壶，
当他们把酒注满它就会再次活起来。

以及乌斯利抄本第 116 首（加尔各答抄本第 345 首）：

当我屈身在命运脚下，
我被从生命的希望中连根拔起，
请注意你只是用我的尸土做成酒杯，
或许斟满酒时我会复活。

还有 1207 年抄本第 170 首（“乐园”本第 427 首）的后两行，和上头两首的后两行都一致。菲茨杰拉德全都转用在陶罐上，这个酒能使之复活的意象，将这组诗自然地引向一个美好的结束。当然，更重要的是，这里暗示放弃那些没有结论的争执，在纵酒中实现人生。这是《鲁拜集》最基本的主题。

90

菲译第一版第 66 首，
1913 年版
132 mm × 95 mm

这是英国插画家、摄影家雷恩 · 布尔（René Bull，1872—1942）的作品。他依据诗意在画面前景中描绘了背扛着陶罐的扛酒人和一堆陶罐，陶罐们期待的弯月正在窗边探望。台阶和建筑物巧妙地增加了画面的纵深感。

XC

So while the Vessels one by one were speaking,
The little Moon look'd in that all were seeking:
And then they jogg'd each other, "Brother! Brother!
"Now for the Porter's shoulder-knot a-creaking!"

【校记】

●一版：列其六十六；
二行作 'One spied the little Crescent all were seeking:'；
四行 'Now for' 作 'Hark to'。
●二版：列其九十七；
二行同一版。

【注释】

At the Close of the Fasting Month, Ramazán (which makes the Musulman unhealthy and unamiable), the first Glimpse of the New Moon (who rules their division [1] of the Year) , [2] is looked for with the utmost Anxiety, and hailed with [3] Acclamation. Then it is that the Porter's Knot may be heard—toward the *Cellar*. Omar [4] has elsewhere a pretty Quatrain about the [5] same Moon—

"Be of Good Cheer—the sullen Month will die,
"And a young Moon requite us by and by [6]:
"Look how the Old one meagre, bent, and wan
" With Age and Fast, is fainting from the Sky!"

【注释校记】

[1] 'division',一版、二版作 'Division'。
[2] ') ,',一版作 ')'。
[3] 'with',一版作 'with all'。
[4] '*Cellar*. Omar',一版作 '*Cellar*, perhaps. Old Omar',二版作 '*Cellar*, perhaps. Omar'。
[5] 'the',一版、二版、三版作 'this'。
[6] 'by',一版、二版作 'bye'。

其九十

言时新月露纤纤，
瓮缶纷然引领瞻。
喜若不禁相倚语，
今期担上一声添。

【注】——

斋月每令回教徒众疲弱躁厉，将终，新月彼为分年之度也，之初睹，久跂足待，而今为一欢呼矣。窖中佣夫结束之声亦可闻矣。奥玛别有佳什言此月，曰：『闷时已过可为欢，直待新光贳酒餐。老月不堪成禁断，羸容惨色送将阑。』

90

陶器们正如此一个一个论辩，
都在期待的一弯小月已看见：
**　他们就互相碰撞着，“兄弟！兄弟！**
就等扛酒人吱吱响起的肩垫！”

【校记】———

●一版：二行作“一个人瞄见了所有人都期待的新月”‘One spied the little Crescent all were seeking:’；

四行“就等”作“去听”。

●二版：二行同一版。

【注释】———

在斋月（这总是让穆斯林很虚弱很躁怒）结束的时候，新月（它决定着他们对一年的划分）的第一瞥早被焦急万分地等待，现在可以大声欢呼了。地窖里运酒者捆扎的声音也听到了。欧玛尔关于这同样的月亮还有另外一首很好的四行诗：

开心吧！郁闷的月份将要死去，
新月给我们的补偿不断持续：
　看那一个老的，憔悴，佝偻，惨淡，
被时间和斋戒折磨，奄奄天际！

【解读】———

第 90 首是这组诗的最后一首，来自乌斯利抄本第 158 首：

赖买丹月过去闪瓦鲁月来了，
增长，欢乐，和讲故事的人来了；
“肩上扛瓶”的时候来了，
他们说——因为搬酒的吆喝着来了。

闪瓦鲁月是回历十月，意为猎月，前一月就是斋月。黄杲炘先生注释说：“伊斯兰教历（阴历）九月封斋后第二十九天黄昏时，如望见新月，第二天就开斋，否则便推迟一天。因此急于开斋的穆斯林等待新月的心情十分殷切。”菲茨杰拉德用这个期待，把这组诗的尾声置于欢快的氛围里，也让主题的表达显得很乐观。

菲茨杰拉德注释里引的那首鲁拜，来自加尔各答抄本第 218 首（1207 年抄本第 183 首，“乐园”本第 305 首）：

要开心！因为你节日的月亮要来了，
欢乐的办法都是吉庆的；
这个月亮已经变得憔悴，佝偻和惨淡，
你会说它在忧苦之中沉落。

91

菲译第一版第 67 首，
1913 年版
128 mm × 136 mm

英国插画家埃德蒙·约瑟夫·沙利文（Edmund Joseph Sullivan，1869—1933）的这幅插图，描绘了生命消逝的“我”被包裹着青翠的葡萄叶放进挖好的坟坑中的情景。

92

菲译第一版第 68 首，
1930 年版
126 mm × 183 mm

匈牙利插画家威利·波加尼（Willy Pogány，1882—1955）在此描绘了墓地的情景。远景中的人物就是诗中说的路过此地的“信徒”或“信士”。

XCI

Ah, with the Grape my fading Life provide,
And wash the Body whence the Life has died,
　And lay me, shrouded in the living Leaf,
By some not unfrequented Garden-side.

【校记】——
●一版：列其六十七；
二行‘the Body’作‘my Body’；
三行作‘And in a Windingsheet of Vine-leaf wrapt,’；
四行作‘So bury me by some sweet Garden-side.’。
●二版：列其九十八；
二行同一版。
●诸版诗后俱有分隔号。

XCII

That ev'n my buried Ashes such a snare
Of Vintage shall fling up into the Air
　As not a True-believer passing by
But shall be overtaken unaware.

【校记】——
●一版：列其六十八；
首行‘snare’作‘Snare’；
二行‘Vintage’作‘Perfume’,句末有逗点；
三行‘True-believer’作‘True Believer’。
●二版：列其一百；
二行句末有逗点。

其九十一

葡萄佳酿请先陈，
一日云殂用洗身。
其叶菁菁相就殓，
不妨葬近满园春。

其九十二

瘗骨成灰正未甘，
葡萄生出蔓先覃。
中天网得圣徒在，
相视欣欣殊不谙。

91

啊，为我凋谢的生命备酒浆，
好去清洗身躯当生命消亡，
埋葬我，用那新鲜叶子裹好，
葬在并非少有人来的园旁。

【校记】

●一版：三行、四行作“裹进葡萄叶的尸布 / 埋我在那些美好的花园边上”。

【解读】

第 91 首来自加尔各答抄本第 12 首（1207 年抄本第 171 首，“乐园”本第 553 首）：

当我死了用酒来洗净我，
拿着纯粹的酒诵读我的葬礼仪文；
如果你希望你能在复活日看到我
你一定要在酒馆门口的泥土里寻找我。

以及乌斯利抄本第 69 首（加尔各答抄本第 158 首，1207 年抄本第 82 首，“乐园”本第 189 首）：

记得把我和酒杯留在一起，
我黄褐色的脸就会像红宝石一般；
当我死了，用酒来洗净我，
用葡萄藤木做我棺材的板子。

但菲茨杰拉德表达得更意气风发，更有神采。这是他那个世界和时代的风格，再不可能回到质朴的古代东方了。

92

那么就算我已然埋骨成灰
也把葡萄网罗向空中抛飞
不会只有一个路过的信士
要被它不知不觉地牵了回。

【校记】

●一版：二行“葡萄”作“酒香”。

【解读】

第 92 首来自加尔各答抄本第 14 首（“乐园”本第 246 首）：

我要喝下这么多的酒以致酒香
会从泥土中透出当我身在其下；
当有酒徒在我身体之上经过，
他会沉醉且在我的酒香中迷失。

酒香变成了葡萄藤的网罗，更有画面感，也更显得华丽夺目。这是风格转变的又一个例子。

这两首写纵酒写到身后，前一首流连，要用酒去洗、用葡萄藤去裹自己的尸身，后一首倔强，要去诱使信士就范，把无奈和淡淡的哀怨掩盖住。

93

菲译第一版第 69 首，
1909 年版
115 mm × 173 mm

这是匈牙利插画家威利·波加尼（Willy Pogány，1882—1955）的作品。画面中一群人在富丽堂皇的宫殿前施施而行。前景中的一对男女正弹琴歌唱，画面右下角的陶罐寓示着美酒，表现的正是第三行和第四行诗句的意思。

XCIII

Indeed the Idols I have loved so long
Have done my credit in this World much wrong:
  Have drown'd my Glory in a shallow Cup,
And sold my Reputation for a Song.

【校记】——

●一版：列其六十九；
二行 'credit in this World' 作 'Credit in Men's Eye'；
三行 'Glory' 作 'Honour'。
●二版：列其一百〇一；
二行 'credit in this World' 作 'credit in Men's eye'。
●三版：二行同二版。

其九十三

长向樽前中圣贤，
人间名誉转难全。
一杯足使浮荣没，
一曲拼教令闻捐。

93

真的，我热爱了这么久的偶像
贻误了我在这个世界的声望：
淹没我的光荣在浅浅的杯中，
还出卖我的体面为一声低唱。

【校记】———

●一版：二行"这个世界"作"人们眼里"；三行"光荣"作"荣誉"。

●二版、三版：二行同一版。

【解读】———

第93首，据赫荣－艾伦说，来自加尔各答抄本第170首：

当我的心情倾向于祈祷和斋戒，
我说所有我的救赎都获得了。
啊！那些净礼都让我的快乐毁了，
我的斋戒也让半杯酒勾销。

不过内容还是颇有距离的，倒是他提及的乌斯利抄本第22首（加尔各答抄本第59首，"乐园"本第433首）的最后一句：

希望的掮客只是为了一首歌就出卖了他。

还能见出些痕迹。乌斯利抄本第22首已经被菲茨杰拉德引入序言，不过，在那里，"song"（歌）变成了"nothing"（无），"乐园"本也没有提到"歌"，而前三行基本一致。更接近的倒是"乐园"本第225首（1207年抄本第106首）：

我出卖了国君之冕和王侯之冠，
缠头巾换得一曲笛声婉转。
拿念珠——这伪善者的标记，
痛痛快快换取美酒一碗。（张鸿年、宋丕方译文）

以及1207年抄本第181首（"乐园"本第270首）的后两行：

我以拜垫换取一杯美酒，
荣辱的瓶儿摔到石上，任它粉身碎骨。（张鸿年译文）

这首从倔强更进一步，显得傲世慢俗，也更动人。

94

菲译第一版第 70 首，
1910 年版
122 mm × 185 mm

英国画家尤恩·盖迪斯（Ewan Geddes，1866—1935）的这幅插图，描绘了一对身着亮丽衣服的恋人在鲜花盛开的草地上漫步的情景。画面展示了诗歌中提到的春天和玫瑰。

95

菲译第一版第 71 首，
1913 年版
128 mm × 136 mm

英国插画家埃德蒙·约瑟夫·沙利文（Edmund Joseph Sullivan，1869—1933）在此描绘了诗人向酒家买酒的情景，卖酒者被表现为一具骷髅的形象。

第九十四首

XCIV

Indeed, indeed, Repentance oft before
I swore—but was I sober when I swore?
And then and then came Spring, and Rose-in-hand
My thread-bare Penitence apieces tore.

【校记】——

●一版：列其七十。
●二版：列其一百〇二。

第九十五首

XCV

And much as Wine has play'd the Infidel,
And robb'd me of my Robe of Honour—Well,
I wonder often what the Vintners buy
One half so precious as the stuff they sell.

【校记】——

●一版：列其七十一；
二行 'Well' 作 'well'；
三行 'wonder often' 作 'often wonder'；
四行 'stuff' 作 'Goods'。
●二版：列其一百〇三；
三行同一版；
四行 'stuff' 作 'ware'。

其九十四

人生多悔誓多申，
只向从前梦梦身。
谁复单丝牵一忏？
万花盈手正临春。

其九十五

行既湎淫名既诬，
事犹不解酒家胡。
卿来卖此忘忧物，
一世欢颜买得无？

94

真的，真的，以前经常地悔罪
我发誓——我发誓时可曾喝醉？
**　然后春天一来临，玫瑰在手**
我那褴褛的忏悔纷纷撕碎。

【解读】———

第 94 首译自加尔各答抄本第 431 首（“乐园”本第 318 首）：

每天我都决心晚上要作忏悔，
为了满溢的杯盏做忏悔；
现在玫瑰的季节来了，我不能忧伤
在玫瑰的季节为了忏悔赐我愧疚吧，哦主！

面对行乐和信仰，偶然也会出现摇摆，海亚姆表达得很坦率，反而更觉得有力度，不时让我们想到陶渊明，——“贫富常交战，道胜无戚颜”。(《咏贫士》七首其一）

95

虽说酒扮演了无信仰的角色，
还把我名誉的外衣剥夺——不错，
**　我还是经常疑惑酒家买什么**
才把他所卖东西的一半抵过。

【解读】———

第 95 首译自乌斯利抄本第 62 首（加尔各答抄本第 196 首，“乐园”本第 308 首）：

虽然酒撕破了我（名声）的面纱，
只要我有灵魂，我就不会和酒分开；
我对卖葡萄酒的总是感到困惑，因为他们——
他们买的什么能比他们卖的更好？

这是对酒的价值的又一个表达，很容易引起共鸣，对于英语读者、中国读者都一样。

96

菲译第一版第 72 首，
1958 年版
125 mm × 203 mm

约翰·扬·贝特曼（John Yung Bateman，活跃期 1946—1958）在这幅插图中描绘了俊男、美女、鲜花、芳草、小鹿、夜莺、诗卷等意象。整个画面洋溢着春天的气息，但所画的夜莺更像是鸽子。

97

菲译第一版第 38 首，
1909 年版
114 mm × 176 mm

匈牙利插画家威利·波加尼（Willy Pogány，1882—1955）的这幅作品，描绘了在沙漠中行进的驼队和珍贵的泉水，整个画面虽朦胧却富有层次感。这幅插图是为菲译第一版第 38 首所绘，但也表现了第五版第 97 首诗的意象。

第九十六首

XCVI

Yet Ah, that Spring should vanish with the Rose!
That Youth's sweet-scented manuscript should close!
The Nightingale that in the branches sang,
Ah whence, and whither flown again, who knows!

【校记】

●一版：列其七十二；
首行 'Yet Ah,' 作 'Alas,'；
二行 'manuscript' 作 'Manuscript'；
三行 'branches' 作 'Branches'；
四行 'Ah' 作 'Ah,'。
●二版：列其一百〇四。

第九十七首

XCVII

Would but the Desert of the Fountain yield
One glimpse—if dimly, yet indeed, reveal'd,
To which the fainting Traveller might spring,
As springs the trampled herbage of the field!

【校记】

●一版：无此首。
●二版：列其一百〇五；
二行 'indeed,' 作 'indeed'；
三行 'To' 作 'Toward'。

其九十六

花自飘零春自归，
锦年香稿掩依依。
枝头听得莺啼尽，
谁晓去来何处飞？

其九十七

疲人一瞥起相招，
沙自茫茫泉自遥。
应似牧场青草偃，
百蹄过尽复扬翘。

96

啊，春天带着玫瑰去无踪迹！
韶年的芳馨篇页也将掩闭！
**　那在树枝之间欢唱的夜莺，**
谁知道，哪里飞来，何处飞去！

【解读】———

第 96 首译自加尔各答抄本第 223 首（1207 年抄本第 12 首，“乐园”本第 157 首）：

啊！青春的书卷已经叠起？
这新鲜的红紫之春被冬天侵袭；
那欢乐之鸟，名字叫青春，
啊！我不知它何时飞来何时飞去。

如果不读原诗，很难理解菲茨杰拉德的“夜莺”究竟何指。在翻译时，受到目的语自身的各种限制，对来源语表达不够醒豁，是常有的情况。

97

沙漠里能把泉水踪迹瞥见——
哪怕尚微茫，只要真的，出现，
**　虚弱的行人也会跃起而往，**
像是踩倒的牧草跃起地面！

【解读】———

第 97 首，赫荣－艾伦说，来自加尔各答抄本第 509 首：

哦！希望有个休息的地方，
或者我们会走到路的尽头；
将来自地心，在十万年后，
我们都希望能像青葱植物一样再次绽放。

实际上并没有意义上的对应。菲茨杰拉德的意思大概是说，眼前的生命远比荒芜的信仰更是迫切的愿望所在。

98

菲译第五版第 98 首，
约 1920 年
82 mm × 127 mm

这是美国画家约翰·沃森·戴维斯（John Watson Davis，1870—1959）的作品。画面中发须花白的书吏一手执羽毛笔，一手握纸卷，若有所思。天使的手搭在书吏的手腕上，寓示着“另外再写，或者，把字迹完全涂抹严实”。

XCVIII

Would but some wingéd Angel ere too late
Arrest the yet unfolded Roll of Fate,
　And make the stern Recorder otherwise
Enregister, or quite obliterate!

【校记】

●一版：无此首。
●二版：列其一百〇六，异文甚多，别出。

II-CVI(V- XCVIII)

Oh if the World were but to re-create,
That we might catch ere closed the Book of Fate,
　And make The Writer on a fairer leaf
Inscribe our names, or quite obliterate!

其九十八

天使翩翩舒翼来，
金縢密册尚全开。
不闻簿吏矜严酷，
笔削相烦曷敢推。

二版其一百〇六

乾坤开辟得重期，
尚及天书未掩时。
名字欲添新样纸，
或央簿吏径除之。

98

只盼有翼天使们别来太迟
赶在命运书卷还没合上时，
　让那严格的书记另外再写，
或者，把字迹完全涂抹严实。

2-106（5-98）

哦如果世界还是能够重造，
命运之书掩卷前我们赶到，
　就让书写人在那新的一页
写上我们的名字，或全删掉！

【解读】

第 98 首，在第二版里更近于波斯原文，赫荣 - 艾伦认为来自尼古拉斯版第 457 首：

我愿主能够完全改变世界，
他应该现在就做，我就能看到他做了；
要么他从卷子上把我的名字划掉，
要么把我的状况从缺乏提升到充足。

菲茨杰拉德后来的改写增添了天使，不提再造世界，也许会让有基督教背景的英国人更容易亲近。

99

菲译第一版第 73 首，
1913 年版
166 mm × 211 mm

这首诗表达了希望天公或造物主能改弦更张，由人自己来安排命运的愿望。英国插画家、摄影家雷恩·布尔（René Bull，1872—1942）描绘了一对恋人在花园中相拥，男士仰望苍穹、若有所思的情景。这幅插图的画面体现了布尔作品的典型构图和风格。

XCIX

Ah Love! could you and I with Him conspire
To grasp this sorry Scheme of Things entire,
Would not we shatter it to bits—and then
Re-mould it nearer to the Heart's Desire!

【校记】

●一版：列其七十三；
首行‘you’作‘thou’，‘Him’作‘Fate’。
●二版：列其一百〇八；
首行‘Him’作‘Fate’。
●三版、四版、五版诗后有分隔号。

其九十九

悯此不仁予美呼，
一同造化运灵枢。
政须宇宙俱颠覆，
始得从心铸作殊。

99

啊我爱，要是你我能跟他协力
去掌握万物所有的可悲设计，
**　我们岂不会把它砸碎——再把它**
重新塑造了好接近心中所欲！

【校记】———
●一版：首行“他”作“命运”。

【解读】———
第 99 首译自加尔各答抄本第 395 首（1207 年抄本第 228 首，“乐园”本第 47 首）：

我要是，像主般，控制了天，
难道我不把天全都消除，
难道我不从头再创造另外的天
因为，自由，每个人都能按照内心的愿望获得它？

这首菲茨杰拉德没有迁就，根据波斯原诗正面写重造世界，显得极有决断。由于诗中激荡着近于革命的热情，自五四运动以来，菲译在中国早已成为名作。

100

菲译第一版第 74 首，
1922 年版
146 mm × 190 mm

英国插画家安妮·哈丽特·菲胥（Anne Harriet Fish，1890—1964）的这幅插图用大面积的紫色来衬托弯月，显得清冷、孤寂，闺阁中的女子似乎正在穿针引线。诗人、画家寓情于景，表达了对生命易逝的无奈和怅惘。

C

Yon rising Moon that looks for us again—
How oft hereafter will she wax and wane;
  How oft hereafter rising look for us
Through this same Garden—and for *one* in vain!

【校记】——

●一版：列其七十四,异文甚多,别出。
●二版：列其一百〇九,异文甚多,别出。

I-LXXIV(V- C)

Ah, Moon of my Delight who know'st no wane,
The Moon of Heav'n is rising once again:
  How oft hereafter rising shall she look
Through this same Garden after me—in vain!

II-ClX(V- C)

But see! The rising Moon of Heav'n again
Looks for us, Sweet-heart, through the quivering Plane:
  How oft hereafter rising will she look
Among those leaves—for one of us in vain!

其一百

明月寻人夜夜来，
盈虚不改此追陪。
凄凉知有谁相遇？
只向空园照冷杯。

一版其七十四

所欢明月几曾虚？
又向中天光景舒。
从此园林多遍照，
年年只是不逢予。

二版其一百〇九

同看寻人月色来，
梧桐影里漫徘徊。
明朝万一成孤另，
叶叶枝枝空照哀。

100

那边升起的月亮又寻找我们——
此后她还会多少次圆缺晴阴；
　还会多少次升起把我们寻找
寻遍这同样的园子，——再无一人！

1-74（5-100）

啊，可知我欢乐的明月长圆，
天空的明月再次升起眼前：
　此后她还会多少次升起来
寻遍这同样的园子——是徒然！

2-109（5-100）

但是看！我爱，天上月亮又升
来找我们，穿过扶疏的梧桐：
　此后她还会几度升到叶间——
寻找我们中的一个也成空。

【解读】——

第 100 首出自乌斯利抄本第 5 首（加尔各答抄本第 7 首，“乐园”本第 47 首）：

因为没有人为你保证明天，
你现在就让这颗痴情的心快乐吧；
在月光中喝酒，哦月，因为这月
将会长久寻找我们，又不会找到我们。

菲茨杰拉德做了很多次修改，看来他非常喜欢这一首。他刻意把这首放在第 100 首的位置，跟第 1 首形成一个对应：太阳升起和月亮升起的对应，从梦里醒来和人离去的对应，——昭示着一个循环要结束了。

101

菲译第五版第 101 首，
1900 年版
78 mm × 115 mm

英国插画家吉尔伯特·詹姆斯（Gilbert James，1865—1941）的这幅插图表现的是“酹酒于地”的情景。这股红的酒显然是葡萄酒。远处的建筑和酒姬的装扮都是东方式的风格。这幅图创作于1896 年，最初的是黑白版，但细节与彩图有些差异。

CI

And when like her, oh Sákí, you shall pass
Among the Guests Star-scatter'd on the Grass,
　And in your joyous errand reach the spot
Where I made One—turn down an empty Glass!

TAMAM.

【校记】——

●一版：列其七十五；
首行作‘And when Thyself with shining Foot shall pass’；
三行作‘And in thy joyous Errand reach the Spot’；
四行‘One’作‘one’。
●二版：列其一百一十；
首行作‘And when Yourself with silver Foot shall pass’。
●三版：首行‘Sákí’作‘Sáki’，
五版末怀特所作校记引三版初稿此行作‘And when Yourself with silver step shall pass’；
三行‘joyous’作‘blissful’。
●一版：‘TAMAM.’作‘TAMÁM SHUD.’。
●二版、三版、四版：‘TAMAM’作‘TAMÁM’。

其一百〇一

谁伴名园露饮来，
翩如星里月徘徊。
欢时请向凄凉处，
为我殷勤酹一杯。

101

啊，行觞人，你如像她一样穿过
在那草地上如星散开的宾客，
在你愉快的差使中到了那里
有我的一席之地——请把酒倾落！

【校记】———

●一版：首行作“当你自己迈着闪闪的双足经过”。

●二版：首行作“当你自己迈着银足经过”。

●三版：首行，五版末怀特所作校记引三版初稿作“当你自己迈着银步经过”。

【解读】———

第 101 首出自乌斯利抄本第 83 首：

朋友，当你们一起聚会，
这是应该的，你们热切地想起你们的朋友；
当你们一起喝着可致健康的酒，
轮到我时，请把（杯子）翻个个儿。

和乌斯利抄本第 84 首：

朋友们，当你们相约聚会，
在彼此倾心中作乐，
当持杯人把穆护之酒拿在手里（轮着）斟遍，
在你祝福时记着某个无助的人。

穆护，是古代伊朗的琐罗亚斯德教教职人员的称呼。“乐园”本第 502 首也有类似的叙写。

菲茨杰拉德把这首诗作为最后一首，以日出始，以辞世终，却用酒贯穿了终始，甚至贯穿到了辞世之后。然而死亡毕竟是归宿，没有乐园，没有来生，再乐观，再夸大，也掩饰不了内在的哀伤。如同菲茨杰拉德在序文里所说：“不管如何，这结果是足够伤感的，……他徒然努力想让自己的脚步摆脱命运，能赶上真正瞥见明天，可还是跌回了今天（这今天比很多的明天都要长！）。那是他唯一可以立足的地方，尽管也很快会从他脚下溜走。”

删稿

Deleted Manuscript

1-37 菲译第一版第 37 首，
1913 年版
129 mm × 160 mm

英国插画家埃德蒙·约瑟夫·沙利文（Edmund Joseph Sullivan，1869—1933）用生动的形象表现了诗中倒酒和时间的意象。旷野中的仪器表明了画中人物的身份。

I-XXXVII

Ah, fill the Cup:—what boots it to repeat
How Time is slipping underneath our Feet:
  Unborn To-morrow, and dead Yesterday,
Why fret about them if To-day be sweet!

1-37

啊，倒满杯子：——那样只会失落
反复地讲时光从脚下溜过：
** 未生的明日，和已死的昨日，**
它们何须忧如果今日欢乐！

一版其三十七

来将美酒满吾杯，
莫恨光阴去不回。
后日未生前日死，
那妨今日笑颜开？

【解读】———

第一版第 37 首出自已经在第 57 首中引过的乌斯利抄本第 20 首（加尔各答抄本第 22 首，“乐园”本第 140 首）后两行，这里根据阿伯里译出全诗：

如河中之水原上之风，
我生命流转的另外一天又已过去：
从来没有为了两个日子的忧虑住我心中——
还没来的日子，已过去的日子。

还有乌斯利抄本第 17 首（加尔各答抄本第 84 首）的后两行：

你不能说昨天，那逝去的，是甜美的，
要开心不要说昨天，因为今天是甜美的。

这个主题在《鲁拜集》里反复讲到，比如，“乐园”本第 113 首（1207 年抄本第 200 首）也讲到。也许菲茨杰拉德为避免重复，后来删去了。

1-45

菲译第一版第 45 首，
1913 年版
121 mm × 118 mm

英国插画家、摄影家雷恩·布尔（René Bull，1872—1942）的这幅插图，表现了三位智者正在争辩的情景。堆着的书籍和仪器，表明了智者的博学多才。

I-XLV

But leave the Wise to wrangle, and with me
The Quarrel of the Universe let be:
　And, in some corner of the Hubbub coucht,
Make Game of that which makes as much of Thee.

1-45

但是让那些智者自去争辩，
让我跟着宇宙的争执相伴：
　而在某个喧嚣的角落躺下，
去和那些谑笑你的对着干。

一版其四十五

智如相辩即成讹，
天地不和吾与和。
嚣内一隅箕踞坐，
戏从肝胆起风波。

【解读】———

第一版第 45 首，赫荣－艾伦认为没有准确对应的波斯原诗，阿伯里说，加尔各答抄本第 71 首可能有些帮助：

没必要在每扇门前胡言乱语，
必要的是设法应对时间的善与恶；
从天堂的碗里拿出命运的一对骰子
不论（它们）出现什么样的点色，都有必要去玩。

还说，“喧嚣”一词一定是想到了《萨拉曼和阿布萨尔》里库尔德的故事，第四页那个问自己的人说：

在所有这些喧嚣中我该怎样，
醒来时再认识我自己？

阿伯里这些引述都和菲茨杰拉德的译文有着相当的距离。1207 年抄本第 204 首（“乐园”本第 155 首）的后两行：

觅一隅之地安然静处，
冷眼旁观人间冬夏春秋。

似乎意思更为相近。这一首稍嫌玄奥，不知道是不是因此后来被删去。赫荣－艾伦认为，删去的原因大概是没有对应的波斯原诗，但这似乎不成为理由，因为在菲译里，好几首都没有对应的波斯原诗。

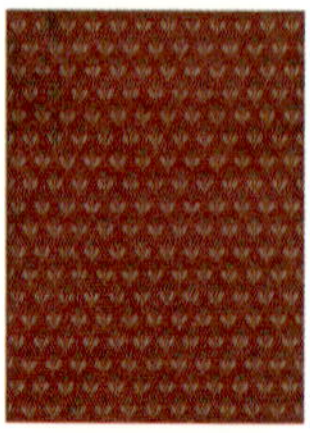

2–14 菲译第一版插图，
1955 年版
76 mm × 106 mm

这幅插图具有波斯细密画的风格，华美而细腻，富有装饰性。画面中男士跪地，给站着的女士献酒，而女士则给男士献花，呈现出祥和温馨的气氛。

II-XIV

Were it not Folly, Spider-like to spin
The Thread of present Life away to win—
　What? for ourselves, who know not if we shall
Breathe out the very Breath we now breathe in!

2-14

还不愚蠢,像蜘蛛一样织着
眼前的生命之丝去换什么?
**　啊? 我们自己,都不知道是否**
将呼出的气就是正吸进的!

二版其十四

效彼蜘蛛宁不愚,
生丝命缕费工夫。
吾人日夜劳呼吸,
气息方同知得无?

【解读】——

第二版第 14 首,来自乌斯利抄本第 136 首(加尔各答抄本第 504 首,1207 年抄本第 245 首,"乐园"本第 192 首):

我们还要烦恼多久为了我有的或没有的,
我们要轻松地度过此生还是不呢?
倒满酒杯,因为我不知道
我是否还能吐出我吸入的这口气。

在波斯文的鲁拜里,气息的呼吸被经常提到,比如,1207 年抄本第 177 首("乐园"本第 122 首)。

2–28

菲译第一版第 72 首，
1909 年版
103 mm × 133 mm

英国插画家吉尔伯特·詹姆斯（Gilbert James，1865—1941）的这幅插图中有大量的红花和白花。男士手拿书籍，若有所思，而女士则手握蔷薇花，正沉醉在花香中。

II-XXVIII

Another Voice, when I am sleeping, cries,
"The Flower should open with the Morning skies."
　And a retreating Whisper, as I wake—
"The Flower that once has blown for ever dies."

2-28

另一个声音，当我睡时，响亮，
"花朵要跟着晨色一起开放。"
**　又是渐远的低语，在我醒来——**
"花朵一度盛开了永成凋丧。"

二版其二十八

睡里先闻传语来，
花颜应逐晓天开。
不知争发终何益？
一寸春心一寸灰。

【解读】———

第二版第 28 首，赫荣 - 艾伦认为在第四版、第五版里被第 63 首换掉了，它们的来源相同。我赞同他这个观点，不过 1207 年抄本第 232 首，在形式上有相近之处：

蔷薇说：我是埃及优素福，在草坪憩息，
我的嘴如同镶着金边的红玉。
我说：你是优素福有何为证？
她答：看，这不是那件被撕碎的衬衣！（张鸿年译文）

也许给了菲茨杰拉德内容之外的启发？

2-44

菲译第二版第 44 首，
1910 年版
174 mm × 223 mm

法裔英籍插画家埃德蒙·杜拉克（Edmund Dulac，1882—1953）这幅插图主要描绘了在花园中相拥的一对恋人。人物的装扮是东方风格的。花园中还有耐旱的仙人掌、剑麻等植物。对于欧洲读者来说，这幅插图充满了异域风情。

II-XLIV

Do you, within your little hour of Grace,
The waving Cypress in your Arms enlace,
  Before the Mother back into her arms
Fold, and dissolve you in a last embrace.

2-44

你呢，尚在短暂的恩宠之中，
手臂缠住如波的丝发青青，
** 趁大地母亲把你抱入手臂**
之前，先消融在这最后一拥。

二版其四十四

应知天眷不多时，
挽起青青柔发丝。
未及坤灵先揽入，
终身一拥且销之。

【解读】———

第二版第 44 首，相近于加尔各答抄本第 189 首的头两行：

要开心！因为时间会到来
（当）所有的身体被埋在地下。

和加尔各答抄本第 195 首：

我全部的心情都在对玫瑰般红颜的投合，
我的手总是抓着酒杯；
我从（我的）每个部分中提取它分派的作用，
直到（我的）那些部分和一切混同。

但都不是很接近。菲茨杰拉德的译文很有惨怖之象，也许因此后来被删掉了。

2–65 菲译第四版第 40 首，1930 年版
127 mm × 183 mm

匈牙利插画家威利·波加尼（Willy Pogány，1882—1955）的这幅作品前景色彩艳丽，表现的是在美人陪伴下饮酒欢乐的场面，“醇酒妇人即是天堂”。

II-LXV

If but the Vine and Love-abjuring Band
Are in the Prophet's Paradise to stand,
　Alack, I doubt the Prophet's Paradise
Were empty as the hollow of one's Hand.

2-65

如果没有醇酒妇人的那帮
别的都去占据先知的天堂，
**　悲夫，我会怀疑先知的天堂**
就是虚无如同把空拳一张。

二版其六十五

先知苦说竟何功？
无酒无欢兴已穷。
若此天堂宁待问，
张拳一看是空空。

【解读】———

第二版第 65 首来自乌斯利抄本第 127 首：
喝酒并在美人的陪伴下厮混
好过去实行狂热者的虚伪；
如果情人和酒徒注定下地狱，
就没有人能看到天堂的面目。

赫荣－艾伦认为，这首被尼古拉斯版第 64 首提示，来自加尔各答抄本第 60 首（1207 年抄本第 165 首，“乐园”本第 343 首）：
他们说酒徒要下地狱，
这是让人厌恶的信条，心里不能相信；
如果喝醉的情人注定下地狱，
明天天堂将空得如同手掌。
“乐园”本第 338 首大致意思也一样，不过表达不同。

根据菲茨杰拉德的序文，他对原文里经常出现的“饮酒和作乐”的内容宁愿保存得更少一些，这首透露出醇酒妇人即是天堂的意思，似乎颇为出格，就删去了。

2–77

菲译第一版第 27 首，
1910 年版
40 mm × 94 mm

这是英国插画家莫里斯·格莱芬哈根（Maurice Greiffenhagen，1862—1931）为菲译第一版第 27 首所配的插图。作品描绘了正在高谈阔论的贤哲们，一位年轻男子正闻着玫瑰花香，听他们在谈论。画面中的服饰和建筑物表明这是在古代波斯。玫瑰也是《鲁拜集》中常出现的意象。

II-LXXVII

For let Philosopher and Doctor preach
Of what they will, and what they will not—each
　Is but one Link in an eternal Chain
That none can slip, nor break, nor over-reach.

2-77

就让哲人和博士们去训诫
他们愿意和不愿意的一切——
**　每个只是永恒链条上一环，**
不能脱节，也不能断掉、逾越。

二版其七十七

且教贤哲道相传，
称意违心只未全。
一节枉从长索觅，
无逾无脱守无愆。

【解读】———
第二版第 77 首，很难找到波斯文的来源。
也许菲茨杰拉德把西方学术中提到的“存在之链”的观念引了进来，后来又觉得过于“归化”，就删除了。

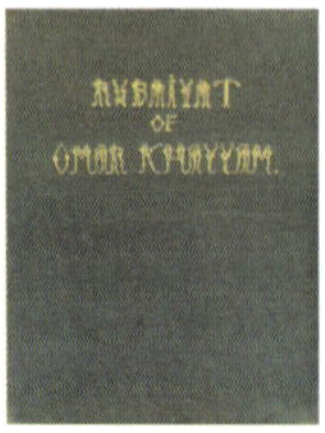

2-86

菲译第一版第 27 首，
1914 年版
172 mm × 220 mm

印度画家梅拉·塞特（Mara Sett）描绘了一群或谈玄或冥想的人。他们或微笑，或沉思或怒目。这幅插图画面中的凤凰和孔雀表明这是东方式的聚会或筵席。

II-LXXXVI

Nay, but, for terror of his wrathful Face,
I swear I will not call Injustice Grace;
　Not one Good Fellow of the Tavern but
Would kick so poor a Coward from the place.

2-86

不，但是，就算他的怒容吓人，
我立誓不把不公正当施恩；
**　没有一个酒店里的好伙伴**
不把这种卑微懦夫踢出门。

二版其八十六

落落由他怒目瞋，
岂将大伪唤为真？
筵前宾客多刚直，
正怕相逢骂座人。

【解读】———

第二版第 86 首来自加尔各答抄本第 8 首：

没有人像他被同胞所唾弃，
（同时）包括好人也怕他的恶意。
如果一个酒徒在慷慨上表现出不情愿，
他所有的酒友都会认为他是个鄙夫。

恐怕和“乐园”本第 432 首也有些关联：

与贫人为伍，但要像帝王般自尊，
扫去阴霾，拂去心上的愁云。
与酒肆的常客交游为友，
我行我素，认清自己是何等人。（张鸿年、宋丕方译文）

这首在菲译里，风格罕见的豪放，不知是不是不符合菲茨杰拉德的审美理想，就删除了。在“词以婉约为正宗”的观念里，豪放不就是被视为“叫嚣”吗？

2–99

菲译第四版第 6 首，
1930 年版
127 mm × 183 mm

欧玛尔·海亚姆的长眠之地“正有斜枝墙外出，一身都为覆花英”。匈牙利插画家威利·波加尼（Willy Pogány，1882—1955）在这幅插图中描绘了花园、穹庐、玫瑰花枝、持酒的美人，令人联想到欧玛尔的陵园。

II-XCIX

Whither resorting from the vernal Heat
Shall Old Acquaintance Old Acquaintance greet,
　Under the Branch that leans above the Wall
To shed his Blossom over head and feet.

2-99

从春日中的阳和去了那里
老友就会跟老友问候致礼。
**　在斜侧伸出墙头的树枝下**
他的花朵把我头和脚掩起。

二版其九十九

将辞春暖赴佳城，
谁与殷勤指旧盟？
正有斜枝墙外出，
一身都为覆花英。

【解读】

第二版第 99 首，赫荣 - 艾伦说，是插在第 98 首之后的，在菲茨杰拉德的序文里提到尼札米和卓所讲关于欧玛尔安息地的故事，估计此诗由此衍出。可能既在序文里提到了，为了避免重复，于是予以删除。

2-107

菲译第一版第 29 首，
1909 年版
114 mm × 171 mm

匈牙利插画家威利 · 波加尼（Willy Pogány，1882—1955）在这幅插图描绘了一位男士在波涛汹涌的大海中漂流的情景。岁月的洪流带给人的是无奈、悔恨和惨痛。

II-CVII

Better, oh better, cancel from the Scroll
Of Universe one luckless Human Soul,
　Than drop by drop enlarge the Flood that rolls
Hoarser with Anguish as the Ages roll.

2-107

更好一点，哦那会更好一点，
从天卷将一不幸灵魂删减，
**　比起一滴滴随着岁月滚动**
涌成洪流嘶哑惨痛地翻卷。

二版其一百〇七

皇天注册本无亲，
何事畸零托此身？
岁久涓流成恨海，
沧波涌处尽颦呻。

【解读】———

第二版第 107 首，赫荣 - 艾伦说，无疑受到尼古拉斯版第 457 首的提示，参考了乌斯利抄本第 54 首：

那笔所写的不能再改变，
忧伤只能带来深切的折磨。
虽然你一生都哭着血泪，
但没有一滴会增大超出它应有的大小。

这首显得过于消极哀伤，似与全集风格不大协调，也许是删去的原因。

五版编辑者注

IT must be admitted that FitzGerald took great liberties with the original in his version of Omar Khayyám. The first stanza is entirely his own, and in stanza XXXI. of the fourth edition (XXXVI. in the second) he has introduced two lines from Attár (See Letters p. 251). In stanza LXXXI. (fourth edition), writes Professor Cowell, 'There is no original for the line about the snake: I have looked for it in vain in Nicholas; but I have always supposed that the last line is FitzGerald's mistaken version of Quar. 236 in Nicholas' ed. Which runs thus:

O thou who knowest the secrets of every one's mind,
Who graspest every one's hand in the hour of weakness,
O God, give me repentance and accept my excuses,
O thou who givest repentance and acceptest the excuses of every one.

'FitzGerald mistook the meaning of *giving* and *accepting* as used here, and so invented his last line out of his own mistake. I wrote to him about it when I was in Calcutta; but he never cared to alter it.'

[This Note, by William Aldis Wright, appears at the end of many Macmillan editions of the Rubáiyát.] [William Aldis Wright (1831—1914) was FitzGerald's closest friend, and after FitzGerald's death in 1883 took on the task of literary executor, publishing *Letters of Edward FitzGerald* (2 vols, 1894), *Letters of Edward FitzGerald to Fanny Kemble* (1895), *Miscellanies* (1900), *More Letters of Edward FitzGerald* (1901), and *Letters and Literary Remains of Edward FitzGerald* (7 vols, 1902-03, expanding on an earlier 1889 edition of three volumes). —KS]
and in stanza 31 [This typographical error was, it seems, neither spotted nor amended: he means in fact stanza 33.]

必须承认，菲茨杰拉德在他的欧玛尔·海亚姆的译本中，相对原文来说有很大的自由度。第 1 首全是他自己的。第四版的第 33 首，（第二版第 36 首。译按：原文误作三十一）有两行取自阿塔尔（见书信集，第一卷第 251 页）。关于第四版的第 81 首，考威尔教授写道："原文没有一句提到蛇，我找遍了尼古拉斯版也没有见到。我总是怀疑最后一行是尼古拉斯版第 236 首的误译，它是这样的：

你知道心中的隐秘那人个个，
你会抓住他的手每当他软弱，
啊神，予我悔心，也接受我悔过，
啊你予人人悔心，也接受悔过。

菲茨杰拉德弄错了用在这里的‘予’和‘接受’的意思，出于他自己的错误杜撰了最后一行。我在加尔各答时就此写信给他，但他从未注意改正。"

案

这个注释是威廉·奥迪斯·赖特写的，出现在麦克米兰各版《鲁拜集》的卷末。威廉·奥迪斯·赖特（1831—1914）是菲茨杰拉德最亲密的朋友，在菲茨杰拉德1883年去世后被委以文稿执行人之责，出版了《爱德华·菲茨杰拉德书信集》（二卷，1894）、《爱德华·菲茨杰拉德致弗妮·肯布尔书信》（1895）、《杂着集》（1900）、《爱德华·菲茨杰拉德增补书信集》（1901），和《爱德华·菲茨杰拉德书信和文学遗集》（七卷，1902—1903，是早时1889年三卷本的增补）。

其中所引的诗，在1207年抄本第95首（“乐园”本第1首）、“乐园”本第3首、第4首、1207年抄本第151首（“乐园”本第24首）都有相近的表述。

五版增注

费氏结楼之译《鲁拜集》也，颇无约束，此不得不言者也。首章全为彼结撰。四版之三十三章，原作三十一章，盖手民之误。二版列其三十六，二句撷之阿特，见书简卷一二百五十一页。四版之八十一章，考威尔教授言，“原文无一句言及蛇，吾遍检尼古拉斯版全书皆未见蛇字。而吾常疑末句误译，盖在尼古拉斯版之二百三十六章，文曰：‘人心危处总能知，无力时为援手时。予悔非苛还受忏，神恩周遍莫须辞。’费氏结楼昧于此处‘予’‘受’之意，出彼自误，杜撰末句。吾在加尔各答时，尝驰书纠之，而彼终未在意更之也。”

案

此注威廉·奥迪斯·赖特撰，缀于麦克米兰诸版之《鲁拜集》末。赖特与费氏结楼至交。费氏于一千八百八十三年卒，委以遗稿。乃刊《爱德华·费氏结楼书简》二卷、《爱德华·费氏结楼致弗妮·肯布尔书》《杂集》《爱德华·费氏结楼续简》。又于一千九百零二、零三年刊《爱德华·费氏结楼书简与集存》七卷，为一千八百八十九年三卷本之增订，《鲁拜集》五版即在此三卷本中也。

各　版　编　次　对　照　表

第一版	第二版	第三、四、五版
I 1	I 1	I 1
II 2	II 2	II 2
III 3	III 3	II 3
IV 4	IV 4	IV 4
V 5	V 5	V 5
VI 6	VI 6	VI 6
VII 7	VII 7	VII 7
VIII 8	IX 9	IX 9
IX 9	X 10	X 10
X 10	XI 11	XI 11
XI 11	XII 12	XII 12
XII12	XIII13	XIII13
XIII13	XV 15	XIV 14
XIV 14	XVII 17	XVI 16
XV 15	XVI 16	XV 15
XVI 16	XVIII 18	XVII 17
XVII 17	XIX 19	XVIII 18
XVIII 18	XXIV 24	XIX 19
XIX 19	XXV 25	XX 20
XX 20	XXI 21	XXI 21
XXI 21	XXII 22	XXII 22
XXII 22	XXIII 23	XXIII 23
XXIII 23	XXVI 26	XXIV 24
XXIV 24	XXVII 27	XXV 25
XXV 25	XXIX 29	XXVI 26
XXVI 26	LXVI 66	LXIII 63
XXVII 27	XXX 30	XXVII 27
XXVIII 28	XXXI 31	XXVIII 28
XXIX 29	XXXII 32	XXIX 29
XXX 30	XXXIII 33	XXX 30
XXXI 31	XXXIV 34	XXXI 31
XXXII 32	XXXV 35	XXXII 32
XXXIII 33	XXXVII 37	XXXIV 34
XXXIV 34	XXXVIII 38	XXXV 35
XXXV 35	XXXIX 39	XXXVI 36
XXXVI 36	XL 40	XXXVII 37
XXXVII 37		
XXXVIII 38	XLIX 49	XLVIII 48
XXXIX 39	LVI 56	LIV 54
XL 40	LVII 57	LV 55
XLI 41	LVIII 58	LVI 56
XLII 42	LX 60	LVIII 58
XLIII 43	LXI 61	LIX 59
XLIV 44	LXII 62	LX 60
XLV 45		
XLVI 46	LXXIII 73	LXVIII 68
XLVII 47	XLV 45	XLII 42
XLVIII 48	XLVI 46	XLIII 43
XLIX 49	LXXIV 74	LXIX 69
L 50	LXXV 75	LXX 70
LI 51	LXXVI 76	LXXI 71
LII 52	LXXVIII 78	LXXII 72
LIII 53	LXXIX 79	LXXIII 73
LIV 54	LXXXI 81	LXXV 75
LV 55	LXXXII 82	LXXVI 76
LVI 56	LXXXIII 83	LXXVII 77
LVII 57	LXXXVII 87	LXXX 80

第一版	第二版	第三、四、五版
LVIII 58	LXXXVIII 88	LXXXI 81
LIX 59	LXXXIX 89	LXXXII 82
LX 60	XCIV 94	LXXXVII 87
LXI 61	XCI 91	LXXXIV 84
LXII 62	XCII 92	LXXXV 85
LXIII 63	XCIII 93	LXXXVI 86
LXIV 64	XCV 95	LXXXVIII 88
LXV 65	XCVI 96	LXXXIX 89
LXVI 66	XCVII 97	XC 90
LXVII 67	XCVIII 98	XCI 91
LXVIII 68	C 100	XCII 92
LXIX 69	CI 101	XCIII 93
LXX 70	CII 102	XCIV 94
LXXI 71	CIII103	XCV 95
LXXII72	CIV104	XCVI 96
LXXIII 73	CVIII108	XCIX 99
LXXIV 74	CIX109	C 100
LXXV 75	CX110	CI 101
	VIII 8	VIII 8
	XIV 14	
	XX 20	XVIII18 注释
	XXVIII 28	
	XXXVI 36	XXXIII 33
	XLI 41	XXXVIII 38
	XLII 42	XXXIX 39
	XLIII 43	XL 40
	XLIV 44	
	XLVII 47	XLVI 46
	XLVIII 48	XLVII 47
	L 50	XLIX 49
	LI 51	L 50
	LII 52	LI 51
	LIII 53	LII 52
	LIV 54	LIII 53
	LV 55	XLI 41
	LIX 59	LVII 57
	LXIII 63	LXI 61
	LXIV 64	LXII 62
	LXV 65	
	LXVII 67	LXIV 64
	LXVIII 68	LXV 65
	LXIX 69	XLIV 44
	LXX 70	XLV 45
	LXXI 71	LXVI 66
	LXXII 72	LXVII 67
	LXXVII 77	
	LXXX 80	LXXIV 74
	LXXXIV 84	LXXVIII 78
	LXXXV 85	LXXIX 79
	LXXXVI 86	
	XC 90	LXXXIII 83
	XCIX 99	
	CV105	XCVII 97
	CVI106	XCVIII 98
	CVII 107	

图书在版编目（CIP）数据

鲁拜集之美 /（波斯）欧玛尔·海亚姆原著；（英）爱德华·菲茨杰拉德英译；钟锦译解. -- 北京：北京时代华文书局，2022.10

ISBN 978-7-5699-4406-8

Ⅰ. ①鲁… Ⅱ. ①欧… ②爱… ③钟… Ⅲ. ①诗歌欣赏－伊朗－中世纪 Ⅳ. ①I373.072

中国版本图书馆 CIP 数据核字 (2021) 第 277562 号

LUBAI JI ZHI MEI

出 版 人：陈　涛
图书策划：陈丽杰
责任编辑：陈丽杰　袁思远
执行编辑：高春玲
特约编辑：吴　伟
责任校对：李一之
函盒插图：安妮·哈丽特·菲胥
插图提供：吴　伟
装帧设计：熊　琼
执行设计：段文辉
责任印制：刘　银　訾　敬

出版发行：北京时代华文书局 http://www.bjsdsj.com.cn
北京市东城区安定门外大街 138 号皇城国际大厦 A 座 8 层
邮编：100011　电话：010-64263661　64261528
印　　刷：天津图文方嘉印刷有限公司
开　　本：787 mm×1092 mm　1/16　　成品尺寸：160 mm×260 mm
印　　张：24　　字　　数：550 千字
版　　次：2024 年 1 月第 1 版　　印　　次：2024 年 1 月第 1 次印刷
定　　价：198.00 元